GOD, ME

AND THOSE

FLYING

& Blue Skies & Fair Winds

MACHINES

Lowell Farrand

As told to

Rebecca McLendon

To:- John
From:- Lowell Farrand
May God Bless you now & always

Those whose hope is in the LORD
will renew their strength,
they will soar on wings like eagles;
they will run & not grow weary,
they will walk & not faint.

Isaiah 40:31

Dedication

Dedicated to my wonderful wife of sixty-five years, Gaylia, and our two amazing sons, Grant and Jim, who have made us proud as they pursued their careers and cared for their families.

We are so blessed.

TABLE OF CONTENTS

CHAPTER 1

Model Airplanes and Early Flying

As far back as I can remember, I carried a love for airplanes. In First Grade I was already drawing model airplane plans. I was soon building small balsa wood models. As I got older, the models just got bigger. As soon as I could ride my bike to the airport, which was quite a long way away, I began hanging out there, just hoping to see an airplane fly.

World War II was in full swing at the time, and instructors came by to schedule one-hour lessons for student's eager to learn how to fly. After the lesson, they left, because there was no FBO—Fixed Base Operation—at the airport. One day after a lesson, an instructor noticed me hanging around rapt with interest in the whole event.

"Hey, kid, would you like to wash the bugs off this plane for a ride around the field?"

It was obvious I was ready. I was so thrilled I was almost up into the airplane before he could finish his question. I had a real job from that point on. I guess I could be considered the CEO of Bird Bathers, Inc. Eventually, he asked me if I could put the planes away after I washed them, because he needed to head out.

1

With a surge of bravado, I thrust my chest out and told him, "Why, of course I can!"

However, I soon realized those airplanes were quite hard to push for a youngster like me, so I figured out how to start them. I was soon cranking up Champs, Chiefs, Luscombes and an Ercoupe.

It wasn't long till the day came where "it" happened. I had washed a Cub and was taxiing it to the hangar. I had the tail up, pretending that I was a pilot. Little did I know, the Cub was lighter than the others, and it took off! I tried frantically to push it down, but the fence was coming up very fast—soooooo—up I went. I flew around up there until I quit shaking and began trying some low passes that seemed to work okay. Miraculously, I came down and landed safely.

As a fourteen-year-old kid, I just said, "WOW! That's no big deal." And then I taxied the Cub to its hangar and put it up. From then on, when I washed any of the other planes, I took them around the field to air dry them.

One day, a student who had recently soloed wanted to rent the Champ for an hour. The instructor shook his head firmly.

"Not today. It's too windy, and there's also a crosswind."

The student's shoulders clearly sagged with disappointment. He had taken off work and wouldn't be able to get another day off for quite a while. The instructor headed for his vehicle and then turned to me.

"Lowell, I have to leave now. Go ride with him, and don't let him mess up!"

"But I—I don't have a license, and I can't fly! I'm not an instructor!" I said, with my heart in my throat.

"I know you can fly," he replied. "I've seen you fly the other airplanes! You fly better than most of the guys here."

So, from the age of fourteen to seventeen, that instructor had me fly with pilots who were having trouble with crosswind landings.

One day a pilot from the Dunlap/Midway Airport was at the Goshen Airport when he got word that the Ercoupe he had rented had run out of gas and landed in a field. Fortunately, it had no damage. He motioned to me.

"Hey, kid! You wanna go with me to recover the Ercoupe?" We took the gas cans and drove to the field where it had landed. We inspected it for damage and fueled it up.

He put the gas cans in the car and said, "Kid, I'll see ya back at Dunlap."

"But, Mister, I can't fly an Ercoupe!" I argued.

"Yes you can, and you're a lot lighter than I am. It'll get out a lot better with you."

Well, of course, I flew it back to the airport. That marked the beginning of my season of picking airplanes up for aircraft dealers for several years. I suppose my love of airplanes was stronger than my good sense!

Back in 1951, in high school, I wanted to impress Gay. So, I borrowed an Aeronca Champ 7 AC tandem seating. I planned to fly Gay to Rochester, Indiana, for lunch. We had a very nice flight, and it was very smooth. As I prepared to land, however, I discovered I couldn't pull the stick back! I was worried at first, and then I grabbed it with both hands. I pulled back hard and heard a loud crunching sound.

I made a good landing, parked the airplane and immediately set to finding out what that sound was and why my stick wouldn't pull back. In that day, those square, boxy, straw purses were popular, and Gay had placed hers on the floor back of the stick! I smashed it completely in two pulling back. I was sure she would never date me again, but we were married the next year, and now, nearly sixty-five years later, we are still married.

I later bought that Champ and flew it 385 hours before selling it. Later on, our oldest son found it again and bought it before he had ever owned a car. He flew it another 385 hours before he sold it. Much later, we found that plane again, but we did not buy it a third time. I had my Luscombe by then and wanted to keep it.

Back in those days we just flew around for fun. But when I turned seventeen, the new FBO operator at the airport decided I needed to make myself legal if I was going to continue in aviation, so I began taking lessons and got my Pilot's License. However, I soon discovered I could not afford to fly.

A friend of mine, Bob Wilden, found a fifty horsepower Franklin-powered J-3 Cub. The raccoons had eaten all the rib stitching out of the wings. We bought it for $75.00, each of us paying half. We rib-stitched the wings right through paint and all and then put two-inch tapes over the stitching. We then repainted it.

The Franklin valves were leaking. I discovered that Dodge truck valves were the same, so we got it running quite well. We soon realized we couldn't afford hangar rent, gas, and other essentials, so we sold the plane and actually made a little money.

I soon decided to build a Benson Gyrocopter, because I could build it in the garage and keep it at home. I flew it a great deal and decided to take it to the Rockford, Illinois, EAA Fly-In. I wanted to fly in to the Fly-In, but not from home, so we trailered it to about three miles from the show. I flew in from there while Gaylia and the kids came in by car.

At this Fly-In, the "fixed wing" people did not like gyrocopters. And, wouldn't you know it? At the show, the cranky old McCulloch would not start. The "fixed wingers" made fun of me. I told them that I would be back the next year and show them that gyrocopters really could fly. It was much harder than I thought it would be, but, by 1970, and my fourth re-make of my gyrocopter, designed now with a Continental engine and a different rotor system, I was ready to prove them wrong. These re-makes spread over a period of nine years. By this time, the Fly-In had been moved to Oshkosh, Wisconsin. And that year, I won the Man and Machine Award.

After that, I flew gyrocopters quite a bit, and we had a very active Popular Rotorcraft Club. I served as Secretary/Treasurer of the PRA Chapter 34.

CHAPTER 2

Notre Dame Aerospace Division and Parafoil Testing

At one of our EAA Chapter 132 meetings I heard about Notre Dame University working with an open-celled type parachute, known as the Parafoil. Domina Jalbert, known in the kite world as the "Father of the Ram Air Cell Airfoil," had apparently designed a kite for advertising signs. The ocean breezes would hold the signs up in the air, however a strong gust pulled the fence post to which Jalbert had tethered the chute. He then anchored it to the back of his truck, but another gust caught it and spun the truck around.

Jalbert realized something was going on, and he carried his chute to the Notre Dame Aerospace and Mechanical Engineering Department and met with Dr. John Nicolaides. They had done wind tunnel and some drop testing with students until their lawyers found out and told them that no students would be allowed to jump them. So, I volunteered to do it, starting a brand-new adventure.

For the first test, I was pulled up by a 750-foot tow rope, in a way similar to a Para Kite. I was then released and came down to a standup landing. Dr.

Nicolaides was excited by the soft landing. Failure to do a soft landing, with the tuck and roll maneuver, could have possibly resulted in broken legs. We were testing in what was then a practice football field, with goal posts.

One morning, they decided it was too windy and wanted to "scrub" the jump.

"I've driven so far that I'd like to go ahead with the jump," I protested.

After I jumped out, the chute opened, and a big gust of wind hit, causing me to jerk on the line really hard. The chute made a quick ninety-degree turn, so I pulled the other line. It turned back ninety degrees the other way. After I got down, I told the Professor that the chute was controllable by just pulling the lines.

The Professor argued, "No, that was just a big gust of wind that hit you!" He was only interested in a soft standup landing. I went up again to jump to show him how controllable the chute was.

I decided to fly an airport pattern—downwind, base and final. I looked up at the chute, to make sure it was making good square corners, and then making the football field. I saw that I might hit the goal posts, so I pulled my feet up. I flew through the goal posts and landed just on the other side.

Dr. Nicolaides came running up and said, "You've made your point!"

That was the day we realized the chute was controllable and capable of a soft landing when both lines were pulled. That day we also decided to split the Aerospace class into two groups. One half of the class would perfect it as a controllable parachute. The other half of the class would perfect it as a powered parachute, with the hope of bailing out and flying the chute back.

To get it powered quickly, I took the rotor of my Gyrocopter and replaced it with the Parafoil, resulting in the first Powered Parachute. This would be the beginning; however, there would be more to the story.

The first test at Notre Dame using my Gyrocopter to power the chute was not as successful as I had expected. With about 115 horsepower available, it didn't want to climb and was hard to control. Our figures showed it should be able to fly with twelve horsepower. We only had one chute that we had been jumping, and the lines were so long that the chute trailed behind at such an angle, that resulted in all drag. The chute would not move overhead. We shortened the lines, which helped a lot, but we needed a specially-built cart to make more tests.

We realized the chute we had was not designed for powered flight, so we took the patterns to the ladies at the awning company, and they said they could sew up our patterns and make up our chute. They claimed they did not know what they were making, but they could do it as long as they had the patterns. From that point on, we joked about going out and flying our "awning."

Wayne Ison, Aircraft designer and a member of EAA Chapter 132, volunteered to design a new craft. My copter, THE LADY GAY was named for my wife who had painted it. It was considered an IRISH FLYER I. Ison designed IRISH FLYER II and IRISH FLYER III. Each design was much improved.

Notre Dame had received a large grant from Wright-Patterson Air Force Base to research a parachute that a person could bail out with and fly the seat back to our safe lines. However, we were never able to achieve this, because no power supply was available, but, in trying, I bailed out in a Martin-Baker ejection seat which came from Great Britain. We had installed an electrically fired JATO Rocket under the seat. The chute opened, and I fired the JATO Rocket.

My first thought was, "This is the END!" Although it was only a ninety-second rocket, the ride seemed to last a lifetime! The chute stayed straight behind and twisted violently from side to side. I thought any minute would be my last, but as the rocket burned out, the chute moved overhead and became controllable, which enabled me to make a safe landing.

In the meantime, Wayne Ison got the IRISH FLYER II built, and I built up a Volkswagen engine to power it. It was a tractor design with the engine up front. It had rudder pedals in slides that, when pushed, also pulled the control lines. It worked well, but it was large, heavy and slow.

You think, aren't parachutes supposed to be slow? Strange enough, everyone wanted it to go fast. It was flying at only twenty-two to twenty-six miles per hour. Wind tunnel tests, however, showed the Parafoil, originally rigged at twelve degrees' angle of attack, when reduced, went thirty-five miles per hour. We reduced the angle of attack four more times, and it went faster each time. At the fourth time, it reached fifty-five miles per hour, but it became violently uncontrollable. It porpoised violently until it hit the ground, knocking me out and dragging me, destroying the IRISH FLYER II.

Wayne then set out to design IRISH FLYER III. This design consisted of a lightweight cart with a two-cycle engine. In the late 1950's, two-cycle engines were new, but not very good. The only one available was the Hirth 600cc. It overheated in spite of everything we tried to do to cool it. In addition, it vibrated so badly that it shook everything.

We built our own reduction drive for it with a 2:1 ratio and a Gates Poly "V" belt. It also shook and overheated, and in about fifteen minutes the belt would get rubbery. It was the best power to weight that we could come up with. Gates had told us our 35 horsepower could not heat the belt, since it was made for 400 horsepower. He did not understand two-cycle power pulses at that time. Two-cycle pulses set up a unique action that causes the belt to heat up more quickly.

IRISH FLYER III was built with a control stick arranged to pull the lines in a wing-warping configuration and flaps for landing, so that the control stick would feel like a real airplane control. On the test flight, it worked up to twenty-five miles per hour but the Parafoil chute became so rigid at the higher speeds that when we moved the control stick, only the cart moved around. The Parafoil never moved at all! It just went where the wind took it.

I was going downwind for the airport, and it would not turn back to the airport. I saw a friend's house coming into view and thought that nice big yard would be a good place to land. I got real low and shut the power off, but the chute kept floating and floating. It turned out I made a great landing in the swimming pool!

CHAPTER 3

Notre Dame and Wright- Patterson Air Force and Testing

Irish Flyer IV was bigger, heavier and powered by a larger VW engine. We learned much from Irish Flyers I, II, and III, and we incorporated all these things in Number IV. We took Number IV to Wright- Patterson Air Force Base in Dayton, Ohio, and flew low-level circles around the Generals in the stands to prove that it was controllable.

We were never successful flying a pilot back after bailing out. A small enough power supply was never developed. However, we did develop radio-controlled pallets of ammo and medical supplies which were dropped out of C-123's and C-47's right at the troops' feet. They didn't even have to walk to pick them up.

In Viet Nam, the winds would carry the old round chutes with supplies to the VC's. They were getting more supplies than we were. Using Radio-Controlled 12-volt gear motors, we could use the Parafoil by pulling on one line or the other to control it and drop the pallets right at our men's feet. The war ended

13

before we could make an impact, but we proved that we could do it!

Because of the wind tunnel testing, and working with the students, I was fascinated by all the equipment Notre Dame Aero Space had to work with. Since I hadn't been a good student in school, I never considered going to college. I grew up with a bad, mean attitude. I didn't like anybody! I didn't do well in school. But, now at Notre Dame I was so fascinated that I found myself helping the students use all the equipment. Notre Dame even asked me to teach a class. Of course, I told them that l couldn't—I thought that l was "dumb as a box of rocks", and it couldn't possibly be legal! They said they knew that, and, for a while, they listed me as faculty! I could "lecture" instead of teach! I really enjoyed this, and we did some great projects.

Some of this was done while the Irish Flyer was being rebuilt, and we were working with the wind tunnel projects. One of the projects was an Inner City Bus developed by General Motors. Right at forty-five mph, it would buffet, so, it wasn't comfortable to drive. GMC supplied us with an exact scale model of the bus, which we tested in the wind tunnel at exactly forty-five mph, and it began to shake and buffet. The smoke showed us that it was the turbulence off the clearance lights that caused the buffet. We recessed them and it ran very nice and smoothly. The full-sized bus was changed and ran just fine. A project for the military was a radar controlled cannon that would shoot seventeen to twenty miles. But, they couldn't hit anything, because the bullets would start oscillating and go wild. At that time, Notre Dame had the only wind tunnel in the world that could get wind speeds to test these bullets.

In the wind tunnel the bullet went wild, so we reshaped the bullet from a blunt-nose to a pointed-nose and balanced the CG the same as we would do a wing. When the military tested, it they said that they could shoot a truck on the road seventeen miles away and decide if they wanted to shoot its front hub cap or the back one. It was that accurate.

In the 60's, students protested any military testing at Notre Dame Aero Space Division. They'd lie down in front of the doorway, so we couldn't get into the class room. That's kind of the way it was in the 60's.

The Parafoil chute opening was refined to eliminate the shock of opening. Steve Snyder and John Iff developed a slider to control the opening. With the chute perfected, Dr. Nicolaides invited the Golden Knights Parachute Team to come and evaluate the chutes. I helped pack the chutes and told them that I'd flown square patterns and did various maneuvers, but not aerobatics. Anything more than that, they would be "test jumpers". On their first and second jumps, they were already doing Figure Eights and wingovers and spins! Sgt. McDermott of the Golden Knights was the first one to jump the chute after our testing. We had pretty much completed the testing of the open-celled Parafoil chute and powered cart.

Me in the Irish Flyer

Flight of the "Irish Flyer II", and improved model over the

Flight of the Irish Flyer II.

This was my first jump as a parachutist landing where the Big Dome ACC Building is today.

CHAPTER 4

Notre Dame Projects Close, Ultralights Begin

While working at Notre Dame Aero Space Department, there were some perks. Gay and I had to attend the Test Pilot dinners. On one occasion, James Lovell sat to my left and Gay to my right and Father Ted Hesburg across the table from us. After dinner, James Lovell told us step by step about Apollo 13. He held us spell bound when describing their return from space. We were given season tickets to all the home football games. We were seated with the faculty on the fifty-yard line and given great box lunches.

To show off the new Parafoil parachute, Dr. John Nicolaides wanted me to jump into the stadium before the Notre Dame- Navy game. It was very windy, and it went well—until I got down to the top of the stadium. The wind over the stadium caused the chute to flutter. I made a very hard, but safe landing.

We had fulfilled our contract with Wright-Patterson AFB for the Parafoil testing, and I was recuperating from the accident with a very long recovery when Dr. Nicolaides moved to San Louis

Obispo, California. There, he patented the Powered parachute as the Nicholas Flier. He made several as a sport chute. One of the grad students manufactured powered parachutes as the Freedom Flier. He only built about four, however, before running into financial problems.

Steve Snyder was the first to start a manufacturing company to build the chutes in large numbers. Unfortunately, Snyder was later killed while flying an F-86 for the movies. It was almost ten years later that a number of companies began manufacturing the powered chutes as PPC's.

While working with Wayne Ison and the Notre Dame project, we became very close friends. We discovered that pilots wanted "bigger, better and faster. Wayne had been designing a very light airplane long before there were ultralights. He asked me to put a light weight engine on it. I used a German JLO two - cycle engine. The plane weighed 235 pounds, and I weighed 235 pounds. We took a lot of kidding about that! The JLO was a very early two-cycle engine that had a lot of problems. It burned up for me while I was flying a demonstration at the Oshkosh EAA Fly-In. I then built up a 1700cc Volkswagen engine. The plane was called the "PDQ-2 (Pretty Darn Quick to Build!)".

Wayne sold kits to about twenty-six countries. At one point, we had sold 3,000 sets of plans and 300 complete kits. That was about the kits – to - plan ratio that was common in the 1960's. Wayne's airplanes all flew very well, and that led to the ISON Aircraft, Co. It then became TEAM Aircraft, and now it's TEAM MINI-MAX Aircraft. I would fly the prototypes for each model. At one time, we had one of each model at my home air strip to fly. Today, the company is in Niles, Michigan, with dealers in China, Australia, New Zealand, and Great Brittan.

Prototype of the Mini-Max Wayne Ison designed and built.
It sits in front of my beloved Luscombe 8A.

CHAPTER 5

My Luscombe Story N71556, N71232, N2077K and N39031

While I was washing airplanes at the Goshen Airport as a kid, there was one dark red Luscombe that took my eye. Compared to the other planes, to me it was a sports car.

"Someday I want one of those," I vowed to myself.

Gay and I were married, and we purchased a double garage. Gay's dad and mom helped us to turn it into a cozy little home. From our house going west was nothing but farm ground. I began thinking that I could land an airplane there! Then I heard of a Luscombe that was for sale cheap and needed some repair. I could afford to buy N71556, so I arranged to pick it up at Chain 'O' Lakes Airport. I also arranged for an instructor to check me out.

However, when the big day came, I waited all day and he didn't show up! I simply jumped into it and flew it back to Goshen Airport. I'd heard all the tales that Luscombes are hard to land, so I was very nervous. I landed so easily at Goshen that I was disappointed. I fully expected something to happen!

Somewhere around 1955, I was flying my Luscombe up the shore line of Lake Michigan to the North and was really enjoying the lakeshore. A sudden storm came across the lake. I tried to fly around the storm, but, in doing so, I got lost. I was truly "sweating this one out." There was nothing but trees in this part of Michigan. But, suddenly, in the distance, I could see a large clearing! As I got closer, I noticed it was the Army Air Force Base at Grayling, Michigan.

Just then, the engine quit. I had no choice but to make the Air Base. Now, this was right in the heart of the Cold War. As soon as I landed, they came at me with guns, confiscated the airplane, and I was interrogated for hours. They insisted that I lied about being out of gas.

The Base Commanding Officer came in, and listened to my story. He had one of the soldiers to go out and check my gas tank. He came back into the office and said, "There is not a drop of Gas in that tank, SIR!"

The Commanding Officer said, "Fill the plane with gas and escort him out of the area." He told me to fly straight out of the area and not to even think about coming back.

I took off with a BT-13 on either side of me. After take-off they moved their wings in right under mine—

real close. I was really sweating it out again. I then looked at them in their cockpits and they were laughing. They must have thought this was funny, but I got mad. I hit the radio button and said, "Try this, guys!" I suddenly pulled the power off and slowed to 35 mph. I watched both of them stall out and dive away.

I pushed the radio button again and said, "Don't mess with a country boy."

Mind you, this took place before my accident and before God got a hold of me. I was mean back then and didn't like being shoved around.

After some minor repairs, it was one of the nicest Luscombes that I ever had. Several years later, when the kids came along, we needed to sell the airplane. We did keep track of it for a while. Two Chicago policemen had purchased it together. Then, recently, a young couple sent us pictures of it. They had just won a Grand Champion Award with it.

After the boys started school, I missed the Luscombe so much that I went looking for one. I found N 71232, of course, needing a LOT of repair, but it was cheap! While inspecting it before flying home, I fell through the fabric-it was so rotten! The engine was worn out, and the exhaust was rusted very badly. I got the engine running well and glued a bed sheet over the hole in the wing. I'd planned to land it in the field behind our house. On the way home the engine sounded like a tractor, burning holes in the rusty old exhaust pipe. I landed in the field, but the field was a lot smaller than I thought. I was headed for the house, and I braked really hard. The tail came up very high and stopped. But then it finally went back down. I stopped about three feet from hitting the house.

Gay and I rebuilt the wing in the tiny living room of the house. The wing went crosswise corner to corner. We spent from Christmas until New Year's rib stitching the wing, passing the needle back and forth with the help of our two little boys. I rebuilt the engine and about everything else and gave it a very nice paint job. It was a beautiful airplane that we flew many hours. Medical bills and kids in school used up our finances, so I again had to sell the plane.

A few years later, I was back to missing a Luscombe. I heard of a completely totaled one at the Wawasee Airport where a student had crashed it. It was almost new. The airport had already gotten a lot of repair parts for it, that were still lying in a corner. I gave them $700.00 for all the pieces and took it to the Dunlap Midway Airport where I had just rented a hangar. The Dunlap Airport had a training school for Luscombes.

The first night, as I was going through all of the parts that I had purchased, the airport owner came out and told me that during their training of students they had turned over two Luscombes and all of those parts were in the attic of my hangar.

"Check them out—there may be something that you can use!"

Amazingly, everything that was bent on mine was okay on those two! I was able to use the windshield, doors, windows, all the landing gear, some of the cowling and many aluminum formers. I could completely rebuild my airplane, and all I had to buy was rivets!

While I was finishing the airplane, the guys at the airport kept asking me "What's he (the airport owner) going to charge you for all those parts?"

He was one of the biggest car dealers in the area and was known to be a "wheeler dealer!" I began to get a bit scared— I didn't have any extra money at all. The airport owner had the hangar next to mine and had just purchased a new twin engine Piper Apache. He didn't fly it much and let the battery go dead. Therefore, I would always hand-prop one engine for him. He would run the engine to charge the battery to start the other engine. When I asked how much I owed for the parts he said, "OH, just keep propping my engine for me!" I just couldn't believe it!

A few days later, N2077K was ready for the FAA Inspection. They were to meet me right after lunch. I waited until 5:00 p.m. and they didn't show up. I figured the FAA doesn't work after 5 o'clock, so I went up on a test flight-just in time to look down and see the FAA fellow drive in! I was so worried that I was shaking, thinking that this was IT for me, but all he said was, "Well, that's one way to see if your work is O.K. Got your Log books?" It passed.

I continued flying N2077K for about fifty years. It became like a member of the family. Many, many memories and stories were made in that airplane. I do not have an instructor's license, but I have taught many, many young people enough about flying for them to "solo".

One nice summer day I took our oldest son Grant flying. After flying for a while the weather started to turn bad. A summer afternoon thunderstorm came up with lots of hail. Grant was getting afraid and wanted down. I didn't say much, but I wanted down, too! It was hailing so hard that I couldn't see forward, but straight below I saw a herd of cows. Knowing that cows stand with their backs to a storm, I lined up on them and landed in the field with them! I called my Dad to come pick up Grant.

By this time the cows were licking the paint off the leading edge of the wings. The field was much shorter than I thought, and I knew that I would have to lighten the plane to fly it out, I took the interior and seats out and drained all of the gas out, then put just enough back in to get me to Goshen Airport. I took all of my clothes off, except my shorts, to save weight. I told Dad to drive to the airport and drive right out to the plane so I could put my clothes back on! I took off okay, but nicked a bush. At the airport, I planned to stay in the plane till Dad got there, but everybody at the airport had heard that I had gone down in the storm, so they rushed out to the plane where I sat, wearing just my shorts.

One time I was visiting my cousin Keith at the Crawfordsville, Indiana, airport and we were watching a fellow trying to hand prop his Luscombe. He was having trouble getting it to start, so I walked out of the office to help him. Just then it started wide open, knocking him down and hurting him. I tried to grab the plane as it went past.

I missed the wing strut, but grabbed the tail. With one hand on the vertical fin and the other hand on the back of the rudder, I pulled the rudder to one side. The plane was running wide open and dragging me around in circles.

A fire department stood on the field very close to us and they watched all of this. They thought they could drown the engine out with a fire hose. They aimed the fire hose at the engine every time it came around the circle. They missed the cowling but always managed to hit me with the water. One the third or fourth try they finally "killed" the engine, but I looked like a drowned rat!

The people standing around were laughing so hard and said it looked like a greased pig contest! It could have been worse, because there was a whole row of parked airplanes that we were only missing by feet. I was a mess. Someone asked me if I wanted to shower. I only had one comment.

"I think I just had one!"

My cousin Keith owned a 1939 Aeronca Chief. We would fly back and forth to visit each other. It was my turn to fly down to Crawfordsville. I pre-flighted my

Luscombe and found a flat tire. I pumped it up and couldn't find anything wrong. I was anxious to go, so I kicked the tire. It was still solid, so away I flew.

I had a nice trip down, and, coming over Crawfordsville, I could see the airport south of town and started to wonder about the air in the tire. I opened the door to kick the tire. The wind was blowing so hard against the door that I was having trouble, so I managed to kick the tire which was okay, but the wind caught my loafer. I watched it spiral down to the big A & P Grocery Store parking lot. I landed at the airport and walked into the office to see if I could borrow the "old airport car" to go into town and find my shoe.

"Sure, you can borrow it, IF you can tell us how you lost your shoe while flying."

I drove to the A & P parking lot and, sure enough, I found my shoe. When I got back to the airport they wouldn't believe my story—so they made up their own story which was a lot more exciting than mine.

With over 3,000 hours in this plane, there are numerous stories that come to mind—too many to tell. I still go into restaurants, and people say to me, "Do you remember me? I soloed in your Luscombe!" I flew 500 Young Eagles for the EAA Young Eagles Program. As parents and grandparents brought most of the kids to our airstrip, I always flew many of them too! So, I probably flew more "old buzzards" than Young Eagles!

I never thought that anything would happen to the Luscombe. It was like a member of our family. However, coming home from the last fly-in of the year in October of 2014, the weather began turning very stormy. I climbed to get above the storm, but upon arriving at home and descending on downwind, I could see a very black line all the way to the ground. Approaching from the opposite direction, I thought that I could beat it to the runway. On the approach, it became the roughest that I'd ever seen. My passenger said that he could hear tearing metal! I was too busy landing. I made a good landing, pulled the throttle back at the same time the storm hit us. It picked us up about 100 feet and turned us upside down and tore the back fuselage and tail off.

Since it went in upside down I went out through the windshield with the cowling and engine on my back. My passenger's seat belt held but he was upside down. I could hear gas running.

I yelled, "Get out quickly!"

He released his belt so quickly that he fell on his head, injuring his back, but got out okay. What had saved us was the corn crop next to the runway. It was the tallest and thickest ever. They had combined all but two passes alongside the runway. The plane landed upside down on the tall corn, which cushioned our crash. God and the corn surely saved our lives!

When I looked at all the pieces lying in my shop hangar, I couldn't believe that it was torn up so badly. The fuselage had torn back of the wings, and the tail had come off in the air. Over the weeks and months that I looked at it I went into depression. I didn't feel like doing anything, and I didn't want to go anywhere. As a DAR for the FAA, I had been doing a lot of Airworthiness Inspections, but I stopped doing them.

A fellow from Valparaiso, Indiana, called and wanted me to do the inspection on his homebuilt. I told him that I had stopped, but he reminded me that I'd told him when he was finished, that I would do the inspection. So, I told him I would do one more. I inspected his plane and gave him his Airworthiness Certificate. He said that he wanted to introduce me to Louie, the IA at Valpo. Louie bought damaged Luscombes. He had more than twelve Luscombes with varying amounts of damage and LOTS of spare parts!

After talking about the parts that I would need to rebuild mine and the time it would take me at my age, which was eighty-three at the time.

Louie said, "At your age-you need to buy, not build!"

Then he showed me a beautiful Luscombe and said, "Make me an offer."

"I can't make you a decent offer," I said sadly. So, we went home. We had no extra money.

A bit later, it was time for our EAA Chapter's Christmas Dinner party. Gay went to the punch bowl, and one of the women gave her a Christmas card and said, "Do not open until you get home."

When we got home and opened it, there was a deposit slip from our bank for the amount of the airplane! We had sent a check in earlier to pay for our dinners. The members said that they knew we wouldn't accept the money, so they got the account number off the check and put it into our checking! The Valparaiso EAA, the Niles, Michigan Chapter, the Elkhart, Indiana Chapter, and the Nappanee Chapter all contributed to pay for the plane. Louie had made the price of the airplane about one-third of the price that the Luscombe was worth. We were overcome with emotion and were deeply humbled that they would do this for us. It was amazing to think that so many people would do this for me, when they all have projects that they could use the money for.

When I went to pick the airplane up, it had been given a complete overhaul—new mags, wires and plugs, plus a rebuilt carburetor and accessories. I got to start it and put the first time on it. The first hour that I flew it, I cried to think of what the Chapters had done. I had to land and get dry hankies. Even now, when I fly and see what a wonderful plane I have, I still get tears.

N39031-everybody calls it "Lowell's NEW/OLD Airplane". It is a 1941 8A/E manufactured July 7, 1941, by the Luscombe Manufacturing Company, West Trenton, New Jersey. The test pilot picked it up on the same day, and did the test flying and delivered it to DeLand, Florida on July 11, 1941.

Until WWII broke out, it was used for private flying, and then it was used for military training until April 14, 1945. The plane turned over a number of times. The original fabric wings were repaired six times, and later it was damaged, and the wings were replaced with metal wings.

On October 14, 1946, it was put back into civilian ownership, where it was used for training. Again, N39031 was repaired after being damaged, and the model was changed from an 8C to 8A. In 1947, a new Continental A65-8 engine was installed.

On September 25, 1958, it was changed to a Research and Development Category to test EDO Floats and a Lycoming O-290-D engine and two wing tanks. It was used for testing until July 23, 1959. The plane was then changed back to a Model 8A/E with a new Continental 85 horse power engine with new wings and a new prop.

On January 13, 1981, after being damaged, a new cabin roof with carry through spars was installed. A new radio, transponder, antennas, electrical system with NAV lights, tip strobes, and landing light were installed on October 10, 1995. Then, on October 18, 2001, all new windows including windshield were installed. Finally, on June 12, 2014, N39031 got new tires, brakes, and tailwheel.

Many more repair orders were filled during the time the plane was used for training.

My "NEW/OLD" Luscombe 8 A/E 1941 – N39031

CHAPTER 6

Luscombe Fly-Ins and Reunions

At the first Luscombe reunion, Gay and I had a nice trip flying down to Moraine, Ohio. Later on we needed to get a ride to the motel. We had been talking with a Catholic Priest. He had driven down in a motor home which his family had lent to him because he needed to take some time off. He chose to come to this reunion because of his love for Luscombes. He said he needed to get some supplies in town and drop us off.

This was a very early model motor home—very big and boxy and hard to see out of. He drove us to the motel and stopped just short of the portico because it was too low to fit under. We visited a while, not knowing that a motorcycle had driven up behind the motor home. I suppose the cyclist thought the motor home would go on and pull forward under the portico, so he parked behind him and went inside the office.

Instead, the priest put it in reverse and backed over the motorcycle. The owner came out of the office. He was bare from the waist up, completely tattooed on his upper body, wearing a green German helmet with a spike on the top and a motorcycle chain around his neck.

"Ohhh, Man, we are dead!" I whispered.

The priest walked up to the biker and put his arm around him, "Buddy, we've got a problem! I just backed over your bike!" The two of them picked up his "chopper bike" with the big long forks in front, and everything looked bent. They grabbed the handle bars and straightened them out, pulled the fenders and some parts out.

"That looks about right," the biker said. "It'll be okay!"

The big guys hugged each other. The priest handed him some money and said, "Here, go buy yourself some beer."

Here I thought we were going to be in big trouble, but they seemed happy and okay. By the way, we had a very good Luscombe reunion that year, with 102 Luscombes flying in.

After a few years, the Luscombe Reuinion was moved from Moraine, Ohio, to Mattoon, Illinois. I had just purchased a new LORAN which was the state-of-the- art navigation in that day. I was going to test it out on this flight. About an hour into the flight, it said my ground speed was nineteen miles per hour! I tapped it and shook it a little and told Gay I didn't think it was working. I looked down and saw that bicycles were keeping up with us!

The wind was right on our nose, and, as I figured our gas, I knew that we couldn't make it to Mattoon without refueling. Monticello, Indiana, had a runway that would be into the wind. As we landed, a bunch of guys came running out. I thought that maybe I had done something wrong, but they grabbed the wing struts and said they would hold us down while we refueled. It turned out the wind had turned over the plane that had just landed before us.

They held on while we refueled and said, "Take off from the gas pump, and we'll hold on as long as possible!"

We got off in one hundred feet! We flew to Mattoon, and, luckily, they had a runway right into the wind. We landed, and I carefully taxied to a tie down. The plane beside me was just tying down. The pilot said his Luscombe had never gone so fast in all its life. He had just flown in from Farmington, New Mexico! I told him I'd never flown so slowly before, and I had flown in from Ligonier, Indiana!

That evening, we were all eating at a long table, and one fellow was using two canes. He had just had both knees replaced, but he was not about to miss the Luscombe Reunion. The next three people told that they had gotten pacemakers recently, but were determined to get to the Reunion. As we went around the table, most of the pilots said they didn't have a current medical!

"Oh, well, what do doctors know?" said one fellow.

"Yes! God takes care of us anyway," I added.

The Frasca Fly In was started in 2002 by Rudy Frasca and Paul Poberezny because Paul was unhappy with so much attention to commercial exhibits at Oshkosh. He felt we had lost the "grass roots" feel of flying.

Rudy had a factory that built Flight Simulators for planes and simulators for boats. It sat on Rudy's airfield in Urbana, Illinois, and could do what he wanted. He had a large family who is all involved in the business. He and Paul started the SAA (Sport Aviation Association).

Nothing would be for sale except gas and oil for the planes. Rudy's wife and some church women made the meals with only a donation box. They just wanted people to show and talk about their airplanes, relax and have a good time.

Gay and I were going to fly the Luscombe, and our friends Brian and Diana were going to fly their Meyers OTW Bi-plane and follow us, as they had never been there. Just as we crossed into Illinois we hit unreported fog. One minute the Bi-plane was right on our wing, and, the next minute, it had disappeared into the fog.

I circled and circled trying to find them and grew quite worried. I was lost, and our GPS wouldn't work in the fog.

By now, our gas was getting low, and I was afraid it wouldn't last until we reached Frasca's. I throttled way back to conserve fuel, and flew real low, following the roads till we got there. I landed and got to a tie down. A fuel truck came and put fourteen gallons of fuel in our fourteen-gallon tank! Our friends in the Meyers landed soon after. They had gone up through the fog and had flown on top in the sunshine! They found a hole right over the fly-in and landed safely.

The Frascas were great hosts! One time we were early birds to the Fly-In, and Rudy took Gay and Audrey Poberezny in his 1953 restored Chevy convertible down the airstrip and all around his property, and the ball field he had given to the school. Paul teased Rudy about taking his wife without permission. We were also able to have a great breakfast with Corky Fornoff, the movie stunt pilot!

Paul Poberezny, right, and me, left, with my Luscombe at the Frascas Fly-In.

CHAPTER 7

Ferrying for Dealers

After High School, flying was too expensive, and, even though I re-built an old cheap airplane, I couldn't afford gas and hangar rent. It seems, however, that circumstances always get me around the rules! My wanting to fly was stronger than my good sense! After I'd flown an Ercoupe out of a field for a dealer, he asked me if I was interested in picking up surplus airplanes for him. I said I didn't have a pilot's license.

He said "that's O.K. The planes aren't licensed either!" They were military surplus and you had to get them back and license them as civilian aircraft— just don't log your time.

As WWII airplanes came on the surplus market I picked up Wacos, Stearmans, lots of PT 19's, PT 23's, & PT 26's , PT13, AT6's/SNJ2, Harvards and also the L series of L2,L3,L4, L5, L16, DGA 15. Some of these were in very bad shape while flying them back, and I learned to fix almost anything that went wrong. Some of the engines were so worn out that when I pulled the prop through, I could hardly find compression. I learned to clean the oil and fuel screens and clean the spark plugs before I started home. Even though I pre-flighted them very well, I still had emergency landings in many fields across Illinois and Indiana. In fact, once on Gay's birthday, we were invited to dinner at our daughter-in-law's parents. I didn't show up, so Gay called the dealer and asked about me.

"The last time I saw Lowell he was down in a field in Illinois!" he said, as if this was a normal occurrence. Well, back then, it was normal.

Of all the planes I picked up, I never scratched or damaged any of them. I repaired all but two of them and flew them home. The other two had to be taken apart and trucked home. After I repaired them, they flew again. I was never checked out in any of them. Remember, they weren't licensed, so no one would check me out in them.

The Stearman seemed awfully big. I developed a method of practicing landing on a cloud while I was getting used to the plane. I would practice a full stall landing on a cloud, the plane would stall and drop through the cloud. Then I would recover from the stall. Doing this helped me to get a feel of the plane, landing speed, stall speed and recovery speed. By doing other maneuvers on the way home, I got more of the "feel" of the airplane.

While that dealer was only interested in military aircraft, the other dealer was interested in civilian aircraft and British and French aircraft. I loved the British Tiger Moth and Chipmunk, the French Stamps and different models of the Jodel, but then, of course, I love all GA aircraft.

As a kid, I picked up my first Bonanza. I was so nervous as I preflighted it, that I went to the coffee shop to calm down. The fellow beside me said, "Is that your Bonanza?"

"No, I'm just ferrying it back for the owner."

The fellow said, "How do you run yours? I run mine 24-squared!"

He was very talkative. You could tell he loved his airplane. I had listened carefully and then flew home just as he had said. It went really well.

The aircraft dealer sent me to pick up a Mooney M-20 that he had purchased. I left to pick it up, but when I got there, I discovered it was up on barrels!

"What's this?" I asked.

"It hit a snowbank and damaged the landing gear. It's been repaired, but we just haven't taken it off the barrels."

I checked it out, and the landing gear seemed to work okay. I had not flown a mooney before, so I asked several Mooney pilot/owners how they flew. They told me that the manual landing gear on the early Mooneys was very stiff.

"If you take off, get some speed and pull the nose up good. The wind on the bottom will help push the gear shut.

This was a very special Mooney. A couple had had it readied for a round-the-world flight, complete with wooden wings converted to wet wings, which means both wings were gas tanks. They also had extra gas tanks installed. Sadly, they both developed health problems and never attempted the flight. They subsequently sold the airplane.

. I took off, but, when I started to pull the gear up, the handle stopped half way, and I heard a big "clunk"! Something was wrong. It wouldn't go up or down. I tried everything, but it wouldn't move! All along the 200 mile trip home, I tried to think about what I should do. I certainly didn't want to "belly" it in. I climbed to 6,000 feet, pointed the nose straight down, but I didn't realize how fast a Mooney could pick up speed. It passed red line.

As I pulled out hard, I thought, "This is a wooden wing Mooney, and I hope they stay on!"

In the pull-out I heard a dunk; the gear dropped down and locked! I had a safe landing at Goshen. Upon inspection, I found that the Mooney uses a very long, narrow wheel well to retract the nose wheel back and up. This is done with a long control rod with ball rod ends. The problem turned out to be the rod and rod end had bent and locked up. I installed a new rod. It was a simple fix.

Our youngest son, Jim was twelve when I took him up in the Mooney and let him fly it. To this day, he says that Mooney is his favorite plane. It is fast and real smooth on the controls.

In 1976, this very same plane would play a part in my life—again. When we had the first fuel crisis, the airports were saving their fuel for student training, etc. The dealer couldn't get fuel locally, but the airport at Vincennes had plenty. I would fly the 'wet" wing Mooney to Vincennes, fill up and fly home, using it as a tanker. I could drain 100 gallons out and still get back to Vincennes for more.

All the planes that I picked up seemed to have a story all their own. For instance, there was a nice little J 3 Cub. When I went to pick it up, it was in the shop after a complete rebuild. It was very pretty and looked like new. The airport was big with a very long taxiway—over a mile to get to the runway. I did the run up and checkout, but noticed the ailerons are hooked up backwards! Because of the distance from the hangar I thought I could fly it back if I stayed just inches off of the ground. Thinking backwards for the ailerons was harder than I thought. I almost lost it while flying back to the hangar. I learned not to try that again! I could have damaged an almost new airplane!

The Piper Clippers were beginning to be popular. They were some of the first short wing Pipers and not everyone was accepting them. I really liked them as they still had control sticks instead of control yokes. I thought they were cute, and I liked the way they maneuvered. They performed very well with their Lycoming O-290 engines.

At that time, there were Rearwin Sportsters, 1930's American two-seat cabin monoplanes, and Commonwealth Skyrangers, the last aircraft produced by Rearwin, that I picked up. Also, the Fairchild 24's, were nice, because they were bigger and heavier with more power. Most of these were flown back to the Dunlap/Midway Airport to be sold.

Years later when the airport closed, it became a shopping center. The last plane out when it closed was a Stearman Hammond which had been sitting a long time and the valves were sticking in the engine. On takeoff, the engine started to miss. The plane hit several trees at the end of the runway and was damaged too much to be repaired.

In picking up airplanes, I learned to like the round engines. They seemed to almost "talk" to you and tell you if something was wrong before they would fail. The Fairchild PT-19's and 26's had Ranger engines in them. They would also run even if they were in bad shape. So, if you lost a cylinder the plane would still take you home. The dealer at Dunlap wanted to buy some P-51's, but he could only get them if he purchased the whole squadron. He was trying to pre-sell some of them to get money to buy them. The trainer that came with the squadron was a Ryan PT-22 that he didn't want. At that time I didn't know what a Ryan PT-22 was, but I told him I would buy it for $1200. It turned out it had only 50 hours on it since new! It had a round engine, and I loved it. I flew it for many hours, however my cousin crashed and totaled it. Luckily, he wasn't injured.

The other dealer bought mostly general aviation airplanes. When a customer came to buy a used airplane, he would always say, "Lowell, take them for a ride in the Stamp Bi-plane"

Giving those rides always seemed to help to encourage them to buy a G.A. Airplane! He also liked Stinsons, so I picked up a lot of them.

"Lowell, you can fly one of the Stinsons, if it sells, you can fly another one."

During that time, I had two Stinson 108-2's and two 108-3's also known as Stinson Station wagons. When our oldest son was about three or four, he stood on the seat between my legs and flew most of the way to Illinois to visit family in the Stinson 108-3

In the late 60s and 70s there was an abundance of used airplanes and unscrupulous aircraft dealers. The rule was BUYER BEWARE! These guys would paint them up and make them look good and doctor the log books.

A fellow called me to pick up an airplane he had just purchased. He had taken some lessons, but he didn't have a license. I went to pick up the airplane, which was a Stinson Station Wagon 108-3. It had been recovered and repainted—not the best job, but it looked okay. It had a Franklin 165 horsepower and the log book showed low time. I took off and was heading toward Elkhart, Indiana, and was about ten miles west of the airport, when there was a very loud bang. The plane became uncontrollable, with the control yoke banging in and out. It took all of my strength to hold it.

I knew this was bad, and I called Elkhart Tower, and declared an emergency. I asked for a straight-in approach. They cleared me for any runway. I tried lowering the power and putting the flaps on. I got it just above stall speed which gave me some control. The tower said I had something long trailing behind me and it was flapping up and down. I knew this was very serious.

"Lord, I'm sure going to have to have your help on this one!" Immediately everything slowed down as if it was in slow motion, and got a little bit more control. I eased it onto the runway and had a very good landing. I knew that it was downwind, but I didn't have enough control to make turns.

It turned out the dealer had quickly covered the airplane with new covering over the old rotten fabric, and then covered that with a new paint job. The old fabric had let go at the firewall and had torn all of the belly fabric back to the tailwheel. I had fourteen feet of fabric trailing behind and swirling in the wind! The plane was left to be rebuilt and recovered at a very top-notch quality shop.

Little did I know, this plane would test me again. After the rebuild, the shop had set the plane outside until the owner could pay the bill. After the bill was paid, I checked over the plane—a beautiful rebuild inside and out! I took off and climbed out, and, as I leveled off, I needed a lot of nose down trim. It kept getting worse. The nose wanted to go up. With full nose-down trim, pushing the wheel in as hard as I could, it was still climbing. I put full flaps on and powered down to just above stall speed. I just barely had control of the plane. I was heading east and didn't think I could make the turn around to go back to Elkhart.

I remembered that about fifteen miles ahead was a little airstrip—one that I had made! It was near the little Amish town of Shipshewana, they had a horse auction every Tuesday. A lot of bidders were there from Montana and had flown in in Cessna 180s. They wanted someplace close to the auction to land. The owner of the auction asked me if there was any chance that we could make a strip close to the town.

I said, "Yes, if you have the land!" They had the land and gave me two horses and a bed spring to drag the runway smooth. They then gave me grass seed to plant, and by the fall of 1957, the grass was growing very well. In the spring of 1958, with the first mowing, the town had a grand opening of the new airstrip.

I knew that strip was dead ahead, and I could make a straight in approach. I prayed, "Lord, I pray you can help me again!" He did. The landing went okay. Once on the ground I discovered they had installed drain grommets in the airplane fabric but had not opened holes in the center of the grommets. We usually do this with a hot nail or a soldering iron point. I opened all the holes, and the plane drained water for half a day. The rebuilding shop had tied the plane outside, and it rained so hard the plane filled with water which all rushed to the back when I took off.

Later, a Pentecostal preacher bought this plane and had Gay and me fly him and his wife to a Pentecostal Conference. He insisted that we sit in the front row at the conference. When one of the lady preachers got all fired up and came flying across the altar rail, speaking in tongues, it was quite a shock to us Methodist folk! The plane turned out to be a good one and flew for many years.

The strip, by the way, is still in use by a crop duster and a number of different airplanes.

CHAPTER 8

Flying with Northern Indiana Air Museum

Each museum plane had its own story. The last South African AT-6 had been robbed of parts to finish the other three, so they could be sold. We had to scrounge the parts needed to complete the airplane rebuild. We took engine, landing gear and propeller parts.

One morning, I walked into the hangar, and all the landing gear parts were laid out on the floor. The museum mechanic asked, "Ya think we can make a landing gear out of these parts?" We did, and they worked.

The next time the mechanic called me to come up, the hangar floor was covered with prop parts—blades, gears, and hubs. He asked, "Did you ever have a prop this disassembled?"

I said, "No." But we managed to put it together.

At this point, the museum had pre-sold the airplane and had two days to deliver it to Tennessee. We finally rolled it out, and I made a twenty-minute test flight. I landed, told them that the tail wheel strut had gone flat, and the engine was running too lean. I told them if they would fix the strut I would work on the engine. They took the side panel off to fix the strut and saw that the elevator control cable had completely missed the pulley.

They fixed the cable and pulley and put nitrogen in the strut, while I set the carburetor richer. By this time, it had started to snow the biggest flakes I'd ever seen. We called Tennessee, and it was seventy degrees and sunshine!

I took off without any more test time, topped the snow at 10,000 feet and flew to Tennessee. I delivered the plane to the buyer, and he took it up for a test flight, came back landed and said, "Boy! Is that a smooth airplane! The engine runs so good, and the prop is so smooth."

All the while, I'm thinking, "If he had only seen it two days before! ALL those pieces on the floor!"

The RC-45 was to be the museum's flag ship. They really wanted it to look nice. I had a paint scheme in mind and thought they should paint it. The others wanted all polished aluminum with very little trim.

"NO, NO! You don't want a polished airplane! Paint is so much easier to take care of." I argued.

I was overruled. So, about twenty people and 2,000 hours later, we had a polished airplane. We bought white paper coveralls for everyone, but they were black by the time the polishing was done. What helped us was that the Snap-on-Tools dealer donated a three-part polish and an air- operated polisher with a ten-foot chrome wand with polishing pads. That made the job much easier. We couldn't have done it without them.

One of the South African A-T6's almost finished after rebuild and painting.

South African SNJ-3 that the NAIM museum rebuilt and sold to make money. I got to fly it several times in airshows before it was sold.

NIAM's NA-50 Bottom: Blowin Smoke in the NAS-50 to entertain folks at EAA Chapter 938 Dinner in the plane which I flew for two years at Indiana and Ohio Airshows.

The NA-50 getting its annual inspection. I maintained the engine and prop and flew it about four years in air shows. Bottom: My last flight in the NA-50.

CHAPTER 9

Early EAA Years, Oshkosh and Some Flying Awards

My years with the EAA began in the 1960s when I worked alongside Paul Poberezny and Tony Bengelis. We held our TEC Counselor meetings at the EAA Museum in Hales Corners, Milwaukee, Wisconsin. Paul Poberezny held the meetings and then would take us all to his favorite pub to eat and tell airplane stories well into the night. The group decided to have the first Fly In at the old Curtis-Wright Airport in Milwaukee. The Fly-Ins were later moved to Rockford, Illinois. Gay and I, along with our boys, made all of the Rockford Fly-Ins.

When the Fly-Ins were moved to Oshkosh, Wisconsin, we made all of those Fly-Ins until 2015. We had always volunteered with the work party group which we enjoyed so much and miss the great volunteers a lot. Our legs are giving out, so we can't do it anymore.

In 2014, Audrey Poberezny invited several of us to her home for a visit. We found her a joy to be around, and we enjoyed the visit very much. It is interesting to note that when Paul purchased the land at Oshkosh for

EAA, the first building he built was "Chapel." If you've never been there for a Sunday service, you should plan to go. Also, check Paul's Memorial Wall and Compass Hill. These are unbelievable places to see.

We've been fortunate to attend Oshkosh in summer heat, rain, tornadoes, floods, cold winds and even ice on the tent. EAA has meant a great deal to us. I received my FAA/ DAR License to certify Amateur-Built Airplanes through the efforts of EAA's working with the FAA. Gay and I have done 628 Airworthiness Inspections through this program. We have made a lot of great friends in the local EAA Chapters, and with the EAA organization we have also made a number of great friends through doing the inspections. We still keep in touch with each other.

One year at Oshkosh, a 19-year-old girl walked up to me and asked, "Are you Lowell?"

"Yes."

She said, "I have a problem with my Luscombe, can you help me out?" "

I said, "Sure, I'll try."

She told me that she had left California for Oshkosh with four or five Cessnas. She had just gotten her plane out of the shop with a complete overhaul. After flying most of the day, she discovered the plane was leaking and using a lot of oil. She told the other planes to fly on, and she would try to get hers fixed. Every time she stopped for gas, she had the FBO look at it. Nothing seemed to help. She got to Oshkosh by buying oil by the case along the way. After she arrived at Oshkosh, she asked who could help her get it fixed.

Someone said, "Since it's a Luscombe, ask Lowell Farrand."

In that huge crowd, I don't know how she found me. It must have been a God Wink! We decided that the plane was safe enough to fly to our home airstrip when the Fly-In was over. She flew down and stayed several days. She didn't want to impose on us, so she slept in her little pup tent, but ate with us. I determined that at the start of her trip the new rings had not "broken in," and, at that time, a lot of fuel was going into the oil and making it so thin that it was leaking out everywhere! I washed the engine down and found everything was loose. I re-torqued the engine and "safetied" everything. We flew it a lot and it stayed completely dry. She had never landed on a grass strip before, so she was so excited that she shot landings for about 1 ½ days. She called her Luscombe Fantasy. Flying home to California she used only ½ quart of oil! The next year after Oshkosh, she flew to our place again and stayed several days.

As a rule, I don't like awards. They are all about things a person should have been doing anyway. I am humbled and don't feel that I deserve all the awards that I have received. My wife Gay says I must include them, and since we've been married nearly sixty-five years, I'd better do what she says!

In 1969, I received two different trophies. One was for the IRA (Indiana Rotorcraft Association), and another at another IRA Fly-In in 1969 for Best Flying. In 1972, at the Oshkosh, Wisconsin, EAA International Fly-In, I received a Man and Machine Trophy for Gyrocopters. Then in 1982, I received a Trophy for "Best Pilot" at a local fly-in. In 2004, I was interviewed for the Timeless Voices for the EAA website about my work with the Powered Parachutes and Notre Dame.

In July, 2013, I received the Tony Bingelis Award at the EAA AirVenture International Fly in Oshkosh in for my contributions as an EAA TEC Counselor. Our son Jim flew in from Oregon to surprise us. He had called EAA and arranged it with them. As Gay and I stood in line for food, I felt a tap on my shoulder.

"Hi, Pops!"

Gay and I both whirled around. My jaw dropped, and Gay just about fainted. To add to that surprise, many of our friends and even people for whom we had inspected planes for had shown up. It was an amazing evening for us.

Our son Jim surprised us at my awards banquet at the 2013 EAA AirVenture Fly-In at Oshkosh, Wisconsin.

In August, 2013, The FAA presented me with the Wright Brothers Master Pilot Award for fifty years of promoting safe flying. Gay also received a Wright Brothers Award for being supportive of my flying.

There is a little story about the Wright Brothers Award. Gay and I flew to an EAA Hog Roast at Duck's Pasture in Michigan, owned by a fellow whose name is Donald Duck. People always give strange looks when we say we are going to see Donald Duck.

As we approached, I noticed right away that there were two FAA fellows there. I told Gay, "This is not good!"

Most of the pilots that go to this out of the way, country fly-in may not have their planes licensed, and may not have current pilot's licenses! This is kind of like "out west," complete with "good 'ole boys flyin' around." There was a big tent with a sound system playing WWII music, and before the dinner, the FAA fellow stepped up to the mic and said he had some awards to give out. He gave three other couples the Wright Brother Awards.

I told Gay, "I don't qualify, because I know the rules, and it says, 'For Fifty years of accident-free flying!' I've been down in most of the fields in Southern Indiana and Illinois."

Much to my surprise, he called us to the mic and gave us our awards. He said, "I've got to explain this about Lowell." He held up a stack of papers about an inch thick and continued, "I have in my hand the reports of the times that Lowell was down in fields around here. When Lowell was picking up airplanes, they were not as reliable as they are today. I studied all the reports and found that Lowell fixed all the planes but two, and flew them out. The FAA made him take the other two apart and truck them out. In checking the reports, they all flew again. So, we could call them all

'incidents' and not 'accidents'." That qualified me for
the Wright Brother Award.

U.S. Department
of Transportation
**Federal Aviation
Administration**

Great Lakes Region
2300 East Devon Avenue
Des Plaines, IL 60018

August 18, 2013

Mr. Lowell L. Farrand
12264 County Road 148
Ligonier, IN 46767

Dear Mr. Farrand:

On behalf of the Federal Aviation Administration, I take great pride in presenting the Wright Brothers "Master Pilot Award" in recognition of your 50 years of aviation flying experience.

This award was initiated by the Federal Aviation Administration in honor of the Wright Brothers who designed, built, and piloted the first powered airplane. In doing so, we are recognizing and honoring those individuals who have demonstrated professionalism, skill, and aviation expertise by maintaining safe operations for 50 or more years. Like you, they are the pilots who have brought the aviation industry forward for the enjoyment and benefit of future generations of men and women who will look to the skies.

This award acknowledges your exemplary service, professionalism, devotion to aviation safety, and recognition by your peers.

I extend to you best wishes in your future endeavors.

Sincerely,

James E. Gardner
Manager, Flight Standards Division

Wright Brothers "Master Pilot" Award, 2013

Gay and me on November 13, 2014. I was inducted into the
EAA-Ultralight Hall of Fame.

Another time at the EAA Hall of Fame Award dinner, Sammy Mason was honored as a World Aerobatic Champion and Test Pilot for Lockheed at Edwards AFB. Since Sammy had passed away, his daughter, son and grandson were there to receive his award. They were seated at the table next to us. She gave me a couple of big hugs and then presented me with a book about Sammy's life. In the book, it told of Sammy testing the rigid rotor helicopter for Lockheed. It seems that while I was recovering from my almost fatal accident, the metallurgist engineer found that a high-frequency harmonic vibration had destroyed the rotor system on the one that I had tested.

Rotor system harmonics are very complicated. A harmonic vibration can destroy metal in just seconds. The frequency of the vibration can be changed by the different thickness of the metal and the thickness of the blade. Also, the frequency can be changed by using dampeners. These vibrations have plagued helicopter designers for years. They redesigned the rotor system which changed the frequency and added dampeners. It was sent to Edwards AFB where Tony LaVere, head test pilot, had flown it just a few feet off the ground and checked all its control operations then turned it over to Sammy Mason to run it through the entire test program, including aerobatics.

He was told to be very cautious, but the Paris International Air Show was just two weeks away. It would take one week to get it there, leaving only one week for testing. Sammy was to demonstrate it at that show. He made a low-speed pass and a high speed-pass. Then, on the next pass, he did two rolls! Everyone was on their feet, because, at that time helicopters were not supposed to be able to do rolls.

After that demonstration, Lockheed called Sammy on the carpet. "What were you thinking? Our whole company's reputation could have been lost. What were you doing?"

Sammy answered, "I was selling helicopters!" And they did.

One year later, Sammy's grandson, Sammy Mason, Jr. was honored at the EAA Hall of Fame as an Aerobatic Champion. He had just found his grandfather's original Stearman, and the first thing he was going to do when he got home was to restore that plane exactly like it was originally.

It would be wrong to close this chapter without mentioning the "Monument Surprise." My wife tells it best:

"In April of 2001, Lowell was gone to a Fly-In and three of his EAA buddies from Chapter 132, Steve Linton, Bernie Yoder and Bill Weaver, came down with a very big wooden crate. They asked if they could put it in the carport. It was a "surprise" for Lowell. They were planning to come the next Saturday to have a "cook-out" too.

"I asked, 'How many people do you expect?'"

"'Probably eight to ten folks,' they answered. They added that they would furnish the grill, burgers and pop.'

"I agreed to get chips, baked beans and table service, and thought, 'This will be great!'

"On April 29—a gorgeous, sunny day, the three guys drive in. The next thing we knew, people started arriving by car, van, truck and airplanes. I found out that someone heard about our Surprise Party and told another, who told another, who told somebody else. In other words, word got out.

"The 'Three Buddies' mixed up cement, uncrated the Monument, created by Steve Linton at his Monument Business, and set up the monument, which is in the shape of a Luscombe rudder. It was beautiful and Lowell was 'flabbergasted'.

"The burgers were on the grill, and we were ready to celebrate—but, in a short while we ran out of everything! We sent a fellow to the grocery store for more food, chips and pop. We were thankful that several ladies had brought cookies, cake and chips.

"Strangers stopped when they saw the planes and all the people, so we fed them too. The very last couple that showed up got the last hamburger to split. It was getting late in the afternoon and some people had left. We realized we needed to take pictures! There were still thirty-five people there to pose with our Luscombe and the monument.

"It was quite a day, and the next day was my birthday!

"It is interesting that, in the weeks that followed, several people stopped by and gave their condolences to me. They were sorry. They actually thought Lowell had passed and was under the monument! Boy, did I set them straight!"

Our "Monument Surprise Party". Top. The "crowd that showed up" under my Luscombe. Bottom: My wife Gaylia and Me with the Luscombe and the Monument.

CHAPTER 10

Flying Young Eagles

I flew a lot of Young Eagles with the EAA organization over the years, and I am sure there is a story with each one, but one young girl stood out from all the rest. We usually consider kids for Young Eagles between the ages of eight and eighteen, but I always flew anybody that wanted to fly. On this particular day I had flown all the children except one six year old girl.

She was so excited, jumping up and down. She wanted to fly! I sat her in the plane, and she said, "I can't reach the rudder pedals!"

I thought, "At six years old, this girl doesn't even know what rudder pedals are!"

So I put a lot of cushions under her and behind her where she was able to reach the pedals. I explained the controls, and then we took off, climbed up and leveled off.

Once air born, she asked, "Can we fly over my Gramma's house?"

"Yes, but I don't know where your Gramma lives."

"Well, I DO!" she insisted.

All the while, I am thinking, "No six year old girl, her first time in an airplane isn't going to know the way to 'Gramma's house."

But she pointed and said, "Just follow this road down here to Nappanee, Indiana."

So, we did, and upon arriving at Nappanee, she said, "Turn your way right down here at this first street! See the house with the swimming pool? That's my Gramma's house. I was swimming in that pool just this morning!"

We flew over "Gramma's house" and then I told her we would fly over some lakes and see the sail boats. She asked if she could fly the plane. I told her to put her hand on the stick and her feet on the rudder pedals. I showed her how to make left and right turns. She took over and flew over the lakes, around the area, and back to our place.

I could not believe how well she flew! I pointed to the dial on the altimeter and told her to descend to the pointer on the altimeter. She surprised me by asking, "Will you pull the power back a little so I can descend?"

She leveled off at the exact altitude, flew downwind, base and final. I never touched anything until she got down to fifty feet on final. I took over and landed and taxied in.

I turned to her and said, "This cannot be your first airplane ride!"

She responded, "I have never been in any airplane, but I fly my computer Flight Sim every day! My Sim has a J-3 Cub and a DC-3. I can land both of them on the computer!"

I will never forget that little girl!

Another time, a neighbor boy who was helping his father do some cement work for us noticed the hangars and the airplanes. He was very interested in them and asked a lot of questions. I took him up for a Young Eagles ride and then, on another flight with him, I wound up showing him how to fly the airplane.

I did not see him for some time. Gay and I were at a meeting at the Goshen, Indiana, airport, and there he was. He was very excited that he had earned his Private License just the day before, and was taking his girlfriend for a ride. She was his first passenger!

It wasn't long before his parents told us at church that he graduated from Purdue University and earned his Private License, Commercial License, Instructor's License and his ATP License! He had just finished his training in Texas for flying airline jets. He married his girlfriend, got a job with the airlines, and bought a home in Goshen. They now had a two-year-old daughter. Gay and I thought, "Wow! That is really working fast! Where did the time go?"

We suddenly felt old!

Lloyd Turner, President of EAA Chapter 938, asked me if I would help fly a Boy Scout Troop for Young Eagles. Lloyd has a Cessna 150 on Wawassee Airport, a small grass strip on the edge Lake Wawassee. I had my Luscombe. I had just upgraded the engine to a 100 hp.

A couple of the boys were very large—one weighing 250 pounds and the other, 285 pounds. We had flown all the other boys, and Lloyd was concerned that the Cessna would not get them off the ground.

"It shouldn't be a problem for the Luscombe," I said. On takeoff I ran almost the length of the strip, but the plane wouldn't get off. It was too late to stop, so I pulled it off and kept it running flat. It finally started to climb a little.

I always fly my Young Eagles over their house and then over the lake. With full throttle, I finally got up to 750 feet by the time I passed over his house in Ligonier, Indiana. I even lost altitude in the turn over his house. I got it back up to 750 feet by the time I got to the lake.

The boy was enjoying his flight so much, but did not know I was "sweating bullets." I took the other boy and it was almost the same thing. He was the lighter of the two, so it wasn't near as bad.

All the boys enjoyed the flights. I blamed the bad performance of the airplane on the hot day,. But the following Monday, I was working in my hangar, and could not find my tool box anywhere.. My first thought was someone had stolen my tools.

Then it hit me! Goshen, Indiana, airport had called me about a problem with a prop seal leaking. As I retraced the events of that day I realized I had left my tool box in the Luscombe's baggage compartment. Now, my tool box weighs so much that it takes a big man to pick it up. I nearly fainted at the thought that the tool box had been riding in the baggage compartment when I flew those big boys. Either I was very lucky or God was surely with me. I am sure it was God!

"And he said unto me, My grace is sufficient for thee: for my strength is made perfect in weakness." 2 Corinthians 12: 9

Back in 2001, a grandfather brought his two grandsons to our home strip for Young Eagle rides. He had owned a Bonanza and was a pilot when he was younger. He wanted his grandkids to know more about airplanes. The boys were ten and twelve years old. I showed them each how to fly and let each one take the controls for about an hour.

I also helped each one build a balsa wood airplane and explained how airplanes fly while the grandfather took pictures of us. Years later, the grandfather came over to give us a picture of that day. In the same picture frame was a picture of the big MET LIFE (Snoopy) Blimp with the older boy at the controls. He had been flying the blimp for quite a while, and his brother was flying corporate airplanes.

Mr. Miller, whose sons farm the fields around us brought
this picture of his grandson. I flew them, and the oldest,
Joel Cox, graduated from Embry Riddle with all of his
pilot ratings and is flying this blimp. 4/17/2001

One day as I was driving home, I saw a huge shadow over our home strip. I couldn't figure it out at first. But when I turned into the drive, I saw the blimp about ten feet above the runway! It looked enormous.

He slowly went up, made a slow pattern around our strip three times, each time, almost touching the runway, and then flew off to the East.

One morning, while having breakfast at a local restaurant, the blimp pilot's dad asked, "Did you see the Met Life Blimp stop at your runway the other day?"

"Why yes I did!"

He told me his son had been videoing a football game and were on their way back to Ohio. He noticed that he was coming close to our strip. He told his crew, "I'm going to show you where I got my first airplane ride!"

How cool is that?

Mrs. Roberta Carpenter, writer for the Goshen Newspaper asked me if I could fly her over the Goshen area one day. She was writing an article about Goshen's expansion in both housing and industrial projects. I flew her over the area, but also, because she was so excited about flying, I showed her how to turn and fly the airplane. She did so well, that I told her she could fly anywhere that she wanted to go. She flew to

Bristol, Indiana, and over a horse ranch called Loveway. She was a volunteer there helping children with disabilities, using horses as therapy.

She later asked if she could bring the children down to see the airplanes. We set a date and all the volunteers brought the children. I explained the airplanes and how they fly. I took each one for a ride and was down to the last child., a sixteen-year-old girl. The volunteers told me she couldn't ride in the plane. She was a beautiful girl, but could not do anything for herself. She couldn't even talk. They said she might try to grab the controls and was very strong. She was always grabbing the volunteers.

"Well, I'm pretty strong, and I think I can handle her," I said. I just could not fly all the others and leave her out.

I was able to get her into the plane and explained everything to her just like I had done for all the other students, even though her "sponsor" said she wouldn't understand anything. After we had flown awhile, she put her hand on the control stick, but very gently. I put my hand on hers and made both left turns and right turns while telling her everything we were doing.

I had been told by the "sponsor" that she was not capable of expressing any emotion, but the huge smile on her face lit up the cockpit! We flew for quite a while, and she smiled the whole time.

Once we had landed and were standing by the plane, she began to pat the cowling—almost like you would pet a horse. I opened the cowling and explained how we check the engine before we fly. She reached in and put her hand on a spark plug wire, following it to the spark plug.

"SPARK PLUG!" she said very loudly and clearly.

"That's the only word she has ever spoken!" her "sponsor" said.

We learned that her father owned a little garage where he repaired cars. He would take her to the garage and tie her in a chair so she couldn't fall out. She watched her dad work on cars all her life.

Sadly, she died at age 19. I am so glad I was a part of her first smile and her first word.

One year when I served as Young Eagles Field Rep at Oshkosh, we organized to fly a group of "Make a Wish Foundation" children in a Ford Tri-Motor. The flights were paid for by David Hartman, Television announcer. We had enough children for four flights. The children ranged from ten to sixteen years old. We had been told that they were all terminal cancer patients. However on this day, they looked like the picture of health and were very excited to fly. They all wore ball caps to cover their bald heads due to chemo hair loss.

We explained to them about the airplane and how it flies. We then did the pre-flight inspection. As we began loading the first group, the FAA showed up and wanted to see the pilot's paper work. They said since the flight was being paid for, it became a commercial flight. The pilot would have to meet the same qualifications as commercial pilots, which is minimum of 500 hours in that type of aircraft. He had thousands of hours but only 395 in a Ford Tri Motor. The FAA grounded the flights.

We all had tears in our eyes and were trying to figure out how to tell these kids they wouldn't get their wish. As we pondered our situation someone showed up beside us.

"I hear you have a problem! Load them up! I'll fly them!" We all turned and there stood Chuck Yeager! We loaded the kids once again and made all four flights. Chuck Yeager was great with those kids and gave each one of them time at the controls.

After we had unloaded the last group, David Hartman stood on one side of the door and I stood on the other. Then Chuck Yeager appeared. He reached out and snatched my EAA hat and autographed it! Then David Hartman grabbed it and signed it too. They autographed all the hats for those kids too!

I reached for my hat and my wife grabbed it. She said, "You can get another EAA hat! I have plans for this one." She purchased a shadow box, lined the background with a sectional chart and placed the autographed hat in it. It hangs in our living room to this day.

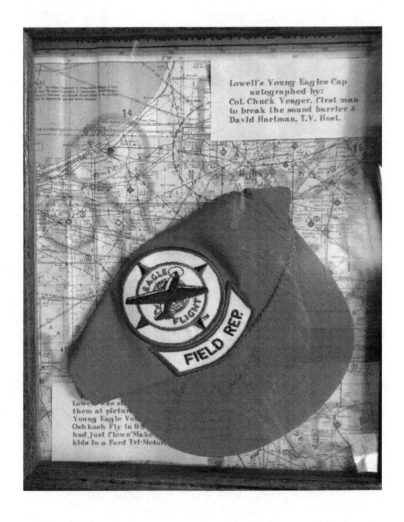

We found out one year later that almost half of those children had passed away from their cancer. But on that one day they were all happy and excited, and, as Gillespie McGee wrote, they had all "reached out and touched the face of God."

We have on hand a huge manila envelope full of Thank-you notes, cards and drawings by some of our Young Eagles.

"Dear Pilot's,

"Thank you for the ride. I reely licked it.

Your friend,

N. S. F."

"Young Eagle"

"Since Lowell Farrand took me flying in an airplane there has been a big change in my life. A change I've never been though before. I mean a change that's took me above everything. Something that's want me to fly day after day.

"By the way my name is A.U. I live in Wawka near Ligonier. I love my plane ride very much. I rode in a Luscombe 8A N2077K.

"Now since I rode with in an airplane with Lowell, I'm a member of the Young Eagles. If you want to know how I got involved with airplanes here it is. One night I was going out to eat with my grandpa and grandma. But I didn't know we were going to Lowell's house. I didn't know but my grandpa planed so my brother I are now Young Eagle's.

Thanks, Lowell Farrand."

Whenever I think of Young Eagles and taking them up, I would always be reminded of this scripture:

But they that wait upon the Lord shall renew their strength; they shall mount up with wings as eagles; they shall run, and not be weary; and they shall walk, and not faint. Isaiah 40:31

After all, flying is a God and me thing, and I loved giving those eagle wings to young kids.

CHAPTER 11

More Ferrying for Dealers

I picked up a Jodel-11 in southwestern Illinois and inspected it well. Everything looked good, and it was a nice airplane; however, I did note an unusually long pointed spinner. I checked, but I didn't like it. I had lost a spinner the day before on a 90 HP Piper Cub, and I knew how violent it can get if it breaks. I was half way across Illinois with the Jodel when the spinner broke. The vibration was so violent that I thought that I might even lose the engine. I Immediately shut it down and landed in the only available field. The landing was okay, but it was a hay field, and the hay was much too tall to take off. I removed the spinner and backing plate and checked the plane again. Everything seemed okay, and, after turning the plane back and forth very carefully, I was able to work the plane through a gate and into the farmer's driveway. I checked the highway in front of the farm and decided that I could take off from the highway if I held the plane down for half a mile—then I could pull up and miss all the wires. The farmer watched the traffic and told me when it was clear. Everything went well, and the trip home was just fine.

Another time, I picked up a Druine Turbulent which had a much smaller gas tank than the paperwork said it had. I picked the plane up just across the river in Missouri, flew across Illinois and just into Indiana when the gas gauge said zero. So, I started watching every field, thinking that I was going to run out of gas any minute. I had just flown over a big farm and noticed a "lean — to" type hangar with a Piper Cherokee in it. Just past that, my engine quit. I made a hard turnaround and landed in the field that had been the farmer's runway. He hadn't used the plane or the runway for three years. He said the Cherokee was full of gas and that I could use the gas, even though it was old.

"Drain the gas out, and fill your plane while I mow the runway," he said. After I got the gas and he got the mowing finished, I thanked the farmer and took off. However, about fifteen minutes into the flight, the plane sputtered and quit!

I immediately thought, "Uh-oh! There's water in that old gas!"

By using the primer and saying a prayer, I got it re-started. It seemed that I went through this procedure about every five minutes until I reached Lafayette, Indiana, where I landed and drained a quart of water out of the tank and got a tank full of fresh gas. I was supposed to be home for Gay and our daughter-in-law

Beth's birthday dinner at Beth's parents' house. The flight home from Lafayette went well but, needless to say, I arrived very late for the dinner.

Another time, I was flying a plane with a pusher engine. I was landing at the Mishawaka Pilots Club where the final approach is across the Robert Young railroad yards. As I turned from base to final, there was an awful BANG! It almost shook me out of the seat! I shut the engine down. I could see the runway, but I was sure that I couldn't make it. Looking down at the railroad yards, I saw two switching tracks that were separated enough that I could probably land between them. The landing went smoothly, with no additional damage to me or the plane. A faring had come off and cut one blade off the prop.

The engine had vibrated and bent the engine mount, but otherwise, there was no damage. The guys from the Pilots Club came over and thought there were enough of them that we could carry the plane over to the Pilots Club.

However, the FAA arrived about the same time and said "NO, you'll have to take the plane apart and truck it out of here!" We tried to argue, but the FAA won.

On another occasion, we were taking the NIAM airplanes to the local Elkhart, Indiana, air show a day early. A Grumman Wildcat F4F-3 came in from

California and was immediately grounded by the FAA.

The Pilot said "OH, boy, what are we going to do for the airshow? And how are we going to get the plane home?"

The Air Boss said, "Let's find Lowell, and he can fix it!"

I was flying the NA -50 that day and had just parked it. I went to check the Wildcat out, and there was definitely something going wrong in the aileron. Now this airplane was one that had been sitting on the bottom of Lake Michigan for sixty years. It had been raised and found to be in excellent condition and was restored to flying condition. This was one of the first air shows it had been flown to.

I removed the aileron, found that the balance weight had torn loose and had damaged all the ribs in the aileron. I stayed up for two days and a night without sleeping, made new ribs, repaired the balance weight, covered and painted the aileron, and filled out the FAA paperwork to show that it had been balanced. I installed the aileron on the plane. The FAA required a test flight before it could be flown in the airshow. For all that they gave me a Wildcat hat.

On a side note to the story, the plane had gone down in Lake Michigan during carrier qualification maneuvers. The pilot was reprimanded at that time for running out of gas! Ironically, when the plane was raised after all these years, the tanks were still half full of gas. They found that the problem was two lower cylinders that had blown. This enabled them to get the reprimand wiped off of his records.

Back around 1960, I was landing my Luscombe at the Goshen Airport and noticed a shadow in my windshield. Looking up, I noticed a nose wheel of a Cessna 172 only about two feet above me! I pushed down hard trying to get away from it. The lady pilot had full flaps on a 172 and was dropping as fast as I was diving. I pushed full rudder and somehow managed to slide it out from under her. We were now wing tip to wing tip, descending at about the same speed. She landed, and I was able to go around and then land safely. She said later that she never saw anybody else in the air. The guys at the airport said that they had noticed her at the same altitude coming up behind me on downwind. They said it looked like she was right on top of me all the way from base to final, just behind far enough that I couldn't see her. They also said that on final, we were so close that it looked like a bi-plane!

Mrs. Huffman had purchased a new Cessna 172 straight tail. She had just soloed and was building time. She had two of the cutest little girls that sat on the rail fence that used to be by the office the whole time that their mother was flying. The guys reported that when Mrs. Huffman flew, she never saw anything else in the sky and never used her radio.

Another dealer wanted me to fly to Ohio and pick up some aircraft parts. He wanted me to fly over in a 160 horsepower Musketeer with the back seats out and pick up a "firewall forward" Mooney engine, motor mount, cowling and prop. It took a long time to get everything loaded and on my way. It started getting dark, and, earlier in the day, one radio had gone out. Now, on the way home, the other radio went out. Besides that, it was getting foggy.

I made an approach at the Goshen Airport and saw the plane's landing lights shining on the roof of a red barn. Looking at the artificial horizon, I saw that I was in a 60-degree bank! Somehow, I was able to recover and stay above the fog, which, by now, was solid. I knew that my only chance was to fly straight south and hope for a temperature change which would cause the fog to lift. By now, both gas tanks were reading 1/4. I "leaned" the maximum and hoped the gas would hold out.

I thought, "I have a 1/2 Mooney in the back seat. If I crash they will wonder where the other airplane came from! The left fuel tank went dry, and I switched to the right tank which said ZERO! I was still on top of solid fog and wondering when the engine was going to quit.

I saw a red light that looked sort of fuzzy in the fog. It turned out to be a red light on the Muncie, IN. Airport! I approached using the red light, found the runway and landed safely! By now it was 2 AM, and I was so shaken up that I walked to a motel in Muncie to stay till morning.

The next morning, I walked back to the plane, checked the tanks which were completely dry—so dry that it wouldn't start to taxi to the pumps. Thinking back, I think I felt it quit while I was descending on the red light. God was surely watching over me!

In 1976, during the gas crunch, I was delivering a Smith Mini Plane DSA-1 to the west side of Illinois. DSA stood for "Darn Small Airplane—single place". Most were built with 65hp, or 85hp engines. This one had a Lycoming O-290D 135hp. The power was nice, but it burned more fuel. I stopped at Monticello, Indiana, for gas. They wouldn't sell me any because of the "gas crunch," so I took off in "kind of a huff!" In about the middle of Illinois the gas gauge read "zero". I knew that it would quit any minute. Fortunately in that part of the state, Illinois was all flat farm ground.

It was the spring of the year, and everything was freshly plowed. I knew if I landed in the plowed field, I'd probably flip over. Up ahead, I could see a horse ranch with a race track, so I landed on the race track. A pickup truck came out, and I apologized for landing on the race track.

However, the lady said, "Oh, this is the most exciting thing that has ever happened to me!"

She had come from England to race and train horses. She showed me each of her horses. The buildings were so beautiful, and so was she, with her cowboy boots and western clothes and big belt buckle. She filled my plane with tractor gas from a barrel and wouldn't accept anything for it. So, as I left I gave her a "mini airshow".

I delivered the Smith Mini-Plane and picked up a Jodel 9 BEBE with a Continental A-40 engine and flew back home. This Jodel, like all Jodel models, was a delight to fly.

CHAPTER 12

The AIRUP Story and Test Flying

The AIRUP was a low aspect ratio flying wing designed in 1933-34 by Dr. Clyde Snyder of Plymouth, Indiana. My friend, Milt Hatfield, an early aerobatic pilot, was the test pilot at the time. In 1929 he did skywriting for PEPSI-COLA, and in 1933, Milt flew the ARUP to the Chicago World's Fair.

The flying wings were extremely far ahead of their time. They would go faster with less horsepower. They could take off shorter, land shorter, and carry more weight than conventional airplanes. The other manufacturers were so afraid that the flying wing would take over the market that they sabotaged the ARUPs.

Gas lines and control cables were found cut. Finally, someone stuffed oily rags into the planes, and they all burned up. Dr. Snyder was never able to recover from the loss, and later, at his death bed, Milt Hatfield told him that he would rebuild the AIRUP in his memory.

Dr. Snyder's daughter, Sylvia Eisenhower, offered me a wind tunnel model and test data if I would build an ARUP in her father's memory. I felt that I didn't understand flying wings well enough, but said, "If Milt Hatfield would build it, I will fly it!"

Milt, who was in his eighties by then, built three ARUPs, and I flew the test flights for all three. Each one improved as we learned from the tests. They all took off very short and landed very short. They cruised faster with smaller engines than most other airplanes. You could get almost parachute type landings with the stick pulled back.

As we were doing the testing, a fellow came and said that he had been the photographer for the 1934 South Bend, Indiana, Airshow. He had just discovered the film in the attic—a 70 mm film that had the ARUP demonstrating short takeoffs and landings. Since it was old celluloid film, it might disintegrate, but we could have the film. I could get twelve minutes transferred to video when it all fell apart. I still have the video of the ARUP doing short field landings at the South Bend Airshow.

Milt passed away while working on the fourth ARUP. It's a shame that all the technology of the ARUP has been lost. I enjoyed flying it so much. It flew like no other airplane. I am perhaps the last person alive who has flown this wonderful flying wing ARUP. This aircraft had the most benign landing characteristics of any I ever flew. Little is known where the ARUP fleet is located, and none of the remaining examples are airworthy.

The Niles, Michigan, High School Automotive/Building Trades classes wanted to build an airplane as a class project. They picked a Pietenpol Air Camper to be powered by a Corvair car engine. They rebuilt the engine and converted it to an aircraft engine. They ran it in on a test stand, painted it bright red with black cylinders and added lots of chrome.

That took one-half year of class time, and it took eleven more years to complete the remainder of the airplane. I followed them and inspected the project a number of times. They asked me to be the "test pilot" once it was completed. The morning of the test flight, teachers and members of eleven years of classes assembled at the airport. After inspecting the airplane, I started the engine, and it was running very smoothly. After some more checking, I took off, and about fifty feet in the air, fire came back out the left exhaust almost to my arm. I saw that I could not get down on that runway, so I made a hard left turn which put me behind a full row of houses. I was just about level with the roof line of the houses.

It was early morning, and a lady coming out her back door with a wastebasket saw me right above her. She threw the wastebasket down, and her house coat came open. She had nothing else on! Only a pilot can see all these details in a crisis and still remember them! On down wind and over the end of a lake fire began to come out of the right exhaust, and I was losing power fast.

The plane was going about fifty miles per hour, but I knew two things: the Pietenpol will fly at fifty miles per hour, and the prop was made by Roger Lorenzen, the world's greatest prop maker, in my opinion. Roger had made the prop and had donated it to the project. Roger was famous for making the world's largest wooden propeller for the Langley Wind Tunnel. I had also flown Roger's props on different planes. It was just like putting a new engine in a plane when you put one of his props on! I knew that if I could keep the engine turning that his prop would get me there safely.

I turned final, and the landing was uneventful, but there were no people around! A fellow came out of the office. I asked "Where is everybody?

"Oh, A plane took off a while ago, and it crashed so everyone went to the crash site!"

I said, "No, that was me, and I'm okay!"

The problem was very simple. They had run the engine in the auto mechanics class on auto gas. It had been sitting for eleven and one-half years. The valve stems had all "varnished" and stuck. After a lot of solvent and cleaner, the engine ran okay. The other test flights went very well, and the plane is still flying today.

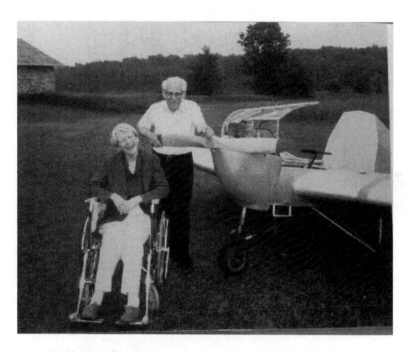

Milt Hatfield, famed ARUP builder and Sylvia Eisenhower, daughter of the original designer, Dr. Clyde Snyder.

CHAPTER 13

Memorable First Flights and Restorations

A local friend built the first plans-built QUICKIE canard aircraft. A canard is unique in construction that features a small forewing, or fore plane, situated forward of the main wing of a fixed-wing aircraft. The term "canard" came to describe the aircraft itself, as well as the wing configuration or the fore plane.

The Wright Flyer of 1903 featured the canard surface, but these designs were not built in quantity until the Saab Viggen jet fighter emerged in 1967. The aerodynamics of canard configuration are quite complex, thus requiring great care during the design planning process.

Building and finishing it required a LOT of sanding. It was hot that summer, and my friend was wiping sweat mixed with fiberglass sanding dust. He got Epoxy poisoning so badly that he couldn't get close to the project because he would break out.

I, along with two other friends, finished the airplane for him. His dream was to get it to Oshkosh, but time was getting close. Back then, the Phase I test time was seventy-five hours, unlike the forty that it is today. I flew the test flight. This was the first time that I'd flown a canard. I didn't know what to expect. The builder was standing on the ramp at Goshen Airport, so I dove down to about ten feet and made a close pass by him.

I went to pull back up, and the plane would not come back up. I had the plane at 160 mph, and the stick full back. There were trees coming up, and I was much lower than them. I squeezed between two of them, flew around the other, and tried to find my way around to line up with the runway. I lined up for final, but couldn't slow down, because the nose would drop consequently, I landed at 150 mph, and it took over 4,500 feet to stop!

It turned out that, being the month of May, I had just flown through a swarm of May flies! They had gummed up the front of the canard so badly that it lost lift. After cleaning all the bugs off and polishing the canard, it flew very well.

Trying to get seventy-five hours on the plane meant I was flying it as much as possible. Two days later, I had flown it constantly for two hours, when I suddenly woke up and realized I had been sleeping! The plane has a bubble canopy, and you sort of recline in the seat which it makes easy to fall asleep.

I looked over the side and thought "WOW, look at all those tall buildings!"

I was right over downtown Fort Wayne, Indiana. I made a quick turn and headed for home, while figuring my gas. It was just enough to get me home safely. We got the seventy-five-hour test time over the day before we were to leave for Oshkosh! The Owner/builder decided that he would try to fly the plane to Oshkosh, and I would follow him in my Luscombe just in case anything went wrong. We flew around some rain showers, but made Oshkosh successfully.

As we were tying the Quickie down, Burt Rutan and Gene Sheean walked up to look it over. Burt Rutan said, "Hey, I'm working on a rain canard, so in the meantime if you fly into rain, turn around and get out of it as quickly as possible as the canard loses lift."

We started laughing and said, "We've already been there and done that!"

Later Burt did develop a cuff for the canard which we installed on my friend's plane. That fixed the trouble.

Gene Sheean had manufactured the Quickie kits, and had his prototype Quickie at Oshkosh, but he asked if he could use my friend's Quickie in the Manufacturers Showcase that night.

"Yours looks better than mine!" he said, chuckling.

The flight home went well for my friend, except for a lot of rain showers which caused him to stop at a lot of airports and wait for the rain to quit.

After installing the cuff on the canard as Burt had promised, it flew very well. However, the owner still had a problem with the fiberglass poisoning. Every time he flew the plane he would break out. Dow-Corning supplied us with a special paint. We painted the whole interior and any other place that he might touch. It helped quite a bit and allowed the owner to fly the plane a total of 385 hours. Then the fiberglass poisoning came back, and he had to sell the plane.

I rebuilt about fifteen airplanes during the winter months. I would sell them in the spring and use the money to fly my Luscombe. In those days, you could get a "barn-find" airplane to restore. Each of them seemed to have their own story. Most of them either went down, or were parked for some problem. After rebuilding them, you had to find the problem. One of them had a history of the engine stopping for no reason. After rebuilding and flying it, which included three road landings, I found the problem. Someone had replaced a fuel gasket with a rubber gasket. Gas caused the rubber gasket to swell up and shut off the fuel. It took a while to find that one!

Another one was a Rearwin Sportster with a Menasco engine that had a history of quitting when the mags got too hot. I completely rebuilt the airplane and painted it bright red with black trim which were the Rearwin colors. I installed two blast tubes to cool the mags. A nineteen-year-old girl from Florida wanted to buy it. I tried to talk her out of it, because it was more of a round the patch weekend kind of flyer. I didn't recommend it for long distances, but she bought it anyway! I told her to keep in touch with us and call as soon as she got to Florida . She called and said that she had a wonderful trip home and loved the airplane. The only problem she had was that every time she stopped for fuel, everyone invited her to stay over and tell them all about her plane, so it took her over a week to get home.

The next airplane that I rebuilt was a Commonwealth Sky Ranger. They were noted for ground looping easily. I rebuilt the damage from ground-looping. I changed the tail wheel to a modern one that would help with the ground-looping. Again, when it was for sale, a young girl wanted to buy it!

I told her about the ground-looping tendencies, but she insisted on buying it! I told her "O.K., but only if I show you how to land it." She learned well and really loved her plane.

The next three airplanes that I restored were Stitts Playboys. Each one had a story. As I rebuilt each one their story would come out. In rebuilding them, I really learned to like the Stitts Playboys. He also developed the only fabric covering system that would not burn. I have covered many airplanes with the Stitts Polyfiber system.

Ray's son built the blue one so that it would be smaller than his dad's Sky Baby. He only flew it once to set the record, then they gave both airplanes to the EAA Museum. Ray was a good friend and a great guy! He passed away in 2016 and is really missed. He designed many airplanes—the Sky Baby, Play Boy, Play Girl, and the Play Mate.

Next, I rebuilt an Aeronca Chief that the wind had blown over and had broken the wing spars. While I was flying for the museum, we could fly the Museum planes, but could not afford the fuel for the big aircraft just to fly for fun. I told them I knew where there was a basket case Aeronca Chief that had been stored for thirty years. Both spars had been broken in a wind storm and it was in pretty sad shape. The good news, however, was I could get it for 500 dollars! Twelve of the volunteers helped on the rebuild for about a month, and then they suddenly stopped showing up.

It took Gay and me about eighteen months to finish it. The engine had been overhauled thirty-one years earlier, just before the wind damaged it. I checked it over, and it ran fine. I made the first test flight over the Industrial Park north of the airport.

There was a big bang, and I thought, "Oh no! I'm going to have to try to land in one of the factory parking lots! This isn't looking good!" Then I thought, "Wait! This is an Aeronca. It will fly on three cylinders. I've only blown one cylinder!"

I nursed it back to the airport. The spark plug threads had corroded, and the spark plug had blown out. I put a new insert and new spark plug, and the next day, I flew another test flight. About the same place, over the industrial park, I heard another big bang! I nursed the plane back to the airport again. I found that all the spark plug threads had corroded. I pulled all the cylinders and sent them in to be rebuilt.

I finally got the plane flying and tested, and also had twelve pilots that wanted to fly, but none of them had ever flown tail draggers. By the time I got them all tail dragger qualified, I had replaced the left wing tip twice, as they always ground looped to the left. I had repaired the left stabilizer and left elevator twice and replaced the tail wheel spring several times. But after all of that they flew the plane constantly. One pilot would get out of the plane, and another would climb in and get ready to take off.

Later the museum went broke, so the Aeronca Chief had to be sold, along with the other planes. It now resides at Albion, Indiana, Airport.

After that came an Aeronca Tri Champ 7FC, A Piper J-3 Cub and others. Our Tri Traveler, had quite a story. The Aeronca Company in Middletown, Ohio, had welded up four fuselages to make the first Tri Champs, but the company was in negotiations to sell to Champion Company in Wisconsin. Three of the fuselages and most of the jigs were sent to Champion. The engineering department at Aeronca kept one fuselage and finished it as a Tri Traveler. It became N9859B. The Goshen College purchased the plane for their Pilots Club. It was delivered to the Goshen, Indiana, Airport in 1958 by a company pilot.

I, of course, was hanging around the airport, as usual. He asked me if I wanted to take the new plane around the field once. I still remember the new smell of the interior, the smell of doped fabric and the eighty-octane Avgas—the red "stuff" we don't have anymore.

Hesston College, of Hesston, Kansas, was associated with Goshen College, so the students made many flights between the two colleges. Later on, Goshen College canceled the Pilots Club program. The plane was sold to an old man, and I kept trying to buy it from him.

"I'll sell it to you if you'll take me for rides in it whenever I want," he finally said. By now the plane had 4,200 hours on it, so I totally rebuilt the engine and recovered the plane. Both of our boys flew it a lot until they got married.

I then had to sell it in order to keep the Luscombe. It was sold several times, but always close enough that the owners said I could fly it. They all still called it "Lowell's Plane." Recently it sold again, and N9859B now resides in West Virginia, owned by Clarence Peters. It was a great airplane and hard to replace.

Milt Hatfield did skywriting for Pepsi-Cola. He knew that I was flying and had not taken training.

"Hey! Have you had any spin training?" he asked one day.

"No, matter of fact, I haven't."

"Well, you're gonna get some today! Go get in that Civil Air Patrol J-3 Cub over there!"

Up we went to do spins. His spins were so nice and smooth. Mine made the windows rattle and sand came up off the floor! It did not feel very good. After an hour of this, I finally got the feel for spins, but I never did like them.

"I didn't want to show you spins so you could go out and do spins," he said. "Rather, I wanted to show you how to keep from getting into a spin!" I believe that one hour of spin training might have saved my life in later years.

After all these years, a neighbor found that same Cub. It has been rebuilt and recovered many times. He now keeps it in the hangar at the other end of our home strip and says I am welcome to fly it whenever I want!

Aeronca Tri-Champ

Top: Gaylia with the restored 1946 Aeronca Chief. She had just taken her first ride in it. Bottom: My Tiger Moth. Couldn't afford one, so I built one!!

My PT-26 I completely rebuilt after it suffered a blown engine on take-off.

The PT-26 engine had blown and the whole engine and airplane was going to need a lot of parts. In researching, so many had been in training at Love Field, in Dallas, Texas. Wondering if they still had any parts, I was able to contact the supply sergeant, and he said, "You are in luck, I have just been ordered to completely clean out all of the old PT aircraft parts!"

He had collected them to be thrown away and was only a week away from their being destroyed. He boxed up and sent me everything I needed to rebuild the entire engine, and all of it was in 1942 boxes! Parts were all wrapped in cosmoline to preserve them. I was able to rebuild the PT into a good airplane, and it won many awards. I went to

the Fairchild Museum where it was on display only to
find the building had just been sold, and all the
airplanes had been sold.

CHAPTER 14

Growing up, My Wife and Kids

I grew up a pretty bad guy. I think it all began on the first day of first grade! My folks had bought me all new clothes to start school, but I came home with my clothes torn and dirty.

Dad asked me, "Son, what happened?"

"The big boys beat me up!"

With that, Dad took off his belt and just beat the tar out of me. I was crying and asking, "Why, why?"

My Dad said, "Every time you come home and have lost a fight, you'll get another beating, until you learn to stick up for yourself!

"But they're bigger!" I argued.

"That doesn't make any difference! You get in the first and hardest hit, and you won't have to worry about them."

I found this to be true, so I hit the first and hardest. This caused me to get kicked out of school, probably more than any other kid! I made up my mind that I would try to be the meanest kid that I could! As I grew up, I didn't get any better. I learned to out-fight and out-cuss anybody else there.

After High School, I went to Chicago and attended Coyne Electronic School and De Forest Technical School, now known as De Vry University. Coyne Electronic School was in very bad part of Chicago. I stayed at the YMCA at Madison and Monroe St. At school, they told us to NEVER walk home from school alone. One night I stayed and helped the teacher clean up. On the way home, I noticed the sidewalk was blocked by a bunch of gang members. They circled me and said they were going to rob me! I started to fight them, but thought I'll probably end up dead! About that time, I looked around, and a lot of the guys were laid out on the sidewalk. I looked up, and there was the biggest kid I had ever seen! His hands were huge! He could grab and throw a fellow with just one arm!

"Are you having some trouble?" he asked.

I was so glad to see him and found out that he stayed at the Y on the same floor that I did. After that, I walked back to the Y with him.

Later, I married my high school sweetheart, Gaylia. We had two sons, Grant and Jim. I loved them so much, but I was still mean to them. I really felt bad, because I didn't want to be mean to them. Once the kids scattered my tools in the yard, and they rusted. I really got mad and used my belt on them. This has always bothered me.

After my accident where I was pronounced dead, God became so real to me, saved me and gave me a second chance. I completely changed and am so different from my "old self." The meanness and cussing were gone. Gay says that now I tend to let people take advantage of me. Our kids started bringing kids home from school with them. Their parents were fighting, getting divorced, etc. Over the years, we had about fifteen kids total. Some were there for a short while others, two girls, were there until we helped them with their weddings. One couple came back and lived with us for a while.

We were always hard up for money, but when the kids got old enough to have jobs and needed cars to get to work, we bought old worn-out $50.00 cars and told them that they'd have to learn to repair them if they were going to drive them. It seems that we spent almost every evening working on someone's car. I tried to teach them all to be good mechanics—even the girls!

Gay often tells that during that year when I was recuperating, we "barely squeaked by." However our parents and grandparents had gardens and brought canned fruits and vegetables for us. That Christmas we told the kids we couldn't afford to buy them anything. However, Gay did have a couple of S & H Green Stamp books and used them for a small gift for each of the boys.

Grant and Jim went down the road about a mile with their friend Lonny to the old abandoned barn where they sometimes "hung out." They found a very old flat top four plate iron stove that burned wood. After they cleaned it with a wire brush, they painted it "stove black," loaded it on a sled and pulled it to our house through the snow. They beamed as they presented their Christmas gift to us! We still have the stove and use it as an end table in our living room.

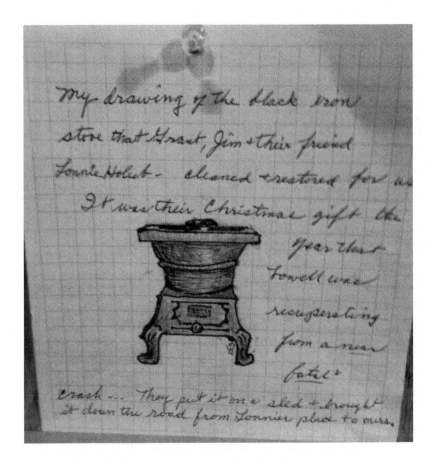

I love music, but I don't have a single note in me! My dad spent most of his life working for the musical instrument company C.G.Conn. I could have any instrument I wanted, but I had no musical talent.

Ironically, while I was servicing televisions, stereos and other electronic equipment for Sears & Roebuck, Sears decided that I would be the person to service their electronic organs. Since I had no ear for music, I was tuning the organs with an electronic tuning device. The device was supposed to be the most accurate, but I had noticed that when a man tuned the organ by ear the organ then seemed to come alive. It was just different. Then I met a man who had perfect pitch! Robert Crumlish helped me out immensely. He worked for CG Conn and tuned all of their pipe and theater organs. Conn had built him a soundproof room so he could check the tuning of all the different instruments. He was definitely a genius.

As we talked together one day, he told me about his problem. He couldn't shut down his mind and could not sleep. Doctors had told him that he would" burn out" and be dead before he reached twenty-five years of age.

He had a wife and six children, so he bought two houses side by side. His wife and children lived in one, and he lived in the other! He knew that no one could put up with him for twenty-four hours a day!

He was also a pilot and had been in the Army Air Corp before WWII. He had been flying the old B-10 bombers two years before WWII. When war broke out, they made him an instructor in B-17's. Since he was a pilot and into electronics, we got along really well.

One day the FAA called me and said that the peripheral transmitting station was out of commission. It was located on a hill south of Goshen.

"Can you get it working by night fall?"

The Chicago tower transmits through this station to line up all airliners coming from the eastern section to "stack" them so that they will line up with the airliners coming from the western section without creating delays. I knew that this could be beyond me so I asked Robert if he would go with me.

This was back when everything was vacuum tubes. There were so many tubes in this transmitter that they heated the building. I was very nervous, thinking that this was beyond me.

We walked into the building, and immediately Robert said "You've got a burned out transformer in this corner!"

"How can you tell by just walking into this building?"

"Just by the smell. Resistors and condensers smell different than transformers!"

Sure enough, a transformer had shorted out! It was a very special transformer, and no way would we be able to get one very soon.

Robert said "Oh, just get me a TV transformer. I'll modify it to make it work."

It worked fine, and the station was back up and running in two hours! He was just unbelievable! After that, Robert and I became good friends, flying together and working on organs.

About that time, Gay wanted an organ. I was going to buy her a small Sears organ, but Robert intervened.

"OH, NO! We'll just build one!"

He brought a huge CG Conn cabinet with three keyboards. two levels of foot pedals and more stops than I'd ever seen on an organ! And all of this was to go into our little A Frame House. There was nothing inside the cabinet! He brought in a really large box filled with all kinds of parts. We worked on the organ in our spare time for one year. One New Year's Day, Robert said he would come down and finish it. We built the whole organ without a schematic, which had me concerned.

Robert said "No problem, I have it all in my head!"

We finished at midnight, and he pulled up the bench and gave us a concert that was unbelievable. His hands and feet just floated across the keys and pedals. Sadly, he passed away shortly after that at age 52, twice as long as the Doctors had thought. The organ was too big for the house, so eventually we traded for a smaller organ. Robert was a really special guy and I missed him terribly.

Example of the Conn 653 Theatre Organ that we built.

One day I was surprised when I came home and saw one of the girls among our kids' many friends had put a clutch in her Datsun, she was lying underneath, trying to put the transmission in. They all turned out to be good mechanics. We were still hard up, and I started working two jobs. I worked an eight-hour job in Goshen, got fast food to eat as I drove a little very worn out VW "Bug," wide-open for an hour to Niles, Michigan, where I repaired all the electronic items on the bench till about midnight, and then drove wide-open to get home for a few hours of sleep!

My life consisted of "WORK-SLEEP-REPEAT!" Many years later when our kids and their families were here, the boys said, "Dad, you were always working or sleeping when we were growing up."

We are so proud of our boys and the other kids that we tried to help. They have turned out to be hard-working, kind, loving people with great families of their own. It took a lot of love, patience and some tears to get through it all. But God was there the whole time helping us! I took them all flying, and Grant, Jim and one of their friends all got their pilots' licenses. Besides that, all the kids could land the plane if they had to.

Our kids had been married about thirty years and were all home for Christmas. We were going through old pictures from the past, and I noticed a picture of the instrument panel of my Aeronca N83655. The altimeter was reading 10,000 feet in the picture, and I said, "I never had that plane to 10,000 feet!"

The kids said "Dad, that's all the higher it would go!!"

The next picture was of my in-laws' cottage near Kalamazoo, Michigan. I said, "How did you get these pictures?"

It was then the story came out how they'd chalk the tires in the hangar, note how the prop was set and what the gas gauge read, so they could put the plane back just like it was! Now, mind you, Grant was fourteen; Jim was twelve, and their friend was twelve. The three of them would go flying in my two-place airplane. Grant would get off the school bus at the airport and taxi to the far side of the airport, where Jim and their friend would get off the bus and jump into the plane and they'd go flying! The plane was always put back exactly like it was—so for all those years, I didn't know what they had been up to! Later, when Grant was sixteen, I allowed him to skip school to solo the morning of his birthday. The instructor signed him off to solo and told him that he could practice a little.

Grant took off and flew to Knox, Indiana, about sixty miles away, to talk to Dave Vallo, the FBO operator, because he'd flown in WWI and liked to tell the kids his stories about flying in the Lafayette Escadrille. He also looked a lot like my dad, and talked like him, too! Grant lost track of time and flew back to Goshen about 5 p.m. The instructor was looking for him!

He said "I okayed you to practice in the airport pattern, not to do a cross country!" I couldn't be too upset with him, because I had done about the same thing.

Later, Grant found an Aeronca L-3 Defender which we totally rebuilt. He really liked it. He loved to do spins, loops, and rolls in it on almost every flight. He said, selling it was the first biggest mistake he ever made. The second was delivering it to Maine.

I went with him to deliver the plane. It was to be a two-day trip—one day out, deliver the plane, and pick up a Piper 160 horsepower Cherokee and fly home the second day. About the middle of the afternoon on the first day, it suddenly got dark as night and started lightning! I'd never seen weather change so fast. We were now IFR in an Antique airplane, no IFR instruments. All we had for a radio was a small wooden box called a "Sky Boy" which we had sitting on the floor.

We called Ithaca, New York. Surprisingly, they responded immediately. They had us on radar and gave us a heading to follow and added a warning. "Be sure you don't fly past the airport, because there are mountains that are higher than you are flying!"

We were flying in a pitch-black sky when Ithaca called again and said we were approaching the airport. We started to descend, and suddenly we saw the airport. We were right over the middle of the runway, but very high.

"We're not going around," Grant said, as he put the plane into the hardest "slip" I've ever seen. We landed on the end of the runway and taxied in. It was raining so hard that we could hardly see the buildings. Guys were standing in the doorway of a huge airliner hangar and motioning for us to taxi right on in. We parked beside a DC-3.

Someone said, "They want to see you in the tower!"

I thought, "Uh-oh! We're in for it!"

However, they just hugged us and said they didn't understand how we got through the storm in that little airplane. They were so glad to see that we were okay. Much later, we found out that a friend of Grant's had been praying for us to have a safe trip.

We were told that this was the first week of the fall solstice, and that means it usually rains for ten days. Every morning we checked with the tower about the weather, and on the tenth day, they said, "We think we can get you out of here today!"

As we looked out, we couldn't even see the end of the runway. They said "Oh, that's okay. Just take off; keep it to about ten feet, and right off the end of the runway, you'll see a railroad, turn left, stay over the railroad, through the mountain pass. We've called ahead—it's clear sunshine on the other side of the mountain range."

We called the fellow who was buying Grant's plane, and he suggested that he'd meet us at Cornell, New York. We delivered the Aeronca, picked up the Cherokee and started for home. By this time, we had both maxed out our credit cards; our wives were upset, and we almost lost our jobs. We were sure glad to get home!

About a year later Grant was billed for taxes on the Aeronca which was still in his name. The lawyer said the buyer parked the plane in hangar, the paper work was still in the seat. The guy, his wife and kids had disappeared in a brand-new car and had never been found.   Grant could get the plane back if he wanted to pay the hangar rent and lawyer fees!

After that first trip, we decided against it.

CHAPTER 15

I'm Not Dead

He went in and said to them, "Why all this commotion and wailing? The child is not dead but asleep."

Mark 5:39

In the 1960's all the engineering talk at that time was about a rigid rotor helicopter. Many had tried, but were unsuccessful. A Chinese scientist came to Notre Dame and said he knew how it could be done. He brought Bendix in to make the tie bars for the rigid rotor. We assembled a test machine, and I said that I would fly it.

On a beautiful morning, I made the test flight and was just thinking, "This is so smooth! We really must have something good!"

And that's when pieces started flying in all directions! I was taken to the ER and pronounced dead—no heartbeat, vital signs, etc. My back and legs were broken. Broken arms consisted of bones sticking out of my elbows with dirt caked on them. Several ribs were broken. The ER Doctor said to the nurse, "too bad we couldn't save this man, but he has too many injuries!"

I wanted to say so badly, "Doc, I'm NOT DEAD!" I then realized that I was seeing this whole picture, but I wasn't in my body! I could see everything that was happening so clearly and I felt GREAT! Then the doctor told the nurse to wheel me back into a hall, tag me and call a funeral home! The nurse kept leaning over me, and then ran back to ER screaming, "I don't think this man is dead!!" The ER Doctor came back and looked at me again.

"No vital signs, he's gone. Sometimes corpses twitch and groan."

With that, he returned to ER, because there had been several very serious auto accidents. The nurse ran back to ER a second time.

"I don't think he's dead!"

The Doctor said angrily, "If it makes you feel any better, go ahead and hook him up to life support. His angry voice caused her to cry.

At that point I wasn't on the gurney in the hall. Instead, I was in a most wonderful place. It was so beautiful. The place was so big, and I was confused. I thought, "I need to figure out what's going on!"

I felt more wonderful than I had ever felt before. I saw a bright, warm glow, and there were lots of people that I felt drawn to. I was walking toward this beautiful place when suddenly a loud voice said, "You don't have to go back, but if you do, you must go right now!"

I kept saying, "I've got a wife and kids, I've got to go back!"

Immediately I was back in my body on the gurney. I hurt EVERYWHERE. I wondered then, did I make a mistake? I saw they were giving me shots. I heard a nurse say, "Penicillin!"

I knew I was allergic to that, but I couldn't speak. Gay and the boys came in to see me and found me in a plastic lined bed filled with ice! I had a very bad reaction to the penicillin, and later my skin got red and began to peel! Later, I woke up in a full body cast. I heard the nurse tell the Doctor that my heart rate was coming up, and my vital signs were getting better.

I heard the Doctor tell the nurse, "You didn't do him any favors by hooking him up to life support. He was out of oxygen for a very long time, and he may be brain dead—just a 'vegetable'. Also, with all the broken bones, he may never walk again." Funny, some say I am still brain dead—Ha!

I thought to myself, "Doc, I'm going to show you!"

It was a long, slow recovery before I could do much or return to work. But during this time I realized that something was different! I was so thankful for the nurses and doctors and the great care that I received.

I need to tell you a bit about my life before this experience. I grew up a very bad person, I would fight; I didn't like people. In fact, I didn't like myself. My language was terrible. I could hardly say a whole sentence without curse words. I especially didn't like school teachers. I was kicked out of school probably more than any other kid. One English teacher didn't like me, and I sure didn't like her. On one test, I made sure that I missed every question! She gave me a passing grade!

"You can't do that," I said. "I know I missed them all. "She said, "I know—you had to know the right answers to miss them all, and, furthermore, I'm not going to put up with you another year!"

I wasn't very nice to my wife and kids. I had a quick temper and blew up often at them. I knew that I was a bad person, fought with everybody, including my Boy Scout troop, where I got my lower front teeth knocked out! But, I couldn't help myself to change and become better, although I was raised in church and went every Sunday. My Mother was the oldest continuous member at 97.5 years of age. She taught

Sunday school, and I'm sure that she prayed for me a lot!

My Dad was a trustee and a Boy Scout leader. I became a Boy Scout Leader when our boys were growing up. After getting married, Gay and I led Junior Church. I prayed for friends, family and the church prayer requests, but I don't think that I really expected an answer. Religion was a "Sunday thing". When church was over, I was as bad as ever.

But, after I woke up from that terrible accident, I realized that something was very different. I loved everybody, and the cursing was gone! All the hatred was gone! I became totally different and confused. After a long recovery, and I was well enough to go to church I told the minister that we had at the time about my "out of body experience and seeing heaven," he laughed at me and said, "That's what we call a fox hole experience—everybody in the war thought they were going to die and had dreams, saw angels, etc." I was so embarrassed that I never told another person for forty years. After recovery and I had a checkup, the doctor sent me home and suggested that I probably shouldn't drive and that I'd never be able to fly again. So, I went home and got the plane out and flew for an hour.

"What did he know?"

I knew I had lived Colossians 1:12-13 because I was "giving thanks to the Father." Who has qualified (us) to share in the inheritance of the saints in the light. He has rescued us from the dominion of darkness and brought us into the kingdom of His beloved Son,…"

Forty years later I was flying an old friend who had been a very good pilot, he could not pilot the plane anymore, and he wanted me to fly him around. He had a very nice Cessna 175 — just like new. It was the best airframe that Cessna ever built with the worst engine that Continental ever built. We were flying a longer trip, and I suddenly felt compelled to tell him "my story".

He said, "People don't know this about me, but I' m an ordained minister, and I can tell you when they pronounced you dead, your old soul died, and God gave you a new soul, because HE has something for you to do."

In fact, in Jeremiah 29:11 the Father tells us "For I know the plans that I have for you,' declares the LORD, 'plans for welfare and not for calamity to give you a future and a hope."

It was like a great weight had been lifted off me, and my life has been so different, Gay and I have found both our lives have changed, so much for the better. We are much happier. We have had so many answers to prayer, God has also brought so many wonderful Christian people into our lives. It is amazing!

After I realized that I had been given a new soul, a pilot that flies from our home strip asked me to ride to Ohio with him to pick up an aircraft engine. He told me of his out of body experience during a kidney transplant. He, too almost died. I, in turn, told him about my experience and how the minister/pilot told me about my new soul. He asked me to tell his Sunday School class about "my story". I now felt that I could share my story without people making fun of me.

Just days later, I was getting a checkup at my doctor's office. When she told how God healed her from an "incurable" disease after the whole church family and friends had prayed, I told her my story. She insisted that I share my story with her Sunday School class. After sharing with her class, one of the ladies was in tears. After class, I talked to her said I was sorry if I had said something to make her cry.

She said, "Oh, no! It's like a great weight has been lifted off me. I was pronounced dead after a car accident about forty years ago. I went to heaven!

She told how beautiful it was, and all the things she saw. When she told her best friends, they shunned her and thought she was crazy and told other people in their church, who also gave her the cold shoulder. She didn't share her story with anyone until that day we both sat down and had a good cry. She was visiting her father from California, and he brought her to that

Sunday School class! What a God Wink! It was amazing that she described heaven almost exactly like I had seen it!

After my accident and long recovery, I went back to flying, and I realized that I was very different. All the bad "stuff" was gone. There was no more cursing, and I liked everyone. Life was different, and I was happy! I saw good in everyone around me. God started to answer my prayers so much that it was kind of scary. God has still answered so many prayers, it is almost shocking.

I began to fully understand what the Apostle Paul meant in 2 Corinthians 5:17 when he said, "Therefore if any man be in Christ, he is a new creature: old things are passed away; behold, all things are become new."

One of the times it happened when the airport called and said that a plane had landed to refuel on a long cross-country trip to home in Idaho. Now, the plane would not start. The airport mechanic tried everything he could think of, and still it wouldn't start. They asked if I might have any ideas, and I told them that I was on my way.

Driving to the airport, I was thinking, "I know their mechanic. He's the best there is! What am I going to do?"

I got there and checked everything. Most of it, the mechanic had already checked. After about one day of checking, I began to feel pains in my chest. It was a very hot day, and at my age, I thought I should back off a little bit.

I heard the pilot talking about being worried. He seemed very upset and really needed to get home, and he wondered how he would get back for the plane.

The FBO Manager told him, "Don't worry. Lowell will have it going in a few minutes!"

I prayed, "Oh, Lord, they have so much confidence in me, and I tried everything! If we're gonna fix it, I sure will need your help!"

At that very moment, it was just like a voice said to me, "Open your eyes! You're looking at the problem!"

I realized that I had been looking but not seeing. There in front of me were mag filters installed like I'd never seen before. They had overheated and shorted out. It was a quick fix, and the plane started fine!

The pilot told me the story. He had had radio trouble before he started the trip, and the radio shop had installed filters. When he was landing at Goshen, the radio cut out again. The radio filters had been installed wrong! I would never have found the problem without God's help!

Other answers to prayer kept coming. I also took care of an old pilot that lived in a very old run-down house. He relied on me to fix everything. The house was really falling apart, and things would break, but he thought I could fix it. One day he called and said he didn't have any electricity. The house had at least 100-year-old wiring, and I started checking for the problem. Everything was shorted. I checked everywhere. I went under the house that had an old stone foundation. Wild animals of all kinds were living there! I was frustrated and dirty as a pig, and I'd checked everything. Since I knew electricity, it should have been easy to find the trouble. I spent most of the day looking and not finding the problem.

Soon, I began to feel weak and began to pray, "Lord, this fellow has no money to go anyplace better. There's no electrician who would come in to this dirty, falling down house. I tried everything, and I'm at my wits end"

While I was praying, the fellow ran his wheel chair from the living room into the kitchen. The wheel chair caught on the molding of the kitchen doorway. I bent down to free the wheel chair and noticed the molding had pulled a hole in the wall. I'm thinking, "Oh, boy, now I'll have to fix the molding and plaster the hole in the wall, but, when I looked into the hole I saw that a mouse had made a nest there & chewed the wires together! It was about ten minutes to fix the wiring, and I realized that, on my own, I would have never looked inside the wall. I didn't even know that there was wiring in there! I thanked God so much for answering prayer, so this old fellow could stay in his home a while longer. These are just two of the answered prayers since I have been changed. There are many more.

Thanks LORD for giving me a second chance!

Trust in the Lord with all your heart, and do not lean on your own understanding. In all your ways acknowledge him, and he will make straight your paths. Proverbs 3:5-6

Man's goings are of the Lord; how can a man then understand his own way? Proverbs 20:24.

145

CHAPTER 16

It's a Wonderful Life!

A really nice day surprised us after a long, rainy and windy spell, so, like most pilots, I took the Luscombe out for an hour of "just local flying" over the lakes and the farm country—no place in particular—just enjoying the beautiful sky. After the winter season the sky always seemed bluer, and the plane seemed to fly smoother. It was such a wonderful feeling to be up there, enjoying the beautiful sky. My mind wandered through all the EAA members and friends that made my "New/Old Luscombe" possible.

I was enjoying the flight so much and thinking that, now in my mid-eighties, I never know which flight might be my last one. After landing back at the home strip and tucking the Luscombe away in the hangar I saw the guys in my neighbor's hangar bringing out two Gyro planes. The memories of my early days flying Gyro Copters came flooding into my mind.

I got a glass of iced tea and sat in the greenhouse to watch the fellows fly. They know that I really like to hear the rotor blades "chop" so they fly right over the top of the greenhouse and slow up to make them "chop" for me. Years ago, we had such a good Gyro

Copter club with about twenty Gyro Copters. We met at Knox, Indiana, or Coldwater, Michigan, about once a month for a lot of flying and supper and sometimes even dancing! Sometimes at Knox the guys flew their Copters to Winamac, Indiana, for a picnic, and the wives would drive there with food.

One summer afternoon we could see the weather was changing, and black clouds were forming. Most of the fellows' wives brought the trailers along to take the copters back to Knox. I decided I would fly back to Knox, but as I approached Knox I could see the sun shining on half of the airport and black rain clouds on the other half! I had been flying with my camera around my neck so I snapped a picture of that! It turned out to be the most beautiful picture. You could see my copter, and, to the left, was beautiful sunshine. To the right, were the very black storm clouds. Needless to say, I got very wet while landing.

At another Copter fly-in at Coldwater, Michigan, we had a full day of flying. In those days, we were all flying target drone engines. In the late afternoon, I climbed out from the airport and blew a cylinder — right over U.S. 12! I turned sharply back toward the airport, past the Drive-In theater screen at about half way up! I barely made it to the end of the runway. About the same time, our club Vice President was approaching from the other end of the strip, which put him over a lake. He blew a cylinder and went into the lake about ten feet from the shore. We all rushed over and pulled him and the plane out of the water. We were all wet, but all O.K. That night, we had a wonderful dinner with live music and dancing.

Later, as I sat in the greenhouse, my thoughts went through all my flying days and I reflected,

"Here I have just put the Luscombe away after a wonderful flight, Two Gyro Copters are flying overhead while an Aeronca Champ warms up at the other end of the strip. A two-place Flight Star has just entered downwind to our little strip, and a Kit Fox is farther out on approach to the strip. A young State Trooper is just getting his Challenger out to go flying. How much better can this get? I have my own Air Show!

"And to make it even better, we have the most wonderful neighbors and friends. A neighbor lady keeps the strip mowed. She loves to do it. Says 'It's my quiet time!'

"The Flight Star pilot also rolls the runway with a vibrating roller. The other pilots always 'chip in' if there are repairs like wind socks, spreading weed killer, repairs, etc. One of the lady pilots and her friend cooks on the grill for all of us about once a month, everybody brings other things, and we have a ball. GOD has blessed us with these friends and neighbors.

I have been dead and lived to tell it. I have been down in places no pilot would want to be. As I have said before, "I've been down in most of the fields in Southern Indiana and Illinois." I've had close calls from flying low to see the ground, but I can say, "Hey, doesn't God say 'LO, I am with you always?'—even when we get corn stalks in the landing gear!!"

It's a wonderful life! God gave it to us. And He has more of it for us to live! Why, He even says it!

I am come that they might have life, and that they might have it more abundantly. John 10:10

Top: Our home, strip and hangars in Ligonier, Indiana.

The day I got to "fly" the Spruce Goose, wearing Howard Hughes' hat! What an airplane that is!

Me, standing with my "Tiger Moth" replica.

Editor's Note

I came in contact with a fellow pilot, Mike Sheetz, from Indianapolis, Indiana, at the EAA AirVenture 2016 in Oshkosh, Wisconsin. It was a complete chance meeting over hotdogs at one of the many concession stands along the way. My husband and I instantly fell into conversation about flying, EAA, and various other "getting-to-know-you" topics.

When he heard I was there to sign my books at the event, he bought my second book. Settling in: At Home in My Skies. He read it and raved about it. We all stayed in contact.

About six months later, Mike called me about possibility of doing a book on the life and career of Lowell Farrand. And asked me to send them a copy of my book. I sent Lowell and Gaylia my first book, The Day I Grew Wings. Lowell and Gay came by their place one day as they made their way to check off their 619th experimental plane. Mike accompanied them to Hendricks County Airport, west of Indianapolis, to watch Lowell do a first-hand inspection process. Of course, they exchanged some more stories as they drove along. Afterward, the Farrands visited with Mike and his wife Dixie briefly before returning home that evening. It was a very enjoyable day to be sure.

After a couple of initial phone calls and emails to

Lowell and Gay, I told him I would be delighted to work with him on this project. A large notebook with pictures and notes soon arrived on my door step, and then Gay began sending me notes from his journals almost daily. As we got more acquainted they asked for my third book and also sent more notes to me

After compiling the notes and doing the edits, I sent the rough draft for their perusal. More and more stories and pictures came, and the book rapidly took form. I set it in my mind to wrap the book up at their home in the summer of 2017.

The place was exactly as I had read about and imagined. The Farrands live in an A-frame house and are closely accompanied by three hangars. His workshop and office have been described as a "pilot's dream." Their living room defines what they are all about, too. Aviation artifacts, pictures, models, wallpaper and even the paper napkins and paper plates remind us all that aviation has been a large part of his life. The presence of scripture reminders and Bibles remind us that his life clearly says, "God, Me and Those Flying Machines!" They live both.

After two long days of perusing the manuscript and working up photos to reinforce the chapters, we called it a book, called it a day and went out to fly his 1941 "New/Old Luscombe." I even wrote up a log book entry and he signed it! It will be a treasure there for years to come. I hope you enjoy Lowell's life story as much as I have in putting it together.

Rebecca McLendon, 2017.

Editor's Note. While I was on premises working out the finishing touches for this book, these two jewels came to Zollinger. In the top two pictures, a Titan Tornado II came by, and of course Lowell had to examine and approve all that went into this project. The pilot was happy and gave us a lovely take off.

The next day, this beautiful Carbon Cub (bottom picture) came in from Kentucky. It was an errand demanding Lowell's quick help to provide the pilot with wires necessary to work on an aircraft down at a fly in in Kentucky! Only in aviation. In the picture, Gay takes a look at all the fancy gadgets in the cockpit.

As for Lowell and fancy gadgets, he still wonders, "Why can't pilots just fly their airplanes and just enjoy looking out the windows?" After flying with him that Luscombe, I am ready to agree! *Rebecca McLendon*

Acknowledgment

God has a way of placing people in our lives that serve as an inspiration to direct us toward what we are to be doing with our lives. In my growing up years I admired Milt Hatfield. He had his own airstrip and shop at home where he worked on and recovered many airplanes. In his early years he was a skywriter for Pepsi-Cola in a 1929 Great Lakes Bi-plane. He was also a test pilot for the Flying Wing (the AIRUP) in 1933-34. He flew it to the Chicago World's Fair in 1933. He later flew Beech 18s and a Skymaster for the city.

Milt was also an instructor, teaching many people to fly. Besides that, he was an inventor and held many patents. He made it a point to get up early every morning and be in his shop at 3:30 am working on inventions until 10:00 am, which was when he would stop working and then play with airplanes for the remainder of the day. He never considered airplanes work, and kept this schedule until well into his eighties. In fact, on his eightieth birthday he borrowed a Christen Eagle plane and gave us an impromptu airshow that held us all spellbound!

After many years of working on airplanes, he had accumulated so many engines and parts that everybody went to him to get the parts they needed.

He was the "go to guy" that all the pilots could get answers to their questions from. He would help fix problems, lend tools, and give parts and advise on flying.

He would usually ask, "Have you had any spin training?"

If you said, "No," he would say, "Well, you're gonna get some today!"

Now that I am in my eighties, it appears that I have taken his job as "go to guy." In fact several have called me that from time to time. Guys come to me constantly for parts, problems, instruction and advice.

I guess it has kind of come full circle!

Lowell Farrand.

JOHN H. BROWN

AUGIE'S WAR

Black Rose Writing | Texas

Third printing

ISBN: 978-1-68433-061-4
PUBLISHED BY BLACK ROSE WRITING
www.blackrosewriting.com

Printed in the United States of America
Suggested Retail Price (SRP) $18.95

Augie's War is printed in EB Garamond

Acknowledgements

You may have heard this before, but writing a novel can be a lonely experience. For me though, I have been accompanied on this literary journey by a whole host of friends. First of all, I need to acknowledge the late Bill Neely, a West Virginia writer who provided early inspiration and acted as a mentor for me when I was first thinking about the book. Bill wrote for national magazines and was a novelist, and he provided me with encouragement and inspiration early on.

A couple of years ago, when I had the time to devote to writing the book, I was ably assisted by Maria Young, my editor at the Charleston Gazette-Mail. Maria has always been a great sounding board throughout the time it has taken me to complete the book. I am also grateful to Maryanne Reed, Dean of the WVU Reed College of Media, for her assistance and suggestions.

Another important person who assisted me early on is my very good friend, Tom Flaherty. Tom was instrumental in helping me structure the story and has always been willing to read and critique the work in progress.

Having folks you respect be available and willing to read and react, as well as provide technical assistance to the various drafts of the story, was a gift I had not expected. I want to thank a slew of friends who served as beta readers of Augie's War over the past year.

First of all, I am indebted to several gentlemen who not only read the manuscript, but who are also Vietnam Veterans who provided assistance with some of the technical and military descriptions in the book: John Rowley (an infantry officer and forward observer); Chris Beall (a public information officer); and special thanks to Air Force C-130 pilot Colonel John Madia (Retired). Also, a shout out to my hometown buddy, Billy May, for his review of a chapter dealing with helicopters. Bill is a retired Army Lieutenant Colonel and was a helicopter pilot in Vietnam.

Others who took the time to read and react to the novel are: Mike Brown, Bucky Evans, Paula Flaherty, Gayle and Joe Manchin, Bill and Paula Vagnoni, Rise Justice, Steve Haid, Jennifer Taylor and Sandy Green. And I want to express a special thanks to my friend Michael O'Connor who went above and beyond anything I expected to give me an in-depth critique of the novel.

I am also grateful to two professional editors who assisted me on the book. Nicole Ayers (of Ayers Edits) completed an exceptional manuscript evaluation for me, and helped me re-think the structure of the novel. And Sheila McEntee provided excellent overall editing for the book.

Of course, the most important and long-suffering victim of my literary venture is my wife Debbie. She has been my daily editor and my constant companion, and she has endured this rocky ride with patience, love and understanding.

This novel is dedicated to you!

AUGIE'S WAR

"The true soldier fights not because he hates what is in front of him, but because he loves what is behind him."
G. K. Chesterton

Prologue

Qui Dong, South Vietnam
15 February 1970

Dear Mom and Dad:

If you're reading this letter, you know that I won't be coming home. I can't imagine what it must be like to get that worst of all possible notifications. But as I sit here trying to write this difficult letter, I am filled with love and gratitude, and I hope my words will somehow ease your pain.

Things have been pretty crazy around here the last several weeks, and I didn't write because I didn't want to worry or upset you. But lately things have gotten a lot worse, and I believe there's a real possibility I won't make it back. In that event, I have had this letter inserted into my personnel file with instructions that it be sent to you. So this may be the last chance I have to tell you some things I should have told you years ago.

First of all, I want you to know that I love you. I don't know if I've ever said that to you out loud before, but this is no time to hold back or be embarrassed to express my true feelings. You gave me opportunities you never had, and I can't thank you enough for your love and support. So no matter what happens, I want you to know that when things got really bad over here, I always flashed back to special memories of you and our family, and all the good times I had growing up in Riverview. Also, please tell Grandpa, Grandma, and my aunts and uncles—especially Aunt Lia and Uncle Sal—how much they mean to me. And let Uncle Dante and Uncle Giorgio know that memories of those years I spent with them working at the bakery keep me smiling even during the hardest days.

I have lost some very good friends over here, and this war has made me understand how precious life really is. That's why I cherish thoughts of home so much. Those memories have gotten me through the worst of times, and I know that if I don't make it back, I have had a very good life.

With all my love,
Augie

November 1969

Sergeant Carson wiped the sweat from his brow and winced as I jabbed the black steel muzzle of the M-16 rifle into his chest. The air, still and heavy in the small room, was moisture laden and oppressive.

"Cumpton, what the hell are you doing here? Put that weapon down," he said, his voice trembling.

It was just before first light, and Carson was lying on his cot in a sweltering room inside the noncommissioned officers' hooch.

"You've been drinking, boy," he said quietly. "Go on back and sleep it off. You go now and I'll forget about this, okay?"

I tried to control my rage and the urge to squeeze the trigger. I knew the world would be a much better place without this cretin, this martinet, who had made our lives so unbearable.

"No way, Carson," I said. My voice quavered as I tried to maintain my balance in the dark. The room was completely black, except for a thin shaft of early morning light that leaked from the outside through a hole in the poncho-covered window. The light cut a slash across Carson's sweating, oval face.

I suddenly felt dizzy. The room seemed to sway and I fought to remain upright. It was as if I was suspended in a void of blackness. Desperately, I locked onto the shaft of light—a steadying influence—and slowly regained my balance. I heard my own voice coming to me, garbled and far off at first, and then more distinct.

"You're going to die, Carson. I'm going to waste your sorry ass right here and now, but I want you to know why. I want you to understand that this is payback for all the things you've done to make our lives completely miserable. And I want you to think about what you did to Frazier. How you're responsible for what happened to him."

I pulled the charging handle on the M-16 and locked the first round into the chamber.

"Oh God, please, Cumpton. No. Don't do something you'll regret."

"Regret?" I laughed hoarsely. "I'll regret doing this about as much as you regret what you did to Frazier."

"You don't understand, Cumpton. I had no choice. Frazier wouldn't listen." Carson was now pleading. "You've got to believe me, Cumpton. I tried to help him. I really did, but he just would not change."

"He was a child, Carson. An innocent kid and now he's a brain-dead vegetable because of you."

"Control yourself, Cumpton. Think, boy. There was nothing I could do. I warned Frazier. I told him what he could expect if he didn't shape up."

"So you warned him. And when he didn't play your lifer games, didn't get with the program, you had him sent out to the boonies. He was a kid, Carson. Just a snot-nosed 18-year-old clerk, and you sent him out there. Now he's lying in some nursing home with half his head gone. You miserable bastard."

I flipped the M-16's selector switch from safety to full automatic with a click that echoed in the small room.

"This is it, Carson. I would have killed you in your sleep, but I wanted to hear you beg."

Carson was now whimpering. "Oh yes, I'll beg. But please, don't do this, Cumpton. Think of what you stand to lose if you go through with this."

"You're the one who's going to lose. Lose your worthless life." I slowly began to squeeze the trigger. A little more pressure and ...

The bellowing bark of the .50 caliber machine gun and the staccato percussion of small-arms fire, like discordant instruments in a steel band gone mad, rudely interrupted my dream and left me feeling as if I had come up one second short of consummating a torrid sexual encounter. It was 5:30 a.m.

"Damn 173rd. Blowing away some more water buffalo," I said, shaking my head to wake up fully and cursing the Signal Battalion troopers who were pulling perimeter guard. I pulled the mosquito netting back, sat up, and peered over the plywood partition at Barlow, who was sleeping soundly on his cot.

"Hey D. Hey D, wake up, man!"

Derek Barlow tried to ignore the intermittent small-arms fire *and* me. But in the very next instant, an earth-shaking explosion lifted him out of his cot and onto the wooden floor.

"Incoming, incoming!" someone screamed. Then the entire billet was filled with crawling, yelling, running men, some in skivvies and others completely naked, all intent on getting to the shelter of the sandbag bunker some twenty feet outside the entrance to the hooch. Another explosion sent shock waves through the area, as we dove headlong into the bunker, cursing the siren that had only just begun to warn us of an enemy attack.

The fear, sweat, and close proximity of unwashed humanity was overpowering in the bunker, as we cowered in blackness. With each blast, dirt and sand rained down on us. Four hundred yards to the west, on the base perimeter, the battle continued with heavy caliber machine guns, rocket-propelled grenades, and small-arms fire erupting simultaneously. Helicopter gunships now joined the fray, firing rockets and expending thousands of rounds of minigun ordnance at enemy soldiers who were attempting to breach the defensive perimeter.

The battle raged for another twenty minutes, and then, suddenly, it was over. The only sounds were the occasional fire of smaller-caliber machine guns and the rhythmic thud of the 155-millimeter artillery battery. All outgoing. The battery continued to fire its mission at the now-deserted enemy rocket emplacements in the mountains five miles to the west of the sprawling army base at Qui Dong. The siren signaling the end of the attack also seemed to welcome the dawn, as the sun, like some spherical pink fish, began to ascend out of the South China Sea.

"Good morning, Vietnam! This is AFVN in Saigon," the voice of an army disc jockey cheerfully announced from a portable radio, as I joined other Administration Company soldiers slowly filing out of the bunkers and back into their hooches.

"Let's get rolling on a really nice day with something from the Beatles new *Abbey Road* album called 'Here Comes the Sun.' This one goes out to Specialist Fourth Class Victor Lopez on line with the 4th Infantry Division somewhere near Pleiku."

As I began to dress, thoughts of home flashed into my mind, taking the edge off my frustrations. I was getting short! In less than four months, I'd be boarding that "freedom bird" back to the World. Back to my family and friends, and away from this purgatory on Earth. Finally, I'd be extricated from this miserable, mosquito-infested swamp of a country, where only the perpetual fear of instant annihilation kept me from being bored to death. And as if the war and this dreadful place were not enough, my fellow enlisted men and I had to endure the incessant, haranguing criticism of a loathsome tyrant: Sergeant First Class Wilber Everette Carson. This place was really getting to me. Not only did I have to contend with Carson during my waking hours, but now the bastard was a regular visitor in my dreams—I mean nightmares.

Augie

My full name is Augustino Lee Cumpton. I was born August 6, 1945, on the fateful day that Little Boy—the first atomic bomb—was dropped on Hiroshima. I was a "victory baby," born at the end of World War II. I was raised in a large, extended Italian-American family in Riverview Addition, a neighborhood of Jeweltown, West Virginia. My father, Harry, worked as a foreman in a glass factory, one of four in Jeweltown, and my mother, Gina, was the fifth of eight surviving children born to Italian immigrants Salvatore and Luisa Costanza. In fact, I was named after one my mother's siblings, who died as a child from scarlet fever. Dad was a third-generation Irish American, whose parents and grandparents had resided in the small West Virginia mountain town of Cork. The town was named by immigrants, many of whom fled the eponymous Irish city during the infamous potato famine in the mid-nineteenth century.

Dad was smitten from the first moment he saw my mother. They met at a USO dance in Riverview, where my dad was stationed as an Army recruiter in early 1943. Mom's dark eyes, slender build, and angular but attractive face lent her a kind of exotic look that my father found alluring and completely captivating. It was uncommon in those times for Italians, or just about any other ethnic group, to marry outside of their own ethnicity. So Grandpa Salvatore and Grandma Luisa viewed this "outsider" from the mountains warily. And while it took several months for dad to be welcomed by the large Costanza family, it was even more difficult for my mom to be accepted by dad's parents, who lived an almost cloistered existence in Cork. There, anyone whose name ended in a vowel was looked upon with suspicion.

My father understood this and thus chose to seek employment after the war in Jeweltown, where there was not only more opportunity but also a willingness on the part of mom's family to accept their unusual alliance. So I grew up in an Italian family with little knowledge of my paternal grandparents. I saw them only on the infrequent occasions dad took me to visit them in Cork.

Both of my parents worked, so I spent my early years in the care of Grandma

Luisa or one of my aunts. All of my aunts and uncles, along with Grandpa and Grandma, lived along the same block in Riverview, so there was always a home I could go to after school. Of all my aunts and uncles, Aunt Lia was my favorite. She was a larger-than-life character. I can hear her right now:

"Hey Augie! Get over here and give your Aunt Lia a kiss. What's wrong, you mad at me? And here, eat this meatball sandwich. You need to put some meat on those skinny bones."

When things get particularly unbearable in Qui Dong, I flip a mental pause switch and flash back to memories of my home and family. I especially remember times spent with Grandma and Grandpa and my Uncles Giorgio and Dante. My uncles worked at the Chestnut Bakery with Grandpa. By the time I was old enough to work at the bakery, after grade school, in the late 1950s, Grandpa had turned the business over to Dante and Giorgio. I worked after school selling bread and pepperoni rolls to my Riverview neighbors. Later, I was allowed to work overnight at the bakery.

I was an only child, but I had a whole slew of first cousins. We spent many hours in the serious pursuit of play. Since glorious memories of the "Big War" were still fresh in the minds of those living in the early 1950s, my male cousins and I spent hours creating war games. Little GI Joes would hunt down little Japs or Krauts on our imaginary battlefields.

On other occasions, Dad took me hunting and fishing. Some of my happiest memories are of frosty autumn dawns spent casting for rainbow trout along the banks of the region's cold and pristine rivers. I couldn't know how much I would cherish these memories much later, in a faraway land, under considerably less pleasant circumstances.

I attended Catholic grade school and high school in Jeweltown. The nuns who taught me at Holy Trinity Grade School, and later, at St. Alphonse's High School, said I had a lot of potential, but that I lacked "academic motivation." I was interested in literature and history, despised mathematics, and tolerated other subjects, including religion, which was incorporated into every course.

"Who made you?" my first grade teacher, Sister Luella, asked.

"God made me," I quickly replied.

"Why did God make you?" Sister asked.

"Because God loves me," I repeated from memory.

"What is the one true church, Augie?" Sister continued.

"The one holy, Catholic and apo, ... apo, ..." I stuttered.

"Apostolic, Augie. Say it, Ap-o-stol–ic."

"Ap-sto-lol-ic."

"No, no. Listen to me and look at my lips. Ap-o-stol-ic," Sister Luella repeated.

"The one holy, Catholic, and Apostolic Church," I said, smiling broadly at Sister.

I occasionally got into trouble when I transitioned from grade school to junior high. On one occasion, during a school assembly at Holy Trinity, I began mimicking the sound a pigeon makes. I perfected this odd ability after months of listening to a neighbor, who could whistle all manner of authentic bird calls. I was able to utter this trilling sound without moving my lips. This made it difficult for my teachers to detect where the sounds were coming from.

As my classmates began to laugh and turn their heads in my direction, I was quickly discovered by a nun, who grabbed me by one of my ears and led me out of the gymnasium to the principal's office. The principal, Sister Fumelda, told me to sit on the floor at the foot of a statue. Staring up at the frightening ceramic countenance of St. Anthony, I was instructed to read aloud an ejaculatory prayer, over and over and over:

"My Jesus, mercy; my Jesus, mercy; my Jesus, mercy; my Jesus, mercy; my Jesus, mercy."

I repeated this prayer for more than an hour, until my voice was hoarse and I had sufficiently paid for my misbehavior. I later thought that I must have freed a million souls from purgatory.

My high school years were uneventful. I was a B-minus student and a fullback and defensive end on the football team. I also wrote for the school newspaper. I dated around, though mostly girls from the public schools. The Catholic school girls were unduly concerned about risking eternal damnation and had rebuked my occasional amorous advances. So I followed the path of least resistance and dated girls whose virtue was more "elastic."

I grew into young manhood a six-footer with an average build, dark eyes and hair, and my mother's slightly angular face. I had been nurtured in a womb of stability and love throughout an almost idyllic childhood, but my life was about to change as I entered the real world.

College was almost too great a change for me. I nearly flunked out my first year. Freemont State College presented me with something I had truly never experienced: total freedom. Too much, too soon describes the transition best. There were girls and booze, freedom to attend class or not, and no one to criticize my descent into intemperance.

My first roommate in the freshman dormitory was a very large, raw-boned hulk of a fellow who was attending college on a partial football scholarship. Delbert Jenkins did not share my penchant for skirt-chasing, boozing, and general hell raising. Delbert came to Freemont State from Elk Cave, West Virginia, an unincorporated village tucked in a mountain hollow, or "holler," as he was wont to call the place on those infrequent occasions when he actually spoke to me. Delbert did not approve of my lifestyle or my occasional use of foul language. He was raised in a Christian fundamentalist household by very strict parents who took him and his two sisters to the Church of Heavenly Rapture for services every Sunday morning and Wednesday evening.

"Taking the Lord's name in vain will get you a one-way ticket to hell, Cumpton," Delbert said to me one evening in our dorm room.

"Delbert, I'm not really disrespecting the lord when I say goddamn it. That's just an expression of my frustration more than anything else. You need to lighten up, man," I replied.

Delbert jumped to his feet and stood over me as I sat on my bed untying my shoes.

"There you go again, Cumpton. Using foul language and taking God's name in vain." The guy stood over me clenching and unclenching his fists.

"Get out of my face, Jenkins," I said, as I stood up and shoved him. Without hesitation, Delbert swung and hit me with a roundhouse punch that knocked me onto the bed. The fight was over quickly when the dorm resident assistant, hearing the ruckus, entered the room and separated us.

The very next day, Delbert and I were assigned new roommates. Mine was an acquaintance who had attended another high school in Jeweltown. Jimmy Reasor, if anything, was even more of a hell-raiser than I was. We spent the remainder of our freshman year in bars, at parties, or just about anywhere but class. My grades suffered and I was put on academic probation. Jimmy Reasor flunked completely out, was drafted, ended up in helicopter flight school, and later went to Vietnam.

I began to settle down during my sophomore year. By my junior year, I had mastered the art of academic survival and transferred to the state university to pursue an English literature degree. Yet, at the university, my grades were still only marginal. I concluded that my primary goal at the university would be to make my educational experience last until the Vietnam War ended.

The university was not a hotbed of student antiwar activism. In fact, during my time there, the war in Vietnam was largely ignored by the student body. Only a few brave souls attempted to foment interest in marches, sit-ins, and other protests. They were often scorned by other students, some of whom resorted to violence to demonstrate their intolerance of the demonstrators. The only time the protestors were given any visibility was when they were arrested, usually after being physically assaulted by both campus tuffs and the police.

It wasn't until 1969 that the peace movement gained wide acceptance on campus, and by that time, my fate had been sealed. But from 1965 through 1968, while I was a student at the university, it was hard to take the peace movement seriously.

My feelings at the time were mixed. On the one hand, I quietly hoped, along with the protestors, that the war would end, but it would have been hypocritical of me to express this view. Like most Americans living in those times, I believed that our nation had the right to wage war when it wanted, where it wanted, and with whom it wanted. This was indisputable. The major justification by our leaders for prosecuting the war in Vietnam was to stop the spread of communism and to prevent something called the *domino theory* from becoming a reality. In other words, if one country (Vietnam) fell to the communists, it would precipitate other nations (dominoes) falling too. So if we didn't stop the communists in Vietnam, we might be fighting them in the streets of the good old US of A.

But I felt no kinship to those—either on my campus or around the country— who were involved in the antiwar movement. They represented such radically different views and expressed those views in such unconventional ways that it was difficult for someone like me to identify with them. In my small-town, Catholic world, fealty to one's country followed only belief in God, trust in papal infallibility, and loyalty to family.

The truth was, I secretly approved of the ultimate goal of the antiwar movement, not because I thought the war was immoral but because I feared for my own safety. I feared bodily injury and death. Even more, I was afraid of how I might perform under fire. As a result of these fears, I felt shame and an immense guilt that I kept to myself.

During my senior year, the war became much more than an abstraction. I remember the going away party for a very good friend who had graduated the year before. Freddy Wilton was a fair-haired, golden boy who had captained the baseball team, dated the prettiest coeds, and excelled academically. We had become close friends and had roomed together during Freddy's senior year at an off-campus apartment. It was there that we engaged in serious conversations about world events, especially the war in Vietnam.

I remember one particular night right before Freddy was scheduled to graduate. As a senior in the ROTC program, he would be going into the army as an officer that summer. Late one night, I tuned into the *Johnny Carson Show*. Johnny was interviewing an army officer who had recently returned from a tour in Vietnam.

"Hey Freddy, come take a look at this. This could be you in a year. This guy is just back from Vietnam," I said.

Freddy sunk down in the beanbag lounger and used the small, metal bottle cap remover to open two bottles of Iron City beer. He handed one to me and stared intently at the TV, focusing on the interview and the young officer. Johnny Carson told the audience the young captain was a Silver Star recipient and then asked the officer to describe the action that earned him the award. Freddy was riveted. After the interview, he stared solemnly at the TV.

"What're you thinking, Freddy? Kind of a scary place, don't you think?" I said.

"Oh, I don't know. I actually hope I get sent over there," Freddy replied. "My dad and his father before him were soldiers and they both fought to defend the country—my grandfather in World War I and my dad in WWII."

"Yeah, but that was different," I said. "The whole world was at war then. From what I see on TV and read in the papers, we're either fighting this to stop the spread of communism, or, if you believe the antiwar folks, we're in it to line the pockets of the military-industrial complex, and we're killing innocent civilians in the process."

"I don't know about any of that political stuff, and I certainly can't understand the motivation of the protestors," Freddy said. "I just know that when my grandfather and dad were called to help defend the country, they did it without trying to figure out the politics of it, or whether it was morally right.

They just went. And that's what I'll do if I get orders to Vietnam."

Later that year, in the middle of football season, Freddy came back to the university on leave. He had just completed officer candidate school and had gotten his expected orders to Vietnam. The going-away party lasted well into the predawn hours, with toast after toast to the newly minted second lieutenant. I remember driving Freddy to the airport the next morning and waving to my smiling, hung-over friend, as he went into the terminal.

Three months later, as I was reading the student newspaper, I was shocked and stunned by the headline "Wilton, U Grad, Killed in Vietnam." I read and re-read the short news story, hoping against hope that it was about someone else named Wilton, or that I would wake up and realize that it was just a bad dream.

But no. It was true. I would never see my friend again. My hands trembled as I wept for Freddie. I cried for the life that he would never lead, for the wife he would never marry, for the kids that would never be born. I also wept for myself. For what might lie ahead. For what fate might have in store for me. Would I end up like my friend?

After a while, I searched for and found Freddy's home telephone number. With great trepidation, I dialed the number. Mrs. Wilton was very composed as she explained that Freddy had been killed by enemy mortar fire—a direct hit on his bunker. They had just buried him three days earlier. She apologized for not getting in touch with his college friends, including me.

"It was just too draining," she said. Then, with a catch in her voice, she added, "It was a closed casket, Augie. We didn't even get to see him one last time."

Freddy Wilton's death brought the war home to me. It was not just something that affected strangers. His death made me acutely aware that my life could also be in mortal danger. Consequently, my most pressing concern was to avoid being drafted at all costs. Then, if I faced that eventuality, I would attempt to enlist in either the navy or air force, where my odds of surviving the war were much better.

Of course, the gold standard for those times was to enlist in the national guard or reserves, but available slots for those options were very limited. They usually went to the sons of the wealthy or to those who were politically connected. I was neither. So I did everything within my power to extend my student deferment in those years by taking the minimum number of credit hours each semester. My hope was to delay graduation until the oft-repeated government promise "to end the war by Christmas" became a reality.

But by the spring of 1968, I had run out of Christmases, credit hours, and time. During that same time, a series of monumental events outside my almost cloistered existence were playing out around the country and the world.

In South Vietnam, there had been a series of major attacks by the North Vietnamese and Viet Cong all across the country called the *Tet Offensive*. These attacks ignited a maelstrom of antiwar protests in what had been, until that time, just a simmering and unorganized peace movement. Then, President Lyndon Johnson shocked the nation by deciding not to run for reelection. A month later, the Reverend Martin Luther King Jr. was assassinated, setting off weeks of rioting and civil unrest around the country. And in June, Senator Robert Kennedy was also murdered.

When I graduated with a bachelor's degree in English literature, my student deferment expired. Within two months, I received my draft notice. Now I was a grown man with a college degree who should have been out searching for a job and embarking on a new career. But Uncle Sam had other things in store for me.

You're In the Army Now

Since I was not able to secure a slot in a reserve or national guard unit, or in the navy or air force, I was drafted into the US Army in September of 1968. I hoped, because of my college education, that I could secure a noncombat type Military Occupational Specialty, or MOS. And even though I qualified for officer's candidate school, I chose to serve as an enlisted man, feeling my chances of survival were better than if I were a green lieutenant out in the bush. And, more importantly, I didn't want to be responsible for the lives of a platoon of soldiers.

Army basic training was physically demanding but invigorating. Early morning runs, midafternoon runs, and occasional after-dinner runs were interspersed with training in combat, marksmanship, military tactics, and military protocol. And there was continual marching. The instructors—drill sergeants— were all Vietnam veterans who missed no opportunity to point out graphically how even little training mistakes could translate into instant death in the jungle.

"You're dead, asshole," they would scream, or, "You just tripped that wire and a gook booby-trap blew your balls off."

Days were filled with forced marches, bivouacking, marksmanship training, hand-to-hand combat, foot care, and cleaning your weapon. We'd drill and drill again. We'd run, eat, shit, laugh, cry, scream, and sing. Everywhere we went, we sang, particularly this little ditty:

> I want to be an army ranger,
> I want to go to Vietnam.
> I want to live a life of danger,
> I want to kill a Viet Cong.
> Sound off, one – two,
> Sound off, three – four,
> Sound off one, two, three-four.
> Sound off!

Eventually, each day became more routine, and, as I got stronger, I was able to go through the physical motions with little difficulty. The emotional and mental strains, though, were intense, totally unexpected, and an unfortunate consequence of my participation in army basic training.

Small-town life had not prepared me for the larger world beyond, and for the culturally diverse environment of the United States Army of the late 1960's. While I was aware of the serious racial problems of the times, particularly after the assassination of Dr. Martin Luther King, those issues were far removed from my daily existence. Until now!

I was shocked and totally unprepared for the abject hatred directed toward me and other white troopers by many of the black soldiers in my basic training company. It was incomprehensible to me that total strangers would hate me for no other reason than the color of my skin. I expressed that thought to one of the more vocal blacks in my basic training platoon.

"Touché, motherfucker," the soldier replied. "You dudes been stepping on the black man for 400 years, and for the same no-account reason—just cause of our color."

I was incredulous. "That's bullshit!" I told him. "Not me. I've never said or done anything to hurt any black person—anywhere, anytime."

"Maybe not. But you can bet your lily-white ass that your daddy or granddaddy did. And now some black dudes think it's come-to-Jesus time for whitey."

I argued, but to no avail, and came to the ultimate conclusion that there were just some wounds that only time could heal. Unfortunately, waxing philosophically did nothing to alleviate the reality of my present circumstance.

As the only college graduate in my entire basic training platoon, I was picked by my drill sergeant as a trainee leader. I was expected to keep the troopers in line and also to keep the peace in my platoon. It was not easy. I struggled through the eight weeks of basic training, oftentimes intervening to stop fights between blacks and whites in my platoon. Most of these soldiers were poor white Southerners, inner-city blacks, or Hispanics, and many of them were high school dropouts. If they had thought about it, they might have come to the conclusion that they actually had a lot in common with each other.

But there was no time for reflection or for group therapy sessions in basic training. The cultural differences, compounded by dissimilar accents and patterns of speech, served to magnify the most obvious distinction among the men—their skin color. It was a no-win situation. I was threatened and cursed by my fellow soldiers and castigated by my twenty-one-year-old drill sergeant—a two-tour

Vietnam veteran—for not showing stronger leadership. It was a thoroughly miserable time and I was relieved to complete basic training.

And I was even more relieved to find out that I would be headed to Fort Lee, Virginia, and quartermaster school. There I would complete Advanced Individual Training (AIT) and, hopefully, land a job as a clerk in the US Army supply system. For once, I counted myself lucky, since three-quarters of my company was sent to Fort Polk, Louisiana, for Jungle School, infantry training, and a direct ticket to Vietnam.

The evening of the same day that I graduated from basic training, I boarded a train for an all-night trip to my next duty station. Fort Lee, located about 30 miles south of Richmond, housed the quartermaster school, where soldiers learned the fundamentals of the army's complex military supply chain.

"You gonna be a REMF," the large, black Private First Class said to me that first cold and snowy morning in late November 1968. I had just found the Quonset building that served as a barracks.

"What's a REMF?" I asked, stomping the snow from my boots just inside the door of the World War I vintage barracks.

"What you want it to be, man?" the soldier replied, glaring down at me and snickering.

I could not advance. The soldier stood squarely in front of me. There was not enough room to move either left or right around him without pushing him out of the way, and I was not prepared to deal with the consequences such an action might precipitate.

I tried again. "I mean, does it have something to do with quartermaster school?"

"You want it to have something to do with quartermaster school?"

"Come on now, what is this shit?" I asked, totally exasperated.

"What kind of shit you want it to be, man?" The PFC moved a step closer and continued to stare wide eyed at me.

I looked around the barracks. The long room was empty except for one other soldier who sat on his bunk indifferently witnessing my bizarre encounter.

"Look," I said, "I just got out of basic yesterday at Fort Knox. I've been on a train all night long and I'm tired. I just need to know if this is Barracks B-4."

"You want it to be Barracks B-4?" the PFC answered, moving to within a foot of me. I moved to the right in an attempt to get around him, but the huge soldier blocked my path. I moved quickly to his left and the PFC did likewise.

"Yeah, you sure enough look like REMF meat. You a college boy?"

I couldn't resist. "You want me to be a college boy?" I said, half expecting the soldier to cold-cock me.

Instead, the PFC moved his huge, oval head to within six inches of my face. His dilated pupils looked like two large, dark islands adrift in a sea of milk. A crazed grin began to spread across his face and I thought the man must be completely insane.

Just then, the soldier on the bunk spoke. "Come on, Rooster, leave the guy alone.

"Hey buddy," he said looking toward me. "Don't pay any attention to Rooster. You're in the right place. This is B-4."

"Shit, man, I was just fuckin' with the dude. He mighta been undercover. Mighta been a MP here to bust us," Rooster said. Then he allowed me to move around him into the barracks.

"Name's Franken," the man on the bunk said as I approached. "Rooster put me through the same routine yesterday when I got here. Take your pick of these fine accommodations." He pointed to the mostly empty room.

I grabbed my duffel bag and placed it on the bunk next to Franken. And then I looked down at the man. "You here for AIT too?"

Franken nodded. Both of us watched as Rooster moved down the aisle to the pot-belly stove at the far end of the barracks and used a coat hanger to stoke the coals until they turned bright red. The bunks, on either side of the long room, were all empty. The mattresses were doubled back, so I sat on the box springs and looked toward Franken.

"Say, Franken, is Rooster going to be in our AIT class?"

"Rooster is just home from the 'Nam. Says he wants to go back, but the army said he needs to get some training first in another MOS. He was a grunt—Eleven Bravo infantry. He decided he wanted to be in supply and so he got assigned here to quartermaster school."

"You gotta be shitting me! Going back? To Vietnam?"

"Yeah. He claims the dope is great and the lifers don't hassle you as much over there. He also likes the women."

"Sounds crazy to me," I said. I didn't see the large soldier ambling back toward us.

"What you say, honky? You say Rooster crazy?" He moved quickly over to where I was sitting and stared down at me.

I briefly entertained the thought of responding Rooster-like but wisely remained quiet.

Franken once again interceded. "Lighten up, Rooster, okay?"

"Sure, man. No sweat." The large PFC grabbed his fatigue jacket and went out the door, chuckling to himself.

I waited until I was sure he was gone and then turned toward Franken. "By the way, thanks a lot. I'm Augie Cumpton. Rooster seems really twisted."

"Ah, Rooster's okay. He was just fucking with you. He gave me the same ration of shit yesterday when I got in. Said he does it to all the new guys."

"What's a REMF, Franken?"

"Rear Echelon Mother Fucker. I guess in the 'Nam, you're either a REMF or a grunt. Rooster put in ten months out in the field as a grunt. Claims he got a case of The Black Clap and got assigned to a REMF unit for his last two months before his DEROS."

"DEROS? What's that?"

"Date Eligible for Return from Overseas. Another fucked-up army acronym. Anyway, after he got transferred to a REMF unit, he decided to re-up for another tour if they assigned him a job in the rear."

"What's this Black Clap bullshit?"

Franken smiled. "Rooster says The Black Clap will rot your pecker off if you don't get it treated right away. He says some VC mamasan gave it to him out in the bush, and he was sent back to the rear to get treatment. He claims it actually saved his life, since a couple of weeks later, his platoon got ambushed and practically wiped out."

I unbuttoned and removed my army greatcoat and began to unpack my duffel bag. I looked toward the small man on the cot.

"Say, Franken, does Rooster think we'll be going to Vietnam after AIT? I thought with this quartermaster MOS we'd have a good chance of getting orders to Germany."

"I wish. Rooster said the class that just graduated got assigned to Germany and that means we'll probably be headed to Southeast Asia."

Despite this bleak prediction about our future, I did pretty well in AIT and completed the quartermaster course without any problem. Yet, while AIT was less physically demanding than basic training, it was more emotionally stressful. It was the last stop before an enlisted man got his (literal) marching orders and his first duty assignment. For more than 50 percent of the soldiers graduating from AIT, that meant an all-expenses-paid trip to Vietnam.

Since Rooster's prediction, I had suspected that I would get orders there once I completed the ten-week AIT course at Fort Lee. But I still wondered how this could possibly be happening to me. In my heart of hearts, I knew the odds were against me. Knew that I would most likely end up in Vietnam.

When the orders finally came, I was almost relieved. In a way, it was as if a great burden had been lifted from me. I had done everything I could to avoid going to Vietnam and had lost to fate itself. I was no less afraid of what the war might do to me, but now I felt a kind of calm resignation, knowing the die had been cast. I had hoped my orders would send me off to Germany or even South Korea, but, unfortunately, Rooster was right. After AIT, I got my orders to Vietnam. It just seemed like yesterday that I was a carefree kid back in Riverview. Now I was going off to war.

The Ruff Avenue Poolroom

The Ruff Avenue Poolroom had a yellow brick facade and occupied the bottom floor of a two-story building in the heart of Riverview. I was six years old when Grandpa Salvatore first took me to the Ruff. I remember Grandpa holding my hand as we walked through the hallowed portal of the poolroom and into a long and smoky room. There was an oaken bar to the right that was situated directly below a huge mirror, upon which all manner of cigarette, beer, cigar, and chewing tobacco advertisements hung in eclectic disarray. On the wall opposite the bar, there was a large blackboard with chalk-drawn horizontal and vertical lines. The lines formed columns and boxes, where the innings of each American and National League baseball game being played that summer day were displayed.

Very near the blackboard, on a wooden shelf protruding from the wall, was an amazing and fascinating contraption. The Western Union ticker tape machine, encased in a small, clear-glass dome, emitted a clattering sound I will never forget. There was a certain regularity to when the machine began to sing, and the men who came to drink, gamble, or play cards at the Ruff were accustomed to it. They rarely seemed to notice when it sounded.

I came to realize that when the fellows did look toward the machine, they did so warily, as if they expected it to bring bad news. And many times it did. It had announced the attack on Pearl Harbor a decade before. It had brought the news of Roosevelt's death. Yet, it had also heralded the end of World War II. And what better news had there ever been to these men, whose sons and brothers had so gallantly defended the flag?

If the ticker tape sounded out of its expected sequence, either too early or too late, dark eyes darted quickly toward it. Over time, and especially during the summer, the ticker tape's expected sounding usually occurred in the time it took professional baseball players to complete one half inning of play. If the machine clattered out of sequence, there was an almost palpable tension in the room. If it sounded too soon, that usually meant one team was changing pitchers. The men who had placed bets on that team would be concerned. If the inning lasted too

Smithsonian
National Museum of the American Indian

CHILD'S GIFT CERTIFICATE

RECEIVE ONE FREE CHILD'S GIFT
when you present this gift certificate at the
NMAI Museum Store at the Museum
on the National Mall in Washington, D.C.,
or the George Gustave Heye Center in New York.

This certificate may be redeemed for one item from a selected assortment. See a store associate for details. Approximate value is $1.00. This certificate cannot be redeemed for cash nor can it be applied toward a purchase.

long, that usually signaled that the batting team was scoring runs. Thus, those who had wagered on that team had cause for hope. In either circumstance, any interruption in the ticker tape machine's natural rhythm caused poolroom patrons to pause and consider its implications.

The Ruff would certainly be an anachronism now. The place was original "old school." It was off-limits to women and it was a sanctuary, where the men of the community could go to socialize and get away from the daily grind. Grandpa visited the poolroom a few times each week to buy his pipe tobacco, chat with the neighborhood men, and place a "numbers" bet. By placing a bet on three numbers, from one through nine, a gambler would try to pick the last three digits of the "handle," or the total amount of money bettors placed on race day at a major racetrack. The numbers game was particularly popular in ethnic neighborhoods, where bets could be placed for as little as a nickel or dime.

After we entered the pool hall, Grandpa picked me up and placed me on the oak bar while he ordered a big, icy glass of draft beer and a tin of Bugler pipe tobacco. I was presented with a six-ounce bottle of Coca Cola and a bag of salted peanuts to occupy my time while Grandpa conducted business with Jimmie Ponza, the proprietor of the Ruff.

Jimmie looked a lot like Clark Gable, with a pencil-thin mustache and slicked-back, black hair. He was a handsome man with a quiet manner. Jimmie was also a bookie. With Jimmie, patrons of the Ruff could place a wager on sports, gamble in card games, and even collect a payoff for skillfully playing the pinball machines. Of course, all of these activities were illegal, but local law enforcement agencies usually looked the other way, as long as the games were peaceful, and as long as the police got their "commission."

"Hey Jimmie," Grandpa said in his broken English. "Putta fifty cents on two, tree, one. Dua, tre, una, okay?"

"Salvatore, every day you play this same number," Jimmie replied. "You been playin' it now for 15 years. You ain't hit it yet. When you gonna change it, Sallie?"

Grandpa smiled his best rogue's smile and said, "You wanna me quit, no? I know this, Jimmie. Firsta time I don't play it, that goddamn number gonna hit. Dua, tre, una, Jimmie."

Grandpa laid a silver half dollar on the bar. I looked around the Ruff. Two ceiling fans rotated lazily, distributing a swirling, smoky pall throughout the pool hall. A step-up in the middle divided the long room. In the front portion were the bar, the ticker tape, the blackboard, a pool table and two pinball machines. In the rear portion, there were several tables where old men sat silently playing cards and sipping wine. They smoked either pipes, like Grandpa, or little black cigars that were short and twisted, and made by a company called Parodi. The pungent odor of the Parodis predominated.

The card players, four to a table, wore dark suits and wide-brimmed hats. As they played, they took the cigars or pipes out of their mouths only long enough to sip red wine from small, round glasses. Only an occasional expletive punctuated the silence, giving vent to their dissatisfaction with the hand they were dealt, or the good luck of their opposing players.

"Mannaggia!"

"Basta!"

"Che Palle!"

"Merdoso!"

That particular day, Muta, who worked for Jimmie as a janitor and lived in a large closet in the back of the poolroom, picked me up off the bar and brought me to the big blackboard. He gave me a piece of chalk and guided my hand, helping me to dip the chalk into an old paint can filled with water. He then helped me form a zero in one of the squares on the board. At first the zero was barely discernible, but then, as the chalk began to dry, the number, like a full moon emerging from hazy clouds, became clearly visible. Muta, who, as his nickname inferred, was completely mute, lifted me high into the air, smiling broadly through broken teeth. Grandpa took me from Muta and sat me back on the bar.

"Hey Augie, you gonna take-a Muta's place?" he asked with a twinkle in his dark eyes. "You gonna writa da base-a-ball scores?"

Jimmie and Grandpa looked at me for a response.

"When I get tall enough to I will," I said, beaming.

There were a few other significant gathering places in the old Riverview neighborhood. The Holy Trinity Parish Hall was one. The hall, located in the gymnasium of the Catholic school, was where families celebrated marriages, got together for community pasta suppers, and held wakes for the dearly departed. Another popular place, particularly for the kids of Riverview, was the local park. The park was an oasis of jungle gyms, swings, and fields, where kids spent hours in the serious pursuit of play.

And, of course, for me, there was Grandpa Salvatore and Grandma Luisa's home, just across the street from the bakery. I spent most of my early childhood in my grandparents' home and in their loving care. Later on, as I grew into adulthood, I would marvel at the challenges they faced and overcame as young, non-English speaking immigrants in a strange land.

Grandpa Salvatore

My grandfather, Salvatore Emilio Costanza, was the founder and proprietor of the Chestnut Baking Company, a business he had dreamed of and saved for during fifteen years of backbreaking labor in the coal mines of north central West Virginia. His and Grandma's journey to, and success in, this country reflect the prototypical American Dream story. And I was able to learn about it in bits and pieces through the years from the adult relatives in my large Italian-American family.

Salvatore Costanza was born in 1883, in San Giovanni, a hill town in the southern Italian state of Calabria. He came to America in 1901, along with thousands of other immigrants, to seek his fortune in "La Bella America." Salvatore's father was a cobbler and he had great hopes that his only son would succeed him in the business. But young Sal was a rebellious sort. He talked of America constantly, much to the chagrin of his parents, who worried that they would lose "this dreamer" to the siren call of a foreign land filled with wild Indians and uncultured heathens.

The Calabria of my grandfather's youth was peopled mostly by agrarian peasants, who worked the farmlands and vineyards surrounding San Giovanni. The land was owned and controlled by a few well-to-do landlords, who managed their property and the lives of the serfs with a kind of benign neglect. The class system was strictly observed, and the padrone of the land was, superficially and publicly at least, accorded the highest respect by the common people, who continued to enrich him through their sweat and toil. As long as this unwritten, but strictly adhered to, class decorum was observed, there was always food on the table and a humble roof over the heads of the working people of San Giovanni. Those who rebelled, however, found themselves banished from their homes and without work.

Grandpa's father paid a significant tribute each month in rent and protection to Don Umberto Luciano, the patriarch of one of the richest families in Calabria. It was Don Umberto's youngest daughter, Luisa, who ultimately made the decision easy for young Salvatore to leave San Giovanni. For Salvatore had committed the unpardonable sin: He had sought to court Luisa and made his wishes known to Don Umberto. The don was greatly offended and promptly had the rakish upstart thrown out of his villa for even suggesting such an outrageous proposition.

But young passions cannot be so easily dissuaded. Salvatore and Luisa conducted a surreptitious relationship that was bound to attract attention in San Giovanni. It did, and Salvatore was forced to go into hiding to avoid the don's roving enforcers, who let it be known that young Costanza had violated the trust of the padrone and would be severely punished.

To avoid great physical harm and to protect his father's business, Salvatore fled in the middle of the night and booked passage on a ship bound for America. He carried with him one suitcase, $100 cash, and the name and address of Vito Serafini, a close friend of his father's and a former resident of San Giovanni.

The seven-day sea voyage was a miserable experience for Salvatore, who, like other immigrants, was crammed into a hold converted to barracks, with bunks stacked four high. Buckets in the rows served as chamber pots. With each roll of the ship, the pots slid and spilled their putrid contents along the floor. Grandpa spent almost the entire trip on the deck, risking the elements and the cold Atlantic spray, to avoid the fetid hold below.

When the ship arrived at Ellis Island, Grandpa, pale and drawn, endured endless lines, countless interviews, and physical exams for another ten days before he was allowed to enter America. Following the instructions of his father, Salvatore bought a train ticket and embarked on the final leg of his journey, which brought him to the coalfields of north central West Virginia.

Arriving in Jeweltown, Grandpa was welcomed by Signore Serafini, who provided him food and lodging, and eventually helped him get a job with the West Fork Coal Company. Grandpa lived in a coal camp adjacent to the mine and worked for a year before Grandma, aided by her sympathetic mother, joined him there. Signore Serafini and his wife served as best man and bridesmaid for the couple, who were married immediately.

The two Italian immigrants began their life together in a company house, amid the squalor of the coal camp. In particularly dark moments, Grandpa would shake his head at the irony of his situation. "La Bella America," he would mutter, feeling as much like an indentured serf as those friends and family he had left behind in Calabria. But here, he would reassure himself, there was still hope.

Here, there was opportunity and Salvatore Costanza would make the most of it.

Grandpa knew that he would not achieve all that he had dreamed about in this new life if he spent his days slaving in a dirty, dangerous, and claustrophobic coal mine. He entered the mine shaft at dawn and spent ten hours digging coal, throwing each shovelful into a large bin. A team of mules pulled the filled bins out of the mine to waiting coal trains.

At the end of each work day, Grandpa left the mine exhausted and walked a mile down the mountain to the coal camp. In the small, company-provided house, he and Grandma started their family.

My mother, Gina, was born in the coal camp, as were three of her siblings. Even though he was required to pay rent for the coal camp home and purchase food from the company store, Grandpa Salvatore managed to save a good portion of his meager earnings. For her part, Grandma planted a small garden that provided her growing family fresh vegetables during the warm months. Grandma also canned vegetables for use during the winter.

Though the family managed, Grandpa knew that he would need to find a way out of the mines. This became all the more apparent when the most devastating mining disaster in US history occurred less than a mile from the mine where he worked.

On December 7, 1907, at 10:30 a.m., Grandpa felt the earth shake and roll under his feet. At first, he and the other miners in his crew thought it was their own mine that had exploded. Only later, at the end of their shift, did they discover that the mine just across the hollow from theirs had been completely destroyed. When Fairmont Coal Company's Number 6 and Number 8 mines exploded that day, 362 mostly immigrant miners lost their lives. This horrific tragedy was an added incentive for Grandpa to leave the mines, but it would take him another nine years to save enough to do so.

Grandpa Salvatore used this time to decide what occupation he would pursue once he left the mines. His father had advised him to start a business that provided a good or service that common people needed in their daily lives. It was a simple philosophy, and it made good sense.

Grandpa decided to establish a bakery, since bread was a dietary staple that everyone consumed on a daily basis. But his bread would be much better than the ubiquitous, bland, and soft white bread that had been their only choice in America. His crusty bread would be especially popular with the hundreds of immigrant families who lived and worked in the region.

Grandpa pondered what he should call his business. One of his fellow miners suggested he use the English translation of his surname. Costanza in English means chestnut. So Grandpa would call his business the Chestnut Baking Company.

Finally, in 1916, Salvatore Costanza resigned his laborer's job at the West Fork Mining Company and moved to Jeweltown. There, he rented an apartment from Vito Serafini, his oldest friend and sponsor. Vito had begged Grandpa for years to leave the mines and work for him at his small restaurant in Jeweltown, but Grandpa knew that he could earn higher wages in the mines.

Now, his dream was closer to reality. He was ready to get started, but Grandpa would still need to work while constructing the building that would house the bakery. For a year he toiled washing dishes and waiting tables in Signore Serafini's small trattoria. In the evenings and on Sundays and holidays, he and a few friends constructed the bakery, where I, much later, came of age.

The Chestnut Bakery opened for business in April of 1917, the same month and year that America entered World War I. Much later, the bakery provided me with experiences that became precious memories and helped me make it through another war.

Farewell

I suppose I suspected all along that I would be going to Vietnam. I had tried to stay in college as long as I could, but there was just no way to avoid graduation. And even if my grades had been exemplary, academic draft deferments for graduate school, except for physician training, had been abolished. Unfortunately, I had passed my induction physical with flying colors and that was that. Basic Combat Training and Advanced Individual Training were in the rearview mirror and now it was time to go. However, the United States Army did grant me a two-week leave, and I used the time to visit with my family in Riverview.

The family all seemed proud that I was going to do my patriotic duty and follow in the footsteps of my father, who had served in World War II, and Uncle Sal, who spent time in France and Belgium after D-Day. Everyone was especially proud of Uncle Sal. He had been seriously wounded during the Battle of the Bulge. I was surprised, then, at his somber demeanor when I went to visit him and Aunt Yolanda one afternoon.

Ours is a family of huggers and kissers, so I hugged Aunt Yolanda and kissed her cheek as soon as I entered their home. When I hugged Uncle Sal, he held on to me for several seconds. When he let me go, I could see tears in his eyes. Then he grabbed me by the arm and walked me into the kitchen. He motioned for Aunt Yolanda to stay where she was. In the kitchen, Uncle Sal leaned against the sink and looked at me.

"Augie," he said, "I don't want to scare you, but all this talk about the glories of war is bullshit. Don't believe any of it. Here's the most important thing to remember: You gotta take care of yourself and watch out for the guys in your unit. Don't try to be no hero or you might not come back. The truth is, rich old men start wars and they make young guys like you fight 'em. So, the most important thing you can do is come back to us with all the body parts you left here with. If you do that, then we'll take care of you when you get home."

"But Uncle Sal, if I come back in one piece, you won't need to take care of me," I said, not fully understanding what he was trying to tell me.

"Listen to me, Augie," my uncle continued. "You may not have any wounds people can see, but war will leave its mark on you. Believe me. It's good that you can't understand this now. If you did, you might not go. Just keep your head down over there and watch out for yourself and the guys around you. And don't worry about winning the war for your country. You win if you come back in one piece. That's it."

Then Uncle Sal hugged me again. At the time, I'm ashamed to say, I was embarrassed for him. I thought he was being overly dramatic. I wondered if he had been drinking. Later, I would appreciate why he acted as he had, but for now, I just wanted to visit all my family at least once before I had to leave. In my mind, I knew I was going to face the unknown and danger, but my way of coping was to look at it as a kind of adventure and not dwell on the worst that could happen to me. I didn't want to reflect on things I couldn't control. On the other hand, it was hard not to remember what had happened to Freddy Wilton.

The other people who tried, but failed, to be stoic about my orders to Vietnam were my mother and father. Even though my dad had not served overseas during World War II, he had attended far too many funerals of friends, classmates, and neighbors from his hometown of Cork. Occasionally, I would catch him staring at me, and when I did, he would quickly turn away. And mom! At the time, I thought she was being overly emotional, even maudlin. On a few occasions I found her with her head in her hands silently weeping. I didn't know how any words I might say would comfort her, so I just quietly left her alone.

For the most part, my parents seemed content to have me with them for at least a little while longer. So each night they hosted a parade of family and friends who came to wish me farewell. One of those visits was from a Riverview neighbor who worked with my father at the glass factory.

Henry O'Flaherty was a 35-year-old fireplug of a man with forearms like Popeye and an engaging smile stitched on his youthful face. His main job at the factory was to polish the molds into which molten glass would be poured. He was also an avid hunter, fisherman, and gatherer of just about anything that grew in the forest. Henry arrived at our house late one evening, just after the last of the well-wishers had gone home. He came into our kitchen carrying a cardboard case of beer containing 24 longneck bottles of cold Stroh's. On the top of the carton was a burlap gunnysack, out of which protruded the green leaves of some incredibly pungent plant.

"Hey Augie, boy do I have a treat for you here tonight!" he said, putting the case of beer on the floor. He then grabbed the gunnysack and dumped the contents onto the kitchen table. The room was immediately suffused with an odor like wild onions and garlic, only stronger.

"Jesus, Mary, and Joseph, what is that?" my mother asked, trying to speak without breathing. "It stinks to high heaven in here."

My father just smiled and his face lit up. "Henry, I didn't think those little lilies were out of the ground yet. Where'd you find them?"

"To tell you the truth, I wasn't even looking for 'em," Henry said. "Gina, these are ramps. I spotted 'em while I was out scouting for turkey this afternoon. The season starts next week, you know. Anyway, I found a mess of these ramps in the same place I get them every year. So I dug 'em right up. Look how small and tender they are. Man, they are gonna be good, Harry!"

"Gina, let's take these to the sink. You can help me clean them," my father said.

"I'm not touching those things. They smell awful," my mother said to dad, who was acting as if he had just discovered gold.

I was totally mystified, as I watched my father unfold several pages of the *Jeweltown Gazette* next to the sink and clean the mud from the bottom of the plants. He then snipped off the very end of what looked like a wild green onion. He put the muddy ends of the plant onto the newspaper to be discarded and the remaining stalks into the sink to be rinsed off.

"Gina, ramps grow in the mountains and are considered a delicacy by folks that hail from my neck of the woods," dad explained. "Heck, we even have a ramp festival in Cork every spring. They fry 'em in bacon grease and add them to fried potatoes or pinto beans."

"Well, I'm going to bed," mom said. "You all open the windows if you cook those things in here. It will surely stink up the whole house. 'Night, Henry. Tell Eloise I said hello."

"Gina, don't worry," Henry said. "These ramps are so young and tender, it would be a sin to eat them any way other than raw, with maybe a little salt and pepper."

And eat them we did! My dad hung with us for about an hour and then he went off to bed. But Henry and I ate every last one of those little buggers, into the wee hours of the morning, washing them down with beer after beer until the last one was consumed and all the beer was gone.

When I awoke the next morning, my head was throbbing and the inside of my mouth tasted like a couple of rats had died there. I was also shivering. My mother had opened every window and door in the house in a vain attempt to rid the place of the smell. I looked out my bedroom window and there was mom, spraying a large container of Lysol into the house from the outside.

On most nights, if the farewell visits ended at a reasonable hour, I went into Jeweltown to the local clubs and partied as if there was no tomorrow—and maybe there wouldn't be. Anyway, two nights before I was due to fly out to California, I was sipping a cold one at a place called the MattaDoor. I spotted a high school classmate of mine who had been the quarterback of our football team at St. Alphonse's. Billy Franco was sitting in a booth at the back of the club, nursing a drink and speaking in hushed tones with the owner of the MattaDoor, Johnny Matta. Johnny was a middle-aged guy who had been serving us icy cold Budweiser draft beer ever since we were old enough to reach across the bar and hand him a quarter. As I looked at the two, Johnny motioned for me to come over. So I ambled to the booth and scooted in.

"Johnny, Billy, you guys plotting something over here?" I asked.

"Listen up, Augie. Billy here has a problem and maybe you can give him some advice, seeing as how you're about to go over to Vietnam," Johnny said and then looked at Billy.

"Hey Augie. I really fucked up, man," Billy said. "I don't know if you knew, but I got drafted about the same time as you. My MOS is Eleven-Bravo-Ten and I'm in the infantry. I really don't want to go. I've been AWOL for two weeks now, trying to figure out what to do. I was supposed to report to the Presidio in San Francisco for processing and then to Vietnam. I don't know, man. I've been thinking about going up to Canada. Don't really know what to do. What about you? I heard you got orders too. You going?"

I looked at Billy and considered my words very carefully before answering.

"You know, I thought about Canada too," I said finally. "I really did. But I knew I couldn't face my family if I went in that direction. That's not to say I'm some kind of patriot or someone who believes in the war over there. Hell, I don't know what to believe. It probably takes more balls to go to Canada and say 'fuck you' to Uncle Sam.

"I don't know, Billy. All I can tell you is I'm going to take a chance and go.

But my MOS is Quartermaster Corps—you know, the supply guys in the army. So I'm not facing what you are. But hey, if you decide to go, we can fly out to San Francisco together. I'm supposed to report to the Presidio too."

I didn't feel comfortable giving anyone advice on something with such potentially grave implications, but apparently my decision had an effect on Billy. I think in some way, he felt better that he had someone to share the risk with, someone he knew who was taking a chance on fate.

Two days later we flew out to San Francisco together. We stayed in town the first night and partied until dawn at the tourist bars along Fisherman's Wharf. The next morning, bleary-eyed and hung over, we reported to the Presidio to begin our great adventure.

I never saw Billy again. He got assigned to the 25th Infantry Division at Cu Chi near Siagon, and I was sent up north to Qui Dong. My father sent me a newspaper clipping a couple of months later with a picture of Billy Franco under a headline that read "Local Soldier Killed in Vietnam." I was devastated. Maybe if I hadn't gone to the MattaDoor that night Billy would have gone to Canada. He would still be alive. It was one more layer of guilt to add to the mounting stress I would feel much later in Vietnam.

Welcome to Vietnam

The journey from Travis Air Force Base near San Francisco to Tan San Nut Airbase on the outskirts of Saigon took twenty-one hours, including two refueling stops—one in Honolulu and another in Guam. My apprehension was building as the stretch DC-8 with 271 souls on board approached the coast of Vietnam. Just prior to landing, I tried to control the trepidation that was about to morph into full-blown panic. As I left the plane and descended the ramp, the extreme heat and nearly suffocating humidity sucked the energy from me.

I was herded with the other soldiers toward several olive drab buses, which we boarded. The fans on my bus blew warm air on us, as I got my first glimpses of this alien place. We drove through a countryside of palm and banyan trees, thatched huts, and villages that looked as if the modern world hadn't touched them. Once I realized I was not in imminent danger, I began to relax.

Soon the bus entered the US Army Command, Vietnam (USARV) post at Long Binh. Except for the debilitating heat and humidity, the base was pretty much like a stateside posting. After I was dropped off at my barracks, which everyone referred to as a "hooch," I unpacked my duffel bag and walked around the post. I was pleasantly surprised to see pizza parlors, swimming pools, bowling alleys, paved streets, and PXs, along with mess halls and EM clubs, where troopers could even buy a beer. My impressions that first day in Vietnam weren't so bad, but the night would be a different story.

I was so exhausted, I fell into bed early that first night. At 1:40 a.m., I was awakened from a coma-like sleep by screaming sirens and a series of ear-shattering explosions all around my hooch. I was completely confused, as I stumbled from my cot. All around me men were sprinting out of the hooch into what sounded like a pitched battle. I felt like a lamb running toward the slaughterhouse, as I joined the flailing stream of hysterical soldiers. All were hoping to reach the relative safety of a protective sandbag bunker outside the hooch. We had to traverse about 50 feet of open ground before we reached the bunker. Our hope was to make it there before an enemy rocket impacted on or near us and blew us to kingdom come.

Within ten minutes, the attack was over. We slogged back into the hooch and tried to sleep, but that proved impossible. There were two more rocket attacks that night and at least one each night for the remaining time I was billeted at Long Binh.

On my fourth day in Vietnam, I lay stretched out on a cot behind one of the sandbag bunkers, sunning myself. I looked up into a cloudless sky, shielded my eyes from the sun, and watched as an F-4 Phantom jet streaked by, banked sharply, and then began making its final landing approach. I followed the silver jet as it descended and until it disappeared behind the bunker. I heard it land with a roar, as it reversed its engines.

I thought about the F-4 and what its mission might have been. I wondered how many Viet Cong or North Vietnamese Army soldiers had been dispatched to gook heaven by the jet's deadly ordnance. I also imagined those F-4 jet jockeys would be having cheeseburgers and French fries at the officer's club before spending the afternoon sunning themselves and deciding which of the bright-eyed, wholesome-looking, all-American nurses to deflower that night.

Except for the nightly attacks, I had no reason to complain though. Since I had arrived in-country, I had spent much of my time basking in the sun and avoiding the myriad nonproductive and time-consuming tasks the army contrived to keep idle soldiers busy until they were given their final orders and duty stations. I had learned how to make myself unavailable when the sandbag filling, K-P assignments, and shit-burning details were being handed out. Except for attending the combat training classes and the exercises I was required to participate in during the morning hours, I spent most of my time relaxing in the sun and wondering where I would be assigned permanently. I hoped to land a job in a supply depot, since that was the MOS for which I had been trained during my time at Fort Lee.

But until then, I laid in the sun outside the hooch, thinking about my family and the good times back home, or reading a paperback novel—anything to avoid speculating on what bad things might be awaiting me. I knew that regardless of where I was assigned in this God-forsaken country, enemy soldiers would be trying to kill me. So it was important for me to focus on the present and more pleasant thoughts.

But living in two worlds is hard to do. I was relaxing, reading, and joking with other soldiers during the day and sleeping fitfully at night, waiting for the sirens that would send us all dashing out to the sandbag bunkers.

Then, in the early afternoon of my fourth day in-country, I got my orders to the 123rd Infantry Division headquartered in Qui Dong. My permanent station was way up in the northern part of South Vietnam, in the Army's I Corps area of operations.

Qui Dong

The C-130 Hercules is a large, four-engine cargo aircraft, but it can also double as a troop transport plane. I sat on the aluminum floor in the cargo hold of the C-130 with more than 100 other soldiers. We were seated side by side in rows, with our duffle bags between our legs. A three-inch strip of red nylon served as a communal seat belt, stretching across each row of soldiers.

The 20 or so officers and noncommissioned officers (NCOs) were luckier. They sat in makeshift red canvas seats on either side of the fuselage, where, if they turned their heads, they could see out of porthole-like windows. The C-130 flew for about an hour over the protective waters of the South China Sea before banking left toward the coast and landing at the large marine airbase at Qui Dong.

Qui Dong lies on an open plain, sandwiched between the South China Sea and a ridge of high mountains. The base camp was five miles long and three miles wide, with the South China Sea as the eastern boundary. The western perimeter snaked along old Highway 1, which ran most of the length of South Vietnam. To the north, the base terminated at the fringes of a small bay, while the southern boundary stretched to the beginning of a peninsula. The peninsula extended eight miles into the sea and provided the area with a large natural harbor—as well as safe harbor for the thousands of enemy soldiers that occupied the area.

Qui Dong was home to the 24th Marine Air Wing, which maintained the airbase, and the army's 123rd Infantry Division. While the marines had landed and secured the base at Qui Dong in 1966, the 123rd Division, formed from a hodgepodge of infantry outfits, established their headquarters at the basecamp in 1967.

The 123rd Division had a glorious history, with history being the operative term. Formed during World War II after Pearl Harbor, the unit had distinguished itself in several Pacific Theatre battles. The newly formed 123rd in Vietnam had a checkered history at best. In 1969, the 123rd had more men (25,000) in Vietnam than any other division. It also had the largest area of operations, extending 50 miles south of the Demilitarized Zone (DMZ) separating North and South Vietnam and westward across the country to the border of Laos. In that same area, the North Vietnamese Army (NVA) and the Viet Cong (VC) had between 50,000 and 100,000 soldiers. However, the 123rd Division had superior firepower and technology on its side, which, according to conventional military thinking, should have more than made up for any disparity in enemy troop levels. Yet, the division regularly suffered more casualties than any other in Vietnam. I quickly came to the conclusion that the 123rd Division was not a very good place to serve.

Later, I became convinced that the division did not acquit itself better on the battlefield because the staff officers, commanded by General "Bullseye" Carp, had their respective heads up their asses. While it's true that my opinion was clouded by a predisposition to discredit and ridicule any soldier who remained in the army longer than required, there did seem to be an inordinate number of incompetent officers running the division. And even though the troopers serving in the division's three infantry brigades fought bravely and endured incredible hardships, those in charge of them were often less than competent, particularly those commanders in the rear areas.

Qui Dong was not Long Binh. Gone were the frills and amenities of that base near Saigon. There were no swimming pools, bowling alleys, pizza parlors, or even paved roads here. From the moment I disembarked the C-130, the oppressive heat and humidity set the mood. I felt a palpable sense of resignation, composed of equal parts physical discomfort, boredom, fear, and despair. As I climbed into the deuce and a half, an open-topped troop transport truck, for the trip to the division orientation center, I wondered how I could endure what was to come and make it back to the World in one piece.

The orientation center was located on the beach, just beyond where the South China Sea's high tide terminated. We newly minted 123rd Infantry Division troopers were billeted in World War II-era canvas tents. Once again—this time for a week—we were required to attend classes each morning. In the stifling heat of larger tents, which served as classrooms, we were regaled with information deemed essential to our survival in Vietnam. From booby-trap identification, to the treatment of trench foot, to operation of the Claymore mine, to warnings of the perils of venereal disease, particularly The Black Clap, we did our best to stay awake in the debilitating heat. The orientation center was a fetid, mosquito-infested inferno and I hated it. But I hated it much more affectionately than I hated the thought of leaving it and the relative safety of the rear area.

The class on Southeast Asian indigenous reptiles was less boring than most other classes, but not enough for me to overcome the effects of the 95-degree temperature in the training tent. I dozed wide-eyed, a trick I had learned in basic training, where closing one's eyes was rewarded with extra duty. I was shaken from my reverie by the sound of my name.

"Is Specialist 4 Cumpton here? Cumpton? One more time, goddammit, is Specialist 4 Augustino Cumpton in this fucking tent?" the now pissed-off NCO yelled.

"Here, I mean, yes, I'm Cumpton." Startled by my own voice, I looked to the door of the tent, where a tall, gangly sergeant glared at me.

"Bout fucking time you answered up, troop. Follow me," the sergeant said, and I quickly left the tent trailing him.

I noticed that the sergeant's jungle fatigues were a light, faded gray, and his combat boots were dusty brown. The sergeant's uniform was in stark contrast to the dark green of my own jungle fatigues and still shiney black boots.

"I'm Sergeant Grotto, 123rd Administration Company up at Division."

"What do you want with me, Sarge?"

"I don't want nothing with you, troop, but somebody in personnel records does. Get your ass in this jeep," the sergeant ordered.

My mind raced as I tried to think of a reason that I would be called to the division personnel records section. It was too much to hope that I might be assigned to an administration job here in the rear.

The jeep traveled away from the beach and began to climb up a small hill, until the ground leveled to a long plateau. As we drove along the plateau, I could see to my right a sprawling cluster of Quonset huts and row upon row of hooches. Several large, airplane hangar-like buildings were in the center of the complex. As we passed one of the large buildings, I saw the letters *PX* emblazoned over the entrance. The jeep suddenly wheeled off the main road and drove another hundred yards before stopping at a large building.

"This is it, troop," the sergeant said, flashing me a smile. "Play your cards right and maybe you can get some REMF duty here at Division HQ." As soon as I got out of the jeep, he roared off.

I was left coughing in a cloud of red dust. I slapped the dirt from my fatigues before entering the building. Inside, large, humming fans rotated noisily, circulating air cooled by large, window air-conditioning units. I walked up to the counter and caught the attention of a private who was typing on a Royal manual typewriter.

"What's up, dude?" the private said and continued typing.

"I was told to come up here and see someone in Division Personnel. Not sure who that would be, but my name is Augustino Cumpton. I'm a Spec 4 and I've been down at the combat center waiting for my orders."

"Cool it here for a few minutes while I check with my captain," the soldier said. He then got up and walked off, leaving me standing in front of his desk.

I waited anxiously for about ten minutes before the private returned and told me to follow him. We weaved our way through rows of desks, where clerks typed away on clattering typewriters. Arriving at a partitioned-off cubicle, the private knocked once and announced, "Captain Wilson, I've got Specialist Four Cumpton here."

"Come on in, Cumpton. Private, you are dismissed," Wilson said.

I entered the small office and walked up to the desk where the captain, with an unlit pipe in his mouth, sat reviewing a file. A thin man with horn-rimmed glasses, the captain, without looking up, motioned for me to sit in the chair in front of his desk.

"You're a college grad, Cumpton. Why in heaven's name aren't you an officer?" he asked, looking at me for the first time.

"Well, sir, I just figured I'd put my two years in as a draftee and then be done with my service. Anyway, I don't think I'm cut out to be an officer. I don't like the idea of having that type of responsibility—you know, for a platoon of guys."

"Well, I guess it doesn't matter anyway. It says here in your 201 file that you're an English Lit graduate. Does that mean that you can write, Cumpton?" The captain looked directly at me.

"Yes, sir. I was a reporter for my college newspaper. I actually wrote an occasional editorial too," I said, hoping to impress the Captain.

"Are you a good typist, Cumpton?

I swallowed hard and then I lied.

"Yes, sir."

"Well, son," the captain said, "we have an opening in our Awards and Decorations Office for a writer here at Division HQ. Is that something you feel qualified to do?"

"Absolutely, sir."

"Okay then. One of my soldiers will get you over to Awards and Decorations and we'll see if they think you can do the job."

At the Awards and Decorations Office I struggled with the typing, but my transformation of the action report into a lucid Awards and Decorations' citation won me the job. I knew that I was fortunate to get this assignment, that I had lucked out. I could have been ordered to some remote outpost in the deep bush. Instead, I would be serving at Division Headquarters in a support position. But I also knew that this was only the beginning. I had to face the jarring reality that I still had a whole year to serve in this stinking and deadly swamp of a country. And I would quickly learn that things could go terribly wrong, even in the rear.

Awards and Decorations

Sergeant Carson was the NCO in charge of the entire Administration Company supporting the Army's 123rd Infantry Division basecamp at Qui Dong. Fortunately for me and my coworkers in Awards and Decorations, several other Administration Company offices were also in Carson's line of fire. That he was roundly despised by everyone was little consolation when he roared through the office verbally carpet-bombing the staff. And his early morning wake-up calls always included shrieking rants about our lack of military discipline.

"You slimy fuckers are why we're losing this war!" he would scream, leaning over the cot and into the face of some half-asleep soldier.

"Grunts out in the field look better than you douche bags! I want your sorry asses up, your living areas spotless, your uniforms starched, and those boots shined. That clear, ladies?"

On one occasion, someone in the back of the hooch responded in falsetto, "Better watch out fellows, sweetie's on the rag again."

This prompted Carson to storm, crimson-faced, toward where the remark came from and, in an apoplectic rage, scream, "When I find out which one of you girls said that, your ass is going to be transferred out to the field. You can crawl around with those miserable grunts in the jungle and get your balls shot off."

But as bad as things were for us in Qui Dong at Division HQ, conditions out in the bush were exponentially worse. While we sustained enemy shelling and occasional ground attacks, these dangers paled in comparison to what infantry soldiers faced daily out in the boonies. In the field, the division's three infantry brigades were in constant firefights with main force North Vietnamese Army (NVA) soldiers. And while they also had to contend with the Vietcong, the NVA were more serious adversaries. They were extremely well trained and disciplined, and had been fighting for more than twenty years. In fact, their communist Vietnamese predecessors, the Viet Minh, had helped defeat the Japanese during World War II, then had fought and defeated the French at Dien Bien Phu in 1954. The victory over the French resulted in the country being partitioned into North and South Vietnam. And the NVA and Viet Cong had been actively engaging the US military since our first army advisors arrived in-country in the early 1960's.

So the fear of being transferred to the infantry was always hanging over our heads, and Carson constantly used that threat to motivate the administration troopers under his command. But everyone in the office also knew that Carson's bite could be much more consequential than his bark. Soldiers in the company who got on Carson's shit list did so at their own peril. One such trooper was Private First Class Alvin Frazier, a slightly pudgy, happy-go-lucky 18-year-old from Idaho Falls, Idaho. Frazier could never seem to please Carson. The sergeant constantly berated the PFC, calling him a slob and threatening to get him transferred to an infantry unit in the bush if he didn't improve his physical appearance.

And then, one day, Frazier was gone. According to our office manager, Specialist Five Hermey Dahler, Carson had made good on his threat to transfer Frazier to the field. About a month later, word drifted back that Frazier had tripped a booby trap and had sustained a traumatic brain injury. He was alive, but he had no chance of ever regaining consciousness. Learning of this, every solder in the company despised Carson even more, but they also knew that he could make good on his threats.

While the soldiers in my unit and the other support troops at the 123rd Division Headquarters were not often engaged in direct combat with the enemy, we were all equipped like our brothers in the infantry. We each carried our own M-16, with hundreds of rounds of ammunition. We also had access to grenades, bayonets, tear gas canisters, flares, and other deadly weapons. Oftentimes we were transported to the base perimeter to help defend and repel the enemy when they attacked our guard positions along the bunker line.

But the main threats to life and limb for guys in the rear, where I served, were the frequent and deadly enemy rocket attacks. The rockets were usually launched toward our positions at night, or in the wee hours of the morning, but occasionally we would be attacked during the day.

The other major threat we all feared was being targeted by one of our own disgruntled fellow soldiers. These random, deadly, and, thankfully, infrequent attacks could be precipitated by just about anything, but oftentimes the trigger was a "Dear John" letter. In fact, during basic training, we would often sing a song while we marched that dealt with an unfaithful girlfriend or wife. One such refrain went like this:

"Ain't no use in going home,
Jody's got your girl and gone."

Whether it was a Dear John letter, or some other real or imagined provocation, the threat of being murdered by one of your own buddies was another frightening fact of life for those of us serving in Vietnam.

The soldiers in Awards and Decorations comprised but one office of the Administration Company, which performed the mundane but necessary functions to keep the division running. In Awards and Decorations, we all worked together to process the division's award recommendations. It could be an interesting job reading the action reports detailing the heroic acts of individuals in the division's three infantry brigades. We were required to work six and a half days a week, and we were ordered to pull overnight guard duty about every seven to ten days.

Hermey Dahler ran the day-to-day operation of the office. He was a good guy who didn't give a shit about the imposition of inconsequential military discipline, like keeping your hair cut, your uniform pressed, or—thank God— shining your combat boots. Hermey was a tall, blonde rail of a man from rural Minnesota and he ran a pretty loose office. All he required was that you get your job done, whether it involved processing, filing, or writing about the hundreds of award recommendations and action reports that came in from the division's combat brigades on a monthly basis.

And Hermey provided one other important function in the office that benefited all the soldiers in Awards and Decorations: He was the filter between us and the bald-headed, martinet-lifer Sergeant Carson. Dahler took the brunt of the daily criticism and ration of shit that Carson directed at us.

In addition to Dahler, the office was staffed by two processing clerks, Private First Class Richard Porter from Jamestown, New Jersey, and Specialist Four George Duber from Orlando, Florida. Porter had been a machine gunner for the 194th Infantry Brigade until he was wounded and then transferred to Division HQ to serve out the remainder of his tour. Duber was a twenty-year-old college dropout who was drafted and fortunate enough to get assigned as a clerk. While Porter was quiet and often morose, Duber was a "hail good fellow" type who had an unusual and annoying idiosyncrasy: He agreed with everyone. I was convinced Duber was schizophrenic at best and, most likely, clinically insane. He was a very pliable fellow; in fact he was so acquiescent, he could take all sides in any dispute.

Private First Class Calvin Vendetti, a nineteen-year-old draftee from the New York City borough of Queens, was a clerk-typist. His mother was a devout Protestant who agreed to marry his Catholic father only if he consented to name their first male child Calvin, after the eponymous Protestant reformist. Vendetti's thick accent reminded me of one of the characters in the Bowery Boys' movies. He even looked like Leo Gorcey, who played Slip, the diminutive, loudmouth leader of the Bowery Boys gang.

Another Awards and Decorations writer, Austin LeMoyne from Colorado Springs, was a University of Missouri journalism graduate. Like me, he refused to go to officer's candidate school and took his chances on the draft. LeMoyne was an odd fellow who I would occasionally find sleeping under my cot, especially after the base had sustained an enemy rocket attack. When I asked him once why he was under my bed, LeMoyne replied, "Isn't it obvious? You're much larger than me."

Specialist Five Tobias Chang, a twenty-two-year-old graduate of Stanford from San Francisco, was second in command in the Awards and Decorations Office. Chang was responsible for editing the award citations before they went to the general's office for final approval, rejection, or demotion to some lesser award. Chang dismissively referred to himself as "CLTC"—short for Chief Lackey Tobias Chang. He was the voice of rational thinking, humor, and wisdom in our office. He was soft-spoken, intelligent, and intuitive, and his observations and opinions were always sought out. At five feet two inches and 115 pounds, CLTC was anything but physically imposing. Yet he was the voice of reason in our often intemperate and violent environment.

Two of my classmates from AIT at Fort Lee, Virginia—Julius Franken and Elvin "Rooster" Washington—were also assigned to the Division Administration Company and were billeted with us. I introduced them to the other guys in the Awards and Decorations Office and they hung out with us. Franken, who, as a child in Chicago, had complained long and often about his parents' insistence that he play a musical instrument, was assigned to be a bugler in the division parade unit and band.

Rooster grew up in the Bedford–Stuyvesant neighborhood of Brooklyn. His father had moved to the area from Alabama after World War II to work at the Brooklyn Naval Yard as a welder. Rooster was the oldest of seven siblings, and he worked odd jobs all through high school to help with family finances. He was an intelligent young man, but he did not wish to continue his education in community college or trade school. I asked him why.

"Shit, man, there's a big world out there and I wanted a piece of it," he told me smiling. "The draft was my ticket out of Bed-Sty, so I took it. Thought I'd be a black John Wayne."

"You weren't worried about coming over here?" I asked.

"Yeah, well, I fucked that up pretty good. Served about ten months out in the field. Lucky I didn't get blown away. Saw a lot of bad shit, man." Rooster looked down and shook his head.

"So why'd you re-up and come over here again?"

"Told the army I'd come back, but only if I could serve in the rear. They said I needed another MOS, so I signed up for supply training. I figured it would be a good job to have over here. That's where you and me met up in AIT at Fort Lee, remember?"

"Hell, yes, I remember. You about scared the shit out of me," I said, recalling our first encounter.

In Qui Dong, Rooster was assigned to work at the division supply depot unloading trucks and planes that supplied the 123rd Division with everything from M-16s to suppositories. Rooster was also a wheeler-dealer. He always seemed to have something to trade to the other offices, including the mess hall, where he sometimes exchanged "excess" supplies for steaks or other hard-to-get edibles.

While I got along well with most of the guys in the office, my best friend was Specialist Four Derek Barlow. Derek had decided on a career in journalism and his dream was to become a foreign correspondent. He graduated from Columbia, where he was a good student and an excellent athlete who starred on the hockey team as a goalkeeper.

But like so many of us, Derek's vocational plans were sidetracked by the war in Southeast Asia. And while he was certainly aware of the risk he was taking, he was also perversely intrigued by the prospect of taking his chances on the draft. Once in the army, he was sent to Fort Dix, New Jersey, for basic training and then on to public information school at Fort Benjamin Harrison, Indiana. He arrived in Vietnam two weeks after I did and, like me, was assigned to the Awards and Decorations Office as a writer.

Derek and the other guys in Awards and Decorations were my community.

They were my de facto neighbors, and most of them became close friends. With the threat of death and injury ever present in Qui Dong, I was glad to have these new friends to commiserate with. But there wasn't a day that my thoughts didn't drift back to my neighbors, friends, and, of course, family in Riverview. They were hard-working, blue-collar, "salt-of-the-earth" kind of folks.

Riverview

Measuring about a half mile in diameter, Riverview is not a suburb of Jeweltown because the city is not large enough to have suburbs. The formal name for the neighborhood where I grew up is actually Riverview Addition. "Additions" were what neighborhoods surrounding a city center were called back in 1950s small-town West Virginia.

And anyway, Riverview didn't fit the suburban stereotype made popular by television shows of the time like *Father Knows Best*. I remember the opening scene of that show, where Father comes home from a day at the office, bounds across the perfectly manicured lawn, and happily enters the front door of a two-story colonial home. He hangs his suit coat in the closet, puts on his cardigan sweater with patches on the elbows, and lights up his pipe. Just then, Mother, in a knee-length, frilly dress, bursts into the room and gives dad a quick buss on the cheek before returning to the kitchen to put the finishing touches on dinner.

I suppose that program and others of its ilk were intended to represent the ideal American family. And while I knew that those shows were fiction, they gave me hope that somewhere, a few lucky people actually lived that storybook existence, and that maybe one day, I, too, could achieve a small measure of the American Dream.

But that was not the reality in Riverview Addition. Ours was a blue collar, ethnic neighborhood with as many apartments as single family homes. Those residences were occupied by folks with surnames like Belcastro, Gonzalez, O'Donohue, and Kowalski. I grew up in an apartment, a second-story flat of about 800 square feet that included a bathroom, kitchen, two bedrooms, and a living room. Grandpa and Grandma had the only single-family dwelling in our large, extended family. That's where we all met, particularly on Sundays and holidays, to share food and camaraderie, and to discuss the issues of the day.

With a population of about 2,000, Riverview was one of five additions that encircled Jeweltown. The city was home to four glass factories, which together formed an industrial base large enough to provide full-time work to anyone willing to perform the exhausting manual labor required. My dad, Harry, was a foreman at one of those factories, and he got me a job there in the summers during college.

That was the hardest job I've ever had because it involved helping tear down and then rebuild the furnaces where the glass was made. In those furnaces, sand was heated to 1,700 degrees Fahrenheit before being transformed into glass. The worst part of that job involved climbing down into the bottom of the furnace and shoveling glass crystals into buckets that were removed from the pit by pulleys. I worked on a team with two other young men, and we were required to wear masks covering our mouths and noses. With temperatures in the pit exceeding 130 degrees, our team rotated 30 minutes on and 30 minutes off with another three-man crew.

During a ten-hour shift, I would spend about five hours down in those hellish pits. Later, when I would occasionally fret about a difficult academic assignment or the discipline required to study and maintain my grades, I would remember my time in the furnace pits and remind myself how lucky I was to be getting an education that would give me better future employment options. Little did I realize that later on, I would need to survive another hellish place to have any future at all.

If you were fortunate enough to grow up in Riverview, you knew everyone and everyone knew you. We had an interesting cast of characters in our little neck of the woods. The kids in our neighborhood, like most children of the 1950s, spent the majority of daylight hours outside. We played hide-and-seek, kick the can, and many other traditional games, but we were also adept at creating our own games, some of which, looking back on them now, seem a little bit strange. Take Fling Cat, for example.

Johnny Trupo...

Johnny Trupo was a burly twelve-year-old with jet-black hair that stood straight up in thick clumps. He looked as if he had stuck his finger in a light socket. He was also the creator of Fling Cat. Johnny, who lived down the street from the bakery, had a bizarre habit of forensically examining previously animate creatures. Johnny was able to do this because he was immune to the physical reactions most kids have to foul-smelling and decaying dead animals. He had no gag reflex.

Instead of avoiding the carcass of a dead dog, bird, or snake, Johnny would poke the rotting creatures with a stick or dissect them with a pen knife. He was particularly intrigued by dead cats, especially ones that had been run over repeatedly by a succession of vehicles for an extended period of time, until the felines had been effectively flattened.

The first time Johnny found one of these unfortunate creatures, he carried it off to a place in the woods and patiently checked on it over a period of weeks. Once the carcass had become completely desiccated, he proudly presented it to us and announced it was time to play a new game he called "Fling Cat." Since the now-flattened feline still retained a slight odor, we were all reluctant to participate in the game, until Johnny demonstrated, with a flick of the wrist, the aerodynamic possibilities of Fling Cat. A freakish cross between horseshoes and Bocce, the object of the game, as Johnny explained it, was to fling the cat toward a goal, usually a telephone pole. The person whose fling resulted in the cat being closest to the goal would be declared the winner.

I remember my cousin Benito quizzing Johnny about the game the first time he introduced it to us.

"Hey Johnny, how many of those cats do you have?" he asked.

"Just this one now, but I'll get some more. Hey, if you find any dead cats, especially ones that got run over, let me know and I'll make some more of these Flingers."

"What about other dead animals? Does it have to be cats? "Benito asked.

"I don't think any others would work. Maybe a rabbit or a squirrel, but they gotta be flat."

So that was the beginning of Fling Cat, a game that was popular until Junior Lacosta, another of our Riverview friends, tried his hand at copying Johnny's formula for creating a Flinger. Unfortunately, he selected a not-quite-flattened and still-ripe skunk carcass. As a result, every kid in the vicinity of the Fling Skunk that day was subjected to a vinegar bath administered by a bevy of angry mothers. That ripe skunk proved the demise of Fling Cat, one of the more unique games we played in Riverview.

Rosie Infantano...

Johnny Trupo was certainly one of the most memorable kids I grew up with, but I also interacted on a daily basis with a slew of unforgettable adults. Many of them came into the Chestnut Bakery to buy a loaf of bread or some pepperoni rolls.

One of the more interesting regulars was Rosie Infantano.

Rosie lived just up the street from the bakery and operated what Grandpa Salvatore called a speakeasy. Her father had, indeed, sold home brew and bootleg liquor out of his basement during Prohibition. Rosie began working in the place as a teenager, assisting the old man in his illegal enterprise.

Now in her forties, Rosie had succeeded her late father and continued operating an unlicensed bar in her basement. It was also said that Rosie offered her late-night male guests more than just home brew and shots of bootleg liquor. For this reason, she was referred to as Regina di Putana (the Queen Whore), a name bestowed on her by Aldo Pantalini, one of the octogenarian regulars at the Ruff Avenue Poolroom. The name stuck and most of the men, when referring to Rosie, used that moniker, but never to her face. In fact, the only person who dared utter the nickname out loud, in public, was Rosie herself. She could hold her own in any verbal and most physical confrontations with the guys at the Ruff.

Rosie was a tall, full-figured woman who wore tight, calf-length dresses that accentuated her curvaceous body. And even though she always had more than enough makeup on her face, she would regularly extract a small case from her purse and enhance the crimson color of her cheeks. Rosie was not a pretty woman, but she was not unattractive either, especially to me, at a time when I was just reaching puberty. So while she was Regina di Putana to most of the men in Riverview, I could never bring myself to refer to her in that pejorative manner. Besides, she always had a smile for me during her daily bakery visits.

"Hey Augie, gimme a dozen pepperoni rolls and two loaves of hard crust," she said one spring afternoon in 1959. "We got some railroad guys coming over tonight for a few drinks and I think they'll be hungry."

"Sure, Rosie. Coming right up." It was hard for me to keep from staring at her and I quickly turned to get her order.

"How old are you now, Augie?" Rosie asked.

"I'm 13, but my birthday is coming up pretty soon. I start high school at St. Alphonse's in the fall."

"Why don't you come over to my place in the basement sometime? I'll pour you some home brew. You do drink beer, don't you?"

"Oh, sure, I sip a cold one every now and then," I said nonchalantly, trying to impress her. "But I don't know, Rosie. I don't think mom would let me do that."

"You a mama's boy, Augie? You tell your mama everything you do?"

"No, of course not," I said hoping I didn't sound embarrassed. "You know how parents are, though."

"Yeah, well, my mom died when I was nine and my old man, he started me working in the basement bar when I was about your age. So I guess I don't know how most parents are."

I looked away from Rosie and changed the subject. "Okay, let's see. That will be 25 cents each for the bread and a dollar for the pepperoni rolls," I said.

"Okay, here you go," she said handing me a dollar bill and a fifty-cent piece. "If you change your mind, you're always welcome to come over and visit Regina di Putana. I promise to show you a real good time." Rosie winked at me and smiled seductively, before turning and walking out the door.

Guido the Gardener...

While Rosie plied her exotic and supposedly scandalous trade, there were other locals who made a name for themselves by simply performing a mundane task with incredible skill and with a superhuman work effort. One of the most amazing people I ever encountered in Riverview was a tiny, illiterate man of indeterminate age who was simply known as "Guido the Gardener." Guido was just shy of five feet tall. He had a wiry build and a grizzled face that was accentuated by a large, bulbous nose. Guido dressed in a brown woolen suit with a stained white shirt underneath the coat, which was always buttoned to the top. He wore a wide-brimmed fedora and kept a large, white handkerchief in his suit pocket. Guido, as his nickname revealed, was a gardener, but of the most rudimentary type. Guido did not plant. Guido did not weed. Guido did not prune. Guido did not mulch. Guido simply—and magnificently—dug gardens for most of the Italian-American families in Riverview.

He accomplished this task with such dedication and perfection that his arrival in early spring was as anxiously anticipated as the end of Lent by everyone in the neighborhood who had a garden. In fact, there was always a wager at the Ruff Avenue Poolroom among the old guys at the card tables as to which garden Guido would till first. Grandpa Salvatore, Lupi Cantalupi, and Jimmie Ponza were always among the first to get a visit from Guido.

Since Guido hardly ever spoke more than just a few words—and only in Italian—he never indicated how he decided whose garden he would visit first, or when he would begin digging. He simply showed up and went to work. When

Guido did speak, it was only to indicate that he needed a glass of water, that it was time to eat, or that he was finished. Mostly, Guido just nodded to indicate what he wanted to do.

The guys at the Ruff all came to the conclusion that Guido decided whose garden to till first based on the quality of the food and the wine he accepted as payment for his work. Everyone had tried to pay Guido a few dollars for his time, but the little man strictly refused their money. He would, however, accept a gallon of wine, a hunk of Parmesan, or a couple pounds of Italian sausage.

Guido would start digging at first light and continue until about ten in the morning, when he would stop to use the bathroom or get a glass of water. Guido never worked fast. He was like a steady machine with no wasted motion and an economy of movement. When he completed his job at the end of the day, the garden was ready to be planted. Row upon row of upturned dirt was proportioned perfectly, like it had been sculpted by some agrarian artist.

But Guido needed fuel to keep his corporeal engine going. So he would stop around noon and go into the kitchen of the family for whom he was working to have his midday meal. Guido had an amazing and prodigious appetite that I witnessed firsthand at Grandma Luisa's house. Guido was a simple man who only required pasta—but a lot of it. He preferred pasta aglio e olio, which is spaghetti with oil, garlic, parmesan cheese, and red pepper flakes. I watched in awe as Guido slowly and methodically ate his way through more than a pound of pasta and washed it down with a liter of Grandpa's homemade wine. He went about eating the way he worked—slowly, methodically, and perfectly. He would spend about one hour at Grandma's kitchen table and then go back outside, sit on Grandpa's metal chair, and smoke a Parodi cigar. Once the cigar was finished, Guido would grab his hat, move out into the garden, and work until he was finished, or until dark.

Tapper Two...

If Guido the Gardner's simple name perfectly described what he did each day, Frankie Secondo's nickname was equally defining, though more flamboyant. Everyone called Frankie "Tapper Two," a stage name he had conferred upon himself when, as a young man, he had visions of becoming the next Fred Astaire or Gene Kelly. Unfortunately for Frankie, tap dancing was on the wane and there was little or no demand for this performance art after World War II. Undeterred, Tapper Two convinced the local school board to hire him to teach tap dancing to grade school students in Jeweltown. This paying job allowed him to pursue his nascent career even though there were few, if any, opportunities to showcase his tap dancing skills. But it did provide him an outlet to keep perfecting his dancing. He taught kids dances like the "Hucklebuck" and the "Cake Walk," all the while keeping alive his dream of one day making it to the "big time" as a tap dancer.

Adding to his unique persona, Tapper Two had an idiosyncrasy that puzzled strangers but endeared him to his friends and neighbors in Riverview, especially those who conversed with him regularly. Tapper Two punctuated each sentence he uttered by whistling, sometimes between each individual word. He might whistle a verse of a song, or make the sound of a pigeon or robin. And sometimes he could actually whistle a word or two. I looked forward to Tapper's daily visits to the bakery, where he would always keep me smiling by whistling and tap dancing his way through the simple act of buying a loaf of bread.

"How you doing, Tapper?" I would greet him as he entered the bakery, and then wait for his melodic response.

"I'm just (a quick whistle) great, Augie," he would reply and then punctuate the last word with another whistling refrain—this one a verse from "Whistle While You Work."

"What can I get for you today?" I asked, and then watched as Tapper did a full pirouette while whistling the theme song to the *Mickey Mouse Club.*

"Two loaves of (whistle) round, Augie," he said and then made the trilling sound of a pigeon.

"That will be fifty cents, Tapper."

"Excellent," he replied, tweeting the song of a chirping sparrow. "Here you go (more "Whistle While You Work"), Augie. See you tomorrow," he said, completing another pirouette and whistling a few notes from "Arrivederci Roma," as he exited the bakery.

Angelina Popata...

I suppose you could categorize Tapper Two as eccentric, but another Riverview local, Angelina Popata, provided our neighborhood with a service that we kids thought was really weird. A middle-aged spinster, Angelina was short and stout. Her most prominent physical characteristic was her extremely large bosom. And while that anatomical feature often caused kids to stare at her just a little too long, what really distinguished Angelina was how she would put those large breasts to use.

Angelina was not blessed with good or even average looks, and she was very shy. As a result, she had never married. Her only regret, as she passed through her childbearing years, was that she had never been able to give birth to a child of her own. So she did the next best thing. She offered her services as a wet nurse to mothers who could not, or chose not to, breast feed their babies. It was not uncommon at the time, particularly in ethnic neighborhoods, for wet nurses to ply their trade and make a living suckling newborns. And Angelina also offered another service to new mothers, particularly ones with several other children, who needed a break from rocking their newborn babies. Angelina would place these infants on her ample bosom and rock them into a peaceful slumber.

But, according to Grandma Luisa and Aunt Lia, Angelina provided an even more important service than wet nursing or rocking babies. She had the power to protect the infants under her care from the curse of the *malocchio*, or evil eye, which a jealous or mean-spirited individual might cast upon a newborn. These spells were said to cause physical deformities like crossed eyes, a sickness, or even seven years of bad luck.

It was common during those years to see Angelina Popata sitting in a rocking chair on the porch of Grandma's house, wet nursing or rocking one of my little cousins, all the while looking to and fro for any sign of someone trying to cast an evil spell. Aunt Lia said Angelina's power came from the special cornettos, or horns, she wore around her neck. These small, gold horns looked like miniature chili peppers. In fact, Angelina wore three cornettos, which represented the Father, Son, and Holy Ghost.

While we kids often joked about Angelina and her purported powers, I now kept a cornetto amulet securely fastened on the same chain as my dog tags, which I wore around my neck. Aunt Lia had given it to me before I left for Vietnam. I am not particularly superstitious, but I wasn't taking any chances. On those long guard duty nights when things got dicey, I would rub that little horn, say a silent prayer, and think of the days of my youth and all the unique characters back in Riverview.

Derek Barlow

Derek Barlow was 22 years old when he was drafted into the army. He was the son of a wealthy vineyard owner who lived in the Finger Lakes region of Western New York State. Derek was the third and last child—all sons—born to Emmett and Louise Barlow. His idyllic childhood, playing along the beautiful lake, orchards, and vineyards of his father's property, was tragically shattered when his parents were killed in an automobile accident shortly before his tenth birthday. Since there were no other relatives to care for the Barlow children, the local court appointed an older couple, who had worked in the family household, as custodians of the property and guardians of the children. While the older couple was kind and caring, Derek could never accept them as surrogate parents. Though he was obedient and respectful, he grew through adolescence into young adulthood never having fully recovered from the loss of his parents, and never feeling a kinship toward his guardians.

His father's will had provided amply for the boys, so when it was time for Derek to go to college, he chose Columbia. He was a good student, and, because of the independence he had developed over the years, he found life in the metropolitan New York area to be a pleasant and exciting change from the rural life he had led. He still loved his country home, but there was always a slight sadness, like a gentle gnawing at the edge of his consciousness, that came to him when he was there and reminded him of his family tragedy. It was as if that place, his home, would not allow him to let go of the pain, and so he chose to stay away as much as possible.

The profits from the orchard and vineyards had grown over the years and a trust had been established for each child, which would easily provide them with a generous stipend for the rest of their lives. Derek's brothers decided to stay on and manage the family holdings, while Derek decided on a career in journalism. His dream was to be a foreign correspondent, but like so many young men of his generation, his vocational plans were sidetracked by the war in Southeast Asia. At Columbia, he was a good student and an excellent athlete who starred on the hockey team. He was a good- looking, sandy-haired six-footer, with an engaging personality and a dry wit. He was also quick-tempered and independent, and he could handle himself in a fight.

Derek was opposed to the war in Vietnam, but he didn't join his fellow students by taking his opposition to the streets. He chose the classroom to express his opinions. He enjoyed the intellectual challenge of arguing dispassionately with his classmates—if he could find anyone so inclined—about his belief that US involvement in the war was a mistake. His opposition was not rooted in morality but rather, he felt, in common sense. If there was a strategic reason to fight a war, Derek would be all in. But, he argued, we were taking sides in a civil war ten thousand miles from home. To stop the spread of communism?

Derek didn't believe in the domino theory. He didn't think defeating the communists in Vietnam was necessary to keep them from invading California. He acknowledged that his views were unorthodox, but he felt they were pragmatic. His opinions angered many of his more emotionally invested friends who opposed the war on moral grounds. But they knew not to push him too far because to attack his integrity or to reduce the disagreement to a personal level could sometimes trigger his volatile temper. Once pushed beyond a certain point, he would not compromise or back down from a challenge. It was both a strength and a weakness, and he had learned, through experience, to sense when a situation was turning bad and to leave before matters went too far.

Derek Barlow enjoyed an active social life and he dated frequently. But his fiercely independent nature was always an impediment to any serious relationship. He enjoyed the camaraderie among his hockey teammates and his male friends, and he especially liked to go out with them and share a few drinks. But he seemed to sense from his earliest experiences with alcohol that he would need to learn to control his drinking. He was frightened by the sense of confidence and the feelings of well-being alcohol produced in him, and he feared he might become dependent on it.

As he approached graduation, Derek knew that he would have to face the prospect of military service. But he was also intrigued and excited about the prospect of serving his country. His oldest brother, who comanaged the family holdings, used his influence to find Derek an opening in the local national guard unit. All Derek had to do was sign on the dotted line and he would spend the war as a certified "weekend warrior." This greatly disturbed him and so, to the chagrin of his brothers, he chose to take his chances with the draft. He could never back down from a challenge.

After he was drafted, Derek Barlow was sent to Fort Dix, New Jersey, for basic training and then on to public information school at Fort Benjamin Harrison, Indiana. He arrived in Vietnam two weeks after Augie Cumpton and, like him, was assigned to the Awards and Decorations Office as a writer.

Now, as he stretched out on his cot in the living area of the hooch, Derek closed his eyes and remembered back to his first month in-country, to the picnic on the island, and to the best day of his life. It just seemed like yesterday ....

* * * * *

It was like a very good dream, and Derek Barlow always concentrated on remembering as many of the details as possible. He remembered waking suddenly, regaining consciousness like an oxygen-starved diver breaking the surface after a long, slow ascent. He rubbed the haze from his eyes and squinted at the brightness, feeling sluggish, heavy, and sore, but at least more oriented.

Derek had only been in-country for a month when he had gotten sick. Malaria. A mild case, he had been assured, and not bad enough to get him sent home, but still a devastating illness. Now he was feeling somewhat better, and he looked forward to getting outside the Med-Evac hospital for a walk in the sun. He remembered the orderly asking how he felt and then telling him of the outing.

It seemed incongruous and certainly out of place, given their location and circumstance, but he was invited to go on a picnic to an island in the South China Sea. He remembered also thinking that he must be dreaming, and he actually pinched himself to be sure it was real. The picnic was real, but his other experiences that day, he would reflect later, truly transcended reality.

The wind rushed silently up through the opened hatch in the floor, chilling the interior of the Jolly Green Giant helicopter. The craft was the largest helicopter used by the US forces in Vietnam. Twenty-four enlisted men, along with three noncommissioned officers from the 123rd Med-Evac hospital, sat silently on aluminum bench seats in the cabin of the chopper, unable to speak above the roar of the engines and the clatter of the giant rotor blades. Derek Barlow shivered slightly, as he peered down through the small opening in the floor of the chopper, at the gentle swells of the South China Sea, four thousand feet below. He looked around at the other passengers. All were clad in light blue pajama tops and bottoms, and everyone wore black sandals made by the local Vietnamese out of old rubber tires. Some soldiers had bandages or casts on parts of their bodies.

Unbelievable, Derek thought. Going on an outing in the middle of the war—a picnic to an island off the coast of Qui Dong.

They had been traveling twenty minutes when the chopper banked sharply to the left and began to descend. Derek looked over his shoulder out the porthole-like window and saw the island emerging through a light morning mist. It looked to be no larger than five miles across, but almost at dead center was a large mountain with a deep crater starting at its crest. A volcano. It had to be inactive because he could see small trees and lush vegetation in the crater, as the helicopter passed over the mountain.

The chopper leveled out and made its final approach, touching down in a large, open field. The hinged rear door of the craft opened and became a ramp, off of which the blue-clad patients were led. Derek walked unsteadily, working to keep his balance. His legs and, indeed, his entire body still felt very weak, as he left the chopper shielding his eyes from the sudden brightness. The NCOs and a few of the heartier patients off-loaded coolers, tables, and cartons of food. Then the Jolly Green Giant lifted off, raising a cloud of dust that swirled like a small tornado.

As the sound of the chopper receded, it was replaced by a din of voices raised in greeting, and by the footfalls of a small army of children, who ran toward the assembled Americans. Derek marveled at the smiling, healthy, and surprisingly clean faces of the kids. The NCOs handed out bubble gum, candy, and, ironically, toothbrushes all around. The children, now satisfied, began mingling with the GIs. Derek looked around at the field, which appeared to be about 200 hundred yards in diameter, and then he heard, rather than saw, the South China Sea. He immediately walked toward the sound, as one of the NCOs called to him not to wander off too far.

Derek could feel the peace settling in on him as he walked through a narrow stand of palms and pines toward the white sand of the beach. As he stretched out on the sand, the rhythmic lapping of the surf at low tide lulled him, within a few minutes, into a sound sleep. When he awoke some time later, the sun was higher and hotter. Stripping the pajamas from his body, he trotted toward the ocean and dove headlong into the surf, tasting the salt and feeling the waves wash over and refresh him. After a short while, he left the sea and lay naked on the sand, letting the sun dry him. After about 15 minutes, he dressed and returned to the field and joined a group of GIs. He drank a beer before setting off to explore the island.

He walked along a path that rose gently toward the volcanic mountain at the center of the island. After twenty minutes of steady but gradual climbing, the trail forked left and right. Derek took the left fork and soon the path began to parallel a small, clear stream. The forest was deeply shaded in a heavy green canopy and smelled of wet earth. There was also an almost intoxicating fragrance of tropical flowers. A single shaft of sunlight, like a radiant arrow, pierced the forest, highlighting a single orchid.

The trail meandered for a while with the stream and eventually led Derek to a clear pool that lay at the base of a fifty-foot waterfall. Here, he sat down with his back to a giant palm. Gazing at the falls, he was mesmerized by the ethereal beauty of the place and the feeling of well-being it engendered in him. It was like being high, he thought, only much better. He sat reflecting introspectively for a long while. Then, behind the spray and mist of the cascading water, he caught a glimpse of movement.

As he strained to clearly observe the scene, two young women emerged from behind the falls. They did not seem to notice him. He watched as they unwrapped their sarongs and dove naked into the pool. Derek was transfixed by their grace and beauty, and he stared wide-eyed as they swam and frolicked playfully in the sparkling water. One was tall and slim, while the other was fuller bodied, but both were exquisitely proportioned. Derek was within 30 feet of the young women, but he was partially obscured by vegetation. He was in an awkward position; if he moved or made any sound, they would surely see him and they would at least be embarrassed and probably frightened. So he watched quietly.

Within a few minutes, the women climbed to the bank and sat down, letting the gentle breeze dry them. They were wonderfully sensuous, with long black hair, olive skin, and small yet full breasts. Barlow felt himself grow hard as desire swept over him in waves.

Then, as if his desire was transmitted by some magical hormonal communication, the tall young woman suddenly rose and walked directly toward him. She was smiling as she approached and Derek wondered if they had known he was sitting there all along. When the woman got to within ten feet of him, she stopped, stared directly into his eyes, and motioned for him to follow her. It was like a dream, and he felt light-headed and giddy. Derek stood and started to apologize, but the woman, with fingers to her lips, indicated that he should be silent.

He followed her then to where the other woman lay and sat down next to her. The taller one went behind him and pulled the pajama top over his head. She got on her knees and began massaging his back, while the fuller-bodied one stroked his cheek lightly, as if he were some new and rare object. He felt gentle hands on his back soothing him, while the hands in front unloosened the tie at the waist of his pajama bottoms and slowly pulled them over his hips, down his legs, and then entirely off his body. Derek had never felt so aroused, as he reached softly for the rounded breast of the woman now kneeling in front of him. She smiled and moved over to him, straddled his body and sat in his lap. She smelled of jasmine and he was gloriously intoxicated by her.

What Derek experienced next he had trouble communicating. He would later describe it as an almost spiritual event. It was so much more than lovemaking, both physically and emotionally, and it transcended anything he had ever experienced. He was left with a peacefulness and sense of security he had never felt before. Time seemed suspended as the three, without speaking a word, gave themselves to each other in a perfect harmony of physical synchronization and spiritual communion. When, for the final time, he climaxed, the light and energy rushed from him, and he fell into a blissful unconsciousness. Sometime later, when he awoke, the women were gone.

A Day at the Beach

"Jesus H. Christ, Cumpton. He'll hang us by the short hairs if we skip inspection," Barlow said, as he passed the container of warm Bloody Marys across the partition from his living area to mine. I took a long drink from the plastic juice container and passed it back.

The hooch inspection was scheduled for 17:30 hours. But I wanted to take a stroll along the beach before heading up to the NCO club to get a good seat for that evening's floor show.

"Screw Carson," I said. "I'm tired of these weekly inspections. This is a war zone and I think we need a little in-country R&R. What do you say, D? He can pack that inspection where the sun don't shine."

I could tell Barlow was warming to the idea. Like the shadow of a cloud crossing a flat rock, a grin began to spread slowly over his face.

"What the hell. What can Carson do? Send us to Vietnam? Okay, we'll check out the PX for some beer, stroll down to the beach, and maybe scope out a little nurse-tang before we head up to the club."

"Okay then, let's do it," I said.

We left the enlisted men's billeting area that afternoon at 5:25 p.m. and set off in the direction of the Division PX, one mile by dusty road to the south. For a while, the road paralleled a portion of the base perimeter. Along the way, we stopped to watch an army patrol enter the open- kill zone between the guard posts on the bunker line and the barbed wire fence barrier some 300 yards away at the tree line. Like a patrol of green zombies, the soldiers listlessly made their way to where the scorched and lifeless remnants of three enemy soldiers hung in grotesque suspension on the razor-sharp concertina wire. We watched as the soldiers went about the grisly task of removing the dead from the wire and dropping them into rubber body bags.

"Holy shit, Derek. How do you fuck up bad enough to get that assignment?" I asked.

Barlow looked out toward the perimeter. "I guess there are worse jobs than shit-burning detail."

After a few moments, we continued our trek toward the PX. An armored personnel carrier (APC) speeding past raised a cloud of thick red dust that enveloped us. I looked over at Barlow. He looked like a rusting tin soldier. The sun blazed in a cloudless sky, pushing the temperature above 110 degrees.

The corrugated tin hangar-like building that housed the Division PX could, at times, be a vast oasis of stereos, cameras, canned foods, suppositories, condoms, chewing tobacco, clothes, booze, luggage, and sundry other items that a soldier might want or need. Just as often, however, the PX was a barren wasteland of row upon row of empty shelves, with an occasional tin of sardines here or a pair of wool trousers there.

Feast or famine. For weeks at a time the place would be empty. Then, overnight, huge Conex containers would be deposited and unloaded at the back of the PX. Unannounced and unanticipated, this bounty would fill the empty shelves with all manner of goodies. Once word spread, crazed and deprived soldiers would converge on the PX like schools of piranha zeroing in on a herd of suckling pigs, ravaging the place with reckless abandon. Spending months of pay like there was no tomorrow (and sometimes there wasn't), the troopers would roar up and down the aisles, grabbing everything in sight. Sharks in a feeding frenzy had better manners.

But this infrequent type of "opulence" was the extreme exception to the rule. Over time, my buddy CLTC had convinced me that it was actually better to have a mostly empty PX. I had to admit that while CLTC's logic was obtuse, it was still sound. It dealt with hope and expectation.

"Hey Augie," CLTC said to me one time. "If the PX was full of all those wonderful products from back in the World we miss so much, it would be even more awful than it is without that stuff. Think about it. When it's empty, like it usually is, it gives us something to look forward to."

In CLTC's mind, an always well-stocked PX represented one less hope and one less expectation. Whereas a usually empty PX gave the deprived GI something to hope for, even though there was little or no expectation that anything good would be arriving soon. So to lift our spirits, every week or so, CLTC would approach me and ask if I wanted to "go check out the nothing at the PX."

This particular afternoon, Barlow and I were lucky. We found a six-pack of Hamm's and set off for the short walk down to the beach. The beer was not cold or even cool, but it was beer just the same. And there was just enough to pass the time until we made our way up to the NCO Club.

But first, we were going to the beach, and the private cove where off-duty nurses and Red Cross donut dollies would be swimming and sunning themselves. At one time or another, all 25,000 soldiers and marines in this portion of I Corps had entertained lustful thoughts about these "round-eye" princesses. The numbers, the chances, the proportions—25,000 horny men to 40 nurses and Red Cross doughnut dollies—were not in our favor.

"Fat chance," I said.

"Still possible," said Barlow, "though the odds aren't real good. But who knows, maybe Lady Fuck, I mean Luck, will smile on us today."

But the only ones who really stood a chance were the young doctors who worked with the nurses at the Med-Evac hospital, located on a cliff above the secluded cove. These dashing officers had rank and therefore the privilege of devoting their boundless energy to seduction and fornication.

Yet it didn't matter to us that the odds of success were long; at least we could stare salaciously at these ladies and fantasize. So we hiked through ankle deep sand, sweating and panting, and made our way around to the private cove.

On this particular afternoon, however, the cove was deserted, except for a solitary marine who sat in the sand smoking a joint. I figured the predawn attack must have caused heavy casualties, which would account for the absence of any nurses. My conclusion was confirmed by the marine, who had pulled perimeter guard near the airbase on the southern end of the basecamp the night before.

"Hell of a way to go, man," he said, taking a beer from me and passing the joint in return. "I was just ready to wake my buddy up to do his turn when the shit hit the fan. Three rockets came in right over us and impacted on the runway, but two others nailed some hooches. The dudes inside didn't have a chance. Then the gooks started hitting us with RPGs. Blew away two guys in the position fifty yards from us."

The marine took a long drink from the beer and stared blankly out to sea. For a few moments, the three of us watched silently as waves crashed wildly on rocks that would soon be covered over by the approaching tide. Barlow broke the silence.

"Did they get inside the wire and make it to the base?"

"Far as we could tell, they all got zapped on the wire. But shit, man, all I know is the fucking officer of the guard wouldn't give us clearance to open up on the dinks until we had four guard bunkers on fire. Motherfuckers! "

I could empathize with the marine because I had experienced the same frustrations. It stemmed from agreements between the Vietnamese village chiefs, who supposedly were loyal to the South Vietnamese Army (ARVN), and US forces. The agreements prohibited us from initiating or returning fire until approval was received from the locals. This protocol was not only cumbersome, it could be deadly. Unless there was an all-out and obvious enemy attack, US soldiers were not permitted to engage the enemy. In order to return enemy fire, GI's on the bunker line first had to call the command post (CP) and officer of the guard (OG), who then contacted the village chief. The village chief would ascertain whether or not any "friendlies" were in the area before giving us the okay to engage.

In many instances, however, the village chief would be conveniently unavailable. This was not surprising, since oftentimes he was busy directing the enemy attack. Despite this obvious charade, US forces, under threat of court-martial, were forced to comply with the absurd engagement protocol.

We left the marine two beers and began the slow trek up to the Division NCO Club, which stood on a bluff overlooking the South China Sea.

"Things are getting pretty dicey now. We're getting short, D. We only gotta keep our heads down for a little while longer," I said and looked over at Barlow. He had a faraway look on his face. He didn't respond. It was as if he was in a trance.

"Hey Derek," I tried again. "You gotta be on that island, right?"

Barlow just smiled at me.

Beginning of the End

The beginning of the end. That's how I would think of it later. A minor infraction. Just a slight transgression. But that small misstep would quickly metastasize into a full-blown infection that would spread with fatal repercussions.

It began early on the morning after we skipped Sergeant Carson's inspection to go to the beach and the NCO Club. Carson, starched and spotless as ever, roared into the hooch at 06:30 to wake us up. It was a particularly rude awakening, since most of us were painfully hung over from a night of overindulgence at the club.

"Get your lazy asses up and at 'em!" he yelled, as he approached my sleeping area. "Another lovely day in Southeast Asia, men. One more opportunity to make America safe from the yellow peril. Up! Up! Up!" he yelled, as he approached my sleeping area.

"You! Augustino Lee Cumpton! Get your butt in gear and be in my office in 15 minutes!" he screamed, leaning over my cot.

Then he looked over at Derek. "That goes for you, too, Barlow. You shitheads skipped my mandatory inspection last night. Well, boys, there's consequences when you fuck up, and now you're in a world of shit," he said and left the hooch.

I pulled on my faded olive-green jungle fatigue pants and grabbed the matching shirt, which everyone, with the exception of Carson, wore untucked, in a futile attempt to lessen the effects of the stifling heat.

"Hey D, looks like it's time to pay the piper," I said and groggily stumbled out of the hooch and toward the latrine to brush my teeth. Sixteen toilets were lined up along two of the four walls in one large room of the latrine, while sinks lined the other two walls. In an adjacent room, 32 individual shower heads, one right next to the other, lined all the walls and served as the community shower room for the Administration Company soldiers—when there was actually enough water to permit personal hygiene.

This particular morning, more than half of the toilets were filled to the top with excrement and unusable. I had learned early on how to brush my teeth and breathe through my mouth at the same time, so I wouldn't gag at the putrid smell. The toilets would remain this way until the unfortunate troopers who pulled the (literal) "shit detail" removed the sawed-off, 55-gallon steel drums from underneath each of the toilets and loaded them onto trucks. The trucks would transport the men and the shit to an open area, where the drums of excrement would be doused with diesel fuel and burned.

As I brushed my teeth, I tried not to think about my living environment. I tried to be thankful for being in a support job and not out in the jungle, where the grunts had to endure not only despicable living conditions but also an even greater threat of death or injury from the enemy.

Still, it was hard not to get depressed. It would be great to just clean up and at least feel good. But try as I might, I could not even imagine feeling good in this place. There were just too many debilitating environmental miseries to deal with. Just about the time I'd get a mental fix on that cool shower, that prime rib, that undulating body—just then the reality of my squalid living conditions would simply render any pleasant thoughts null and void.

So if you were fortunate enough to be stationed in a rear area, you counted your blessings daily. But there was a price to pay that I summarized into four words: flies, dogs, water, and shit. These disparate terms had real significance for me and for the frustrations they represented each day, as I struggled to cope with my alternately boring and terrifying existence in Qui Dong.

Flies...

Flies everywhere. In the latrines, in the mess hall, in the office, in the oppressively hot out-of-doors. Great flying squadrons of these large, black, winged insects attacked human flesh, sortie after sortie. They came, not swiftly like dive-bombers, but ponderously like slowly descending condors, impervious to the flak of continual human swatting. Wave after wave of these putrid horseflies would strike, Kamikaze-like. They sacrificed their individual existence for their mindless mission to suck the life blood out of, and to inflict pain and irritation onto, the bodies of sweating American soldiers.

Dogs...

Sleeping, lying, lethargic, stinking, lazy, apathetic, and hairless dogs. Not as numerous as flies, but, in concert with them, they were another debilitating and depressing fact of life that contributed to the general malaise, and sapped the spirit and will out of us.

These dogs were not the Fidos and Bowsers so lovingly cute and loyal back in the World. No, these nondescript mongrels congregated in large packs only in rear areas, where they instinctively knew that as competition to even army chow, they came in a distant second.

In the bush, they would feed a hungry village for a week. Filet de Bow-Wow. Canine Cacciatore. But in the rear, these hairless hounds lazed about with impunity, impervious to any attempts by we soldiers to befriend them. It was this unresponsiveness that got to me. These creatures were like canine robots. All our attempts to buddy up to them were repaid with total indifference and apathy. They would not even fetch balls or sticks, and they would not bark. I had always been an animal lover, but I was depressed by the unresponsiveness of these canine zombies.

Water...

There was never enough of this life-preserving liquid for more than just hydration and occasional personal hygiene. Never again would I complain of rain. Rain in any form—hurricanes, typhoons, deluges, downpours, floods, thunderstorms, or even broken water pipes—would be forever appreciated. I would almost welcome being hit with a water-filled condom, dropped on me from the heavens above, like some celestial wad of angel spunk. And I would gladly endure the humiliation of an enema (a dreaded treatment administered to me regularly as a child by family members who were convinced enemas were the panacea for all ills) in exchange for enough water for just one weekly shower. The rationing of water in Qui Dong was appalling and left me with very infrequent opportunities to keep myself clean, and this kept me constantly dispirited and petulant.

Shit...

So much of it. Literally tons of it. In the latrines, where it clogged the toilets in great stinking mounds; in open pits and steel drums, where it was burned with diesel fuel (the ultimate barbecue for flies.); and throughout the Vietnamese countryside, where it was used as fertilizer, shit had universal utility and was everywhere to be experienced. Locked in the sensory memory banks of each veteran's mind, shit, particularly burning shit, will forever be the perfect metaphor for a tour in Vietnam.

So, after once again thinking these depressing thoughts, I left the latrine bleary-eyed, disheveled, and totally stressed. Now it was off to receive an ass chewing from Sergeant Carson.

Barlow and I entered the Quonset hut, where the sergeant occupied a small cubicle that served as his office. Several other cubicles dotted the long room, where a single, large, rotating fan recirculated the warm, water-laden air. Carson looked up and then motioned for us to come into his cubicle.

"I'm tired of your constant insubordination," he said in an unusually quiet tone, looking at each of us. "You men don't realize how fortunate you are to be here in the rear. Maybe you would like to get orders for some line duty. Maybe with the 194th Infantry Brigade?"

We had both been threatened with grunt duty before by Carson, and this seemed like just one more idle threat. Barlow tried and failed to suppress a smile and Carson exploded.

"You think this is funny, Barlow? You think I'm bullshitting you guys? We'll see. Anyway, for skipping my inspection last night, I'm issuing each of you an Article 15 that will be enforced immediately. You'll also be fined one month's pay. You dickheads can, of course, refuse the Article 15 and request a court-martial, if you'd like."

I knew that an Article 15 is considered nonjudicial punishment in the Uniform Code of Military Justice, or UCMJ. It's similar to a civil action, like a fine in civilian life. A soldier can refuse the Article 15 and request a court-martial, but the consequences of losing are exponentially more severe than just accepting the nonjudicial punishment.

"What will it be, troopers?" Carson then glanced down at us. His eyes got very wide and his face turned nearly purple. "Cumpton, Barlow? Are those Spec-Five pins I see on your collars? Are you actually impersonating noncommissioned officers?"

In our haste to get to Carson's office, we had both forgotten to remove the Spec-Five pins from our fatigue shirts and replace them with our proper Spec-Four insignia.

"Sarge, you gotta know that every enlisted man in the company does this to get in the NCO Club," I said. I was convinced that Carson, like all other Administration Company officers and noncoms, chose to look the other way when it came to this violation of the UCMJ.

"Bullshit! This is a serious crime!" he replied. "Impersonating a noncommissioned officer? And in a time of war? You guys are going to fry for this."

Then Carson smiled and said, "Forget about the Article 15's. I've got something better in store for you. Just wait, you'll see. Dismissed." He motioned for us to leave.

We left the office and quietly made our way toward the mess hall for breakfast. It was a while before Barlow broke the silence.

"There's no way he can push this," he said, trying to convince himself as much as me that Carson could not make the charge stick.

"Hell, it's the unwritten rule," he continued. "Every enlisted man who's considered permanent party here puts on the fake pins to go to the club. Augie, remember, you're the one who told me how you almost got killed the first time you went to the enlisted men's club."

"Yeah, I know, but I have a bad feeling about this, Derek. Carson has always looked for ways to fuck us over. He doesn't like our attitude—the way we give it back to him. Most of the other guys go along to get along. Not us. This could be a problem."

It surely would be a problem. But it was one I figured we could resolve with other, more reasonable officers and noncoms. And after several months in-country, Barlow and I had begun to adopt the fatalistic but sage advice of Rooster, who always told us, "Live for today 'cause tomorrow might not come." Perhaps we wouldn't have to pay for it too dearly.

But I was depressed and feeling sorry for myself. I needed something to pick me up—something to brighten my outlook—and so I thought of better times. Like when I worked with my Uncles Giorgio and Dante at the bakery. I wondered what they would have to say about all this. Whatever it was, I knew it would make me smile.

The Chestnut Bakery

The Chestnut Bakery made four types of Italian bread loaves: a round one with a medium crust; eight- and twelve-inch-long hard crust loaves, like baguettes on steroids; and a rectangular loaf with a soft crust. The last one Grandpa called "Snuffie" bread because it was the closest thing to the bland, faux-crusted, white bread that nonimmigrant families preferred. The bakery also made pepperoni rolls, hoagie sandwich buns, and partially baked pizza shells that folks could take home, top with their favorite ingredients, and bake themselves.

By the time I was old enough to work at the bakery, Grandpa had turned the business over to two of his four sons, my Uncles Dante and Giorgio. The workday began about 10:00 p.m., when Dante and Giorgio, along with two other full-time workers, would begin the process of making the next day's bread. The men took several hundred-pound sacks of flour and poured them into a large electric mixer. They added water, salt, and yeast, and then switched on the machine, which would turn the mixture into dough. They then took the dough out of the mixer using six-inch-long stainless steel bench scraper tools.

They put the dough into an eight-foot-long, four-foot-deep tub and covered it with a long cloth sheet. There it would sit, fermenting and rising for about two hours. They then took the dough out of the tub in large pieces and placed it on a wooden table. There they cut it by hand into smaller pieces, weighed it, and formed it into loaves. They covered the loaves and allowed them to rise a second time before placing them in the oven with long, wooden, shovel-like paddles, called peels. The loaves baked for about 50 minutes. Then, the finished bread was placed on trays in upright racks and allowed to cool before sacking.

My after-school job at the bakery had been to sell whatever loaves of bread were left after the bakery truck returned from making its deliveries to grocery stores in and around Jeweltown. But all that changed the day I enrolled at St. Alphonse's High School. When I got home from school, my mom told me to go over to the bakery and see Uncle Giorgio.

"What's up, Mom?" I asked, wondering if I had screwed something up at the bakery.

"I'm not sure," she said, but I could see she was doing her best to hold back a smile.

This could not be bad, I thought. I felt relieved, as I made my way across the street to the bakery.

When I entered the building, Uncle Dante was in his cubbyhole of an office perusing a sheet of paper.

"Sominabitch. Them bastards still won't pay their bills," he muttered to himself. I stuck my head in the office. Uncle Dante looked up at me and stared quizzically.

"What're you doing here, Augie?"

"Uncle Giorgio told Mom he wanted to see me. What's up?"

Dante pointed in the direction of the main working area. "He's in there cleaning up the mixer. Gettin' ready for work tonight."

I walked over to where Uncle Giorgio was standing on a small ladder and bending into the mixer, using a damp rag to remove remnants of dough from around the large blades that turned the flour, water and yeast into the amalgamation that eventually became bread.

"Hey Uncle Giorgio, you wanted to talk to me?"

Giorgio kept working for another minute before turning and descending the two steps from the ladder. He looked down and stared at me with his dark eyes. Flecks of dried dough were embedded in his thick, bushy eyebrows.

"Big day today, huh, Augie? You started high school over at St. Alphonse's, right?"

"Yeah. I'm a freshman," I proclaimed with barely concealed pride.

"You know, Augie, Dante and me, we never got past grade school. Pop put us to work right here soon as we graduated from eighth grade at Riverview Elementary," Giorgio said.

I nodded and my uncle continued talking.

"Yeah, Pop let your other uncles go to high school. And hell, your Uncle Rodolfo even went to college on that GI bill after he got back from the army. That's how come he's a teacher over at Jeweltown High. But, you know, I don't have no regrets. Workin' in the bakery has been pretty good. I mean, we ain't gettin' rich or nothin', but we was always able to put bread on the table. Right, Augie?"

My uncle smiled at me. I wondered where this conversation was going, but then my uncles never got to the point right away, unless they saw you do something stupid, wrong, or dangerous. So I just listened.

"Well, you know, me and Dante was talkin' to your mom the other day. She said she and your dad have been tryin' to save some money so's you could go to college. You want to go to college, Augie?"

"Sure, I guess so," I replied. "But I'll probably have to make pretty good grades in high school to get in. And even if I do qualify, I'm not sure Mom and Dad will have enough money to send me."

Giorgio smiled widely. "That's right, Augie. College costs a lot and your dad don't make much over at the glass factory. And goodness knows, Gina ain't gettin' rich workin' for that insurance guy. But there might be a way you could help too."

"How?" I asked, wondering what my uncle had in mind.

"I know you've been workin' at the bakery for the past few years. You like sellin' bread for us after school, don't you?"

"Yeah, I guess so. But now that I'm in high school, I won't have time since I'm going to try out for the football and basketball teams at St. Alphonse's."

"Yeah, that's right. You won't have no time after school, but you might have some time on Friday's to work the night shift here with us, wouldn't you?" he asked with a little twinkle in his eye.

I was shocked. I had always wanted to work at the bakery with my uncles, but they and mom always said that I was too young, that the job was not for kids.

This must mean I'm not a kid anymore, I thought to myself.

"Hey Uncle Giorgio, you know I've been begging you and Uncle Dante for years to let me work at night. Can I start this Friday?"

"Well, now. Hold on there, Mister Go-getter. We got to make sure you understand that this ain't no picnic. The job is hard. You gotta get up at two o'clock in the morning and work until nine or ten. And you can't be fuckin' around. This here is serious work. You think you can handle it?"

"Sure, Uncle Giorgio. I'll work hard. You wait and see."

"You ain't even asked about pay. I guess that's good, 'cause you ain't gettin' no pay. We're going to give your mom the money you earn so she can save it to help send you to college. That okay with you?"

"Sure. Heck, I work for nothing now anyway. I guess you've been giving mom my salary for the work I've been doing for the last three years."

"That's right. And since you done such a good job, we decided to promote you to chief sacker. You think you can sack bread, pepperoni rolls, and hoagie buns fast enough to keep up with what comes out of the oven?"

"Sure, I can do it, you'll see," I said, smiling broadly.

It was always comforting to reflect on home and family, especially the times I spent with my uncles at the bakery. They could always lift my spirits and make me laugh too. And they could spin a yarn.

Arriba Roberto

You could really learn a lot if you did something that most kids never do. I mean, almost all children have an insatiable curiosity that compels them to ask one question after another, until frustrated adults either lose their voices or their patience and stop answering. But most kids are so busy asking questions that they don't listen to and absorb the answers. I guess maybe I listened more because the adults in my family liked to talk and tell stories. They could actually wear a kid out, and that's, literally, saying a lot.

In telling their stories, the adults in my family employed a trick that most adults never used: the buddy system. In other words, when my Uncle Giorgio's story waned and he paused, my Uncle Dante would pick up the tale without skipping a beat. I later came to realize that this was not only a brilliant way to teach kids a thing or two, but also a sly technique to wear out the ones who kept asking the questions.

The adults in my family, along with their Italian-American compatriots in Riverview, were all adept at using the buddy system. "Snuffies," which was a mildly pejorative term used by some members of my family to describe neighbors with names like Wilson, Smith, or Brown, didn't know, or maybe just did not care to use, the buddy system. But "Tallies," which was what Americans of Italian descent called each other in my old neighborhood, could and would spend inordinate amounts of time regaling my cousins and me with detailed stories. These tales were laced with minutia, filled with hyperbole, and suffused with bombast, and they held us in rapt attention and rendered us speechless.

My Uncles Giorgio and Dante were especially skilled at telling stories using the buddy system. Uncle Giorgio and Uncle Dante managed the day-today operations of the Chestnut Bakery now that Grandpa had retired from the business. Though neither man had graduated from high school, they were very worldly wise. While Giorgio was tall and wiry with dark features and a prominent Roman nose, Uncle Dante was a short, squat, roly-poly gnome of a man with big ears and light, brown hair the color of sand. He had Grandma's piercing blue eyes, which could never disguise a twinkle and lit up his face with humor, even when he attempted to scowl. Giorgio was two years older than Dante, and the two were the second and third of the four brothers in the Costanza family. There were also four sisters in the family, including my mother, Gina.

This particular day in 1959, as they toiled forming loaves of bread from newly risen dough, they told me once more the story of Grandpa's arrival in West Virginia from the old country, and of the perilous adventures he experienced in those wild days. And, as usual, this recantation added a new twist to the story.

"Hey Augie! When your Grandpa come to West Virginia, he went to work in the mines over at Highland in Marion County. I mean to tell you, Augie, them rats was as big as deer in that coal camp," Uncle Giorgio said with a flourish, using his large hands to show me just how big the rats were.

"Honest to God, Augie, them Snuffies in that coal camp hated the Tallies, treated 'em worse than the Indians that used to attack the camp," Uncle Dante chimed in.

"And one time when Grandpa, who couldn't speak no English, tried to ask 'em a question by making signs with his hands, they drawed their guns on him 'cause they said he was giving them the evil eye and telling them to go fuck themselves," Giorgio added.

This was definitely a version of the story I had not heard. And I had heard quite a few of my uncles' yarns. Like how Uncle Sal, Grandpa's oldest son, could, by reading the stars, know when to go hunting mushrooms and always seemed to find bushels of the sweetest wild fungi. And like how Rosie Infantano gave the clap to Benito Mussolini's son, who had somehow found himself in her Riverview bordello. But in all my fourteen years, I had never heard about Indians in the coal camp.

My heroes in those days were the Pittsburgh Pirates and, in particular, a young right fielder named Roberto Clemente. I was also infatuated with a new form of music called rock'n'roll and a swivel-hipped singer named Elvis. And I never missed a Saturday afternoon shoot-'em-up starring cowboy heroes like Roy Rogers or John Wayne, who chased off the bad guys or the Indians. Since I considered myself somewhat of an expert on Indians, I was more than a little skeptical about my uncles' revelations regarding Indian forays into the northern West Virginia coal camps.

"There couldn't have been Indians then in Marion County, Uncle Dante," I said, with more than just a trace of doubt in my voice.

"Sure there was, Augie," Dante insisted. "They was the Arriba Indians and they come from up near Pittsburgh. Grandpa can tell you about how they used to come down in the winter and sneak in the mines to get out of the cold."

"Augie, Dante's right," Uncle Giorgio chimed in. "When it got real cold up there around Pittsburgh, those Indians headed south. All the way down the Monongahela River they come, walking on the ice, until they got to where the mines and the coal camps was. At night, they snuck into the camps, stole what they could, and then headed for the empty mines to hold out until spring."

"Uncle Dante, I take American history and I've never heard of any tribe of Indians called the Arribas," I said, showing off my superior education to these two grade school drop-outs.

"Oh, so Mister Smarty-Pants, you ain't heard about no Arriba Indians. Well, I guess you ain't heard of the Pittsburgh Pirates either in your history book," Dante said, punctuating the air with his index finger and leaving little, white flour contrails.

"What do the Pirates have to do with history?" I asked.

"Well, now, the Perfesser here don't seem to know about the Pirates and how they settled Pittsburgh back a couple hundred years ago," Dante said, his eyes twinkling at Uncle Giorgio.

"Yeah, Dante, it don't seem like Augie here knows much about history or he'd know why they call them Pirates—THE Pirates. He'd know that it was real pirates that come to Pittsburgh and set up the first camp of white men where Forbes Field is now."

This story was getting really interesting. But where, I thought to myself, was it going?

"Okay, let's say I can believe that real pirates settled Pittsburgh. What do pirates have to do with Indians, and how does any of this have anything to do with Grandpa, the coal camp, or baseball?" I asked, hoping to get my uncles to finish the story.

Uncle Dante tossed a big glob of dough onto the wooden work table and looked to his brother while pointing at me.

"The boy still don't get it, Giorgio. What do them nuns teach you up at St. Alphonse's, Augie? Look, I'll explain it to you plain and simple. When them pirates landed at the Point in Pittsburgh, guess who was waitin' for 'em? You guessed it. The Indians. And after three days of bloody fightin', where hundreds of pirates and Indians died, them pirates finally chased the redskins off and set up camp. Now these pirates was from England, and for sport they played this game called, ah, ah ... hey Giorgio, what'd they call that game?"

"Cricket," Uncle Giorgio said without missing a beat.

"Yeah, that's right, cricket," Dante continued. "Anyway, after about six months of fightin', the Indians and pirates called a truce. They spent about four days gettin' drunk and cohabitatin'—if you know what I mean—and then the Indians started playin' cricket with the pirates. Now if you ever seen them limeys play cricket, it looks a lot like baseball except the bat's real flat. Anyway, after about ten years, the game sorta changed. You know, the pirates broke their wickets. That's what they called their bats. And the Indians give them their clubs and, over time, the game changed."

I looked from Uncle Giorgio to Uncle Dante, searching for a trace of a smile or for any hint that would give away the ruse, but these guys were pros. This was a story that seemed to get more fantastic with each twist and turn, even though I knew it was a complete fabrication. Or was it?

"Now wait a minute," I demanded. "What year are we talking about Uncle Dante? I know that baseball wasn't even a game until the late nineteenth century."

Uncle Dante just shook his head and looked at Giorgio. Then he looked back at me with pity. "This boy, Giorgio, he gets mixed up real easy, don't he?"

"Yeah, I know, Dante. Once I seen him try to wind his ass and scratch his watch," Giorgio said, winking at his brother.

"Look," Dante continued patiently, "This here is a history lesson. History is in the past, right? And way back then, history was kept by people telling each other about things that happened. By word of mouth. You know, from one person to the next. Anyhow, this one Indian, his name was Chief Doubleday, really invented the game we now call baseball. Yes sir, Chief Doubleday of the Arriba Indians invented baseball right there in Pittsburgh. Later on, when them Indians come down the Monongahela to spend the winter in the coal mines, they always brought their balls, bats, and gloves with 'em."

"Tell him the best part, Dante," Giorgio prodded his brother.

"You mean about his hero?" Dante asked, turning to look at me.

"Yes, Dante. Tell him how his hero, Roberto Clemente, is really an Indian."

My chin must have hit my chest as I tried to absorb this last piece of information. I didn't know whether to laugh or snicker, so I just shook my head in disbelief.

"I can see the boy don't believe you, Dante," Giorgio said.

"Look, Augie," Dante said, "These Indians actually come from those islands south of Florida. You know, Puerto Rico, Cuba, and places like that. They mingled around with the slaves that them Spaniards brung over and before you know it, the people was a cross between Indians and Negroes."

"You're trying to tell me that Roberto Clemente is a descendant of those Indians that you're talking about?" I asked incredulously.

"Why do you think he's playing now for the Pirates?" Dante asked.

"Come on, Uncle Dante, you think I'm going to believe that?" I asked and smiled smugly at my uncle.

Uncle Giorgio smiled just as assuredly right back at me and nodded toward Dante. "Prove it to him, Dante."

"Okay, Mr. Know-It-All. What do all the fans yell when Clemente comes up to bat? Come on now, tell me, Augie. You know."

And, of course, I did know—that, once again, they had me. For whenever Roberto Clemente, the greatest right fielder ever to play the game of baseball, stepped into the batter's box at Forbes Field in Pittsburgh, the crowd screamed in unison: "Arriba, Roberto! Arriba!"

The Club

It's pitiful to admit this, but the closest thing to a neighborhood gathering place in Qui Dong was the NCO Club. I spent most of my off-duty hours there. As a matter of fact, I almost got assigned a job at the club. It was a doorman-type position, which involved making sure the GIs entering the club had checked their M-16's, grenades, K-bar knives, or any other deadly weapons outside the building. It was not uncommon for things to get out of hand pretty quickly at the club. Cheap booze could easily incite lonely, stressed-out GIs to vent their frustrations on one another. But fist fights and even all-out brawls were preferable to firefights within the tight confines of the club.

The NCO Club was located at the far end of the Administration Company compound and stood on a bluff overlooking the South China Sea. It was a large, plywood building with a tin roof and a five-foot-high, wire-screened window that completely encircled the club, providing occasional cooling sea breezes. On a day when one of the regular employees of the club had rotated back to the World, I happened to be lounging at the bar after work with two other soldiers, sipping lukewarm cans of Schlitz. The club manager, a staff sergeant named Roy Shaver, walked up to us and announced that he needed one of us to agree to replace the doorman. When no one volunteered, the portly sergeant looked directly at me and said, "You'll do."

I was shocked. The last thing I wanted to do was spend whatever free time I had working. "Sergeant, I really appreciate the offer, but I don't have time to do this," I said, shaking my head.

Staff Sergeant Roy Shaver looked me up and down for a few seconds.

"Son, I know you're an enlisted man, so what the hell are you doing in my NCO Club?" he asked sternly. "Wait a minute, is that a Spec-Five pin I see on your collar?"

I about choked on my Schlitz trying to respond. Before I could get a word out, the sergeant held up both hands.

"Don't get your shorts twisted, trooper. I know half the swinging dicks in this place are enlisted men, and that's okay with me. And I really don't want to tell Sergeant Carson that one of his goonies is impersonating a noncommissioned officer." Roy Shaver paused and waited for me to respond.

When I didn't reply, he continued.

"It's real simple. You come here and take this job and my lips are sealed. And anyway, it's only three nights a week from five p.m. to closing. And you can drink for free when you're not working."

Before I could react to the sergeant, I was bailed out by the guy sitting next to me.

"Hey Sarge, I'll do it," he said, obviously enamored with the prospect of drinking free for the remainder of his time in-country. Shaver nodded his ascent and that was that.

In Vietnam, soldiers in the bush wore only olive drab or black patches on their uniforms to indicate their rank. This was to make it difficult for the enemy to identify them, particularly our NCOs and officers, who were the primary targets for the NVA or VC. In rear areas, we wore a small, black, plastic rank insignia that could be easily pinned to the collars of our uniforms. Since the club was reserved for noncommissioned officers, or those soldiers who had achieved the rank of Specialist Five or above, enlisted men like me should have been refused admittance. But through the advent of the removable insignia, we "permanent party" enlisted men simply replaced our true rank with plastic Spec-Five pins we purchased at the PX. Most of the enlisted men who were permanently assigned to Division Headquarters used the NCO Club. There was a Division Enlisted Men's, or EM, Club, but because of dangerous conditions that existed there, most soldiers avoided the place.

Like the Long Branch Saloon on Saturday night, the EM Club was not a place for the squeamish, weak of heart, or even sane. And like cowboys after a hard month on the trail, enlisted men from the division's three combat brigades regularly descended on the club to drink, fight, and occasionally kill one another—or anyone else who happened to be in their way. It was almost understandable. The frustrations and fears of being in the bush, of watching their friends get killed and maimed without much chance to exact revenge on an almost invisible enemy, often left these grunts in a foul mood that was sometimes relieved by cathartic rampaging in the rear. The EM Club provided the perfect setting for this mayhem, as I, unfortunately, discovered during my first week in Qui Dong.

The EM Club was an enlarged plywood and tin hooch that emptied into a square, cinderblock-walled, open-air courtyard. Like the exercise area in a dwarf's prison, the courtyard offered just enough room for soldiers to get to and from a bar that was situated in one corner of the enclosure. I had wandered into the club late one afternoon. The place was crowded with GIs, who stood drinking and loudly chatting with one another. As I ordered a beer from a crater-faced Vietnamese bartender, I watched a black soldier dance by himself to Aretha Franklin's soulful rendition of "Respect," which issued forth loudly from a classic Wurlitzer jukebox. As the soldier danced, a white grunt from another unit bumped into him. What ensued left me badly shaken for weeks afterward. Verbal insults were traded by the two, followed by a fight that quickly escalated into a brawl. Tin folding chairs and beer cans were hurled through the air, crashing with sickening thuds into the heads and shoulders of fighting soldiers.

At the height of the mayhem, I dropped to the floor and crawled on my hands and knees toward the exit, seeking shelter. Just then, I saw an object roll across the cement floor. A grenade, looking like some armor-plated dragon's egg, had been tossed into the midst of the tangled humanity. The lucky ones, like me, who saw it, had just enough time to crawl away before the blinding flash and stunning roar of the explosion. Moans and weeping followed, as dazed and bleeding GIs scrambled aimlessly through the smoke in search of the exit. I was bleeding from the nose and ears, and I was afraid to move, for fear of finding that I was more seriously wounded. When I did stand to leave the club, I was quickly triaged by a medic, but I couldn't hear what the man was trying to tell me. Later, I was examined by a doctor at the Med-Evac Hospital, who assured me that my injuries were not serious.

Twelve others, two of whom were killed outright, were not so lucky. Afterward, I vowed that I would rather spend a week out in the bush than another minute at the EM Club. From that point on, I decided to do my drinking at the NCO Club, even if it meant impersonating a Specialist Five noncommissioned officer.

Sergeant Roy Shaver

Staff Sergeant Roy Shaver was a freckle-faced, pot-bellied, 52-year-old lifer who had spent his career operating off-duty clubs for the US Army throughout the world and through three wars. He had learned a lot. Ostensibly, his job was to provide entertainment in the form of drinks, floor shows, movies, and slot machines to any soldier who had achieved the rank of E-5 or better. His was the largest NCO Club in the division and by far the most popular, since he provided at least four floor shows a month to the lonely, sex-starved troopers who frequented the place.

The fact that many of the soldiers who used the NCO Club were enlisted men was overlooked by the club manager. As long as they wore the appropriate NCO insignia on the collar of their jungle fatigues, Shaver did not question them. But there was another reason for the sergeant's benevolence: Roy Shaver was an intensely greedy man who would rather have these men, regardless of rank, alive and spending their money in his club, rather than in the Enlisted Men's Club, where they might get killed or incapacitated. In that event, Shaver would be deprived of having them spend all their spare money in his establishment on watered down drinks, rigged slot machines, and skinny whores with acne and VD. Over the years, Shaver, a high school dropout, had developed astute marketing tactics to get soldiers to his club. He explained his business philosophy to Administration Company clerk Jeremey Anvilhammer on one occasion.

"Give 'em drinks, a place to gamble, and the illusion of sex, and you got 'em by the balls every time," he bragged to Anvilhammer.

And Roy Shaver also regularly provided another treat that was guaranteed to fill the club with salivating and frenzied troopers: "Round-Eye Night." It was evidence of his clout that he was able to occasionally procure American, Australian, or European round-eyed women to provide the entertainment for troopers at his off-the-beaten-track NCO Club. These ladies were a part of groups touring the regular, safe, floor show circuit of Saigon, Vung Tau, Phu Bai, Cam Rahn Bay, and Danang. But Roy Shaver had connections, and he was often able to get the round-eye shows to divert to Qui Dong and the sometimes hostile, always miserable, 123rd Division.

Here, the women would dance, sing, and gyrate in the most sexually explicit manner for his painfully horny patrons. And, despite the great logistical, environmental, and bureaucratic obstacles he faced, Shaver got these round-eye princesses in during monsoons; he got them in during periods of heightened enemy activity; he got them in during typhoons; and, occasionally, he got a few lucky troopers in THEM. The demand to observe these occidental females, writhing teasingly and seminude on his stage, was so great that men would wait in line in front of the club for hours to get a good seat for Round Eye Night.

No one could ever figure out how Roy Shaver did it. When asked how and why he went to such great trouble to provide this type of entertainment to the troops, he would modestly reply, "I just want to give the lonely GI, far away from home, a place to forget his fear for a while."

Everyone, though, agreed on one thing: Roy Shaver was a kind and paternal man who would gladly kill any soldier who complained about the sergeant's right to cheat him by short-pouring his drinks, rigging the slot machines, or overcharging him for the skinny Vietnamese whores he pimped.

Short-pouring drinks required a bartender with manual dexterity. The job review process was an exhaustive exercise, where no stone was left unturned in appraising each applicant's background and suitability for the position. Only after a man's unrepentant corruptibility was established did Roy Shaver consider him a candidate for a bartender job. And, through the club manager's tutelage, a bartender's manual dexterity and sleight of hand were perfected to an art form. This enabled the bartender to pour one half ounce of spirits into a shot glass and almost simultaneously into a paper cup for mixture. This process had made SSG Roy Shaver a rich man, since the US Army specified that exactly one full ounce of liquor was to be poured into each drink.

Roy Shaver was dedicated to the army and loudly proclaimed to his staff that he would never do anything to keep the government from making its rightful profit from his club. On the other hand, once the army had received its specified profit, Shaver rationalized, there was no reason not to spread the rest around. It was the American way: 100 percent for the army and 100 percent for Roy Shaver and his partners, Chauncey Ogden Cleo, commanding officer of the 123rd Division's Administration Company, and First Sergeant Elroy "Buck" Tosser.

Shaver also ran a whorehouse, but you had to be really horny to pay for the pathetically skinny, pockmarked peasant whores who were pimped by the club manager. Still, many paid the $50 tariff and so, the sergeant found another means of enriching himself. To complete the unholy triumvirate, Shaver employed a communications section whiz kid to rig the slot machines to electronically decrease a soldier's odds of winning. This scheme allowed Shaver to keep anything above and beyond the army's take.

But like some peripatetic huckster, the sergeant was always restlessly pursuing new endeavors that would inevitably lead to more opportunities. His latest venture allowed him to reinvest the profits from his club operations into a racket that would be self-perpetuating, as long as the war continued. It was also a way in which he could invest his ill-gotten gains back into the division. And this gave him a sense of civic pride, to know that he was contributing to the economic development of I Corps. But most importantly, it was an operation in which he shared profits with no one. It involved the principle of barter. And since barter had always flourished in less civilized regions of the world, his new venture succeeded greatly on the battlefields of the division, where whiskey was almost as scarce as round-eye pussy.

After reserving some of the booze he acquired through short-pouring, Shaver would fly out to the division's forward firebases and trade the whiskey to the grunts for captured enemy trophies, such as AK-47 rifles, Russian SKS carbines, or Chicom .51 caliber machine guns. Since the grunts hardly ever got to the rear, where they could buy booze, Roy Shaver's infrequent visitations were greatly anticipated by officers and enlisted men alike. But the visits were not without risk to the NCO Club manager. Shaver's helicopter had once been damaged by enemy fire as it was attempting to land at a desolate American firebase deep in the bush. The chopper had to make a forced landing outside the base perimeter. Shaver was "scared shitless," he later admitted. But the troops at the base, knowing who and what was aboard the helicopter, fanatically assaulted dug-in enemy positions and were successful in extracting both Shaver and his precious cargo.

What encouraged the NCO Club manager to continue these oftentimes dangerous missions were the huge profits he could make by trading the booze for the enemy weapons. In the rear, he would trade the weapons to the local Vietnamese for marijuana and other drugs, which he would then sell to US soldiers. The Vietnamese civilians would give the weapons back to the NVA or the

VC, who were often their fathers, brothers, or uncles, to use against the grunts, who eventually killed them, stole the weapons, and traded them back to Roy Shaver for booze.

As long as the war continued, the cycle would continue, and no one understood this better than Roy Shaver. Almost everyone was happy. The grunts got drunk, the REMFs got high, the enemy got their weapons back, and Roy Shaver got rich. Only the peasants got fucked because they were caught in the middle. And after all, Roy Shaver surmised, peasants had been getting fucked for centuries.

Guard Duty

Jeremey Anvilhammer was five feet, three inches tall and weighed ninety-seven pounds. Just seventeen years old, he claimed to be the last living descendant of an obscure tribe of Indians he called the Croakies. He had Bugs Bunny-like buck teeth, along with straight, black hair that hung over his ears, and he wore silver-rimmed officer's sunglasses.

Anvilhammer was the Administration Company clerk and, as such, he was in charge of managing the guard duty roster for the troopers in the unit. Each solder in the company was required to pull regular dusk-to-dawn guard duty to provide security for the division basecamp at Qui Dong. For most soldiers, that meant regularly checking a duty roster at the company "Head Shed," to see if their name was on the guard list for that evening. Soldiers were assigned to posts either on the perimeter along the bunker line, to beach bunkers along the South China Sea, or to walking posts inside the base and around the Administration Company.

Everyone dreaded being assigned to the bunker line. It was the most dangerous posting because it was the one most frequently assaulted by the NVA or Viet Cong. Recognizing this, Jeremey Anvilhammer instituted a clandestine and illegal system that lined his pockets. For a fee, any enlisted man in the company could purchase his way out of guard duty altogether, or secure a safer and more desirable posting from Anvilhammer.

To avoid duty along the bunker line, soldiers could pay Anvilhammer $25, and then they would be assigned to guard the beach. The elevated beach bunkers were seldom attacked, for to do so would require an amphibious assault. Anvilhammer assured concerned troopers that "most gooks can't swim anyway."

The second option, and the most desirable duty, was a walking post. These posts only required that a soldier patrol relatively secure locations within the Administration Company area, such as the PX. Walking posts, which could be purchased for $50, required that a soldier stand guard for only four hours before being relieved. Of course, the best guard duty was no duty at all. Anvilhammer charged a flat fee of $100 per month to any soldier who could afford the price of "omission."

Spec Four George Duber routinely chose the $50 option.

"Don't you have any goddamn opinions, Duber?" Jeremey Anvilhammer asked the handsome soldier one afternoon, when he came to the Head Shed to buy a walking post.

"Of course I have an opinion, Jeremey. I agree with you."

The little Indian clerk was persistent. "You agree that we oughta send them B-52's up north and bomb the shit out of the gooks?"

"Yes, I do."

"Then how can you agree with your asshole doper buddies who say we oughta get out of the 'Nam and leave the dinks alone?" The clerk smiled slyly at Duber.

Duber had no logical response, but he had never allowed logic to inhibit his desire to reach a compromise.

"Any thinking man must be open minded," he replied, repeating a statement he had heard expressed earlier by someone in some other argument who had had no logical response.

Jeremey Anvilhammer was getting angry. "Okay, smart ass, I guess you won't argue with me if I put you on the bunker line tonight instead of letting you have that walking post around the PX."

Anvilhammer had struck a chord. Duber went pale. There was nothing like fear to give a man a jolt and knock him right off the fence.

"Listen here, Jeremey, I paid you $50 for that walking post and I better get it," he said, echoing the threatening tone always used by First Sergeant Buck Tosser when he addressed subordinates.

Like a Cheshire cat with a serious overbite, Jeremey Anvilhammer smiled broadly, flashing a mouthful of over-sized teeth.

"Now that's more like it, Duber. And don't worry about that walking post; you got it. You know, if you was willing to pay me a cool hundred a month, you wouldn't pull no fucking guard duty at all," the little Indian offered as an afterthought.

Duber pondered the idea for a few seconds before answering.

"I certainly admire your salesmanship, Jeremey, and the way you've set up your organization." Duber, now out of danger, was back to being agreeable and obsequious. "But I feel I have a duty to perform, and I just don't think I could face myself in the morning if I didn't pull my share of the load."

As Duber turned to leave the Head Shed, Anvilhammer said, "You certainly are."

"What?" Duber asked.

"A load," the diminutive clerk said, smiling into his typewriter.

*   *   *   *   *

Nightly guard duty along the bunker line could be both a boring and terrifying experience for the troopers assigned to protect the 123rd Division and the marine airbase from an enemy ground attack. It was serious business, yet soldiers sometimes had to fight to keep from being lulled into a false sense of security. I had been lucky so far. I had experienced no enemy ground probes during my times along the bunker line. On a few occasions, my guard sector had received sniper fire, and this had both frightened and frustrated me. The gooks were almost invisible, and the SOP for returning fire was positive identification of an enemy combatant who was firing his weapon at you or your position. So unless there was an all-out enemy assault, troopers almost always had to wait to return fire while the NCOs and officers observed an agreed upon engagement protocol.

This procedure required the Americans to contact the local Army of the Republic of Vietnam, or ARVN, officer, or a local village chief, to seek permission to open fire. It didn't matter to the OG, I thought, if some soldiers got their shit blown away; if there was no authorization, you did not engage.

Thankfully, most of the time, guard duty was uneventful. At best, it gave me a chance to do some serious reflection on the things back in the World that meant a lot. At worst, these reflections could trigger a deep, dark depression that left me feeling hopeless and impotent to do anything to improve my situation. The only escape was a ticket home, but not, God forbid, in a rubber body bag.

Everyone had to find his own way of coping. I decided to just lock into the present and deal with existence day to day by bitching, moaning, drinking, doping, and working. And if that didn't work, I could always flash back to memories of good times back in Riverview.

On this particular evening, Duber and I gathered our gear and began the quarter-mile trek to the guard inspection area near the company Head Shed. It was nearly 6:00 p.m., and rifle and gear inspection would commence at 6:15. After that, we would be loaded into deuce and a half trucks for a ride to our assigned posts. Mine was situated along the southern end of the army's area of operations, near the marine airbase. I had cleaned my M-16 quickly, without bothering to break it down. I had loaded 18 magazine clips with 19 rounds each and fit them into two cloth bandoliers, which I wore crisscrossed—Pancho Villa style—across my chest and over my ten-pound flak jacket.

"Hey Cump, you wanna do a jay?" Duber asked as we made our way to guard inspection in the stifling early evening heat. Duber was a handsome, twenty-year-old college dropout from Orlando, Florida, and he was totally without conviction. He was pliable, amenable, gullible, and amoral. He was every man, or tried to be, and he had a terminal case of end-stage vacillation.

Duber had a knack for adapting to any situation by adopting the mannerisms, mood, and personality of anyone he was with. He thought his easy good looks, compliant nature, and vacuous, yet harmless, banter was a ticket to peer acceptance. But to the soldiers he lived and worked with, he was a pain in the ass. Duber tried on demeanors like a man in a clothing store tried on suits, and he agreed with everyone who argued with him about his reluctance to disagree.

Earlier, Duber had bought a walking post from Jeremey Anvilhammer, so he would be spending four hours strolling around the perimeter of the Administration Company. As Duber and I walked toward the guard inspection area, two Marine F-4 Phantom jets were on final landing approach. I watched as the two planes banked gracefully overhead, their silver wings momentarily reflecting flashes of pink light from the setting sun, as they descended toward the marine airbase at Qui Dong.

"What do you say, Cump old buddy? Let's do a number. Kind of set the mood for tonight," Duber said, looking sheepishly toward me.

"Fuck off, Duber," I shot back. "I'm going down on the bunker line tonight and the last thing I need is that opium-laced shit you smoke."

"Sure, Cump. Good point. Gotta keep your wits down there. Dope settles me, though. You know, cools me out."

Cools me out. I knew Duber had heard that phrase used before by some other soldier. Then it came to me. It was Rooster. I looked over at Duber and shook my head. How could a guy who looked as good as Duber need a personality crutch? The man was a sociopathic personality thief and a thought parasite. The poor bastard had never had an original idea.

We arrived at the headquarters company assembly area and stood waiting for inspection. Sergeant First Class Willie Streak, who was as black and thin as a licorice stick, was sergeant of the guard that evening. He was a solemn man who took his job seriously. As NCO in charge of the Casualty Office, he had a unique awareness of what the enemy did each day to hundreds of GIs in the division's area of operations. I thought dealing with human injuries and deaths as cold statistics must be as terrible as it seemed if Willie Streak's morose countenance accurately reflected what he felt in his heart.

Officer of the guard that evening was First Lieutenant Waldo Dunning. A graduate and an accounting major from a small college in South Dakota, Dunning worked in Finance as executive officer. After a cursory rifle inspection, Dunning went over the rules of engagement, gave the password, "Yankee Clipper," and informed us that a yellow alert, signifying possible enemy activity, would be in force that night. Willie Streak then read the list of guard assignments. There were twelve beach bunkers strung along a two-mile stretch of coastline and fifteen elevated bunker line posts along the perimeter that faced inland toward the mountains. Each bunker would be manned by three soldiers. There were also several walking posts around interior areas of the Administration Company and other support operations, but they were always sold out well ahead by Anvilhammer. Duber would have one of these.

The overall defense of the sprawling 123rd Division Headquarters and marine airbase began several miles inland with a series of small firebases. The firebases provided artillery support for US platoon-strength infantry patrols, which worked the area day and night. They also formed a comprehensive and interlocking system of fire support and, along with the army and marine infantry patrols, acted as an enemy early-warning system. The tactical goal of these patrols was to spot and engage enemy forces before they were able to mass for a large-scale attack on the main basecamp at Qui Dong.

Unfortunately, the patrols were only marginally effective, due to the overwhelming numbers of Viet Cong main force troops and NVA regulars operating in the area. And while there had yet to be a successful, large-scale enemy assault on the basecamp, NVA sapper squads carrying high-explosive satchel charges had frequently attacked and occasionally breached the basecamp perimeter. They did this by quietly slipping around and avoiding the US patrols.

The mere mention of the word sapper struck fear in the hearts of anyone pulling perimeter guard. Their ferocious and daring attacks were legendary, and the death and destruction they left as a bloody legacy after their nocturnal visitations was well documented throughout Vietnam. Most GIs thought of them as dope-crazed, suicidal lunatics, who kept attacking without regard for their own lives. Qui Dong had felt their deadly sting periodically, and with the Lunar New Year of TET approaching, enemy activity, most likely in the form of sapper attacks, was sure to increase.

The basecamp at Qui Dong was situated along the coastal plain with the South China Sea to the east and a small bay to the north. To the south, the defensive perimeter ended at the beginning of a peninsula that extended like a bent finger out into the sea. To the west, the camp faced inland, to the gently rolling land, and extended through rice paddies, villages, forests, and to the base of a range of 3,000-foot mountains. The mountains commanded a majestic view of the entire coastal basin and provided excellent firing positions for the enemy rocket crews. With great regularity, they launched their high-explosive ordinance on a trajectory in the general direction of the giant basecamp. It was a hard target to miss.

The clerks, like me, who manned the bunkers along the southern section of the basecamp, were fearful their luck was about to run out. This night, I was sharing the bunker with two troopers new to Vietnam. The deuce and a half truck rolled down the dusty road and stopped, allowing the three of us only a few seconds to jump from the bed of the vehicle. I was the last to climb into the bunker. The guard duty was divided into three watches: 6:00 to 10:00 p.m., 10:00 p.m. to 2:00 a.m., and 2:00 to 6:00 a.m. Since the most likely time for an enemy attack was near dawn, and since I would be unable to sleep then with two rookies in the bunker, I volunteered for the 2:00 to 6:00 a.m. shift.

Each bunker was equipped with an M-60 machine gun and 5,000 rounds of ammunition, a box of grenades, a grenade launcher, and an apparatus for firing the command-detonated claymore mine. There were also CS, or tear gas, canisters in firing tubes, which were mounted on top of the bunker and which could be activated by simply pulling on a string that hung inside the guard post. In addition, each soldier carried an M-16.

The bunkers were elevated on thick, wooden stilts and stood ten feet off the ground. They were reinforced with sandbags all around, and while they were effective in protecting against small-arms fire, they were woefully inadequate in shielding the soldiers from RPGs or armor-piercing rounds. To the rear of the bunker line and spaced a half mile apart, three giant humming generators provided the power for illuminating the area. Search lights mounted on telephone poles constantly swept over the open kill zone, between the bunkers and the concertina and barbed wire barrier 300 yards distant at the tree line. The bunkers were located one-eighth mile apart, with foxhole fighting positions in between. These would be manned by reinforcements during an enemy ground attack.

My bunker mates and I exchanged small talk while the last light of day faded pinkly behind the now dark mountains. I lit a Marsh Wheeling stogie and blew the smoke along my arms and down my open shirt front, hoping to blunt the voracious appetites of the huge mosquitoes that had begun to buzz noisily in the bunker. The army-issue insect repellent was totally ineffective, and human flesh, marinating in the stuff, was a particular treat for the legions of mosquitoes that feasted hungrily on exposed body areas. One of the soldiers switched on a small, battery-powered portable radio and dialed it to AFVN in Saigon. Soon the strains of "Purple Haze" issued forth almost hauntingly in the darkening bunker.

I stared out into the dusk toward the tree line and reflected on my situation. Things had been more tense than usual during the last couple of weeks, with nightly enemy rocket attacks and frequent assaults on the bunker line by little men in pith helmets firing RPG's and AK-47's. With less than 50 days (and counting) left in-country, I tried to imagine what fate might have in store for me. Would I end up like Frazier—a vegetable? Or worse? No, nothing could be worse than lying locked in your own useless body, helpless and unable to communicate. Unless, God forbid, Frazier's mind was somehow functioning and no one was able to detect it. What if he lay there, imprisoned within himself, in the worst imaginable solitary confinement?

The walkie-talkie crackled, and I was grateful for the opportunity it gave me to interrupt this negative train of thought. I put it to my ear and responded to the routine bunker check from the OG at the command post. This would be a long night, so I went to one of the cots, removed my flak jacket, and, placing it under my head for a pillow, stretched out to get some sleep. It would be difficult, but sometimes I was able to drift into sleep by allowing the deep, humming sound of the generators to lull me into unconsciousness. Like the drone of aircraft engines or the rhythmic roll of tires on pavement, the sound of the generators could sometimes transport me soothingly into a deep sleep.

This night, though, I slept fitfully at best. Heat, mosquitoes, sweat, helicopters, flares bursting and lighting the sky, Phantom jets taking off and landing, and dreams—always dreams—made it difficult to get any real rest. My dreams were usually just fleeting cerebral vignettes that left me frustrated and tired, but tonight's dream was a nightmare:

In the wilting heat of a mountain jungle, I am pursued relentlessly by an NVA soldier. After a long and an exhausting chase, I find refuge by climbing up into a small tree. As the enemy soldier approaches, I aim my M-16 directly at the man and wait for him to move within range. I can see him clearly now, dressed in a khaki uniform and pith helmet and carrying an AK-47 automatic rifle. I cannot possibly miss the soldier at this distance. I hold my breath, flip the selector switch from single fire to full automatic and squeeze the trigger.

Though I smell the cordite and see the ejecting shell casings, the rifle makes no sound and the rounds seem to go right through the man with no visible effect on him. No blood, no wounds, no death. I fire again and again, magazine after magazine. The bullets streak soundlessly and impotently through the soldier, but still he stands unharmed.

Now out of ammunition, I look over the smoking rifle barrel, the stench of cordite stinging my nostrils, and see the enemy soldier raise his head and look directly up at me. The soldier stares at me and then, as he raises his rifle and aims it at me, he begins to smile through uneven, yellow teeth....

"Wake up, man. Come on, your time now." The voice, hollow and soft, brought me out of my dream.

My mouth was dry and I was sweating heavily, as I struggled up off the cot to begin my turn on guard. The night air was thick and still. I stared out into the semi-illuminated kill zone. The soldier I replaced mumbled that everything had been quiet. Then he fell onto the cot on which I had lain. For the next two hours, I watched and listened, checking in periodically with the CP. It all seemed to be going fine, until a little after 4:00 a.m.

I was scanning the wire for the hundredth time, peering through the starlight scope mounted on my M-16.

Damn, there is something out there, I thought. There it is again. Movement.

Through the eerie, green illumination of the scope, I could discern a lone figure, working feverishly along the barbed and concertina wire almost 300 yards directly to the front of the bunker next to ours—Perimeter Three.

"Son of a bitch," I whispered to myself. "A gook, a sapper." I quickly picked up the radio, but before I could speak, the walkie-talkie crackled. I listened in on the communication.

"Alpha One, Alpha One, this is Perimeter Three, over," the soldier spoke tensely into the radio.

"Perimeter Three, this is Alpha One. Go ahead, over," the command post responded.

"Alpha One, I got a target on the wire directly to my front. Request permission to open fire, over."

"Perimeter Three, this is Alpha One, can you confirm NVA or Victor Charlie? Over."

"Alpha One, he ain't advertising his politics, but the son of a bitch is out there and we didn't ask for no fence repair, over."

"Okay, okay, be cool Perimeter Three, we have to check this out with the townies. We'll get right back, over."

I had lost sight of the enemy soldier now. I looked desperately up and down the wire for a sign of movement that might help me locate the man. I quickly checked the M-60 machine gun and woke my two sleeping comrades. All three of us now stared anxiously out into the kill zone.

*   *   *   *   *

It had taken the enemy sapper just twenty minutes to cut through the wire and crawl on his stomach over almost 250 meters of open ground, pushing a bandoleer of high explosives in front of him with one hand and dragging his AK-47 assault rifle with the other. The man was clothed only in shorts, and the rest of his body was blackened with mud. He was aided in his mission by a very dark and cloudy night with no visible moon.

He was now within fifty meters of the American guard bunker. He had calculated that even if he had been seen, it would be some time until the Americans were given permission to fire on him. He knew that the Americans would need to get permission from the local village chief to engage him, and he had been assured that particular official would delay responding to the

Americans.

The sapper could now hear the hum of the giant American generator. He silently cursed it and the searchlights it powered, which swept over the kill zone, where he was hoping to avoid detection. Now twenty-five meters from his target, he located the deadly enemy claymore mine just to his left and moved to it. Satisfied that the Americans had not booby-trapped the mine, he gingerly picked it up, turned it around 180 degrees and angled it up toward the bunker directly in front of him.

It was time. He had been trained well and now, he thought to himself, he must be courageous and go through with the plan. He would live to tell about the experience, his leaders had assured him, if he followed their instructions. Slowly he stood, directly in front of the enemy bunker, raised his AK 47, and aimed it at Perimeter Three.

* * * * *

I stared transfixed and open-mouthed at the dark figure now standing in front of Perimeter Three. Then, suddenly, the man raised his automatic weapon and fired a quick burst at the guard bunker. One of the soldiers in Perimeter Three pressed the triggers to detonate the Claymore mine, unaware that the enemy sapper had turned it around and directed it back at them. There was a flash and a small explosion, as the mine discharged more than 700 shotgun-like steel pellets at Perimeter Three.

Without hesitation, the enemy soldier then ran toward Perimeter Three. In the next instant, I saw a bright flash and was flung to the floor of my guard bunker, landing atop the other two soldiers who were also on the floor of the emplacement. Lying on my back, I could see flames shooting into the air and feel the intense heat on my face and forehead. Curling into a fetal position, I firmly grasped the cornetto attached to my dog tags that Aunt Lia had given me to ward off evil.

With an almost paralyzing fear, I realized what the second explosion had been—a satchel charge. The enemy soldier had rushed toward Perimeter Three once the Claymore mine had detonated and thrown his satchel charge full of explosives into the guard bunker. I struggled to my feet and saw that the conflagration had completely engulfed the disintegrating remnants of Perimeter Three.

And then, almost immediately, the entire bunker line seemed to erupt with an outpouring of fire. I joined in, mindlessly firing the M-60 machine gun in long bursts out into the pre-dawn emptiness of the kill zone. For over three minutes we blasted away, expending thousands of rounds of ammunition in a profligate and cathartic act, a purging of our collective fears and frustrations.

But the relief was only ephemeral. For after the firing had subsided and we saw the first gray light of dawn, it became obvious that the sapper had gotten away. No enemy body or even blood trail could be found.

Still trembling slightly, I watched as soldiers began gathering around the smoking skeleton of the guard bunker. In a daze, I stared transfixed as a medical unit began slowly and gently collecting the body parts of the three soldiers who had occupied Perimeter Three. I watched in horror as the detail gathered a helter-skelter scattering of legs, arms, heads, and unrecognizable chunks of flesh. In an almost formal and solemn manner, they carefully placed the human remains into olive-drab body bags. Several soldiers stood nearby and observed the macabre scene, many with handkerchiefs pressed to their mouths and noses. Others bent retching onto the blood-soaked earth.

As I climbed up into the deuce and a half for the ride back to my hooch, I tried hard to erase the awful images of carnage from my mind. At times like this, I struggled to focus on good memories of home and of my childhood in Riverview. This awful day, I thought of the one person who was the architect of all that was good in our large family—Grandma Luisa Costanza. Her wonderful Sunday dinners, so lovingly prepared, were the best of times. Reflecting back on those special family gatherings always made me feel better, and I needed something right about now to obliterate memories of the last few hours.

Grandma Luisa

If ever there was a saint, it was Grandma Luisa Costanza. My most enduring memory of her will forever be frozen in my mind: Grandma in the kitchen of the two-story home directly across the street from the bakery, sitting at the head of the long dinner table and wielding a sharp knife. Directly in front of her and stacked like garlic-infused kindling were foot-long rolls of pepperoni, to which she adroitly applied her knife, slicing the aromatic salami into four-inch-long, pencil-like pieces. These pepperoni slices were later folded into freshly made dough and baked to produce the delicious and fragrant pepperoni rolls for which the Chestnut Bakery was famous.

Pepperoni rolls were created by Italian Immigrants who came, family after family, to north central West Virginia, and whose fathers and sons worked as coal miners, laborers, stone masons, or in glass factories. According to Grandma and Grandpa, the pepperoni roll was devised to provide a quick, stomach-filling, and delicious alternative to the traditional Italian lunch, which had always served as the main meal of the day. Time and the circumstances of New World jobs would not allow for the traditional Italian lunch, so the pepperoni roll was created. No one knows who first inserted slices of pepperoni into bread dough and baked the first roll, but all of the Italian bakeries in Jeweltown claimed the distinction.

The Italian workers, including Grandpa, were uniformly puzzled and disgusted by the food in the lunch boxes of their American coworkers. These working-class men would consume sandwiches that appeared to the Italians to consist of soft, white, textureless bread; yellow and tasteless cheese; and something they referred to as baloney, which was blasphemously spelled on packaging as "Bologna." To an Italian of any class, Bologna was the sacrosanct epicurean capitol of Italy, a holy place where cuisine was revered. There, the exquisite salumi and formagio panini was the sine qua non of sandwiches. The repulsive food amalgamations eaten by their American co-workers were abominations to the Italians, who considered it heresy to call them "Bologna" sandwiches.

Grandma had made sure that Grandpa had an appetizing meal when he descended into the mines years ago. Indeed, she was a culinary artist of the first order, who did far more than just slice pepperoni. In fact, her dinner table had become famous for the wonderful edible delights she prepared, particularly each Sunday around noon, right after Mass at Holy Trinity Catholic Church. I cherish memories of those Sunday meals, where everyone in our very large family—uncles, aunts, and cousins—as well as neighborhood friends and sometimes even perfect strangers, were invited to the table to feast on Grandma's lunch. And what meals they were!

Grandma would rise at five a.m. each Sunday morning and quietly go into the kitchen, where she would begin making pasta. Within a few minutes, Grandpa would emerge from the bedroom, pour a steaming cup of coffee for himself, stir in a teaspoon of sugar and a shot of Four Roses whiskey, and sit in his favorite spot next to the kitchen window. There, he could observe the dawning of another day, while Grandma Luisa toiled at the kitchen table.

To make her pasta, she combined flour, eggs, and a little water, and then kneaded the mixture, working with her bare hands for half an hour and finally making several grapefruit-sized balls of pasta dough. Covering each with fine linen dinner napkins from her hope chest, she would then allow the dough to rest, while she began making her pasta sauce. Using one or two pork ribs or a chicken neck, she would sauté the meat in vegetable oil—always Contadina, for olive oil was virtually unavailable in those days and also prohibitively expensive. After the meat browned, she would add her *soffritto* of onions, diced carrots, and sliced garlic to sauté. Then she would open several quart jars of homemade tomato sauce and pour them into the pot. The small, sweet plum tomatoes with which the sauce was made were grown in the large garden outside the kitchen. Near the end of August, the tomatoes were harvested, cooked into sauce, and canned by Grandma, with help from my mother and aunts.

Once the sauce was simmering in the large stainless steel pot, Grandma would fetch a five-foot-long, wooden pole from her bedroom closet and begin the arduous task of lovingly transforming the dough balls into pasta. After cutting a fist-size piece from a ball of dough, she would begin rolling the pole over and over the dough, until it was flattened into a large, rectangular sheet. She repeated this process until all the dough balls were transformed into sheets of pasta. Then she cut them into quarter-inch-wide, eight- inch-long pieces of linguine. She then carried the pasta to her bed and placed it on clean, white pillowcases to dry.

But pasta was just the first course. The meat course that followed usually featured meatballs, homemade Italian sausage, and roasted or fried chicken. On holidays or other special occasions, we were treated to roasted baby goat or sometimes a beef pot roast, which had been simmered in tomato sauce. More often than not, the meat we consumed was from animals butchered in Grandpa's basement. The last course was a salad of greens, sometimes dandelions that grew in the lawn, with tomatoes, onions, and carrots, in a simple vinaigrette dressing. Fruit and cheese would conclude the meal, as our family lingered over coffee and the last of the wine.

The adults enjoyed the Sunday meal around the large table in the kitchen, which also served as the dining room. The kids ate in the large living room off the kitchen, where we were seated at smaller card tables. And everyone, even the children, had a small glass of wine, though ours would be diluted with water by Grandma. Still, I remember how proud we kids were to hoist our watered-down wine and raise a toast with Grandpa and the rest of the adults. We toasted each other and the spectacular feast we were about to consume.

But there was one other tradition observed at each of these Sunday meals. Grandpa would select one of the children to fetch a gallon of wine from the earthen-walled basement wine cellar. I remember the first (and only) time that I was chosen by Grandpa for this sacred task. Handing me an empty gallon jug, Grandpa said, "Hey Augie, you go getta the wine today." While I was proud to be the one among the twenty or so grandchildren present to be selected, I was also frightened of venturing down the stairs into the dark and musty cellar.

I remember that day like it was yesterday. Gathering my courage, I rushed down the steps into the dark and dank basement, opened the door to the wine cellar, and pulled the string on the single, hanging light bulb to illuminate the room. The first thing I saw was a huge black spider munching on a fly that had been caught in its web, which hung from one of the legs of the wooden barrel rack. Anxious to get out of the room as quickly as possible, I turned the spigot on the barrel and filled the jug. When the jug was full, I yanked the string that turned off the light, rushed back upstairs to the dinner table, and proudly presented Grandpa with the jug.

Before the toast, which signaled the start of the meal, we kids stood behind our respective parents. Grandma pointed to my cousin Teresa and, in her broken English, said, "You giva us the prayer." Teresa made the sign of the cross as she recited the traditional Catholic blessing: "Bless us, oh Lord, for these, Thy gifts, which we are about to receive from Thy bounty, through Christ our Lord, Amen."

As always, Grandpa was anxious to toast his family and get on with the meal, so he poured himself wine from the jug I had handed him. He passed it to Uncle Giorgio, who filled his glass and passed it to the relative sitting next to him. The process was repeated until everyone, including we children, had a glass of wine.

Then Grandpa, looking around the table, raised his glass and uttered, "Salute." Taking a big sip, he nearly choked. He spit the wine onto his dinner plate and let forth with a stream of Italian epithets that caused Grandma's face to turn crimson. It seemed that in my haste to get out of the wine cellar, I had filled the jug from the wrong barrel—the one that held vinegar. I was, of course, embarrassed, but at least I was never again asked to go down into that scary cellar to fetch the wine for Sunday dinner.

CLTC

It was early evening. Barlow and I were sitting on the floor of CLTC's living area, shooting the breeze and sharing a fat, cigar-sized joint called a "101." Back in the World, the cigarette companies had just introduced a brand of long cigarettes known as *100s*, which referred to their 100-millimeter length. But Chesterfield had produced the "101," which the company claimed in their TV ads was "a silly millimeter longer." The term was quickly hijacked by soldiers in-country to describe the long and fat marijuana joints the Vietnamese villagers sold us. Tobias Chang's living area was now thick with the 101's dope smoke, which hung in the still air of the hooch like a psychedelic cloud. As we passed the joint back and forth, CLTC lay on his cot, just under the intoxicating pall, and told us a story:

"For the first thirteen years of my life, I thought that I was Japanese. No kidding. Mom and Pop had never told me anything about my Chinese ancestry, and I just assumed that I was Japanese. You see, my folks were domestics in the household of a very wealthy Japanese-American, Yoshuro "Spark" Matsununga. In fact, Mom and Pop lived in a small section of the house before my brother and I were born. The Matsunungas were, of course, orthodox Jews and insisted, as a condition of employment, that Mom and Pop agree to raise their children as Jews. So it was not until after my bar mitzvah that I found out that I was actually Chinese.

"Now, I can see by your questioning looks that you are having trouble believing this story. It is, nonetheless, true. Let me back up a little and maybe you will understand.

"You see, when Mom and Pop came to San Francisco in 1931, they settled in Chinatown with distant relatives. For six years Pop struggled to make ends meet. My older brother and sister were born during this period and times were really tough. You know, it was the time of the Great Depression and even occidental WASPs who could trace their proud lineage all the way back to Barbary Coast whores and English thieves were having a tough time making it.

"Well, Pop was working anywhere he could for whatever anyone would pay him, but the family was still on the verge of starvation. Things got so desperate that one day, Pop, in a fit of acute depression, threw himself in the path of a speeding car on Grant Street. Well, to be truthful, the car wasn't actually speeding. In fact, it was in heavy traffic and barely moving.

"Anyway, Pop threw himself onto the hood of that car, which, I might add, was a 1935 Cadillac limousine, and began to moan in agony. Pop was a very talented actor. In 1926, he toured the warlord palace circuit in Outer Mongolia with the Shanghai Players. So his painful groans seemed very real to both the chauffeur and the owner of the car. Turns out the owner of the car was Spark Matsununga, a very wealthy zipper manufacturer in the Bay Area at the time.

"I can see from your sinister round-eyed expressions that you are probably wondering how a zipper manufacturer—and a Jap at that—could become wealthy in depression-plagued San Francisco. Ah, but you will recall the Levi Company. Well, old Spark's business provided the zippers that closed the gap on the most favored work trousers of the time. His little zippers held back the collective genitalia of Bay Area laborers from WPA workers to coolies.

"Anyway, Spark fell for Pop's act and wanted to take him to the hospital and get him checked out. But the old man just sort of slid off the hood of Spark's car, limped over to the zipper magnate and told him he would be okay. Well, old Spark asked if there was anything he could do for Pop. Bingo. So Pop asks him for steady work. It turns out that Spark was looking for someone to cook, clean, and generally manage his household. The deal was struck and my family moved into the Matsununga home.

"But old Spark was a pretty shrewd dude and, as a condition of employment, he demanded that Mom and Pop forego any use of the Chinese language and never impart any aspect of Chinese culture to us kids. He also insisted that they raise us as Japanese.

"You see, Spark and his old lady were unable to any have kids, and I suppose the guy wanted to see his culture live on, even if the kids had no genetic link to him or to Japan. Spark reasoned that the white man didn't know the difference between a Chink and a Nip anyway. We all have slant eyes and buck teeth, right? Unfortunately, this reasoning would later prove to be all too true. But I'm getting ahead of myself."

Chang reached above himself to the reel-to-reel tape deck and switched it on. The strains of Beethoven's Fifth seemed to rejuvenate Barlow and me, and we both stretched and straightened. Chang lit a Salem and continued his story.

"Now, there was one more condition of employment that Spark insisted upon. Mom and Pop also had to agree to raise their kids as Jews. He did this out of respect and in honor of Mr. Levi, who was Jewish and who had given Spark the exclusive contract to make zippers for the jeans company. Spark himself had forsaken his Buddhist beliefs in favor of Judaism, and Mom and Pop were forced to follow suit. This was a small accommodation for starving people to make, so they readily agreed.

"Well, things went okay for several years, since the family now had a roof overhead and plenty to eat. But then along comes World War Two.

"After Pearl Harbor, as even you undereducated graduates of inferior colleges know, all the Japs were rounded up and sent off to internment camps. Despite the relative wealth and influence of Spark Matsununga, and notwithstanding the attempts by Mr. Levi to intercede on his behalf, Spark was sent away too. And along with him went his oriental house staff. Remember, we all look alike. And no amount of pleading by Spark could convince the authorities that our family was anything but baby-killing Japs. So off we went.

"Well, not all of us. I had yet to be born. However, it was not long until my folks adjusted to the new living conditions at the relocation center. In fact, I am organic proof of their adaptation to the public dormitory accommodations. For in early 1943, I was born at the Manzanar Relocation Center near Death Valley.

"We all existed there as best we could, but old Spark was shattered and humiliated. His business, of course, collapsed and he lost everything. Soon he was reduced to a mumbling half-wit. When we left the camp after the war, Spark and his wife came to live with us back in Chinatown, and I was told they were my grandparents. Pop was a very loyal man, and so I was raised to speak only Japanese at home, though I obviously spoke English in public. We also were raised as Jews and, as I said, it was not until my bar mitzvah that I was told of my Chinese ancestry. Meantime, Pop got a job as a cook in a Chinese restaurant and, within a few years, he had saved up enough to open his own place.

"Later, I worked in Pop's restaurant and did pretty well in school. I went down to UCLA and got a BA in liberal arts and then I got my MA in English Lit at Stanford. And, like you two unfortunates, I was invited by LBJ to join the army. End of story."

Barlow and I stared at the little man through dope-glazed eyes and then smiled at one another.

"That's some damn story, Toby," I said.

"Yeah, man," Barlow added. "If I didn't know you to be a man of unquestioned truth and honor, I would think you were shitting us."

"Derek, Augie, you have my word as a former Samurai-Zionist. You guys want to see my circumcision?" the little man asked.

"We'll pass," I said.

"Okay, then, I'll prove to you my story is true. I'll say something for you in Japanese-Hebrew."

Chang paused for a few seconds and then jumped to his feet and screamed, "Tora, Torah, Tora!"

Later, as I lay on my cot under a canopy of mosquito netting, trying to fall asleep, I thought about how good it felt to laugh and how infrequently there was anything to even smile about in Vietnam. Toby's story had lifted our spirits, if only for a short while. The timing was good because things were going to get a lot more complicated tomorrow.

Dire Consequences

Rin Tin Tin, our Vietnamese hooch girl, rushed into my living area and shook me from a lunchtime nap.

"Up! Up! Get Up! Colonel and First Sarge want see you and Barlow at Head Shed. Oh, you in big trouble. Numbah 10 shit. You go, vite! Vite!" she said excitedly.

Actually, the hooch girl's name was Lin Tin. But CLTC, using his best ersatz Chinese-accented English, added another "Tin" and named her for the canine star of the 1950s TV series *The Adventures of Rin Tin Tin*. And, of course, from that day on she was called Rin Tin Tin.

I looked at the small woman dressed in black pajama slacks and an army olive drab fatigue shirt. As with most Vietnamese peasant women, it was hard to tell how old she was. She might have been seventeen or fifty. Unlike the pretty and delicate-looking bar girls who worked at the NCO Club, Rin Tin Tin was wrinkled and unattractive. Her flat face was scarred, like moonscape, from the long-departed ravages of acne, and her teeth were blackened from chewing betel nut, an addictive stimulant, kind of like smokeless tobacco. Her shiny black hair played host to legions of lice, and I marveled at the simian-like ritual that took place each day, as the hooch girls took turns picking the tiny insects from each other's heads.

I had been expecting there to be negative consequences after Barlow and I were caught by Sgt. Carson wearing unauthorized NCO insignias. Carson had promised us swift and severe punishment, and now we would have to face the wrath of the Division Administration Company's commanding officer and the unit's first sergeant. I left the hooch and walked to the office to get Barlow for the visit with the first sergeant and company commanding officer.

Chauncey Ogden Cleo, commanding officer, or "C.O. Cleo, CO," as we called him, was a short, wiry, silver-haired, hawk-nosed, ex-infantry officer who exuded exceptional military presence. He had achieved the rank of major before the brass began to take notice of him.

What they began to notice after twenty-eight years of military service was that Cleo was a shrewd but incompetent megalomaniac who had cleverly covered a trail of disasters that followed in his wake from World War II to Vietnam. Since he had always covered his tracks, the army was unable to fire him and never had enough evidence to prosecute him. So instead, they promoted him to lieutenant colonel and assigned him to command the Administration Company for the largest infantry division in Vietnam, the 123rd. While the division was the largest, it was also the most obscure and least distinguished. The 123rd was simply the unit of last repose for officers who either had no previous division affiliation or who were misfits, miscreants, or general screw-ups.

C.O. Cleo, CO and First Sergeant Elroy "Buck" Tosser were waiting for us as we entered the Head Shed. Jeremey Anvilhammer, the company clerk, escorted us from the outer office into a room where three window unit air conditioners manufactured a numbing, arctic coolness. The machines droned noisily in the dimly lit room, and I began to shiver from the now icy sweat rolling in rivulets down my body. First Sergeant Tosser, his deeply wrinkled face as worn as dried leather, scowled evilly at us and then nodded his head in the direction of two metal chairs. We sat down.

"Sgt. Carson," Tosser began, "has charged you two with some very serious offenses. Colonel Cleo here will be making a decision on what to do with you, so you better listen up."

Tosser looked toward the silver- haired ex-infantry officer. Cleo was staring with his back to us out a small, crooked window, which, I could see, framed the dark green mountains to the west. It looked like a nice watercolor painting hung off center in a cheap frame.

Without turning to face us, C.O. Cleo CO spoke. "First Sergeant, I would estimate that the temperature here on the coast today is approximately 105 degrees. I suppose the reason it feels so comfortable has something to do with the ocean breezes."

The Colonel's deeply resonant voice was almost soothing. "But I imagine that inland, up in those mountains and beyond, the temperature today exceeds 120 degrees."

Cleo stared silently for a long moment before continuing. When he began to speak again, there was a threatening sharpness in his tone.

"No, there aren't any cool breezes up there. No fans either. No hooches. No refrigerators." Cleo's voice now rose with each phrase. "No sodas ... no beer ... no clubs ... no laundry." He was speaking more rapidly now. "No hooch girls, no booze, no beach, no donut dollies, no nurses, no...."

C.O. Cleo CO left the last word hanging, then turned suddenly and screamed at us.

"You are going to die! I'm going to send you up there!" he said, pointing out the crooked window toward the mountains. "To the 194th Infantry Brigade at Ton Fuc, where men are dropping dead from heat stroke, where fresh water is as scarce as round-eye pussy, where casualties are higher than anywhere else in this worthless fucking country, where the NVA regulars are thicker than flies on water buffalo shit, and where US troops are getting wasted and having their balls cut off and stuffed into their dead mouths by dope-crazed gooks!"

The colonel's face was now beet red and he was out of breath. Barlow and I looked at each other. We were shocked at the outburst and both shaking from the tomblike cold and from the words of the enraged ex-infantry officer. Tosser sat passively on the edge of Cleo's desk, lit another Marlboro, and grinned crazily at us.

C.O. Cleo CO turned once again and stared silently for a long while out the small, wooden framed window. When he finally began to speak, his tone was once again calm.

"Yes, I'll simply sign the appropriate orders and you two will be on a resupply chopper to Ton Fuc. In a short while, you'll be out humping the boonies with the rest of those pitiful grunts."

Again, there was silence. C.O. Cleo CO continued to stare, as if mesmerized, out toward the mountains. Then, suddenly, like the sound of a hundred tree frogs barking, Cleo let loose with a staccato burst of farts.

"What's that?" he asked absently. "You say something, Top?"

Tosser immediately rose to escape the room and the overwhelming stench of rotten eggs and vinegar that was issuing forth from the tortured bowels of the colonel.

"No sir, I didn't say nothing. I was just going to take a piss," he said.

"One moment please," C.O. Cleo CO replied. Tosser winced and I could see he was trying to hold his breath as he sat back down. Within a few seconds, though, he was forced to inhale a breath full of the malodorous air.

Barlow looked as if he would be sick. I was too frightened to be sick and would later reflect that the assault on my olfactory sense seemed somehow appropriate, given the rotten nature of our circumstances.

C.O. Cleo CO turned and addressed Buck Tosser.

"Top, have you checked the records of these two soldiers?"

Tosser's face was greener than tarnished brass. "Yes sir. I checked and they're both clean. First offenses. However, Sergeant Carson has told me that they do not display a proper military bearing and attitude. On the other hand, he did say they were pretty good writers over at Awards and Decorations."

Barlow and I both looked imploringly toward the hawk-nosed ex-infantry officer like condemned men hoping for a last-minute reprieve that would save us from certain death. We faced the ultimate REMF fear of being reassigned to the field as grunts. And there was no possibility of appeal. It galled and frightened me that this insane lifer had total control over our destiny. I felt completely helpless.

C.O. Cleo CO now addressed us once again.

"I think it will be necessary to go through with this," he said. He turned to Tosser. "Top, go ahead and have the papers processed. I want them out of here ASAP. How long will it take to get them reassigned?"

"A few weeks, sir," Tosser answered.

"Okay then," the ex-infantry officer said, looking at us. "You will be given Article 15's and fined $250 each, and you will be assigned to the 194th Infantry Brigade. Dismissed."

Then C.O. Cleo CO turned again to face the dark green mountains.

As we rose and left the office, stunned and pale, I saw that Tosser was bent over whispering to company clerk Jeremey Anvilhammer. As we passed him, Tosser motioned for us to take seats in front of Anvilhammer's desk. Then he left the room.

* * * * *

Jeremey Anvilhammer was dressed in cut-off jeans and sandals, and he wore a pea green T-shirt with orange letters announcing "Custer Sucked Sitting Bull's Balls." The small Indian was able to dress and act unconventionally for two reasons: he had balls and he had C.O. Cleo CO by the balls. He actually ended up in Qui Dong by forging the orders of a soldier friend of his who had been posted to Vietnam. His acquaintance was heading to Canada to escape the draft, and so Anvilhammer doctored the orders using his own identity in place of the AWOL soldier's. He took this desperate step to escape the vindictive wrath of a small-time hood whose daughter the little Indian had knocked up. Through good fortune, wily intelligence, and an uncanny knack for adapting to unfamiliar situations, he had made it to Vietnam and been assigned to the Administration Company as company clerk.

But Anvilhammer had the presence of mind to recognize that his ruse could not last indefinitely. So he devised a plan that would protect him from prosecution, grant him freedom from the yoke of military discipline, and, not incidentally, allow him to implement his illegal guard duty scheme. Indeed, he only implemented his plan after having first witnessed the blatant corruptibility of C.O. Cleo CO and Buck Tosser, whose respective shady dealings he marveled at daily in the company Head Shed.

Anvilhammer knew that for his illegal operations to continue, he would need the approval of these higher-ups. He was confident that a deal could be worked out to their mutual satisfaction. He was also counting on the assumption that lifers like Cleo and Tosser would find it difficult to turn him in for impersonating a soldier, since that would reflect poorly on them. But he needed time to establish himself in the company.

So for the first two months he served as company clerk, Anvilhammer maintained his disguise and was a model of military decorum. During this same period, he implemented his illegal guard duty operation. When it became popular among the troopers, he knew it was time to talk with C.O. Cleo CO. The opportune moment arrived when Cleo, impressed with the company clerk's military attitude and discipline, remarked that what the army needed was more men with the diminutive Indian's dedication and patriotism, if the United States was to defeat the yellow peril.

"Boy, what we need are more soldiers like you with dedication and patriotism to defeat the yellow peril, which is threatening our way of life," the colonel said.

Jeremey Anvilhammer stared derisively at Cleo. "I ain't no fucking soldier. I'm a Croakie Indian and I knocked up the lily-white daughter of a made man. I had to get out of town fast, so I switched places with some GI on his way over here."

C.O. Cleo CO's mouth dropped open and he grabbed the edge of Anvilhammer's desk for support. Before speaking, he farted loudly.

"Son, do you realize the seriousness of what you have done?"

"Yeah, knocking up a white chick ain't so good for an Indian."

"Not that. Don't you realize that you can go to jail for impersonating a U.S. soldier, for stealing his records and for boarding that plane to Vietnam?"

"I didn't steal no records. The dude was happy to give 'em to me. Anyway, going to jail is better than being dead."

"Where is your home and what is your real name, son?" Cleo asked in a paternal tone.

"Name's Anvilhammer and I don't have no real home. I was raised in an orphanage in San Mateo," the little Indian lied.

C.O, Cleo CO was perplexed. On the one hand, the boy was a military imposter and should be turned over to the MPs for prosecution. On the other hand, and not insignificantly, he had completely deceived everyone, including the commanding officer for whom he worked. While Cleo was pondering the Indian's fate, Anvilhammer interrupted him and dropped the bomb.

"I got to tell you something else."

"What's that?" the colonel asked absently.

"I got this little scheme going. I been selling guard duty."

C.O. Cleo CO's face began to turn purple and he looked as if he might explode. And then he did as a rapid volley of farts, like detonating firecrackers, escaped his lower tract and diffused the room with eye-watering fumes of hydrogen sulfide. Cleo spoke hoarsely and with great difficulty.

"I'll have you hung for this, you outrageous little heathen! Why, I'll have you breaking rocks! You'll get a dishonorable discharge."

Jeremey Anvilhammer waited for the ex-infantry officer to regain his composure. Then he smiled, looking up at the man.

"I ain't in your fucking army, sir," he said. "And if I hang, so do you for allowing a civilian, and a crooked one at that, to be your company clerk for over two months. And, by the way, I seen a lot of illegal shit going on in this company too."

Cleo thought for a long while and considered all his options before concluding that the Indian had him by the short hairs.

"I guess you think you have me by the short hairs," the colonel said. "Well, Anvilhammer, maybe something can be worked out to our mutual satisfaction."

And they did work something out. Anvilhammer was allowed to stay on as company clerk, but his records were further falsified. He was listed as a civilian defense department employee working with the Administration Company. He was also permitted to continue his guard roster scheme, but he had to share his profits with both Cleo and Tosser.

The Deal

Jeremey Anvilhammer looked up at Barlow and me and smiled. "The CO and Buck are on your asses like stink on a dink," he told us. "But it don't EVEN mean nothing. You ain't gotta sweat them lifers."

Barlow and I both recoiled in horror at the Indian's recklessly provocative words, spoken loudly enough for anyone in the Head Shed to hear. C.O. Cleo CO's door was suddenly slammed shut from within. Once again, Anvilhammer smiled widely, his beaver-like teeth gleaming whitely.

"Listen here, guys," he continued. "I gotta process these Article 15's. That's a pretty stiff fine. And in about two weeks, you'll be on the line humping the boonies with the grunts. Holy shit! You couldn't have picked a worse time to fuck up."

"I heard Cleo talking about this S-2 intelligence report. Something about an NVA regiment in the area for an all-out offensive during TET. Now, I took the liberty of looking at your records and I can see that both of you are getting awful short. You'll be going back to the World soon. Question is, do you want to get home in one piece sitting up, or in a bunch of pieces in a pine box?"

I looked at Barlow and then back at the little Indian. We had heard rumors about the company clerk and knew of his guard roster scheme, but we had been warned to stay as far away as possible from the company Head Shed.

The Indian then said, "You know, we might be able to work something out, if you two was willing to do me a favor." Anvilhammer pushed the sunglasses from the bridge of his flat nose up onto his head and stared squinty eyed at Barlow and me, waiting for a response.

"What kind of favor?" Barlow asked barely audibly.

"Well, old Buck here don't have no awards for valor, and it sure would do him some good if he had a Silver Star when he rotates back to the World. Anyway, this guy's in a position to forget about the Article 15's and that transfer to the field, if you was to do him a little favor. Know what I mean?"

I stared wide-eyed at the outrageous-looking little clerk. What he was proposing was insane. If we were discovered fabricating an award, it would mean several years of breaking rocks in the maximum security slammer down at Long Binh Jail, or LBJ, as the troopers referred to the prison near Saigon.

"Hey Anvilhammer," I said. "We'd like to help you, man, but you've got to understand what you're asking for is impossible." I spoke so quietly that the little clerk asked me to repeat myself. I did, but Anvilhammer was unimpressed.

"Nothing is impossible," he persisted. "You guys will find a way. I can sit on these orders for a few weeks or so, no sweat. But you gotta make up your minds soon. Remember, TET is coming up, and you don't EVEN want to be out there pounding the ground with the grunts now. You can dig what that means. Total heavy shit. Gooks go nuts this time of year. Gonna win it all for Uncle Ho during the year of the fucking jackal. You can bet your asses the dinks are going to be on the warpath. Yeah, man, you want to be away from that action, especially now that you both are so short."

We knew Anvilhammer was right. The next few weeks were going to be bad enough in the rear. Out in the field, it would be hell.

Anvilhammer continued. "Here's Buck's full name and serial number in case you guys decide to help me out."

The clerk handed me a soiled and folded piece of paper and stood up. "You think about it and let me know real soon."

Barlow and I got up and left the office quickly. We were both in shock as we walked back to the office.

"Hard to believe this all started when we got busted for wearing bogus Spec-Five pins," Barlow said.

"Yeah, that started a shit storm that's turned into a fucking hurricane," I replied. "I don't know how we can do this without really putting our asses way out there. If we get caught, they'll put us so far under the jail we'll never see the light of day."

"And if we don't at least try to get Tosser's Silver Star, Cleo will send us up in those mountains with the grunts," Barlow said, pointing at the distant green peaks.

We had to make a decision soon because things were starting to spin out of control. We were going on R&R tomorrow, so we'd at least have some time to try and figure things out.

R & R

It was 2:00 a.m. and I was devouring an early-morning dessert. I was savoring every bite of a hot fudge sundae, the first ice cream I had consumed since leaving the United States more than ten months ago—and I was enjoying it in the luxury of a king-size bed. Lying next to me was a perky, attractive red head, Priscilla McClaren, whom I had met earlier at a Welcome to Sydney event called Colonial Night, sponsored by the Australian R&R Hospitality Services.

"Damn, this is good," I said between mouthfuls. "This is the best sundae I've ever had."

"Come on now, Augie, surely you've had better," Priscilla said. Then she straddled me and put a spoonful of ice cream into her own mouth. "Isn't this a better way to enjoy your sundae?" she asked and smiled down at me.

I put the ice cream on the night stand. "I've got to admit, you're the best topping I've ever had on a sundae," I said.

Rest and Recuperation, or R&R, could not have come at a better time for Barlow and me. We had selected Sydney for our one-week minivacation from the war. The US Army granted an R&R leave to all soldiers serving a tour in Vietnam, and GIs had a choice of nine destinations that included Honolulu, Sydney, Bangkok, Hong Kong, Kuala Lampur, Manila, Singapore, Taipei, Taiwan, and Tokyo. Relief from the tension, boredom, and misery of daily existence in Qui Dong, if only for a brief time, was something we had been looking forward to for months. It also gave us time to think clearly and make a well-reasoned decision on what to do about the Silver Star for Buck Tosser.

Our R&R odyssey had begun when we boarded an old Marine C-47 "Gooney Bird" aircraft, which featured a four-inch-wide canvass strap across a hole in the plane where the door should have been. It was a one-hour flight from Qui Dong to Cam Rahn Bay, where we traded our jungle fatigues for army khaki uniforms and exchanged our army currency (called military payment certificates, or MPCs) for US dollars. I also packed some civilian clothes my mother had mailed me to wear in Australia. Then we boarded a jet for the nine-hour flight to

Sydney.

We had been planning this R&R visit for months and arrived in Australia bleary-eyed but happy. Our planeload of soldiers was whisked through customs and taken immediately to the R&R Center in the King's Cross section of Sydney. There, we were given a briefing on Australia by an army sergeant, who also warned us to stay away from prostitutes and to refrain from using drugs.

At the center, we were also briefed by a female representative of the Australian R&R Hospitality Service on the many activities and attractions available to us on our visit. We were then handed a brochure titled "Things To Do in Sydney." One of the first suggestions from the brochure read, "Do plan to attend our mixer party because we've invited 200 young ladies from in and around Sydney to come and enjoy the evening with you."

I smiled to myself, thinking the brochure statement was an obvious exaggeration, but Barlow and I decided to attend the mixer anyway. Along with 150 other GIs, we paid $12 a piece and were bussed to the Colonial Night mixer party. The party was held in a renovated dungeon of one of the city's historic prisons, which had been transformed into a nightclub and restaurant. For the first hour after our arrival, we enjoyed drinks and nibbled on chips, cheese, and veggies.

"Very nice," I said, "but where are the ladies?"

"Holy shit, Augie," Barlow said and punched me in the arm. "Look at those round-eye beauties. I've died and gone to heaven."

I turned and watched as dozens of young Australian women, like angels descending into a den of iniquity, walked down the steps into the dungeon/nightclub to greet and meet the unruly mob of civilization-deprived and megahorny US soldiers.

That's where I met Priscilla. She introduced herself to me and put me immediately at ease. Of course, it helped that she was pretty and that I was physically attracted to her.

Smiling at me, she borrowed a phrase from an old W. C. Fields movie and, in her best Mae West voice, said, "Hello, sailor. Buy a girl a drink?"

I was speechless for a moment before regaining my composure. Doing a less-than-perfect Humphrey Bogart impression, I responded, "Kinda shy aren't ya? And I ain't no sailor. But I'd sure like to buy you that drink."

I was immediately infatuated. Priscilla was a great conversationalist and she actually seemed to like me. We spent the first hour quizzing each other about our respective countries and our lives. She also matched me drink for drink through the cocktail hour, a buffet dinner, and the dance that followed. Around midnight, buoyed by several beers, I asked Priscilla if she wished to accompany me back to my hotel. To my complete surprise, she agreed.

During the cab ride to the hotel in King's Cross, Priscilla turned to me and, without a word, kissed me deeply. At the hotel, we went straight to my room and, for two hours, we made love. I was insatiable. I could not get enough of Priscilla. I suppose, on reflection, that it was much more than just a physical release I needed. It was as if the act of making love was also an emotional exercise and a kind of catharsis; it was an attempt to regain something that had been taken from me by the war.

Priscilla and I slept for a few hours and then decided to spend the day at Bondi Beach, sunning ourselves and watching the surfers navigate through the giant, twenty-foot-high waves. We lunched at a small café, where Priscilla surprised me by inviting me to meet her parents and then accompany her to the popular American musical *Hair*. I felt conflicted. I had just met her. Why would she ask me to meet her parents? I really liked her, but things seemed to be getting a bit too serious and moving a little too fast.

Priscilla looked at me as I pondered her offer. It was as if she read my mind. She took my face in her hands and smiled at me.

"Augie, I can see you must be thinking 'She's moving things along too quickly.' But really, the R&R Service people have encouraged us, if we truly like and trust our American friends, to take them home. Give them a sense of what it's like to be back with a family, like how it might be at their own home.

"I really do like you a lot, but I'm not trying to force you into anything. This is not some engagement meeting, where I'm bringing you home to meet the future in-laws," she said, giggling.

I shuffled my feet uncomfortably. "Okay, I understand," I said. "And I really like you too. But it's just so different from what I'm used to back in the states. I've never been invited to meet the parents of girls I date. But hey, I'd really like to meet your mom and dad."

Later that day, Priscilla came by the hotel, picked me up, and brought me to her house. She lived in a Sydney suburb about five miles from downtown. Her home had a spectacular view of the Sydney Harbor. We stood on the patio of the one-story rancher, admiring the scene. But it still seemed awkward to be meeting the parents of a girl who, until yesterday, had been a complete stranger to me. What was even more amazing was that I was in Australia, that I was dressed in a suit, and that I was about to attend an antiwar musical at the Metro Theater in King's Cross.

It had been a whirlwind forty-eight hours: The nine-hour flight from Cam Rahn Bay to Sydney, the culture shock of civilization (like being beamed up from hell for a temporary visit to heaven), and then this pretty Australian lass who insisted that I meet her parents. It was all overwhelming for me. Now I stood uncomfortably on the patio, in the presence of a middle-aged couple whose daughter I had spent the better part of the last twelve hours with in bed.

"It is indeed nice to meet you, Augie," said Priscilla's matronly looking mum.

"It's a pleasure meeting both of you too," I said, somewhat sheepishly.

"Where are you from back in the states?" Priscilla's father asked, without a trace of friendliness in his tone. He was a tall, angular-faced man and he looked directly into my eyes.

"West Virginia, sir. A small town in the northern part of the state. "

"Oh, yes," Mrs. McLaren said. "I've heard of Virginia. It was among the first of the colonies in your country, wasn't it?"

"Well, yes and no," I stumbled. "I mean, yes, Virginia was one of the first thirteen colonies, but West Virginia is a different state. It was originally part of Virginia until the Civil War. That's when it split off from Virginia and became a separate state."

"Well, Priscilla assures us that you are a gentleman, and we do want to welcome you to Australia. We also want you to know that we support your efforts in Vietnam," Mr. McLaren said. He then reached for my hand and shook it vigorously.

"Thank you, sir. It seems like the only people saying anything at all about the war back in the states are those who are against it," I said. "And you're the first person who's ever thanked me for serving."

"Well, we're a lot closer to where you're fighting the war, and besides, we've got several thousand of our own boys up there too," Mr. McClaren said.

Priscilla and I enjoyed the musical and then spent the next two days together at the beach, at dinner, and in bed. But on the fourth day, Priscilla did not call or come to the hotel. She had not given me her phone number, so there was no way for me to contact her. I was sitting in the hotel bar drinking by myself when Barlow scooted onto the seat next to me.

"Hey man. Where's Priscilla?"

"Haven't seen her. She didn't call today or come by," I said somberly.

"Cheer up, Dude. There's lots of fish in the sea. Let's go out and sniff around. What do you say?"

"I don't know, D. It just kind of bums me out. It's not like I'm in love or anything. It was just nice being around a girl after so many months without even talking to one. I guess the other thing is, I can't stop thinking that we have to go back in a few days. And we have this issue of Tosser's Silver Star to deal with too. I'm going to miss this little taste of civilization."

Derek looked at me and shook his head. "Yeah, well, what the fuck. Not much we can do about that, is there? You know, I read in the local paper about an underground group here in Sydney that helps guys on R&R who want to desert. Hides them. I guess the downside is you can't ever go home."

I looked over at Barlow. "I wouldn't even consider Canada as an option when I got drafted," I told him. "Wouldn't have been able to do that to my family. Hell, my Uncle Sal was seriously wounded in World War II and my Dad served too. But you know what? After almost ten months in Qui Dong, I'd almost think seriously about staying here." I was shocked by my own words.

"You can't be serious, Augie. You just got a little taste of what we're fighting for—all the things that we take for granted back in the World. I guess we're the ones that need to keep the bad guys from changing the way we do things."

"I'm not sure I buy that bullshit about keeping the commies from taking over the world," I said. "I think the domino theory is a ruse. I'm beginning to believe the reason we're fighting the North Vietnamese has nothing to do with ideology and everything to do with economics. We're a country of capitalists, and the Russians, the Chinese, and their allies, like the North Vietnamese, are socialists. We want trading partners so we can buy and sell stuff, and they want to influence people by forcing them to think a certain way. That's the problem. That's why we're in Vietnam. It has everything to do with markets and dollars and nothing to do with keeping Uncle Ho and Chairman Mao from invading San Francisco."

"Man, that's some serious thinking, Augie. You get a little strange and you sound like John Kenneth Galbraith." Barlow was grinning at me.

He continued, "With all due respect to your political views, you would never desert. I know you and I come from different backgrounds. I mean, you were raised in a large, ethnic family and I was your stereotypical WASP. But regardless, I think we both share a common trait and our upbringing was pretty traditional. Even though I lost my mom and dad in that car accident, the folks that raised me believed in God and country above all else."

JOHN H. BROWN **123**

Barlow paused a moment, deep in thought, before continuing. "At Columbia, I was a pretty good student and I played on the hockey team. But you know what? I was opposed to the war too. I tried to keep my political views to myself and I didn't take my opposition to the streets or even into the classroom.

"Don't get me wrong. I didn't mind debating reasonable people about the war. But I'm opposed to it for very different reasons than most people. In fact, my opposition has nothing to do with morality. It has more to do with reality, or my view of it. I think backing the South Vietnamese is impractical and futile. They're corrupt and they don't have a chance of winning, or even staying in the game without us. That's why I think we should cut our losses and leave."

I was shocked at Barlow's statement. "You can't be serious, Derek. I mean, allowing the fucking North Vietnamese to just take over the whole country? Hey, I'm against the war, but what would the consequences of that be?" I asked.

"Look, I know this sounds radical, but I think having the North Vietnamese win the war could be a good thing for us in the long run," my friend replied. "First off, it would upset the balance of power in the region and drive an even bigger wedge between China and Russia. If the North wins, the Soviets are the real winners. They've been bankrolling the North Vietnamese, and they would have enormous influence over them. By the way, the Vietnamese have never gotten along with the Chinese. It's an ethnic or racial thing. And the Chinese would be even more concerned about increased Russian influence right on their border. They're already fighting an undeclared war with the Soviets along another one of their borders. So, a North Vietnamese win here could cause the rift between the Soviets and China to worsen and that's to our benefit."

"Damn, man," I said. "If I'm John Kenneth Galbraith, you're Niccolo Machiavelli. But neither of us probably knows what the hell we're talking about anyway."

"You're right about that, Augie," Barlow said. "I'd rather be planning how we can maximize what little time we have left here in Australia. Like someone said in the Bible, let's eat, drink, and be merry."

"Dude, I think you got that wrong," I said smiling at Barlow. "Let's eat, drink and make Mary."

And we did. For the next three days, we took advantage of as many civilized luxuries as we could cram into our remaining time in Sydney. I never saw Priscilla again, but later, back in Qui Dong, I would smile whenever I thought about her and our short, sweet time together.

The Medal of Honor

After the long flight from Sydney to Cam Rahn Bay, Barlow and I were put on an old DC-3 for the short hop to Qui Dong. We got back to our hooch around 2:00 a.m. and fell immediately asleep.

At 6:30, Sergeant Carson, sparkling and starched in his jungle fatigues, strolled into the hooch and screamed at us to get our asses in gear.

"Another day, girls," he said and wiped the ubiquitous beads of perspiration from the no man's land where his forehead ended and his baldness began.

"Inspection this morning at zero-seven thirty. Buckles polished, boots shined, and clean fatigues. Got it?"

"Get it, Carson," someone said and the hooch burst into tension-relieving laughter.

"Just be ready, girls. You fuck-ups better get your shit together. Extra perimeter guard and KP for any trooper not looking real good," the sergeant said as he left.

We were definitely back in Vietnam. I struggled to find a clean pair of jungle fatigues and did the best I could to shine my belt buckle and polish my dusty and dirty combat boots. I must have looked better than some of my buddies in the hooch because I was not the target of Carson's thundering rant that morning. And while the burden of deciding how to deal with Buck Tosser's Silver Star filled my waking hours, I still had to show up and work at the office. On this day, I had a really special project to complete. I had been working on crafting an awards citation for a potential Congressional Medal of Honor recipient before I left for R&R.

I had received an action report filed in the division's area of operations by the commanding officer of an infantry company. Captain Lester Rockwell, Company B, 1st Battalion, 46th infantry, operating out of Quang Ton province, sent in the award recommendation for one of his troopers, Private First Class Clayton Livingston. This was the only Medal of Honor recommendation that had come to the office during my entire tour, and I felt privileged to be chosen to draft the formal wording for the citation.

What made this award recommendation unique was the fact that Livingston had actually survived the incident for which he was being honored. In far too many cases, citations for Medal of Honor nominees included the sad fact that the award, if approved, would be presented posthumously. This award had earlier been approved at the company, battalion, and brigade levels, and now was nearing the final approval stage. At this point, the battlefield incident would be transformed into a formal written citation by the division's Awards and Decorations Office.

It would be a badge of honor for me and, indeed, the entire office, if the division commanding general and his boss at the Military Assistance Command Vietnam (MACV) in Saigon gave final approval for the award. I had been toiling on the wording of the action report for most of the day, and I was finally satisfied that I had done all I could to convey how the courageous actions of PFC Livingston deserved the country's highest military honor. The citation read as follows:

Citation:

Rank and Organization: PFC Clayton Livingston, U.S. Army, 1st Platoon, Company A, 1st Battalion, 46th infantry, 123rd Division operating out of Quang Ton province, Republic of Vietnam, 13 June 1969. Entered service at: Atlanta, Georgia, Born: 23 February 1951, Tuscaloosa, Alabama

For conspicuous gallantry and intrepid action at the risk of his life above and beyond the call of duty. PFC Livingston distinguished himself during the period June 13 and 14, 1969, while serving as a squad leader, 1st Platoon, Company A. On June 13, 1969, PFC Livingston was leading his squad in an attack to relieve pressure on the Battalion's forward support base when his unit came under intense fire from a well-entrenched North Vietnamese Army enemy battalion. Despite continuous hostile fire from a numerically superior force, PFC Livingston repeatedly and fearlessly left cover in order to locate enemy positions, direct friendly supporting artillery fire, and strategically position the men of his squad. In the early morning, while directing his squad into perimeter guard, he was seriously wounded during an enemy mortar attack. Refusing to leave the battlefield, he continued to direct the evacuation of the dead and wounded and to lead his squad in the difficult task of disengaging from an aggressive enemy. In spite of painful wounds and extreme fatigue, PFC Livingston risked heavy fire on two occasions to rescue critically wounded men. He was again seriously wounded, but undaunted, he continued to display outstanding courage, professional competence, and leadership. He then successfully extricated his squad from its untenable position on the evening of June 14. Having maneuvered his squad into contact with an adjacent friendly unit, he learned that another six-man squad from his platoon was under fire and had not reached the new perimeter. PFC Livingston unhesitatingly went back and searched for the men. Finding one soldier critically wounded, PFC Livingston, ignoring his own wounds, lifted the man onto his back and carried him to the safety of the friendly perimeter. Before permitting himself to be evacuated, he ensured that all of his wounded squad members received emergency treatment and were removed from the area. Throughout the engagement, PFC Livingston's actions gave great inspiration to his squad and were directly responsible for saving the lives of many of his fellow soldiers. PFC Livingston's extraordinary heroism above and beyond the call of duty is in the highest traditions of the U.S. Army and reflects great credit on him, his unit, and the United States of America.

I was pleased with my handiwork, but I knew the citation faced an uphill battle at Division HQ and then at MACV, where it was very rare for an enlisted man to be awarded such a high honor. I suspected the award might be downgraded to the second-highest medal, the Distinguished Service Cross, or even to a Silver Star. But PFC Livingston deserved to be recognized for his courageous actions, and I thought the kid, barely eighteen, was a true hero. No matter how the division ruled, I had decided to memorialize the occasion by toasting the young soldier that night at the NCO Club. And I would have company.

"Hey Augie," Spec Five Hermey Dahler said as he sat typing at his desk in the Awards and Decorations Office. "You finish that CMH award yet?"

"Just got it done," I said. "I'm going to grab some chow at the mess hall, then I'm going over to the club. Maybe we should all meet there and have a drink in honor of PFC Livingston. And anyway, they have this Australian group tonight and word has it there are three or four round-eye chicks in the band."

"Count me in," Dahler said. He then announced loudly to the rest of the guys in the office, "Any swinging dick not pulling guard duty tonight needs to meet us at the club. We're going to toast the grunt Augie's going to get the Congressional

Medal of Honor for, and then we're going to be entertained by some gen-u-ine round-eye poon-tang."

So the stage was set. The office crew would meet at the club for the round-eye floor show that evening and then top off the night by grilling whatever food we could "appropriate" from the mess hall.

But first things first. Tonight I was intent on celebrating at the club. Hermey and I got there early enough to secure an excellent table to view the special round-eye floor show. As guys from the office filled the metal chairs around the rectangular table, the barmaid, Lan Le, scurried back and forth delivering drinks to the thirsty troopers.

Lan Le, unlike the Vietnamese mamasans who worked in the hooches, was attractive, with delicate facial features and long, flowing black hair. Her traditional, neck-to-ankle Vietnamese dress accentuated her slim but well-proportioned figure, as she moved gracefully among the tables of rowdy GIs.

"Hey Lan baby," Porter yelled, waving a five-dollar MPC note at her as she moved passed him. "Get us another round."

Instead of coins or cash, soldiers in Vietnam were issued small, paper military payment certificates, or MPCs. MPCs were issued in various denominations, and the troopers used them to buy their drinks and anything else while they were in Vietnam.

Lan Le glared at Porter. "You not say please, you no get," she said, as she passed out drinks and collected MPC scrip from the soldiers sitting at the next table.

"Oh, please, please, Lan," Porter said smiling at his buddies, "get us another round."

Lan Le ignored Porter but soon returned with various cans of beer, as well as paper cups of mixed drinks. The band from Australia began to play, leading off with a set of Supremes songs. But the three round-eye women were not quite as accomplished as Diana Ross, Florence Ballard, and Mary Wilson. They butchered their rendition of "Baby Love."

But none of the men at our table came for the musical entertainment. We were elated just to stare with prurient interest at the women, as they glided across the stage, bumping and grinding to the driving beat of the song. As the song reached its climax, the women's contortions and pelvic gyrations had the men in a frenzy. They stood up to dance in the aisles, cheer, and sing along with the band.

When that song ended, the group immediately launched into "Stop in the Name of Love." Each of the women began mimicking different sex acts using guitars, microphones, and drumsticks as phalluses. The room went insane when one trooper jumped on stage and began dancing with the women, who immediately surrounded him. One of the girls was on her knees with her face in the soldier's crotch. Another was behind him, rubbing the microphone on his ass, while the third woman shook her breasts in the lucky guy's face. The place went wild. Then other soldiers clamored up onto the stage and began dancing with each other and the female band members.

At that point, several MPs rushed to the stage and began pulling soldiers off of it. The band had stopped playing and the members were cowering on the stage, fearful for their own safety. The three round-eye chicks were surrounded by four MPs and spirited off the stage.

Without the music and the women, order was quickly restored and the solders went back to their tables. But after about fifteen minutes, the band returned to the stage to finish the show with the two songs that ended almost every floor show in Vietnam. The first was the Tom Jones classic "Green Green Grass of Home." At the conclusion of this maudlin tune, every man in the club was on his feet singing along with the band, and many of the soldiers were wiping tears from their eyes.

Then, with the men still standing, the band launched into what many soldiers thought of as the anthem for a tour in Vietnam: Eric Burdon and The Animals' hit "We Gotta Get Outta This Place." I joined my buddies from Awards and Decorations and sang along, hoping against hope that we would each, indeed, get out of this place—upright and in one piece.

Later, as we were leaving the club, Vendetti reminded us, "The night is young, dudes. Time for a little barbecue back at the hooch."

The Barbecue

Organizing a barbecue event in Qui Dong required considerably more creativity than arranging one back in the World. I was amazed at the lengths to which the soldiers in Awards and Decorations would go to continue this great American tradition—even in a war zone. The late-night barbecues were the brainchild of Calvin Vendetti, who came up with the idea after an encounter with an MP at the Administration Company mess hall. His plan required a little cunning and a lot of larceny, but it offered buzzed-up soldiers with a serious case of the munchies an opportunity for a midnight snack.

The Administration Company mess hall was kept open and operated with a skeleton crew in the evening to prepare a meal for soldiers who worked the overnight shift at Division HQ. But admittance to midnight chow was strictly limited, and only those troopers who worked the cat-eye shift were allowed to partake. Everyone else was refused admittance. That rule did not sit well with Private First Class Calvin Vendetti, who, a few months back, had attempted to grab a late night snack and was rudely turned away by a very large MP. Vendetti was outraged and angrily confronted the MP.

"What the fuck, dude," Vendetti shrieked in his nasal New York City accent. "I missed dinner earlier and I'm hungry. You gotta keep me strong so's I can kick some dink ass tomorrow."

"Dink ass my dick," the MP said. "You're just another Admin REMF trying to get a free meal. It happens every night. You ain't gettin' in, so get you sorry little ass down the road." The MP towered over the much smaller Vendetti.

"Fuck you, mag pie," Vendetti said. "Get it. M. P.—mag pie."

"Magpie is one word, moron," the MP said.

I was standing next to Vendetti, witnessing the escalating encounter, so I stepped between the two men before things got seriously out of hand.

"Hey Sarge, don't pay any attention to Cal here. He's got a load on. I'll get him back to the hooch right now. Okay?"

"You better get him outta here. I'm about to haul his lyin' butt down to Qui

Dong jail. He can sleep it off with the rest of those drunken pukes."

I gently moved my friend out of the mess hall doorway, as Vendetti simultaneously blew a kiss at the MP with one hand and gave him the finger with the other.

Calvin Vendetti never forgot an insult. It was the way he was brought up in his Queens neighborhood by his Sicilian father and uncles. Derek Barlow got a first-hand look at the degree to which Vendetti would go to revenge an assumed insult.

"We were walking back to the hooch from the NCO Club about midnight, and all Vendetti could talk about was how hungry he was," Barlow told me.

"We were sharing a 101 and I could tell the wheels were turning in Cal's head. He seemed agitated as we walked past the rear of the Administration Company mess hall. We could see through the screen door that two cooks were working at a steam table, but they couldn't see us," Barlow said.

"There was a really big and loud exhaust fan on the floor near the cooks, so they couldn't hear us either. We could also see that there was another door to the right just inside the screen door. Cal stopped and looked into the mess hall, and then he told me he was going to sneak in the back door and see what he could find in that other room.

"Before I could stop him, he took off. In a couple of minutes, he came running out that door with two very large cans. He handed me one and then he started laughing and running away from the mess hall."

Barlow looked at me, smiled, and said, "You know the rest of the story, Augie."

I did know the rest of the story. What Vendetti had purloined were two Number 3 cans, each containing six precooked hamburgers. When he reached the hooch, I heard him yell, "Barbecue time! Anybody hungry?"

That night started a tradition among the guys in our hooch, and we enjoyed many midnight snacks after that. Everyone was sworn to secrecy about the source of food for these occasional barbecues. Stealing from the US Army was a serious offense, but if you wanted to dine at these late-night feasts, you had to agree to take a turn at supplying the food. And every man in the hooch did.

Most of the time, these forays into the supply room netted something that was at least edible, especially if the mess hall walk-in cooler had recently been stocked with pork chops, steaks, or chicken. But even when the pickings were limited, we would use a little ingenuity, along with large dollops of hot sauce, ketchup, and mustard, to whip up something at least edible. While very few of my hooch mates had discriminating palates, sometimes the purloined bounty from the mess hall required a bit of culinary magic to make it even marginally acceptable.

Take, for example, the time PFC Richard Porter proudly presented we hungry troopers with a bag of onions and a box containing twelve cans of lima beans. Weird, but no problem for Spec Four Austin LeMoyne, who possessed the best skills for making bland food taste better. It was LeMoyne's job to take these odd ingredients and do something with them.

What he did was mash the limas up, chop and add the onions, and then stir it all up in a helmet, into which he poured a can of beer, some hot sauce, and a bottle of ketchup. Forming the mixture into patties, he cooked them on a three-legged, wobbly, old charcoal grill some guys had found under the hooch where we lived.

"What do you think, guys?" LeMoyne asked, looking hopefully at the assembled soldiers, who were just beginning, with varying degrees of trepidation, to take small, tentative bites.

"Not bad, Austin," CLTC said, taking a delicate bite of the patty he had placed between two pieces of white bread. "I have to say, this beats plain old lima beans."

"Yeah, LeMoyne, I guess this is better than a shit sandwich," Rooster said, dousing his lima burger with more hot sauce.

LeMoyne's burgers were judged a success. But sometimes the menus at the midnight barbecues were just strange. One night, it was George Duber's turn to raid the mess hall, but he was so fearful of being caught that he grabbed whatever he came across as soon as he entered the supply room. What he came across was a one-pound bag of pig intestine sausage casings, a large bag of carrots, and a container of chicken livers. The smell was so putrid from the sausages LeMoyne created out of these strange ingredients that the men gladly went to bed hungry that night.

What eventually put an end to the late-night barbecues had nothing to do with the quality of the food, however, but with the lack of fuel for the grill. The major problem with our barbecues was finding an adequate supply of wood to grill the food. There were no trees on the sandy, coastal plain where the Division

HQ was located, so we were always scrounging around for wooden boxes, discarded ammunition crates, or any other type of wooden containers. Just anything made of wood. The pickings could be very slim, so it was important for guys to always be on the lookout for any available fuel to use for the grill.

The night my friends in Awards and Decorations celebrated by toasting PFC Livingston with round after round at the club, we ended the evening with the best barbecue ingredients yet, thanks to Derek Barlow. That night, Barlow scored the ultimate culinary treat by finding a case of rib-eye steaks in the mess hall walk-in refrigerator. It would truly be a memorable celebration. Word spread quickly among the guys from our office, and soon we went off in all directions to find wood so the grilling could begin. It became obvious, though, that every piece of scrap wood in and around the area had been used up.

Things were looking bleak until Hermey Dahler stepped up to the plate and saved the day. Hermey came out of the hooch carrying a machete. As he walked down the three steps to the ground, he looked to the heavens, howled like a wolf, and then immediately turned around and started hacking and whacking away at the wooden stairs. At first we were speechless, thinking the Minnesota noncom had totally lost it. But then we understood and soon we all began to chant "Her-mey! Her-mey! Her-mey!"

Others then took turns with the machete until only the two parallel vertical braces supporting the steps remained. The wooden step pads got the fire started, and within a short while, they produced glowing embers, over which the thick steaks were grilled to perfection. All of us ate until we were completely sated. Then we all went around to the opposite entrance of the hooch, climbed the steps, and went immediately to sleep.

Sometime later, our chef de cuisine, Austin LeMoyne, rose groggily in the middle of the night to relieve himself at the piss tube located just outside the hooch. Unfortunately, his first step down found no purchase—except thin air— and he fell painfully on his face. The next day, the charcoal grill was gone, and a work party of hung-over soldiers from the office was ordered to replace the missing steps.

Our late-night barbecues were an attempt to make at least some of our in-country experiences pleasant, and, in some feeble way, to approximate those we had all grown up with. It was a way to manufacture a sense of normalcy in an otherwise very abnormal environment.

I had to smile, thinking about Hermey Dahler and his impromptu decision to chop down our steps, all the while howling like a timber wolf. Hermey's howl was actually pretty good, but it paled in comparison to that of an old man who frequented the Chestnut Bakery.

Visitors to the Bakery

The Chestnut Bakery was a sanctuary for night owls, drunks, policemen, neighbors, and insomniacs. It was not until I reached adulthood that I realized what a refuge the bakery provided for its odd assortment of characters. One such individual was Gaetano "Lupi" Cantalupi. Lupi was an eighty-seven-year-old immigrant and naturalized citizen who, like many others of Italian descent, had made the long journey from the Calabrian mountain town of San Giovanni in Fiore. The town grew up around an abbey that was built there in 1188 by the Calabrian monk Joachim of Fiore.

Lupi followed a long succession of poor San Giovanni inhabitants who left the town to seek coal-mining or factory jobs and a better way of life for their families in north central West Virginia. Lupi found a job in the mines, but he never married. He lived in a small, two-bedroom house, not far from the bakery. He had one older sister who had joined him in Jeweltown, but she had died a few years back.

Lupi was short and squat, with a full head of white hair, and his body was riddled with arthritis from years of digging coal by hand. He was a regular visitor to the bakery, especially in the winter months, when his arthritis flared up and caused his whole body to ache. Because of this, Uncle Dante placed a small, metal chair in the three-foot-wide space between the two brick bread ovens. He did this so that Lupi could come and sleep for a few hours whenever he felt the need. The warmth from the ovens soothed his aching body and allowed him to rest.

In addition to napping between the ovens, Lupi had a unique idiosyncrasy that endeared him to his neighbors in Riverview. He was an accomplished howler, whose wolf calls were legendary in their authenticity. You knew when Lupi was coming your way because he sometimes would announce his impending arrival with a wolf howl.

To those who experienced the sound for the first time, it was baleful and chilling, yet pitch perfect and menacingly genuine. He explained that this peculiar howling habit came naturally to him because his surname, Cantalupi, roughly translated meant *singing with the wolves*. He explained that his father and his uncles were renowned howlers. They would end most evenings, particularly after consuming a fiasco or two of vino rosso, with a howling contest that would cause every dog within several kilometers to join in the chorus, much to the dismay of their neighbors in San Giovanni.

On one cold, winter night, as I placed warm pepperoni rolls into small, white paper bags with the Chestnut Bakery logo displayed on them, I heard the signature howl presaging Lupi's approach. A minute later, I looked up to see the old man enter the building brushing snow from his mane of curly white hair.

"Hey Lupi," I said, as the old man walked past me. "Uncle Dante has your chair ready for you. You want a pepperoni roll?"

"No, no, Augie. Grazie. I just wanna warm these old bones up," Lupi said and shuffled toward his chair, shedding his winter coat as he sat between the ovens.

Uncle Giorgio looked down at Lupi as he manipulated the long wooden bakery paddle to place loaves into one of the ovens.

"Lupi, how's the arthritis tonight?"

"Giorgio, this suminabitch is aching like a sore tooth," he said, rubbing his hands together to warm them up.

Just then, Uncle Dante walked over and handed Lupi a shot glass filled with a clear liquid.

"Here, Lupi, take a drink of Mom's anisette. It will help you sleep."

Lupi took the glass, raised it, and said, "Salute." Then he swallowed it down in one gulp.

"Grazie, Dante."

"Hey Giorgio, you think Lupi's howl is a little bit off tonight?" Dante asked and winked at his brother.

"You know, I was thinkin' it sounded a little bit weak," Giorgio replied. "What do you think, Augie? You think Lupi's got a frog in his throat?"

"He sounded pretty good to me," I said, missing the cue from Uncle Giorgio.

"Aw, fuck. Only thing Augie hears is the sound of that girl tell him 'no.' You know the one, Dante. She goes to that Protestant school and she's always telling him 'no, Augie, no!' " Uncle Giorgio said in falsetto.

Uncle Dante chimed in. "Yeah, he don't hear, he don't see, he don't even think. He only has one thing on his mind. Ain't that right, Giorgio?"

"Yeah, that's right, Dante. He's young, dumb, and full of cum."

How did this conversation about Lupi's howl turn into a dialogue on my love life—or the lack thereof? Well, I had learned long ago not to fall into this trap, so I tried to get things back on track.

"I just think Lupi's wolf call was perfect tonight. In fact, it was in perfect pitch!"

Lupi looked up and smiled in my direction.

"Augie, Lupi can't pitch," Uncle Dante said without missing a beat. "He can't even pinch hit or play no baseball at all with that arthritis."

Giorgio said, "Holy shit, Augie! You think Lupi can throw a perfect pitch? Hey Lupi, get up. Let's see what you can do. Dante, go git that baseball you keep in your desk drawer. I wanna see this guy throw." Giorgio pointed to Lupi, who was doing his best to keep from smiling.

I tried not to respond, but I couldn't help myself. "You guys know what I meant. I just mean Lupi's wolf howl sounded good tonight. Pitch means he was howling just right. It sounded just like a real wolf."

"Oh, now I git it," Dante said. "Davy Crockett here knows what real wolfs sound like. That right, Augie? You been up in them mountains huntin' critters and you heard a wolf holler?"

"No, of course not," I countered. "But I heard them on TV and in the movies, and Lupi's howl sounds just like them. As a matter of fact, I don't think there are any wolves left even out West anymore. I think the pioneers and shepherds killed them off in the last century or drove them up into Canada."

"Bullshit, Augie," Giorgio said. "I seen that *Wild Kingdom* guy on TV and he caught one of them wolfs. They was even milking that one she wolf. Him and his buddy, you know, that guy Jim. He's the one always rasslin' them big snakes. Anyway, that guy Jim with the big muscles was holdin' that she wolf down while the main guy ... what's his name...?"

"Marlin Perkins," I said.

"Yeah, for once you're right, Augie," Giorgio said. "Anyway, they was milking this wolf and this Marlin guy was talkin' about how that critter was caught right in downtown Pittsburgh. Right near Forbes Field. Guess he liked the Pirates too, huh Dante?"

Of course I knew the story was a complete fabrication, but now I wanted to hear where it was going.

"Come on, Uncle Giorgio, you expect me to believe that a wolf was caught in downtown Pittsburgh near Forbes Field by Marlin Perkins and Jim, and they were milking it?"

"This boy, he's so smart, Dante. We can't pull no wool over his eyes. In fact, you're right Augie. It turns out they wasn't milking that wolf, they was yanking on its fur. Tuggin' and pullin' to beat all hell. And that wasn't no wolf either."

"Yeah, Augie, that was a sheep," Uncle Dante said.

"That's right, Dante, tell him what was really going on," Giorgio said and smiled knowingly at Dante.

"Augie, you heard that old saying 'a wolf in sheep's clothing'? Well, this here was a sheep in wolf's clothing. So you're right for once. There ain't no wolfs here no more, but there's plenty of sheep and this one had been caught by them *Wild Kingdom* guys. They was paid by the government to catch a wolf someone saw runnin' around in Pittsburgh. But it turned out to be a sheep someone dressed up to look like a wolf."

I looked over at my uncles who were now bent over laughing. Just then, Lupi let loose with a resounding wolf howl that was truly authentic. I just had to smile.

Porter

Maybe it was the stress of war or the distance from home, but I witnessed, and even participated in, some extreme behavior during my tour in Vietnam. Every one of us seemed to act out from time to time. On this night, it was PFC Richard Porter's turn to provide the evening's drama.

It was a week before the first-ever Christmas I would spend away from Riverview and my family. I was trying not to remember how much I missed home. I was struggling against a gnawing depression, as Derek Barlow and I slowly made our way toward the NCO Club in the half-light of dusk.

Derek lit up another joint and passed it to me. The marijuana helped. I was feeling mellow, high, and detached, as the two of us headed toward the club to join our friends, who would be taking advantage of happy hour, when beers and mixed drinks were ten cents and fifteen cents respectively.

By staying buzzed as much as possible during off-duty hours, we were able to live for the minute, string the minutes into hours, the hours into days—and then months—and soon the time to go home would arrive. That was the way I did it. If you could find a way to escape, if only temporarily, from the physical environment, you could lose that particular period of time. It was as if you weren't there, as if you cheated the lifers out of those few precious hours. Your body was present but your mind was AWOL. It was especially important now to escape reality, if just for a little while, since Barlow and I were being pressured by Anvilhammer to manufacture the fake Silver Star for Sergeant Tosser.

We entered the club and looked for our buddies. Six large ceiling fans rotated lazily, circulating thick clouds of cigarette smoke in the room. The smoke obscured and softened the figures in the dimly lit club and seemed to transform them into apparitions and otherworldly creatures.

Finally, Barlow spotted our group seated around a large, wooden table near the front of the room. He motioned for me to follow him. We joined the others at the table and watched in amazement as Private First Class Richard Porter caught a small, green lizard, decapitated it with his pen knife, and added it to a glass brimming with cigarette butts, dead insects, paper, and a variety of remnants of mixed drinks and beer.

"How much?" he asked the group at the table.

"You gotta be shitting me, Porter," Vendetti said. "Even you ain't drunk enough to put that trash in your mouth. Come on, man. Throw that shit away."

Duber chimed in. "Don't listen to him, Rich. You can do it. Hell, it's all biodegradable anyway."

Porter stared quizzically at Duber for a few seconds. "Hey man, I don't know nothin' about no bio-whatever shit you said, and I ain't afraid to drink this stuff. But you dudes gotta come up with some cash."

Franken looked up from the paperback thriller he was struggling to read in the noisy room, disturbed that the group was able to distract him.

He said, "Look, Richard, you won't prove anything to these boobs by demeaning yourself like this, except that you're even crazier than they are."

"If I want any shit outta you, egghead, I'll bust your shell," Porter said. With that he downed a shot of vodka and chased it with a long drink from a can of Schlitz.

Franken shook his head and went back to his thriller. The rest of the group stared at Porter, who was beginning to weave slightly in his chair.

"You guys come up with thirty bucks," he slurred, "and I'll even take a bite outta this glass and eat it too."

Since Franken would have no part of the action, that left me, Barlow, Vendetti, Duber, and Rooster, who had just joined the group, to come up with the $30.

"Say, man," Rooster said, "you want me to kick in to see you kick off? Shit, you ain't worth thirty bucks anyway."

"Look, spade, you put up the cash or slide outta here," Porter said and winked at the huge black man.

Rooster smiled a barely perceptible half smile. He and Porter had shared a common experience—the bush—and there was an easy friendship between the men that was more nonverbal than anything else. They were allies, and their alliance was cemented by the fact that they were the only two ex-grunts in our group. Their commonality of experience in the war trumped the volatile reaction that a racial epithet would have had under any other circumstance.

Rooster reached for his wallet. "I never, ever had to pay to see a honky suffer out in the field. But this is the rear and I s'pose a dude gotta pay for his pleasure."

Rooster laid a five-dollar MPC note on the table and each of us did the same.

Porter looked at the pile of money in the center of the table and shook his head. "That's only twenty-five, assholes. I ain't too fucking drunk to count. Come on, cough up the rest."

"You gotta swallow that stuff," Vendetti reminded Porter as he added another coupon-sized dollar MPC to the rumpled pile.

"Don't worry about me swallowing that stuff, you little guinea weasel," Porter said to Vendetti. "I'll keep it down too. If I don't, you guys can have your money back."

"If Calvin has faith in you, Richard, I'll certainly go another buck," Duber said and smiled nervously at Porter. The rest of us at the table followed suit.

PFC Richard Porter had endured a pretty tough upbringing, according to Rooster, who told me about the PFC one evening at the club. He said that Porter was from Jamestown, New Jersey. His father had been a laborer before a serious drinking problem cost him a series of jobs and, eventually, his life. Porter had joined the army as a seventeen-year-old, before his senior year in high school. His father had gladly signed the papers. The old man was a veteran of WWII, and he was one of those men who could never put his military service behind him.

Porter told Rooster that serving in the army had been the highlight of his father's life. The old man spent hours reliving his war experiences in the working-class bars where he spent most of his time and money. His father's bouts of drinking sometimes ended badly for Porter and his mother, who were often the recipients of brutal beatings from the old man. In fact, Porter joined the army as much to get away from his father as anything else. Porter told Rooster that in the few months after he enlisted, his father's attitude toward him seemed to soften. At times, the old man actually seemed friendly. But then his father had died, and shortly thereafter, Porter was off to Vietnam.

Rooster said Porter's first six months in-country were spent in the deep bush near the Laotian border. His infantry unit was assigned the monumental task of trying to slow the North Vietnamese Army's infiltration into the country, and to disrupt their transportation system along the Ho Chi Minh Trail. It was a disaster. Within a week of Porter's arrival in his platoon, half the unit was wiped out in an ambush. His time in the field was a nightmare of booby-traps, distended entrails, sleepless nights, bloody limbs, endless physical exhaustion, and, of course, death. It was only when a severe case of trench foot got him transferred to the rear and to an administrative unit that he was able to fully reflect on his time in the bush.

It was then, too, that he felt the guilt. His father had been an infantryman in another war, yet the old man had only spoken of the glories of combat. When he was drunk, Porter would ask Rooster if he was some kind of a coward for feeling only revulsion and fear for his own combat experience. But drinking helped him forget it all: the fear, the revulsion, and, especially, the guilt.

Porter was assigned to a stenography pool that served many of the Administration Company offices. There he typed endless official forms by day. At night, he could almost always be found at the NCO Club, where he usually drank himself into a mumbling stupor, punctuated by occasional pleas of help for a fallen comrade in his former grunt existence.

"Help, please help him!" he would cry to no one in particular, and then drop his head onto his arms on the table. At times like this, Rooster or one of the other men from the office would help him back to the hooch, where he would fitfully sleep it off.

But tonight he was just drunk, and his bizarre offer to ingest the assorted living and nonliving things in his beer glass broke the monotony of an otherwise boring evening. It was a diversion. Change was precious for us and diversions precipitated change. Any departure from routine was welcomed, except the one that was most frequent—an enemy attack. And even that terrifying experience sometimes left us shaken survivors feeling alive again, if just for a little while.

The physical environment contributed as much as anything else to this pervasive sense of misery and boredom. Steam bath-like heat or torrential rain alternately sapped our strength. Jobs were performed mechanically. I almost felt like two different people. On the outside, I tried to keep up the facade of the dutiful worker at his task, but it was just a physical operation with minimal cerebral involvement. On the inside, daydreams consumed most of my conscious thought and were the lubricant that kept my mind from grinding to a halt. Dreams of home, family, friends, food, and, of course, sex. My conscious reverie enabled me to passively accept, in most instances, my fate.

Those who could not dream, or who chose not to, would eventually go over the edge. They would either go quietly and without resistance, like a person who cuts their wrists in a tub filled with warm water, or in a rage of violence that physically threatens anyone within the range of an automatic weapon, grenade, knife, or fist.

But most of us adapted after a period of sometimes traumatic adjustment. This was an alien environment, and most of the men in my office used the NCO

Club to help them obliterate the reality of their circumstance. The club was our means of escape, and we cherished the reprieve it offered us from the boredom, fear and drudgery of our daily existence. But I knew that outside this temporary asylum, fate was waiting. Like a being without form or substance, fate was the schizophrenic phantom that stalked us all relentlessly.

PFC Richard Porter spoke a booze-thickened dialect that sounded almost like a bad imitation of a German accent. "Nudder drink, hon," he yelled to the Vietnamese barmaid who walked by with a tray of beer cans.

The noise level in the club had increased considerably, as a Filipino rock 'n' roll band blasted its way through the Beatles' "I Wanna Hold Your Hand." The group consisted of two guitar players, a drummer, an accordion player, and a female singer/exhibitionist who seemed to be performing fellatio on the microphone. But no one at our table paid any attention to the band or to the suggestively swaying singer. All our eyes were riveted on Porter and his glass, brimming full of an obscene array of floating matter—a cornucopia of flotsam in a sea of booze.

Through a mind haze of booze and reefer, I reflected on the scene I was witnessing. We were gathered around a table, ten thousand miles from home, excited by the prospect that our friend, deranged by war, was going to entertain us by ingesting a concoction of booze, paper, insects, cigarette butts, and one decapitated lizard. Just for the sake of our entertainment? Bullshit. For the money? No fucking way, man. Money was cheap over here. You didn't need money if you couldn't think beyond today—if you couldn't project yourself into the future. No, I thought to myself, it wasn't for entertainment or for the money. It was a reaction to the fear and boredom, a diversion from routine. It was a ritual act demonstrating how crazy it all was and how near to irretrievable our collective sanity was.

Porter had been through hell and he relived that hell each night, played it over and over in his mind like a song you can't stop remembering. He was crazy, no fucking doubt about it. "Dinky dau," the gooks would say. Certifiable, I thought. But it wasn't a very long trip to loony land. And who among us sitting at this table could pass a sanity test? Here we were, waiting with bated, fucking breath, for a seriously impaired soldier to chug-a-lug a glass of animate and inanimate things. How could Porter do this? Hell, the only way I'd drink that stuff was if it would get me back to the World.

I shook my head, trying to clear my mind, and then swallowed my cup of warm vodka in one drink. I looked around at the group at our table. Vendetti grinned crazily and flicked his Zippo lighter on and off. Barlow was staring off into space, a faraway look on his handsome face. Probably off at his island picnic again. Duber alternately smiled and frowned, constantly checking everyone's reaction to be sure his accurately reflected theirs. Franken, locked into his paperback, seemed totally oblivious to what was happening. Only Rooster stared with what appeared to be genuine concern for his grunt buddy.

"Okay, assholes, showtime," Porter slurred. The band was even louder now, playing a frenzied instrumental as the Filipino woman singer's body undulated sensuously, doing a bump and grind with the microphone stand to the driving beat of the music. Like a beast about to attack, Porter looked wildly around the table and then grinned crazily at Vendetti. "Ta your guinea ass," he toasted drunkenly and put the glass to his lips.

Everyone now stared at Porter. Even Franken looked up from his book. The music continued to build toward a climax, as the singer, who was now sitting on her heels with her head arched back, hunching the microphone to the pounding beat, seemed about to bring herself off. The troopers all around us were now into the performance. They screamed, whistled, and urged the dancer on with unbridled lust. "Do it, baby! Oh yeah, do it!" they shouted. Only our table was quiet, each man's eyes riveted, watching intently as Porter now began to take slow sips of the stuff in the glass.

"Oh, shit," Barlow said, wincing as Porter took cigarette butts and insects into his mouth and, without as much as a grimace, began chewing and then swallowing them.

"Goddamn," Rooster exclaimed as his grunt comrade sucked a cellophane cigarette wrapper out of the glass that was now half empty. Porter slurped another two butts and a matchbook cover in his mouth, chewed them briefly and then swallowed. And now only the headless body of the three-inch-long green lizard remained, obscenely bobbing up and down in the yellow liquid. With a loud gulping sound, Porter swallowed the slimy critter and slammed the empty glass down on the table, as the singer on stage gave one more furious grind and the music ended.

Loud screams and cheering now filled the club, and for the first time, Porter seemed to notice his surroundings. He assumed the applause was meant for him. He turned and smiled cockily in acknowledgement, stood up wobbling, and bowed to the raucous crowd. Then he plopped back down on his chair, closed his eyes, and seemed to be almost peacefully asleep.

"Holy Mother of God," Vendetti said, his face ashen. "You gonna be alright,

Porter?

Porter sat expressionless for almost a full minute while we stared at him with deepening apprehension. And then, an audible rumble, soft at first and then building in intensity, began to issue forth from his stomach, up, up, up... Every man at the table moved back quickly, expecting...

And then "Buuuuuuuuuuuuuuuuuuuuurrrrrrrrp!" The sound issued forth from Porter's now widely opened mouth. It sounded like a large tent ripping. Then the PFC grinned and opened his eyes.

"Hadja wurrid, assholes," he said smiling that crazy smile. "Thought I was gonna ralph. You know, rrrrrrralph," he said, imitating the universal sound of someone vomiting.

Rooster grinned and said, "Jesus H. Christ. My man, you done it."

"For you, ole buddy, I got an encore. Jus for my spade grunt buddy, I'm gonna eat this fucking glass."

"No, man, don't do that," Rooster shouted and he grabbed across the table for Porter's glass.

But before he could get it, Porter had taken a large bite out of the top and was chewing, oblivious to the warm, red liquid now running down his chin. We stared in horror at the gushing blood. Rooster grabbed a bundle of cocktail napkins and ran around the table, putting the napkins to Porter's mouth.

"Somebody call a fucking medic!" the large black soldier yelled and Franken took off. Porter, now aware of the blood, tried to spit the glass into the napkins Rooster held to his mouth.

"Whatsa maar?" he asked, as Vendetti helped Rooster get him to his feet and move him to the exit.

"Bad scene, huh guys?" Duber said to me and looked toward Barlow. We both ignored him.

"One more?" I asked Barlow and nodded to the bar.

"Yeah, just one more," Barlow said. "We gotta get up before breakfast tomorrow." We left the table and Duber for the bar and one more.

Christmas

It was Christmas Eve and I was assigned to pull guard duty. But I would not be standing watch on the bunker line or even in a beach guard bunker. No, I would have the best of all guard assignments: a walking post. This was a Christmas present I purchased for myself from Jeremey Anvilhammer.

I had seen my name on the guard duty roster at the Administration Company Head Shed. I had originally been assigned to a guard post on the worst of all possible places: the bunker line on the perimeter of the sprawling base at Qui Dong. The officer of the guard had already issued a Code Yellow alert for Christmas Eve and Christmas Day, noting that the S-2 Intelligence guys had confirmed increased enemy troop movement toward Qui Dong in the past few days. But I had made plans for a Christmas celebration with my buddies from the office, so I decided to do something I had vowed never to do: pay Anvilhammer for a walking post. And, of course, I knew the little clerk would pressure me to agree to manufacture the fake Silver Star for Tosser. This was not going to be a pleasant experience.

"Hey Anvilhammer," I said, as I entered the Head Shed a week before Christmas. "I'd like to buy a walking post." It was hard for me to hide my contempt for the little twit. Anvilhammer had constantly lorded his power over the enlisted men in the Administration Company. He had the authority to determine who would be assigned guard duty on any given day and where that soldier would be posted.

Anvilhammer was sitting at a metal desk with his feet up on the desktop, reading a *Sgt. Rock* comic book. He looked up at me and smiled smugly.

"I knew you'd come around sometime, Cumpton. It being Christmas Eve, I guess you didn't like that bunker line duty you was posted to, huh? Well, maybe I can do something to help you out. Fifty bucks will get you a walking post around the admin area. Or, I tell you what, you and Barlow won't ever have to pull no guard duty again if you was to agree to do what I asked."

I reached into my pocket and showed Anvilhammer three MPCs—two twenties and a ten.

"We're still trying to figure that out," I said, and added before he could respond, "I want the early shift. Six to ten. You give me that and I'll give you this." I pointed to the MPCs.

"No problem, dude. You got it." Anvilhammer took the money from me. "You know, you need to make your decision pretty soon. I can't keep stalling. The CO is going to want to know why you guys haven't been transferred to the field yet. And you sure as hell don't want to be out in the bush now humping the boonies with the grunts." He winked at me.

I wanted to yank the obnoxious little shit right out of his seat and throw his ass out of the office. But instead, I just turned and left the Head Shed.

On Christmas Eve, I left the Awards and Decorations Office around five o'clock and went to the hooch to clean my M-16. I had to be at the Administration Company parade ground near the office before 6:00 p.m. to report for guard duty. I didn't have time to go over to the mess hall for dinner, so I grabbed a can of C rations and used my P-38 to open the container.

The P-38 was invented during World War II and it's one hell of a useful, all-purpose tool. It measures about one and a half inches long and a half inch wide, and it's the army's official tool for opening cans of C rations. But it could be used as a screwdriver, to open packages and letters from home, strip electrical wires, clean muddy boots, and to even sharpen pencils. Soldiers also found many other uses for this versatile little tool. I wore my P-38 on the same chain that held my dog tags and the small cornetto Aunt Lia gave me to protect me from harm.

I used my P-38 that evening to open a can of "ham and motherfuckers," a name the troopers bestowed on the most hated can of C rations in the army. The meal, consisting of boiled ham and lima beans, smelled awful and tasted even worse. I doused the open can with several squirts of Tabasco and forced myself to eat a few spoonfuls, as I thought of my plans for the next twenty-four hours.

I would pull guard duty and then join the guys from the office at the NCO Club later that night. Tomorrow was Christmas, so everyone in the Admin Company would have the day off. A bunch of us planned to hike over to the amphitheater near the Med-Evac hospital, where Bob Hope would be entertaining the troops. I liked Bob Hope all right, but my real goal was to get close to the stage, to get a good look at the bevy of round-eye princesses who would be part of the show, especially actress/singer Ann-Margret. An image of her scantily clad body stared salaciously down on us every work day from a poster taped on the wall above Calvin Vendetti's desk.

But first, I had to complete my guard duty obligation. It proved to be a memorable night, even though I would not be able to remember most of it.

It was a miserable evening, when I began my four-hour shift at six o'clock. As I traversed the perimeter of the Administration Company, the monsoon rain began to fall harder. So I stopped under the eaves of an office hooch to unravel the canvass poncho I had stuffed into my trousers and under my fatigue shirt. I removed my helmet and, using the strap on my rifle, inverted the M-16 on my shoulder, positioning it so the muzzle pointed to the ground. I then pulled the poncho over my head, replaced the helmet, and moved back out into the blowing monsoon.

For more than an hour I trudged through the mud and rain puddles, trying to focus on happier times. I remembered last Christmas Eve at Aunt Lia's house, enjoying the Feast of the Seven Fishes with my family. Memories of family and better times had sustained me through the darker moments of my tour in Vietnam. And even when thoughts of home and family couldn't keep depression and self-pity completely at bay, I would reflect on how fortunate I was to be in a rear area. Just a few clicks away from where I was enjoying the relative safety of Qui Dong, my brothers-in-arms were facing an exponentially more dangerous existence.

But this night, I couldn't shake it off. My mood was dark, and I slowly slipped into a deep funk. It was around seven o'clock and night had fallen on the basecamp swiftly, snuffing out all light. The lack of visibility was exacerbated by the raging monsoon, and I struggled to see even a few feet in front of me during that first hour.

But then I saw a light in the near distance. It was coming from one of the office hooches. As I approached the building, I could see there was a roomful of men, and I could hear the sound of laughter. I stopped and peered into the office. Gazing through the pouring rain, I saw soldiers who were raising cans of beer and bottles of booze and toasting one another. I was glad someone was having a good time. As I began to walk away from the office, I heard the screen door slam shut.

"Hey dude, hold up," a voice called to me.

I stopped and turned around and saw a soldier wearing a green fatigue undershirt, Bermuda shorts, and flip-flops motion for me to join him under the shelter of the office roof. I slowly trudged over and then noticed that the guy was sporting a headband fashioned from some sort of white rag. The front of the headband was emblazoned with a crudely drawn peace sign, under which was written "Make Love, Not War."

"Damn, bro, you pulling guard on Christmas?"

I didn't respond. I just stared at the soldier as he lit a small joint. He inhaled deeply and then held it out to me.

Exhaling, he said, "Go ahead, take a hit. This is some good shit."

I looked at the small, pale man, who sported a handlebar moustache and a head of hair much longer than regulation allowed.

"Thanks, but I can't do it now. I'm on this walking post for the next three hours."

"Oh, I gotcha. You're here to protect us from the dinks—from a sneak attack on Christmas Eve," the man said, smiling at me. "Well, let me tell you then, one hit of this shit will turn you into a fucking mean, green, fightin' machine. The dinks won't stand a chance." The soldier winked at me and once again offered me the joint.

I considered the offer. What the hell, I thought. It might cheer me up, and anyway, this guard posting is a joke. Might as well get a little reefer relief.

So I took the small joint from the soldier and inhaled deeply. I held the smoke in my lungs for about ten seconds before exhaling. I took one more hit and then coughed as I exhaled.

The soldier, still smiling at me, said, "That's some good shit, man. Laced with O—you know, opium. Gooks dip it in the stuff and then sell us these little numbers. Best weed in the 'Nam."

Then the man took the joint back from me. "Merry Christmas, man," he said, as I walked back out into the rain and wind.

I remember stumbling away from the soldier, but a serious mind fog seemed to descend on me. The last thing I remembered was a kaleidoscope of colors that lit up the path in front of me and formed a corridor that I glided weightlessly toward, and then, darkness.

*   *   *   *   *

"Hey man. Hey buddy, you okay?" The voice seemed to be coming from miles away, as I struggled to regain consciousness. I was lying spread-eagle in the mud, staring up into a stinging rain that was falling in torrents around and onto me. I rolled over onto my side and tried to use the butt of my M-16 to provide leverage so I could get to my feet. Half way up I fell back into the mud.

"Here, man. Let me help you," the soldier said and grabbed both of my hands, pulling me up to a standing position. The soldier held onto one of my arms to steady me.

"What happened to you? I thought you were dead when I came up on you."

I looked at the man. "I really don't know what happened. What time is it?" I asked.

The soldier looked at his watch and pressed a button on its side to illuminate the face. "It's 9:07," he said. "What are you doing out here in the rain?"

"Holy shit. I'm on guard duty. A walking post around the Admin HQ. You sure it's after 9?" I asked. Panic was starting to set in.

"Yeah, man. You need me to help you over to the Med-Evac Hospital? Let them check you out?"

"No. No. I'm fine. Must have tripped and fallen. Probably hit my head when I hit the ground. But I'm okay. Just a little headache. Thanks for helping me." I removed the soldier's hand from my arm.

"Sure, no problem. You better get yourself checked out, though. Might have a concussion or some other kind of injury," he said as he walked off.

I was disgusted with myself. I had really fucked up. Lucky for me, the sergeant of the guard had not found me passed out. Christ. I had been out for a couple of hours. That opium soaked joint put me completely out of it. I bent over and grabbed my helmet, which was lying in a rain puddle. I shook the water out of it and put it back on my head. My clothes were completely soaked and I began to shiver involuntarily. I forced myself to continue walking around the HQ perimeter and tried to move quickly to warm myself. It was the longest hour of my life. At the stroke of 10 o'clock, I went to the parade ground and found my replacement waiting for me there.

"It's all yours," I said to the soldier and then quickly stumbled away from the area.

When I got to the hooch, I immediately ripped the sodden clothes from my body, toweled off, and got under my army blanket. What an awful night. My plans to join my friends at the club were now a distant memory. I was completely exhausted, and I was still in the dumps. I tried to refocus on more pleasant thoughts. It would be Christmas in a couple of hours. Some of my fondest memories were of holiday seasons past, celebrating with my family. I closed my eyes and concentrated, willing my mind to remember those happy times back in Riverview.

Aunt Lia

Aunt Lia had a great, if weird, sense of humor. She loved an off-color joke and she could swear like a sailor. She also had a cigarette-enhanced wheeze that followed each of her hearty guffaws. Her belly laughs were infectious. She always encouraged me and my cousins to regale her with funny stories or embarrassing incidents—the more outrageous and scatological the better. I remember one particular incident that says it all.

Our large family would often gather on summertime weekends for day-long picnics at Grandpa Salvatore's camp, located along a river not too far from Jeweltown. But there was one particular picnic that will forever be etched into my memory. That afternoon, as I walked past the front door of the camp house, I heard loud laughter, so I went inside to see what was happening. There, lying on his back on the floor was my older cousin Frankie who was Aunt Lia's son. Aunt Lia was leaning over her son and imploring him to "do it again," while several members of the family looked on.

"Come on, Frankie. Let's see you do it one more time. I can't believe this is possible!" Aunt Lia exclaimed, trying to speak between her hysterical laughter and raspy wheezing. Everyone in the room began chanting "Frank-ee! Frank-ee! Frank-ee!"

Frankie was the family clown who was frequently admonished by the nuns at St Alphonse High School for disrupting class. He was a tall, skinny kid and a very good basketball player, but his main talent was his offbeat sense of humor that kept everyone around him in stitches.

Aunt Lia said, "This is better and funnier than that ventriloquist on *The Ed Sullivan Show*. What's his name, Gina?"

"You mean Senor Wences?" my mom replied.

"Yes, that's him. Frankie, show us again!" Aunt Lia bent over to get a closer look at my cousin, who had now spread his legs.

I could see Frankie reaching in the pocket of his shorts for something. It was a small book of matches. Frankie tore a match from the book and lit it. Everyone in the room now gathered around him, and Aunt Lia peered even closer, as her son lifted his bottom off the ground and placed the lit match up against it. He strained and then farted loudly, igniting a blue flame that shot three feet in the air. Aunt Lia screamed in laughter, but everyone else in the room recoiled in horror and involuntarily moved away from her.

Everyone stopped laughing except for Aunt Lia who couldn't see that the ignited fart had burned her eyebrows completely off and singed the hair on the front of her head. Fortunately, the damage was only cosmetic, and Aunt Lia would not be deterred from her mission to make sure that everyone in the family got to see Frankie perform his amazing feat many more times that day.

Aunt Lia was also probably the most opinionated member of the family when it came to food and the preparation of it. And that's saying something, when you consider that our family was composed of world-class "capa tostas" (hard heads), who not only considered themselves accomplished cooks, but who felt qualified to provide very vocal appraisals of a dish.

We took our food seriously and, eventually, almost everyone in the family had at least one special dish that the others grudgingly attributed to them. But this was only after years of constant, and not so subtle, input by other family members whose rendition of that same dish had been panned even more harshly. In the end, the specialty dish was usually ascribed to the family member who persevered, and who was not easily deterred by criticism.

Our family loved to eat and of all the special, food centric celebrations throughout the year, the eight-day holiday season that extended from Christmas Eve through New Year's Day was the most revered by everyone. It was truly the Olympiad of all the holiday celebrations. I am convinced that Italian-American families can eat and drink the way elite athletes run and jump. I know this because as a youngster growing up in Riverview, I learned from the accomplished eaters and drinkers in my family the difference between a sprint and a marathon. You had to be in it for the long haul to survive, so it was essential to savor the feast in "moderation," a term with an elastic definition, kind of like spandex, for the adults in our family, especially the men.

The holiday season was not only a time to exchange gifts, count our blessings, and embrace the Christmas spirit. It was a time to feast! And it was primetime for Aunt Lia and my other aunts, uncles, and adult cousins, who were all excellent cooks. They would bake, boil, fry, and roast all manner of edibles and then share their culinary bounty with the family.

Aunt Lia was renowned for many dishes. Her stuffed squid and other seafood treats, which she prepared on Christmas Eve, were truly delicious. But Aunt Lia did not like following recipes. She viewed them only as a guide and objected to following them strictly, feeling they would inhibit her culinary creativity. She could also find fault with certain food traditions, even sacrosanct ones. For instance, she didn't really object to participating in the Feast of the Seven Fishes on Christmas Eve; she was just offended that the saints had limited the feast to only seven edible sea creatures.

"Hey Gina," Aunt Lia complained to my mother one time as they were planning the Christmas Eve dinner. "What the hell were those apostles thinking when they told us we could only cook seven fishes to celebrate the birth of Baby Jesus?"

This was more than just a rhetorical question for Aunt Lia, since nothing, except God and her children, was more sacred to her than food and the preparation of it.

"So where do they get off telling us what we can and can't eat?" Aunt Lia went on. "I mean, they scare the shit out of us by saying we're going to burn in hell for eternity if we eat meat on Friday. That it's a mortal sin. But then they tell us it's okay to eat fish. Isn't fish meat? I bet it was Saint Peter that made that rule up. He was a fisherman, right?" Aunt Lia looked pained in her exasperation.

"Lia, why do you worry about things you can't control?" my mother said, mildly admonishing her sister. "You know the rules. It's just something we have to do. And there are consequences for us when we do the wrong things."

"I understand the consequences of breaking the law. If I steal a car and I get caught, I'll probably have to go to jail. That's not the same as burning in the fires of hell forever because I ate a meatball sandwich on Friday," Lia said. "And anyway, getting back to Christmas Eve dinner, I don't think it would be a sin to cook more than seven fishes, do you? If it's a sin at all, it's gotta be a venial sin."

"I wouldn't worry about it, Sis," Mom said. "I think the leaders of the Catholic Church, including Pope Pius the Twelfth, have bigger problems to deal with than how many fishes you cook on Christmas Eve."

But like all of my aunts and uncles, Aunt Lia was not so much interested in understanding the reason why things were the way they were as she was in beginning a dialogue, or some might say, starting an argument. But if you gave in and agreed with her, she would immediately find something else to keep the dialogue moving.

It didn't matter what the subject was; the adults in my family never let ignorance of an issue or, for that matter, logic get in the way of a loud debate. No subject was too grand, obscure, or off limits. Like my Uncles Giorgio and Dante, Aunt Lia could argue for hours about any subject. They would debate everything from presidential elections to the size of Angelina Popata's breasts. And those who prevailed usually did so not because of knowledge or eloquence but because of their vocal enthusiasm. To the rare outsiders who were infrequently invited to our holiday celebrations, the decibel level of this enthusiasm must have been a bit disconcerting.

But of all the subjects debated, the most frequent topic of discourse was food. And there was no better time to discuss food than during the holiday season, given the family's tradition of visiting each other's homes, which began Christmas Eve and extended through New Year's Day. In a one-hundred-yard-long block of Riverview, there were eight homes and apartments where my loving grandparents, uncles, aunts, and cousins all lived, argued and (especially) dined with one another.

The family festivities began with a visit to Grandma's home, where you risked bodily harm (from Grandpa) if you refused to eat something. It really didn't matter what you ate—an olive, a piece of cheese, a biscotti, or a crust of bread— just that you ate something and, if you were an adult, had a glass of wine. Then it was off to visit each other family member's home.

And while each dining room table was heaped with the edible bounty of the season, family members especially showcased the dishes for which they were renowned. That's not to say that our family was shy about suggesting ways to improve the dish, but only up to a point. For to be too critical of, say, Uncle Sal's stuffed artichokes was to elicit an epithet-laced tirade that could shatter crystal. So, day after day, morsel after morsel, we consumed the holiday feast with our adult relatives who debated the merits of the food, as well as any other topic that came to mind. By the end of New Year's Day, most of us required the Italian version of Alka-Seltzer—called Brioschi—which was administered to us by the women in the family who practiced a form of culinary restraint less elastic than the men.

Rotor Charlie

"I seen it with my own eyes, but I still can't believe it," Rotor Charlie said, shaking his head. "I mean, a pink fucking APC way out in the bush and smack dab in the middle of the NVA badlands. I know you shitheads don't believe it. Chrissakes, I still don't hardly believe it my own self. But looky here."

Rotor Charlie took a soiled photograph out of his equally soiled flight suit and laid it on my desk for the small group in the Awards and Decorations Office to examine. Charlie was a chief warrant officer (CWO) and helicopter pilot who called North Georgia home. He was assigned to the 163rd Aviation Company and flew reconnaissance missions in a small chopper, the OH-6 Light Observation Helicopter known as a *Loach*. Rotor Charlie had come by the office that day to pick up the company's awards for the month.

"Now the detail on that picture is a little bit blurred, but by God that's an APC, and I'll be dipped in shit if it ain't pink."

Barlow shook his head. "It might be an APC, Charlie, but I can't tell if it's pink. But what the hell, stranger things have happened over here."

Rotor Charlie radiated indignation.

"You REMF pussies wouldn't know an armored personnel carrier from a Corvette," he said. "Listen up now and I'll try and spell it out for you. A couple a weeks ago, I'm on this here recon mission flying in my little old Loach, looking for Charles. I got Johnny Cash wired into my headset and I'm groovin' on the "Orange Blossom Special" when I look down and see all these fucking gooks – NVA gooks. Now git this, these dinks are running full bore—not one of 'em carrying any smoke—and not a single sumbitch the least little bit worried about me. Well, I'll tell you, boys, it was the weirdest goddamned thing I ever seen. So I cut the Johnny Cash off, get my map, check the coordinates, and call in to the division CP for some artillery, or an air strike. And just then I seen the APC."

Rotor Charlie pointed to the photograph.

"You can't see the gooks in this photo 'cause the APC is separated from them by about a hundred yards. But I'll tell you this, them bastards was running to beat hell toward that APC and didn't one of them boys look mad."

"What are you trying to say, Charlie?" I asked skeptically

"What I'm saying is that them gooks was awful anxious to get to that APC and I think I know why." Charlie smiled wolfishly, flashing a yellow, snaggled canine tooth.

"Before I tell you what I think that APC was doing there, listen to what happens when I call in for the ordnance. I give the dude at division the coordinates and tell him what I'm looking at. He asks me to repeat the coordinates and then he goes off the line for what seemed like an awful long time. Meantime, I'm flying over a zillion gooks and I figure pretty soon some of that hot Chi-Com .51-caliber shit is going to be coming my way.

"When the dude finally comes back on the line, he asks me again to tell him where I am. Now I'm really gettin' pissed. Then the dumb sumbitch asks if there is anything different looking about the situation. Well, I goddamned exploded. Yes, I scream at him, there's something different looking about the situation. There's a regiment of NVA gooks running around without weapons, like luna-fucking-tics, toward a pink APC.

"After another moment of silence, the asshole orders me to get out of there ASAP. Well, at first, that's exactly what I wanted to hear. So I banked her hard, gave her full throttle, and started hauling ass back home. But then I got to thinking, why's that shithead asking me about 'Did I notice something different?' Does that prick know something he ain't telling me? Now don't ask me why, but I turned that Loach right around and headed back there for one more look. And this time, I decided to take a few snaps of the situation with my trusty old Yashica-Electro 35 camera."

Rotor Charlie had everyone's attention now and he paused to catch his breath.

"Well, let's see. Where was I? Oh yeah, well, I got back there and you would not fucking believe what I seen. The gooks had reached the APC by now and they was standing in a long line, waiting to get in the thing. I mean, there was a dink single file stretching from that APC over a hill and probably all the way to Laos. I flew in as close as I could and snapped a couple of pictures with one hand. That's why it's so blurry. But looky here at this one."

Rotor Charlie pulled another photograph out of his flight suit and everyone crowded around to have a look. Sure enough, there was the armored personnel carrier and it truly appeared to be painted pink. And stretching out of the picture was a long line of pith-helmeted soldiers. Not one of them was carrying a weapon. On top of the vehicle stood a woman in a very short miniskirt.

"What the hell is she doing there, Charlie?" Barlow asked

Rotor Charlie looked solemnly into the eyes of each of us standing around the desk before declaring, "That APC is a whorehouse! A mobile, pink, fucking whorehouse! And Division Headquarters knows about it or otherwise they would have had an air strike or artillery on that target like I asked."

Rotor Charlie's wild contention, that there was a mobile whorehouse operating out of a pink armored personnel carrier and servicing elements of the North Vietnamese Army with the full knowledge of Division Headquarters, would have been met with disdain, disbelief, and maybe a chuckle, if it had not been for the photographs. But there they were: indisputable graphic evidence substantiating the helicopter pilot's wild tale.

Rotor Charlie smirked as he put the photos back into his rumpled and stained flight suit, picked up his company's awards, and bid our startled group "Later," before strolling out of the office. But no one saw Charlie later—or ever again, for that matter. For within twenty-four hours of his visit to our office, he was gone, and no one seemed to know where. He got "vanished" according to Rooster, who claimed to have seen it happen before to grunts out in the field when "someone fucked-up real bad, man."

In reality, Charlie was "derosed," or sent back to the World immediately, when word about his wild revelations filtered up to the commanding general's office later the same day. It seems Rotor Charlie had stumbled upon a top secret operation run by the division and born in the gray labyrinth of Lawton "Bullseye" Carp's deranged brain.

Operation ThunderClap

A couple of months before Rotor Charlie told his wild tale, General Lawton "Bullseye" Carp sat pretending to listen attentively to the division chaplain who was briefing his commanding general on unit morale. Bullseye Carp had been commander of the sprawling I Corps Division for seven frustrating and embarrassing months, during which time his troopers had been severely bloodied and beaten at every turn. His division had been outmaneuvered, outmanned, and outfought, and he would soon be out of luck and, most likely, a job, unless he was able to do something to stem the tide and slow the advance of the NVA.

Bullseye Carp was six foot five inches tall and weighed 270 pounds. He had a shiny, bald head and a Buddha-like pot belly. He also had a booming, baritone voice that fit his overbearing countenance perfectly. This day he was not a happy man.

The chaplain was reciting a litany of horror stories, from rising suicides and murders to an almost epidemic problem with venereal disease throughout the division. Chaplain Nessle was a tall, pale, extremely thin man with a long neck and large ears that protruded from his head like undersized wings on a giraffe. Bullseye Carp was bored and extremely impatient as the chaplain droned on.

"You see, sir," Chaplain Nessle was saying, "these poor boys are lonely and depressed. They've taken an awful physical, as well as psychological, beating, and they seek human warmth and affection. They're searching for a wholeness of spirit wherever they can find it, and with whomever will provide it to them."

"You're right there, Padre," Carp roared. "They'll stick it in any hole that's available—anywhere, anytime."

The chaplain blushed deeply. "But sir, we must do something. Surely this high incidence of venereal disease must be affecting battlefield effectiveness."

And then it hit Bullseye Carp like the recoil from a 155-millimeter howitzer.

"Padre, you're a goddamned genius," he said to the stunned minister, who was unaccustomed to anything but scorn and ridicule from the division commanding general.

"Sir?"

Carp sat in quiet contemplation for a full two minutes before he spoke. "Thank you, Nessle. You just gave me an idea that could help turn the tide of battle in this division, and maybe in the entire war."

"I did?"

The chaplain stared incredulously at the general. What, he wondered, could he have possibly said to give this bully of a man some sort of inspiration?

"Yes. Now, we'll have to keep this quiet, Padre. Top secret stuff. We'll have it battlefield tested here and then, by God, we'll send it down to General Abrams at MACV in Saigon. Hell, he may have it implemented throughout this whole miserable fucking country."

The chaplain blushed once again. "Sir, I don't quite understand."

"Yes, yes, Padre. Now run along. I'm sure there are many souls to be saved yet today," the general said dismissively.

Chaplain Nessle could feel his anger begin to rise, but he suppressed it, turned, and began walking toward the door.

"Oh, Padre," Bullseye Carp called to the retreating cleric.

"Sir?" Chaplain Nessle turned to face Bullseye Carp.

"Do you suppose the sin of lust is pervasive among all peoples?"

The chaplain looked at the general with a puzzled expression.

"Oh, shit. Look, do you think the NVA and VC get as horny as our boys do? I know they're kinda small guys and probably have little dicks, but I have to think they must like to do the dirty deed too 'cause there's so fucking many of them. What do you think?"

This time the chaplain didn't blush and when he spoke, he didn't mask his pent-up anger.

"Sir, I would not know about that, but I can say that lust, or, for that matter, any sin, is not the sole province of any one nation or culture. It is, unfortunately, pervasive among all the peoples of this Earth."

Bullseye Carp considered this for a few seconds and smiled broadly to himself before addressing the departing chaplain.

"Then hallelujah, Padre! Hallelujah!"

What the chaplain didn't know is that he had provided the inspiration for Bullseye Carp's brainchild, which the general would code name "Operation ThunderClap." Over the next few days, Carp put his plan together and Operation

ThunderClap began to take shape. It would require stealth, cunning, and the knowledge of only a few discreet and corruptible individuals who were not afraid to bend military rules. Carp knew just the guy who could help him make Operation ThunderClap a reality. In the past, he had frequently depended upon C.O. Cleo CO to provide him with various unorthodox services, including Vietnamese prostitutes. And since Operation ThunderClap would involve the use of such women, the general called on Cleo and ordered him to supply the bait for the operation.

Cleo, for his part, immediately contacted Staff Sergeant Roy Shaver and conveyed the wishes of the commanding general to him. Shaver was dumbfounded and miffed at the general's outrageous request.

"You gotta be shittin' me, sir," he said to the hawk-nosed ex-infantry officer who commanded the Division Administration Company.

"Roy, I can assure you, General Carp is serious about this. He needs four of the best-looking girls you can find, and he needs them to be infected with the worst case of venereal disease in the division's area of operations."

"Hell, sir, we done our best to keep these dink whores clean for the general in the past. Is the old man losing it?"

"Roy, I don't think these women are for the general's personal use. All I can tell you is that they will be taking part in a highly classified and important mission."

Staff Sergeant Roy Shaver looked perplexed and worried. "Damn, colonel, I don't know whether I can come up with this one. How am I going to find four beautiful Vietnamese girls with the clap?"

"I'll leave that up to you, sergeant. But I'll tell you this, if you don't get this done for the general, I would be willing to bet that the MP's will be down here looking at our operations real close."

Shaver's face went pale as he quickly considered the consequences of not accomplishing this strange mission for the general. He, along with Cleo, Tosser, and Anvilhammer, were getting rich because the commanding general was looking the other way. Things could go terribly wrong for them if he didn't come through for Bullseye Carp.

Shaver swallowed hard and nodded slowly to C.O. Cleo CO. "I'll get 'em somehow, sir," he said.

In his 29 years in the army, Roy Shaver had been called on before to fulfill strange requests, but this was definitely the weirdest he had ever received. But Shaver was a pressure player, and when the CG made a request, regardless of its nature or difficulty, he knew he would have to find a way to deliver. Besides, this general was allowing him to run his illegal operations with impunity.

Shaver had been all over Vietnam during his five tours, and there had never been a division or a general so willing to look the other way at the manner in which he ran his NCO Club. Shaver was rigging the slot machines, short-pouring the drinks, and running a brothel. And he was using his ill-gotten gains to trade booze for captured enemy weapons that he got from grunts in the field. He then gave the weapons to the local Vietnamese in exchange for marijuana, which he sold to the enlisted men in the Administration Company. Everyone was happy with the arrangement. As long as the war continued, the potential for profit was unlimited. And, of course, C.O. Cleo CO and Administration First Sergeant Elroy "Buck" Tosser were happy because Roy Shaver shared most of his booty with them.

Roy Shaver spent two hours thinking the problem through before arriving at a solution. It would be difficult. Getting the girls would be no problem. Getting them with a case of the clap—and THE BLACK CLAP at that—would be the hard part.

But then it began to come to him. Shaver called the NCO in charge of medical records at the Med-Evac Hospital for a little help. He promised the man some free, round-eye nooky the next time a floor show came through if the NCO delivered Shaver a list of GIs currently being treated for severe venereal disease. After looking the records over, Shaver called the man in medical records back.

"Hey Rupert, I gotta have someone with The Black Clap. I mean, some dude whose wanger is about to fall off but also someone who can still get it up."

"Sarge, most of these guys are seriously hurtin'. They can't even piss without morphine," the NCO said.

"Holy shit, Rupert. I gotta have one of them guys just for one night."

"Wait a minute," the medical records man interrupted. "Most strains of VD will go into a sort of remission where everything seems normal for a while."

"You got anyone like that?" Shaver asked hopefully

"Not here. We usually ship them off to Japan. Keep 'em isolated."

There was a pause before Rupert spoke once again. "But maybe. Yeah, maybe."

"What, for Chrissakes, tell me," Shaver pleaded.

"We just sent a guy down this morning to Cam Rahn Bay to catch a Med-Evac flight to Japan. The flight doesn't go until tomorrow, according to this chart."

"Give me his name. I'll have his ass back up here if I have to drive him back through the bush by myself."

And Staff Sergeant Roy Shaver did go after the man personally. He commandeered a helicopter and roared down to Cam Rahn Bay early the next morning. There, he grabbed the startled GI, who was on the tarmac ready to board his jet to Japan, and spirited him back to Division Headquarters.

The young GI turned out to be just what Shaver needed. The guy was afflicted with one of the most severe, mysterious, and, so far, incurable forms of VD on record in the division. The disease was so bad, it seemed to feed on penicillin and other antibiotics. Shaver told the nineteen-year-old grunt that he had been brought back so they could test a new type of drug that just might cure his VD. Since the VD was in temporary remission, the kid agreed to participate. But only after being assured that, if he were cured, he would not be sent back to join his infantry unit in the bush. And so the stage was set.

In the meantime, Shaver had arranged to bring four of the loveliest Vietnamese whores he could find to Division Headquarters. For all their youthful appearance and beauty, the women were experienced hookers. They were also clean and free of VD. But not for long.

The young GI was given a sugar pill that he thought was the experimental new drug and told that, to test its effectiveness, he would have to take part in a unique experiment involving having sexual relations with four women. The women were told that the young man they were to entertain was the son of a very important general, and that they would be paid handsomely, but only if each of them were successful in having relations with the young soldier. On the appointed evening, the young GI needed no encouragement to exercise his diseased but enthusiastic manhood on each of the four flowers of the Orient.

Bullseye Carp was elated to hear that things were going so well with Operation ThunderClap. The four women were now ready. They had been successfully infected with VD and had survived the early stages of the disease, which had gone into remission. The young GI was told the drug did not work, and he was sent off to Japan, a little disappointed but with a smile on his face.

And now the commanding general could proceed with the commencement of Operation ThunderClap.

The Vietnamese prostitutes were told that they would be cured of the disease only if they cooperated with the army. They were then trained to operate a stripped-down armored personnel carrier. The APC had been customized with two small waterbeds, a wet bar, and a small refrigerator. It had also been painted pink. The girls were then taught how to read a map and how to operate communications equipment. Finally, they were told that their mission would be to provide sex to the North Vietnamese Army operating in the division. They were encouraged to charge whatever they could and keep all of the money for themselves, but they were warned never to stay in one area for more than a day at a time.

"But what if they shoot us?" asked one of the girls.

"Don't worry about that, ladies," Staff Sergeant Roy Shaver said to them. "We'll be keeping an eye out for you, but the only way you'll make it out of there is if the NVA find you attractive and useful. Keep them happy and you'll stay alive and make a lot of Piasters. Tell them about us and they'll kill you. And if they don't, we will," the sergeant said, smiling all the while.

After the first week of Operation ThunderClap, there was a noticeable decline in enemy activity in the region where the pink APC was operating. With each succeeding day and in each new area that the APC was deployed, the level of NVA combat operations slowed down significantly. And no one was more appreciative than Bullseye Carp, who was heard to exclaim, "Not even a goddamned gook can fight with a sore dick!"

General Phan

General Binh Duc Phan had been commanding a North Vietnamese Army force of more than 50,000 troops for three years in the US-designated I Corps region of northern South Vietnam. General Phan was both feared and respected by the US and South Vietnamese forces, who considered him an exceptionally bright and formidable opponent. Only General Vo Nguyen Giap, who was a national hero and the commanding general of the entire North Vietnamese Army, was more revered than General Phan. Giap, of course, had been the architect of the victorious battle against the French at Dien Bien Phu in 1954. But now it was Phan's turn. For the past three years, his 340th NVA Division had harassed and bloodied the American and South Vietnamese troops they opposed each day in the jungles and mountains of I Corps. And it was General Lawton "Bullseye" Carp, Commanding General of the Army's 123rd Division, who bore the brunt of General Phan's aggressive military operations.

But General Phan had no respect for his US Army counterpart, whom he considered ineffective and predictable. Ineffective because the infantry brigades Carp commanded were reactive and uncoordinated, and did not seem to have any strategic objective. And predictable because while General Phan knew that the US soldiers and marines his troops faced daily had fought aggressively and bravely, General Carp had wasted their effort and sacrifice by continuing to rely less on them and more on air strikes and superior weaponry to win on the battlefield.

As a result, General Phan had been able to prevail in a series of bloody engagements against infantry elements of the US Army's 123rd Division. This enabled Phan to slowly and methodically mass his forces closer and closer to the American basecamp at Qui Dong. In fact, during the seven months that Bullseye Carp had commanded the 123rd Division, General Phan had become increasingly confident that he would be able to launch a large-scale assault on, and possibly overrun, the sprawling basecamp. His goal in attacking the entrenched army division headquarters and the marine airbase would be as much a political and psychological victory as a military one. At the very least, it would prove demoralizing to the MACV leadership and General Creighton W. Abrams in

Saigon. Even more importantly, he surmised, this bold attack would further stoke the ever-growing antiwar sentiment in Washington.

But General Phan now had a problem. It was a circumstance so novel, yet so effective, that he had to grudgingly admit that the Americans had found a way to slowly, if temporarily, gain the advantage on the battlefield. This new tactic had become a real impediment to his plans and was slowing down his timetable for the attack on the basecamp at Qui Dong. General Phan prided himself on being the ultimate professional and one who resisted, as much as possible, the urge to allow emotion to enter into any military decision. But this latest tactic by General Carp, and the negative effect it was having on his ability to carry out his mission, had caused him embarrassment and fueled a desire to make the US general suffer personally. He knew that it was wrong to conduct any military operation for personal reasons, but he thought he might have a way to achieve the battlefield objective and exact a measure of pain from General Carp too.

It had begun a month earlier when, for then unknown reasons, soldiers in his division began to fall ill. At first it was isolated to one platoon, but within a week it had spread to a regiment and was now affecting soldiers throughout the 340th NVA Division. Initially, the diagnosis was that an infectious disease was the culprit, since all the men stricken had presented with high fevers and debilitating fatigue. But later, these same soldiers began experiencing excruciating pelvic pain, and within a short while, the problem was diagnosed as an acute form of venereal disease. This strain of VD was so virulent that the antibiotics used to treat it were totally ineffective.

The problem was compounded by the fact that all medicine was in short supply in the 340th Division and throughout the entire North Vietnamese Army, for that matter. And since there were no mobile field hospitals to accompany the infantry units, treatment options were very limited.

Finally, after a couple of weeks of frantically trying to diagnose the source of the problem, General Phan was told a story so fantastic that at first he thought it was a joke. But this was no laughing matter, especially since nearly a regiment of his best infantrymen were put permanently out of commission. What was even more incredible, General Phan discovered, was that the rash of VD cases was not an accident but rather the result of a devious and unorthodox military operation that was instigated and supported by the US Army. In fact, Phan had been advised that this strange military mission was the brainchild of General Lawton "Bullseye" Carp.

It was hard for Phan to fathom, but apparently his soldiers had all visited the same brothel—a mobile, pink armored personnel carrier—and had been infected with a seemingly incurable strain of venereal disease. With the full knowledge, approval, and participation of some of his own officers, soldiers throughout the NVA Division enthusiastically engaged in sexual intercourse with four diseased prostitutes. The prostitutes were eventually captured and admitted that they had been threatened with execution by the Americans if they refused to operate the mobile brothel. So for weeks they drove the APC into the NVA's area of operations and then enticed and serviced as many soldiers as possible.

During their interrogation, the women also recounted the fact that before leaving the American base, they had all been forced to have sex with an American soldier. Phan surmised that that man had infected the women with a virulent strain of VD that they had then passed on to his soldiers. The women also revealed they had overheard the Americans refer to the mission as "Operation ThunderClap." General Phan was humiliated, disgusted, and outraged by Operation ThunderClap, and he secretly vowed to make Bullseye Carp pay.

General Phan had often dreamed of leading his troops to victory in a battle that would turn the tide of the Vietnam War and result in dire and monumental consequences for the enemy. His mentor and commander, General Giap, had accomplished such a feat with the victory at Dien Bien Phu in 1954. That single battle had forced the French colonialists to leave Vietnam for good and resulted in the birth of his own nation, North Vietnam.

Defeating the Americans at Qui Dong, the largest US base in the entire country, could have a similar effect and would surely hasten the enemy's withdrawal from Vietnam. He had been planning the attack on the giant basecamp for the past two years and had gotten the final go-ahead from General Giap. He was not going to allow this small but embarrassing setback to change his plans. He would go ahead with the attack, but he would alter the tactics slightly to accommodate his personal desire to exact revenge on Bullseye Carp.

Phan's strategy was simple: He would direct a withering artillery and rocket barrage onto the southern end of the basecamp, where the marine air wing was located, and then immediately launch a massive ground assault in the same area. The Americans would react by moving most of their rear echelon support troops down to where the main attack was taking place. This would leave the Administration Company area and the Division Headquarters behind it vulnerable to an attack by a platoon-size unit of his 11th Sapper Battalion.

The objective for the thirty sappers would be to overrun the lightly defended American guard positions, then proceed through the Administration Company area to the Division Headquarters and finally to the living quarters of the senior officers. All along the way, they would use high-explosive satchel charges to destroy buildings and kill as many Americans as they could, including, Phan hoped, General Bullseye Carp. The sappers would be aided in their mission by maps drawn by civilian Vietnamese workers who were employed at the base. The maps detailed where various elements of the 123rd Division's command and control operations were situated, as well as where the commanding general and other senior officers' living quarters were located.

Now it was just a matter of time and weather. Phan needed a moonless and dark night to launch the attack, and he would try to take advantage of the monsoon season that would soon be ending. If the weather was particularly cloudy and foggy, that would inhibit the effectiveness of the American air response. General Binh Duc Phan was about to launch the most important military operation of his career, and he was hoping for a glorious victory for his country. He was also excited by the possibility of getting even with Bullseye Carp for launching Operation ThunderClap.

A Fateful Day

Barlow, Chang, and Vendetti were walking through plumes of red dust kicked up by passing military vehicles, as they made the one-mile trek from the Administration Company toward the giant corrugated tin building that housed the Division PX. Next to the PX was a small Korean tailor shop and the division's dentist office. The soldiers had been ordered by Sgt. Carson to get their 123rd Division unit patches sewed onto their jungle fatigues or face nonjudicial punishment in the form of an Article-15, which would trigger a serious fine. Carson had been after the soldiers to get the patches sewed on for several months and now he had finally laid down the law.

Chang, always the voice of reason, urged his comrades to look on the bright side. He said, "I am truly excited. So much anticipation. It's almost overwhelming. Just think, we are about to experience, yet again, one of the most predictable occurrences in the United States Army. I can almost visualize the nothing overflowing at the PX."

"I agree, Toby. It's almost sexual," Barlow said. "I can't wait to walk through those giant doors and feast my eyes on all the unfilled space. I get a woodie just looking at the shelves not piled high with boxes of Oreos, cartons of Cap'n Crunch, or half gallons of Johnny Walker and Jim Beam."

"You are so right, Derek. No cases of Hamm's or Budweiser stacked to the ceiling. Just bountiful and aesthetically pleasing volumes of emptiness. It is so encouraging and uplifting to observe that huge space where no consumer products vie for shelf space," Chang said.

Vendetti just shook his head. "You fucking guys are nuts. I hate going down to the PX. There ain't nothing there. Ever. All I know is, it would be nice to score a pint of Calvert Reserve or even an ice cream cone every once in a while. Pisses me off."

"Exactly, Calvin. That's it. That's why I'm so excited," Chang said. "I love the way this works out. Think about it. This country is not a very nice place. It's hot, humid, and there are no creature comforts. No movie theaters, no drug stores, no baseball fields, no air conditioners, no steak houses or even mom-and-pop restaurants. This place is full of other miserable guys like us who are forced to burn their own excrement. And we're the lucky ones to be back in the rear, where there is usually at least drinkable water.

"Then, to top it off, there are little yellow men, like me, trying to kill us every day. So you have to look on the bright side. Having a PX that is full of nothing is kind of appropriate. Why would you want all those things that we take for granted back in the World to be available here? It would just make you more miserable, right? Make you think even more about home, your folks, and that girl you left behind."

Vendetti was not impressed. "I don't know about any of that shit. And I really don't want to go down to that Korean sewing shop and wait in line out in the fucking sun so those slopes—er, sorry Toby—those Koreans can sew a patch on this shirt."

"No worries, Calvin. Chief Lackey Tobias Chang understands that to the esteemed great white conquerors, we Orientals all look alike. And while I might be a little yellow fellow on the outside, I'm all red, white, and blue on the inside. Anyway, this little walk gets us away from the office for a while, and we can all use some time away from that place."

"And besides, Cal," Barlow chimed in, "you could use a little exercise and some sun. You're getting pale and pudgy. Losing some of that natural guinea tan."

"Go fuck yourself, white bread. We I-talians got the groove. The chicks back in the World are all after a hunk of this Italian sausage," Vendetti said and grabbed his crotch.

"Shit, Cal, I seen that little thing you call your dick," Barlow said. "Looks like a penis only smaller. Hell, I saw you putting that potato in your pants too. Trying to fool those dink chicks into thinking there's something more than what's really there. Only problem is, you gotta remember to put it in the front of your pants."

Vendetti fired right back. "Yeah, I seen you checking out my manaconda, Derek. You going the other way, D? Been in the 'Nam so long the troopers startin' to look good to you? Make you want to cop some serious trouser viper, right?"

"Fellows, fellows. A little decorum, please," Chang said, as the three approached the PX.

"Shit, man. Look at all the dudes waiting to get in that sewing shop. Must be ten of 'em," Vendetti said, as he made his way to the back of the line.

"Hey D," Chang said. "Let's you and me check out the PX and let this line shorten up a little. What do you say?"

"Okay by me. You want to come with us, Cal?" Barlow asked. "That line's too long right now and the sun is blazing. That sewing shop ain't going anywhere."

"No, man. I want to get this over with. Then I'll take a stroll around the PX. You guys check it out and let me know if there's anything in there worth a shit."

"Okay. We'll do a little recon for your sorry ass. They probably got a sale on some nice wool socks and long underwear," Barlow said and entered the large building with CLTC.

*　*　*　*　*

As Chang and Barlow strolled around the nearly empty PX, and as Vendetti waited, sweating, in line, three small men dressed in Khaki uniforms and wearing black rubber flip flops and pith helmets readied four 122-millimeter Russian Katyusha rockets for launch. They worked silently in a small, cleared area of the jungle, on the steep slopes of the mountain range, five miles across the flat coastal plain, much of which served as the location for both the sprawling marine airbase and the Army's 123rd Division Headquarters.

The hundred pound rockets, packed with high explosives, were aimed in the general direction of the US base. Mortar fire would have been more accurate, but mortars had a much shorter range than the rockets and could not reach the base from the mountains. And while the accuracy of the rockets in hitting specific US targets was spotty, the projectiles would always strike somewhere within the US base, occasionally with devastating consequences for American soldiers and marines.

These NVA soldiers had received fairly accurate target information from one of the local Vietnamese civilians working at the base. The crudely drawn map had been given to the local Viet Cong commander who, in turn, passed it along to his contact in the North Vietnamese Army. The map highlighted various buildings within the US Division Headquarters area, including the PX building.

The enemy soldiers worked quickly, using the information to estimate the trajectory and distance. They knew that their presence in the open might be spotted at any time by US reconnaissance aircraft, which flew daily missions over the area. They also knew that once the rockets were fired, they would become the target of an almost immediate response from US artillery, as well as air strikes from helicopter gunships, jet fighters, and even B-52 bombers. Their goal was to arm and fire the rockets, and then run as quickly as they could to nearby spider holes that led to underground tunnels. They would wait in these subterranean bunkers and hope to be protected from the American bombardment that would surely follow.

*   *   *   *   *

Derek Barlow was examining a large, three-pound can of Louisiana's Best okra when the PX building shook violently. This was followed instantaneously by a thunderous explosion that knocked out all power in the building and sent shelves and goods cascading onto the floor. Barlow shook his head and stumbled around disoriented in the dark building.

"Toby! Toby! You okay, man?" he yelled, walking toward the daylight he saw streaming through a gaping and jagged hole near the front of the PX.

"Derek, I'm here, man. Right behind you. Keep moving to the light," Chang said. "We need to find Vendetti."

Vendetti had been standing in line for about 15 minutes and had advanced to within four feet of the entrance to the sewing shop when he heard the last sounds he would ever hear—the high-pitched whine of a rocket's engine and then silence as the engine cut off. He instinctively looked up and then everything went black.

The rocket impacted directly onto the PX right above the sewing shop. It blew shrapnel and building remnants through four people in the shop and three others, including Vendetti, who were waiting in line outside. Shrapnel from the rocket also decapitated the driver of a jeep passing along the road in front of the PX.

Barlow and Chang, along with several other GIs, stumbled out of the PX and immediately into the carnage of the rocket kill zone. The scene was chaotic, with soldiers hopelessly trying to provide aid to what little was left of Vendetti and the others in line with him.

"Jesus, Jesus, God!" Barlow screamed. "Cal! Cal! Where are you, man?" He turned in circles looking for his friend.

Chang grabbed Barlow by the arm. "D, we got to leave this place. Now. We need to get out of here. You hear me, Derek?"

Barlow let out a low moan as Chang gently pushed him out of the puddles of blood and gore and away from the PX. A caravan of fire trucks and emergency vehicles, sirens blaring, now approached the PX, raising up clouds of dust as they screeched to a halt. Chang grabbed Barlow's arm and led him up the road back toward the Administration Company area. Barlow was disoriented and in a state of shock as he stumbled onward, whimpering to himself. After about a quarter of a mile, Barlow seemed to become instantly alert and he stopped. He turned and looked directly into Chang's eyes.

"Toby, I'm going to waste that fucking lifer. Carson is gonna pay for this. Cal is dead! And it's Carson's fault," Barlow said.

"Derek, you can't do anything like that. You need to keep your cool. Killing Carson will just get you busted—for good. Think about it. Take a deep breath," Chang urged his friend.

Barlow didn't respond. He just turned and started running. Chang took off after him but could not catch up to his friend, who was now sprinting in the midday sun. Barlow ran past the Awards and Decorations Office and then toward his hooch. Chang stopped briefly at the office and quickly told the guys what had happened, and then he followed Barlow toward their living quarters. Chang was about to reach the hooch when Barlow came out of the door and down the steps carrying his M-16.

Chang nearly ran into Barlow, stopping him in his tracks. Porter and Dahler from the office fell in right behind Chang. Barlow stopped and jammed a fully loaded magazine into the rifle and then pulled the charging handle, which inserted a round into the chamber.

"Derek! Derek! What the fuck are you doing?" Dahler said. "Think about it, man. You going to ruin your life to blow that worthless asshole away? Come on, man. Cool down." Dahler cut in front of Chang to within a foot of Barlow.

"Get the fuck out of the way, Hermey," Barlow replied, fighting back tears. "That bastard Carson sent Calvin to his death, all because of some bullshit regulation about getting a unit patch sewed on his sleeve. There isn't even anything left of Cal to put a patch on."

While Dahler and Chang tried to reason with their friend, Rooster slipped behind Barlow and grabbed him in a bear hug. The rifle fell to the ground and Dahler snatched it up. Barlow tried to break free of Rooster, but the big man held him tightly. Eventually Barlow went limp and slumped to the ground, sobbing.

Chang looked around and noticed that other soldiers had come out of their hooches and the latrine and had witnessed the scene.

Chang leaned over and put his hand on Barlow's shoulder.

"Come on, Derek," he said calmly. "Let's go inside the hooch and talk about this. What do you say?"

"Leave me alone, man," Barlow said. "Just leave me alone."

The Silver Star

I had been out of the office delivering award citations to Division Headquarters the morning Vendetti died in the rocket attack and Barlow had tried to revenge his death by going after Carson. It had been a week since then and Barlow was still very morose and almost uncommunicative. I had tried to engage him in conversation several times to get him back on track, to get my friend to stop dwelling on the tragedy. Besides, we needed to focus on the major decision we both had to make right now: whether or not to manufacture a Silver Star for Buck Tosser.

"Hey D, we got to get back to Anvilhammer right away on the Silver Star," I said to Barlow as we sat in the Awards and Decorations Office. "We're running out of time, man. Gotta shit or get off the pot."

Barlow stared vacantly out the screened window at the falling rain. It was still monsoon season. The wind was howling and the rain was coming down in sheets. It was actually a very cool, gray, and damp day, and Barlow shivered.

"That fucking Carson has got to pay for Calvin," he said.

Others in the office had attempted to strike up a conversation with Barlow too. They were concerned about the man and had tried to help him get over the attack that had killed Vendetti. But Barlow was inconsolable and he just ignored them. When Barlow did speak, he could only talk about revenging the death of his friend. He wanted to make Carson suffer.

Once again, I tried to get him to focus on our problem. "You need to forget about Carson, Derek. We have to give Anvilhammer an answer right now. What are we going to do?"

"I don't know. I just can't believe Cal is dead, and I can't stop thinking about getting him some payback," Barlow said.

"Look, man, first things first. Are we going to do this? If so, it gets pretty complicated and there's a lot to do. We'll need to write the Silver Star citation and then figure a way to get the necessary signatures and orders signed and into Tosser's personnel file. It's that, or we take our chances out in the field and hope we survive the next 30 days."

A light seemed to come into Barlow's eyes. "You're right, Augie. I only have about a month left in-country. That's just 30 days, and I'll need time to figure out a foolproof way to get even with Carson. Won't have much chance to fuck Carson up if I'm out in the boonies. Yeah, I say we take our chances and forge the award."

Barlow seemed almost enthusiastic. "Okay, I'm in," he added. "Let's do it."

"Holy shit, Derek. You making the decision to do this so you'll have time to screw with Carson? You sure it's worth the risk? If we get caught, we'll be going to jail."

"I was thinking how to do this before Cal got blown away," he said, smiling for the first time since Vendetti's death. "They won't catch us. You write it up and I'll take care of getting the forged signatures. I know a dude at Division HQ. This guy is in personnel and he has access to the signature stamps for all the commanders. He's from upstate New York too. I played football against his team in high school, and we've become friends over here. Met him at the club. I think I can make it worth his while to help us out."

"Okay, I'll let Anvilhammer know we're in, and then I'll draft something up for you to look at tomorrow," I said.

So the stage was set. I went over to the Admin Company Head Shed and told the little Indian we would work on the Silver Star. Anvilhammer confirmed that Buck Tosser would honor his end of the bargain too. I had to smile when Anvilhammer uttered the word "honor" because that was a word that had no meaning to the utterly corrupt scumbags I was dealing with. Buck Tosser would keep his end of the bargain because if he didn't, he knew we would simply tell the officers at Division HQ that we had been coerced into forging and manufacturing a Silver Star for the first sergeant.

Anyway, the die was now cast. I began drafting the bogus action report that would become the Silver Star citation for one Elroy "Buck" Tosser, the 123rd Division Administration Company first sergeant. I began to write: "For conspicuous gallantry and heroic action against

* * * * *

For his part, Derek Barlow, with renewed focus and purpose, went about enlisting the assistance of his friend, Staff Sergeant Jason Cupernick. The staff sergeant worked in the commanding general's office and was the NCO in charge of Division Personnel. In this job, he had access to the personnel records of all the men serving in the 123rd. He was also one of only three NCOs who had access to the signature stamps for the division's officer hierarchy, including Commanding General Bullseye Carp.

Once I completed the official award citation, Barlow would take it to Sergeant Cupernick, who would forge the appropriate officer's name by using the signature stamp and affix it to the official Department of the Army document. The "official" award order and citation would then be placed into the personnel, or 201, file of Sergeant Buck Tosser, who would, like all officers and men departing Vietnam, be required to carry it on his person to his next duty station. For his work, Cupernick accepted $500 in cash from Barlow, who kept the greenbacks secured in a footlocker under his cot back in the hooch.

The next morning, in the Awards and Decorations Office, I motioned for Barlow to come over to my desk. I handed him the typed draft of the forged Silver Star award citation to review. As Barlow began reading, a loud siren began blaring and was almost instantaneously followed by a violent explosion nearby.

"Out to the bunker, guys!" Hermey Dahler screamed, as he ran out of the office. "Right now! Get your asses outta here!"

Two more explosions followed, as everyone else in the office and in the entire administration area now rushed toward the sandbag-reinforced bunkers situated between each of the plywood and tin-roofed office buildings. Barlow dropped the award citation on my desk and ran, following me out the door. More blasts followed, but this time, they were off in the distance and away from the Admin area.

It was clear the enemy rocket attack was targeting the commanding general's and other senior officers' living quarters. Those billets were built on cliffs above the South China Sea, some 200 yards beyond the Administration Company offices, which were located just short of the enemy's actual target.

Most of the attacks during the past several months had been carried out after midnight. It was rare for such an event to occur during the day. But recently, the rocket attacks were occurring more frequently and with less predictability. And daylight attacks, like the one that killed Vendetti, were becoming more common, representing an alarming new escalation by the NVA on the basecamp at Qui Dong. Monsoon season in I Corps would be ending soon and Tet, the Vietnamese

New Year, was coming up. And the enemy had traditionally begun new offensives during Tet in the past.

Within ten minutes of the first rocket impact, the attack was over. The six of us in the bunker waited another five minutes until the all-clear siren sounded. As we filed back into the office, I saw that Sergeant Carson was standing over my desk, reading from a sheet of paper. My heart sank and I knew instantly what he was reading. Barlow, who didn't see Carson, looked at me with concern.

"Man, looks like you just saw ghost. What's up, dude?" he asked. Then he saw why my face had gone pale.

Carson looked at us as we slowly approached my desk. The sergeant's face was beet red and he spoke quietly, with barely controlled rancor.

"This your handiwork, Cumpton?" he asked. "I picked this citation up off your desk, so I assume you typed this fiction. That right, troop?"

I was speechless. I just looked at the sheet of paper in Carson's hand and then at the enraged sergeant. Barlow stared at Carson with undisguised hatred, clenching and unclenching his fists. I quickly blocked him from advancing toward the sergeant.

"This piece of unbridled bullshit is your ticket to LBJ," Carson seethed. "You know about Long Binh Jail, right Cumpton? I'm taking this over to the Head Shed right now and we'll see what Colonel Cleo has to say about it. Tosser put you up to this?"

Carson paused for a few seconds, in deep thought, and then spoke as if he were talking to himself.

"Okay, now I'm getting the picture. I'm the one that told Tosser about your fake NCO pins, and I know he's processing orders to send you guys to the field. I also know he's about to DEROS. I can't believe that the first sergeant would stoop so low...."

Carson was putting one and one together pretty quickly. Without a further word, he turned and bolted past the two of us and out the door.

Barlow and I just sat dejectedly and tried to figure out what would happen next.

"We're fucked now," Barlow said.

"That might be an understatement, Derek," I said.

Later, as I crossed the company parade ground on the way back to the hooch, I watched a couple of soldiers tossing a baseball back and forth, as if they didn't have a care in the world. I remembered a time when I was footloose and fancy free too. Back in Riverview, playing "tapeball" with my cousins Frankie and Benito.

A Stroke of Genius!

Playing a traditional baseball game required equipment, like balls, gloves, and bats, as well as a team of kids and someone to organize the game. Lacking most of these essentials, my cousins and I created our own form of the game, which we called "tapeball." It was an abbreviated version of the national pastime, and it required no bats, balls, or gloves, and only three players: a pitcher, batter, and fielder.

In tapeball, the three participants competed against each other and took turns either pitching, batting, or fielding. The rules mimicked baseball with a few caveats. Cleanly fielded grounders and caught fly balls counted as outs, as did one swing and a miss. There were three outs to an inning but no bases. It was simply a nine-inning game of pitching, fielding, and hitting. Disputed calls were settled by the loudest and largest players.

A minimalist and inexpensive sport, the game only required a homemade ball, a bat, and players. To make the tapeball, we used the small, red rubber ball from a jacks game, which served as the core. This core was wrapped with white adhesive tape until it measured about the size of a peach. The bat was a sawed-off broom handle, about four to five feet in length, and we used our bare hands to field the ball. The game was simple. A muffed fly ball or mishandled grounder counted as a single. There were no doubles or triples, and a ball hit over Mrs. Agnotti's hedge was a home run.

One hot, late-September day, it was my turn at bat. My cousin Frankie was pitching and my cousin Benito was fielding. Frankie and Benito were both three years older than me and, of course, loved critiquing my every move.

I approached the "batter's box," which was directly in front of a window without glass in the basement of Frankie's apartment building. The three-foot-square window hole also served as the strike zone. If the hitter did not swing at the ball and it went into the hole, then that counted as an out.

"Hey Augie, why are you holding the bat like Monica Tremonti?" Benito taunted me.

"That's 'cause he swings it like a little girl, right Augie?" Frankie said, as he fired a pitch at me. I swung and missed.

"One out, Miss Augie!" Benito loudly announced.

Frankie smiled as he wound up mightily. But this time, he threw a slow pitch, a changeup. Expecting another fastball, I got way ahead of the pitch. Once again, I swung and missed.

"That's two outs, Augie! You okay, Benito? I bet you about got blowed over by the wind from Augie-girl's mighty swing," Frankie said.

I was getting mad, but I knew better than to respond. Instead, when Frankie fired another fastball, I timed it just right and hit a high fly, which Benito lost in the sun. It landed just short of Mrs. Agnotti's hedge.

Just a single, but it was enough to quiet the taunts from my cousins—or so I thought. Benito ran to retrieve the ball, but before he could get to it, the little orb rolled in the gutter and then into a storm drain.

"Holy shit, Frankie. Augie just lost our tapeball."

"Get your little ass in that drain and get that ball right now!" Benito yelled.

I went over to the drain, got on my hands and knees, and peered into the four-foot-deep cement hole. The ball was nowhere in sight.

"It's not there. It must have gone down in the sewer," I said.

"Augie, you have fifteen minutes to get us another ball," Frankie said, reaching in his pocket and extracting a roll of white adhesive tape. "Here, take this tape and bring us back a new ball. If you don't, you'll be sorry."

I was in a pickle, as my two older cousins graphically described the consequences, if I did not immediately replace the lost ball.

"You don't get us a new ball, your ass is grass, Augie!" Frankie shouted.

"Yeah, and I'm the lawn mower!" Benito added.

I looked at my cousins, both of whom had scowls on their faces. They were 13 and I was 10. I knew I had to do something, so I took off running, trying to think where I might find another jacks ball to use as the tape ball core.

I quickly realized that finding a jacks ball was going to be impossible. I needed to find something else that would provide just the right weight to form the core of the tape ball. Stones or rocks were simply too heavy. Paper was too light and soft. A golf ball would have been perfect, but because the socio-economic roll of the dice had not favored our fathers and uncles, golf balls were not an option.

No sireee. If it wasn't a baseball, football, basketball, or tapeball, we weren't playing it. This was shot-and-a-beer, homemade wine-swilling, and parlay-betting country. Roberto Clemente, Sam Huff, and Jerry West were the heroes of the day. And kids like us spent long summer afternoons happily playing tapeball, our version of the national pastime, in the streets of our working-class neighborhood.

As I ran past Aunt Lia's apartment, a thought, like a bolt of electricity, struck me. I stopped and thought to myself, could this idea work? The more I thought about it, the more I was convinced it could.

Sneaking into the kitchen of my Aunt Lia's apartment, I opened the small freezer compartment of the old Kelvinator refrigerator and extracted the perfectly round answer to my problem. Everyone knew that Aunt Lia was an amazing cook and that her meatballs were the stuff of culinary legend. Surely she wouldn't miss one frozen meatball.

Sacrilegiously, I snatched one of the circular little treasures that had sealed my aunt's reputation in our neighborhood as the "meatball queen." It was about twice the size of a jacks ball, but I thought it would work. It would just require less tape.

As I wound the adhesive tape around the frozen meatball, I realized that with stealth, cunning, and a little larceny, I could provide our gang with an endless supply of tape ball cores. And when the meatball thawed out and the ball became squishy, we'd simply put it in the freezer overnight and have a new tapeball—solid and ready to go. I was excited as I ran back to my cousins and proudly tossed the meat, er, tapeball to Frankie.

"Feels about right. Where'd you get the jacks ball?" he asked, looking suspiciously at me.

"Found it in my room. Under the bed," I lied.

Frankie threw the ball to Benito and then said, "Okay, let's finish the game."

For another hour we pounded the ball, smacked it, and sent it soaring through the air. It performed flawlessly. Our playing area was catty-corner to my Grandpa's house, and on that particular day, he was out in the front yard with Uncle Dante and Uncle Giorgio, crushing zinfandel grapes that would soon become wine. The purple grapes had just arrived that morning by train from California.

While Grandpa and my uncles worked, a sudden rain shower began to fall. And as we continued to play, fate stepped up to the plate in the form of Benito, who whacked a hanging curve (meat) ball with a tremendous stroke, which lofted it at least 100 feet in the air. At the apex of its trajectory, the ball began a rapid descent toward Earth. Like some miniature meatball asteroid, the small, round object streaked into the vat of grapes that grandpa was crushing.

My grandfather was startled by the impact, which immediately created a splash that stained his upper torso purple. Reaching into the crusher, he fished out the broken, meatball-oozing tapeball, sniffed it, and said in broken English, "Sominabitch! Eat-sa rain meat-a–balls!"

The Confrontation

Five minutes after Sergeant Carson discovered the bogus Silver Star citation, he was standing in front of Jeremey Anvilhammer in the Administration Company Head Shed.

"I need to see the CO right away, Anvilhammer."

"The CO is out right now, Sergeant. How 'bout I get Buck out here? He can help you with whatever you need," the little Indian offered.

"No, I prefer to take this to the commanding officer."

"What's this about, Sarge?"

Just then, Tosser, who was sitting at his desk in the office right behind Anvilhammer's, came into the room.

"What do you need, Sergeant Carson?" He stared at Carson and then lit a Marlboro. "I'm sure I can help you with whatever it is."

Carson could not control himself any longer and he lashed out at Tosser.

"I was just in Awards and Decorations, and I actually read a Silver Star citation with your name, rank, and serial number on it. It was on Spec Four Cumpton's desk. I know you haven't done anything to warrant that award, and I think you had Cumpton, and probably his buddy Barlow, too, write you up the Silver Star. I think you made a deal with those troopers. I think you told them you would rescind the orders sending them to the field if they forged an award for you. Well, first sergeant, your conduct is beyond the pale. I'm taking this to Colonel Cleo and we'll see what happens."

As Carson turned to leave the office, Tosser moved in front of him.

"Wait a minute, Carson. You think I would stoop to something so low? Come on, now. It's obvious what's happened here. It's just the opposite of what you think. Those guys are pretty smart cookies, right? Both of 'em college grads, and the last thing those pussies want is to be sent out to the field. So they get a bright idea. They fabricate this fake award and then they figure all they need to do is take it to you, or someone else in charge, and claim I made a deal with them. They think this bullshit lie will keep them out of being reassigned to the infantry. That's what's happened."

Carson looked at Tosser and then to Anvilhammer. "We'll see about this," he said. "What you are suggesting is possible, but I still want to speak to the CO about it. I won't take this any further until I get a private sit down with the colonel." Carson then turned and left the building.

Tosser paced the floor for a moment and then looked at Anvilhammer. "Any ideas, Jeremey?"

Anvilhammer, who was wearing an olive drab boonie hat and a flower- print Hawaiian shirt, stared off into the distance for a moment. Then he began to smile, flashing his Bugs Bunny-like teeth.

"Don't worry, Buck. I think I can get this straightened out, but I'm going to need your help in a big way."

"Just tell me you can fix this and I'll do whatever it takes," Buck Tosser said and smiled his most evil smile.

Carson

In the millisecond before billions of interconnected nerve cells in his cerebral cortex were forever terminated, Wilber Everette Carson's last thought was that he had been expecting this specific type of circumstance to end his life. Wilber Carson was born in 1930, during the Great Depression, and spent his early childhood years living in the Dust Bowl of rural Oklahoma. He was raised by his unwed mother in the boarding house where she was employed as a maid and cook.

Carson was isolated from other children, except for the ones he met at school. Since he had very little contact with these children, or with any others outside the classroom, he was awkward and uneasy around them. He did not develop the skills necessary to socialize and make friends. As a result, he grew into adolescence and young adulthood silently accepting the psychological wounds inflicted on him by a succession of bullies, from grade school and all through high school.

After high school, Carson, who could not afford to go to college, set his sights on a career in the military, enlisting as a seventeen-year-old right after graduation. He was a tall, pear-shaped young man with a wholly unremarkable face and a receding hairline. He was quiet and socially withdrawn. This combination of physical and social limitations might have prevented Carson from succeeding in almost any occupation, including service in the United States Army.

But Wilber Carson had two traits that enabled him to overcome these limitations: He was extremely intelligent and he was stoic, having persevered through years of constant criticism directed at him as a child. His ability to compartmentalize and sublimate things that were unpleasant served him well, particularly during army basic training, where everyone had to endure constant criticism and verbal taunts from the army drill instructors.

Once Carson moved on from the hell week-like existence of basic training, he embraced the regimen, structure, and order of military life. He excelled in the administration branch of the army. He was rewarded for his diligence, intelligence, and strict adherence to the orders and rules of the army.

Carson received regular promotions as he rotated stateside postings with tours of duty in Korea, Germany, and then Vietnam, where he was promoted to sergeant first class. At every duty station during his twenty-two-year career, Wilbur Everette Carson had always exceeded the mission goals of his commanders. He accomplished these goals by mercilessly driving the men who worked for him. He threatened them with extra duty and denial of weekend passes, if they did not meet his rigorous performance demands.

And while his management style was demeaning and abusive, what really engendered hatred for him among his subordinates was his insistence that the troopers maintain a "proper military bearing" at all times. This meant cleaned and pressed uniforms, weekly haircuts, polished brass belt buckles, and spit-shined boots. While it was difficult for the enlisted men under his command to maintain this type of personal grooming during stateside duty, it was nearly impossible for them to do it in war zones like Korea and now Vietnam.

Nevertheless, Carson was relentless in his insistence that the men he commanded in the Administration Company at Qui Dong adhere to his strict rules regarding their personal appearance. He was a martinet and if you ignored him, you would eventually pay the price.

Alvin Frazier, who had been a clerk when Augie arrived in the office, was a tragic example of what ignoring Carson's directives could precipitate. Frazier was now in a permanent vegetative state because he had defied the sergeant's orders to improve his personal appearance. When he did not meet the sergeant's strict standards, Carson had the man transferred to an infantry unit in the bush, where he had been severely wounded. For his part, Sergeant Carson never mentioned Frazier again, and he certainly accepted no responsibility for what happened to him. Even acquiescing to Carson's demands, as the late Calvin Vendetti eventually had, could result in tragic consequences.

Cumpton and Barlow, along with every soldier in the Awards and Decorations Office, despised Carson, but they also knew that he could make good on his threats. After Vendetti's death, Barlow had vowed publicly to make Carson pay. Now someone had, and the prime suspect was Barlow.

Word spread quickly through the Administration Company that Carson had been fragged. In Vietnam, fragged was the term often used to describe the killing of an NCO or officer by an enlisted man using a hand grenade as the murder weapon. But fragged was also the general term used to describe any murder of a superior officer or noncom by a subordinate.

In this instance, the weapon was an M-16 rifle that someone used to ambush the sergeant. The murder occurred as Carson left his quarters in darkness, the morning after his visit to Jeremey Anvilhammer and Buck Tosser. While there were no tears shed for Sergeant Carson in Awards and Decorations, there was immediate concern for Derek Barlow, who was presumed by everyone to have perpetrated the crime. As it turns out, Barlow did not show up for work on the morning of Carson's murder.

AWOL

I was in a state of panic when I found out about Carson's murder. I needed to find Barlow, so I left the office to search for him. I didn't know how I could help him, but I knew that I had to try. I searched all around the Admin Company area, as well as the NCO Club, and even down to the beach, where we had spent time ogling the nurses from the Med-Evac Hospital. But I couldn't locate him. I returned to the office and tried to work. Later, after dinner, I went back to the hooch and tried to think where Barlow might be hiding. I was frustrated and worried when I finally turned out the light in my living area and I fell into a fitful sleep.

Later, I felt someone shaking me and speaking, but I couldn't hear or understand what they were saying.

"Augie, wake up, man. It's me and we need to talk." It was Barlow and he was whispering.

I sat up on my cot and wiped the sleep from my eyes.

"D, where have you been? Everyone's looking for you. The MP's came into the office after Carson was wasted and they want to talk to you. What happened, man? You didn't do it, did you?"

"Fuck! Wish I had been the one, but no, it wasn't me. It might as well have been, though, 'cause every swinging dick thinks I did it."

"Derek, you need to turn yourself in. If you didn't do it, you should be able to prove that. It happened before first light yesterday morning. Where were you then and can anyone confirm they saw you?"

"That's the real problem, Augie. I was late getting up yesterday, and I didn't see anyone early in the morning who could say they saw me before Carson was killed. And then, at breakfast, I heard some guys talking about it. I knew real quick that I was going to be the prime suspect and I didn't have an alibi, so I've been hiding."

"Shit! You can't hide forever. You have to give yourself up and defend yourself," I pleaded with my friend.

"No fucking way, man. They are going to pin this on me," Barlow replied. "I made it clear to anyone within shouting distance that I was going to waste that lifer. I said it again and again. And you know what? After I found out about the murder, I was still going to turn myself in and take my chances. But when I went back to the hooch before work yesterday and reached for my M-16, I noticed that the barrel was warm. It had been fired. Some son of a bitch used it during the night to kill Carson and then put it back under my cot. So I took it and got the hell out of there. Been hiding in one of those caves above the beach." Barlow finished his story and wiped tears from his eyes.

"What did you do with the M-16?"

"I broke it down and threw some of it in the South China Sea and buried the rest in a cave," he told me. "Hey Augie, the reason I'm here now is to tell you that I didn't do it, and that you need to follow through with getting the fake Silver Star for Tosser.

"When I get the chance, I'm going to write to my brothers and tell them about this. But just in case I don't make it, I want you to get in touch with them when you get back to the World and let them know what happened. Pretty soon they'll be notified by the army that I'm missing, or that I've deserted, and I want them to hear my side of the story. So when you get back, please give them a call and let them know.

"I'm not giving myself up and I'm not going back home," Barlow said, his voice choking up.

"Holy shit, D, where are you going to go?" I asked incredulously. "You're a million miles from home in a country where people are trying to kill guys that look like us."

Barlow looked directly into my eyes. "I got a plan," he said. "A good plan, but I can't tell you about it. Everyone knows you and I are buddies. You need to have plausible deniability. The lifers are going to come after you and they're going to sweat your ass. I know you'll promise not to rat me out, but they will threaten you until you give in. So just believe me when I say I've thought this through, and I'm pretty sure I can make my plan work."

"How can you make it work? You're in Viet-fucking-Nam! Please, D, think this through."

"Believe me, I have it all worked out. And I have this Silver Star award for Tosser greased with my friend Cupernick. All you have to do is go over to the personnel office and look him up. I gave him a carbon copy of the citation you wrote up and he is going to put it on an official form. I told him to expect you. I paid him and he knows to give you a copy of the signed orders authorizing the award that you can show to Tosser.

"Augie, if you don't follow through on this, that lifer Tosser will send your young ass out to the bush. He won't let you off the hook unless you get him that Silver Star. You have less than a month left in-country and you do not want to risk it out in the boonies, especially during TET. Now I've got to get out of here."

Barlow suddenly grabbed me in a bear hug and then quietly left the hooch. I was stunned. I could not sleep, so I just laid on my cot and tried to fathom where Derek could possibly hide in this country. It wasn't like he could just blend right into the populace. He was a tall, white man in a nation of small oriental people, some of whom had dedicated their lives to killing guys like him. Flying out of the country would be impossible because the army would alert all the airports to be on the lookout for him. He might be able to get away on a boat, but where to?

Then it came to me in a flash. The one place that Barlow had mentioned to Chang and me and probably no one else—the island. The place they took him the time he was sick and recovering from malaria. A picnic to that island just off the coast of Qui Dong. Barlow had described the experience as almost surreal. That's where he had met the two young women by the waterfall. Yeah. That had to be it. But how would he get there and how could he survive?

I was worried and depressed about Barlow, and I needed a mental and emotional escape. So I did the only thing I could to leave Qui Dong and the insane realities I was facing. I thought about Riverview and happier times.

Pasquale Fritti

Pasquale Fritti shuffled the deck of cards and passed them around to his three playing partners at the small, square table tucked away in the rear of the Ruff Avenue Poolroom. Pasquale was a short, thin man who, like his octogenarian Italian immigrant compatriots, had worked in the glass factories and coal mines of north central West Virginia. He now spent a good bit of his retirement at the Ruff playing Briscola, an Italian card game.

While the game could be played by just two individuals, it was usually played at the Ruff by teams of two men each. The teams competed against one another for a small-stakes bet, usually not more than five dollars. It took me years to understand the many arcane rules of Briscola. But there were other less obvious nuances to the game that were not in the rule book. For example, partners at the Ruff often communicated with one another by using facial tics. An arched eyebrow, a wink of an eye, or a pull at an ear might signal that a partner was holding a specific card, and this created a game within a game.

At times, the contest devolved into a farcical and humorous series of facial contortions and manual gesticulations among the teams. There were hardly ever any words exchanged by the players or team partners, except for an occasional epithet mumbled to express their dissatisfaction with the hand they were dealt. And then only a word or two would be uttered quietly, either in Italian or heavily accented English:

"Cazzo! Stronzo! Bastardo! Prick!" they would mutter in frustration.

It usually took three hands for a team to acquire enough points to win in Briscola and collect the wager that was at stake. While the old guys played, they sipped dark red, homemade wine that Ruff owner Jimmy Ponza allowed them to bring into the poolroom. Of course, Jimmy expected the winning team to pay him a tribute, usually ten percent of the winnings.

Pasquale Fritti and his closest friend, Aldo Pentalini, were the reigning Briscola champions at the Ruff. Their ability to communicate nonverbally was renowned throughout Riverview and, indeed, in pool halls all around Jeweltown.

I loved to stand to the side and observe Pasquale and Aldo wink, nod, and scratch their way to Briscola victory in the room thick with a pall of cigarette, cigar, and pipe tobacco smoke.

Though gambling of any kind was prohibited at the time, the Ruff Avenue Poolroom and other pool halls in Jeweltown were given a pass by the local police and the county sheriff, as long as the businesses were discreet, and as long as the local constabulary was provided with a monthly cash stipend. However, every now and again, the state police would feel the need to raid an establishment or two, in order to placate the occasional complaint from a prominent citizen with a surname like Smith, White, or Allen.

One such doyen of upper crust Jeweltown, whose delicate sensibilities had been offended, was a banker's wife and president of the Women's Christian Temperance Union. Mrs. Smith had penned a letter to the editor in the *Jeweltown Gazette* to complain about widespread gambling in town. In her letter, she stated that "stringent actions must be taken by the authorities to rid our community of the blatantly illegal activities so prevalent among the lower classes."

And so, occasionally, the state police would feel pressure to take some action and, in a symbolic and unenthusiastic gesture, would raid a local bar or pool hall. Then, news of the raid would be prominently displayed on the front page of the *Gazette*, and those offended would be placated, for a while at least.

But it was not good for business if news that your establishment had been raided was splashed across the front page of the local paper. Jimmy Ponza had always kept the Ruff from becoming a target of a raid. He accomplished this by sweetening the tribute he paid monthly to the sheriff, who had a say in deciding where the raid would take place. However, on one occasion when the sheriff was out of town, the state police, without warning, chose to direct their raid on the Ruff Avenue Poolroom. On that particular afternoon, I happened to be in the pool hall and witnessed the raid. It became part of the legendary lore of the Ruff. Here's what happened:

Late in the afternoon, three West Virginia State Police troopers barged into the Ruff and immediately walked toward the rear of the room where Pasquale, Aldo, and two others were engaged in a vigorous game of Briscola. Pasquale looked up to see the troopers standing over them. One particularly large officer reached out and scooped up several coins that were neatly stacked in the center of the table.

Aldo Pantalini was shocked. He looked up at the officer and said, "Whata you do? Why you taka the coins? We always give the tribute to Jimmy, no? He senda you 'cause we ain't givin' him enough? That sominabitch."

The trooper looked at Aldo. "You gentlemen are under arrest and will have to come with us," he said in a stern voice, trying to keep from smiling. "You should know that gambling is against the law in West Virginia."

Now Pasquale chimed in. "Hey Aldo, these polizia di stato, they got it all wrong. They think we gamble," he said and he picked up the deck of cards. "We no gambling, mister. We justa play the game for fun."

The officer was not convinced. "If you're just playing for fun, why was that money in the middle of the table? And where did you get that wine? You can't legally buy wine in this poolroom or anywhere in West Virginia other than the state liquor stores."

"Signore, this is not wine," Aldo said, holding up the small glass. "This is Grapette. We pour ina our glass froma the bottle we buy here."

"And those coins isa for the telephone," Pasquale said, shrugging.

"Look, men, we caught you gambling red handed," the policeman said.

Aldo looked down at his hands and then at those of the others sitting at the table. "Nobody's hands isa red," he said. "Maybe justa little drop fall ona hands froma the Grapette."

The state trooper was beginning to get impatient. "And you," he said, pointing at Pasquale, "were dealing the cards. If you weren't gambling, then why was there money on the table and why do you have that deck of cards in your hand?"

By this time, everyone in the poolroom was watching the encounter.

Pasquale looked at his friends and then he stood up. He held the deck in his hand and looked right at the officer.

"I tella you, I no gambling. I just have dick ina hand," he said imploringly to the state policeman, pointing to the cards.

The entire room erupted in laughter, and the policemen were doing everything possible not to join in. Pasquale looked quizzically around the room, amazed that something he said had evoked such a mirthful response.

"Okay, that's enough," the policeman said to Pasquale. "I'm not going to argue with you anymore. It's time for you and your buddies to come with us."

Rising from his chair, Aldo Pentalini raised his glass of "Grapette," looked up at the large officer, and said, "Salute, Commendatore," and finished the drink in one long gulp.

Then, as Pasquale and the other old men shuffled slowly out the door toward a police paddy wagon, one of the men in the poolroom patted Pasquale on the back and said, "Don't worry, Dick Ina Hand, we'll come and bail you out."

From that day forward, Pasquale Fritti was forever known as Dick Ina Hand.

The Baby

After Derek Barlow left the hooch, I had trouble falling asleep. When I finally drifted off, my dreams were like a kaleidoscope of disparate images: Derek sunning himself on his island; Vendetti's mutilated body lying in the shadow of the PX; The female singer in the Filipino band hunching a microphone; Sergeant Carson lying dead in a pool of blood.

But this all changed in an instant when, at 4:40 a.m., the whistling whine of 100-pound rockets played their brief warning melody and then began to rain down on us. The rockets exploded in thunderous roars, indiscriminately spewing chunks of hot metal that landed harmlessly in open areas or tore through structures and into sleeping human beings. If you heard the impact, you were safe, at least for the next few seconds, and usually able to scramble outside your hooch into the protective bunkers.

Sometimes, guys like me, who had been in-country for months, could sleep through a minor attack, particularly if we had done some heavy drinking or drugging the night before. But the sheer intensity of this bombardment had set off the auxiliary alarm in my mind and had brought me to an immediate, panic-filled consciousness.

Rolling out of my cot, I ripped the mosquito netting and in a rush, fueled by pure adrenalin, I stumbled out of the hooch and fell hard, tripping on the wooden steps. I was vaguely aware of men running over and around me. I lay there for a few seconds unable to move. Stunned by the fall, I was now also paralyzed by the sensory overload, as the sights, sounds, and smells of the attack overwhelmed me. I drank it all in: the bright white flashes and red flames, the searing heat, the acrid burning stench, and the deafening explosions.

Then, suddenly, the paralysis was gone and I was crawling painfully, toward the bunker. With a lurch, I tumbled into the enclosure. My head throbbed and I felt a dull pain in my left wrist, as I tried to lift myself to a crouch. All around me my friends huddled, most in silence, some praying and all cringing with each explosion. We were trying not to think of what a direct hit on our bunker would do to us. I thought this must be the heaviest rocket attack I had yet experienced, and I willed myself not to scream, not to give in to the almost obsessive desire to let it all go, to strip my soul bare and to use my voice to implore the enemy, God, anyone, or anything to make it stop. The blasts seemed to be coming once every few seconds now, and they seemed to be all around our bunker.

This was the type of circumstance, I thought, that would compel even atheists to seek relief from God by promising to stop drinking, smoking, stealing, fornicating, masturbating, cheating, lying ... or anyfuckingthing. Just let me survive this one time. This was my foxhole prayer! There was no joking around this time. No tension-relieving bullshitting this black morning. No sir. I knew this was serious shit. No one wanted to waste their precious breath on superfluous banter when each life-sustaining breath might be The. Last. One.

Then, suddenly, as quickly as it had begun, the intensity of the attack abated. The intermittent fire was now all outgoing, and even the small-arms clatter along the bunker line had begun to die out. A few more minutes passed and still no incoming rounds. Could it be over, I hoped? Small waves of relief began to wash over me, as hope turned to confidence that the barrage had truly ended.

And then, just as I was about to leave the enclosure, a devastating explosion threw me backward and a gust of super-heated wind blew through the bunker. The intensity of the heat caused me to shiver involuntarily, like a person who emerges from the cool shade into bright sunshine. It was obvious that a tremendous fire was raging nearby, but it was impossible to tell exactly where without leaving the bunker. No one seemed anxious to risk a look, except Rooster, who cautiously stepped out of the enclosure.

"It's the latrine," he said, ducking quickly back into the bunker. And sure enough, as soon as Rooster spoke the words, we could smell shit burning like a sulfur-enriched megafart that would not disperse.

"Holy shit," Franken yelled.

"Ain't no shit holy," Rooster replied, coughing and gagging on the smoke that was now drifting into the bunker. "I'm haulin' my black ass outa here," he roared and quickly climbed out of the bunker.

Now we were all coughing or retching or both on the malodorous smoke. Within ten seconds we were scrambling out of the bunker. And while the incoming fire had resumed, it seemed to be directed toward the airbase three miles to the south. The other soldiers in the Administration Company area had also left their bunkers, willing to risk enemy rocket fire on the outside rather than be asphyxiated by the putrescent smoke that had engulfed the protective enclosures.

I joined Franken and Rooster, who were sitting on the ground with their backs to the hooch. We watched as the latrine, fueled by human excrement, burned furiously to the ground. We listened as the distant attack subsided, and as the first hint of dawn to the east became perceptible. In the administration area, thick, black clouds of smoke rose from the now-smoldering remnants of the latrine and hung suspended below the descending morning mist.

The mist seemed to float on the smoke for a while like oil on water. Then it fell in black, putrid droplets on all of us below. I sat staring, totally drained, while the mist continued to descend through the smoke, coalescing with it and bathing the compound in shit dew. An appropriate conclusion, I thought absently, to the night just completed. I noticed then that Rooster and Franken had left me.

God, I was tired. Completely exhausted. My body and mind seemed to be operating on a low-yield battery that provided just enough juice to keep my heart beating and to make me aware of my throbbing left wrist. I sat a while longer and then, gathering strength I didn't think I possessed, rose and walked, zombie-like, to the Awards and Decorations office.

The attack had knocked out the power. There was very little light filtering into the office from the day, which was slowly dawning, gray and ugly. The mist had turned to a light but steady drizzle, which played softly against the corrugated tin roof. I was alone. I just sat there waiting for the day to begin and thought about Barlow's visit to me the night before. The pitter-patter of the rain obscured the sound of the heavy footfalls that approached my desk.

"That you, Augie?" Spec Five Hermey Dahler asked, looking with concern toward me. I was momentarily startled and then looked up at the non-commissioned officer and nodded.

"You're here early. Power's off, you know. Boys from Signal are supposed to be fixing it now. Should be on right away." Dahler squinted down at me and asked, "You okay?"

"Wrist hurts," I managed to mumble.

Dahler looked closely at my wrist and saw the swelling. "You better get down to the hospital and get that wrist x-rayed. It could be broken," he said. Then he stared through the wire mesh window at the rain.

"Looks like monsoon season just won't quit," he added. Then, turning back to me, he said, "Go on down to the hospital and get that checked out, buddy."

I stared at Dahler and, in a voice just above a whisper, said, "Okay."

I looked down at my wrist. It was now throbbing painfully. With great effort, I struggled to my feet and walked out into the rain. Dahler watched me leaving and then asked, "Hey Augie, you seen Barlow? Everyone's looking for him. You see him, let me know, okay?"

I didn't respond to Dahler, I just continued walking toward the Med-Evac Hospital, which was a mile to the south of the Administration Company compound. I trudged through the steady drizzle and along the muddy road like a robot, impervious to the worsening weather. Thoughts flickered through my mind in slow motion, switching with no warning from scene to scene, like bits of old films spliced together: The club and Porter's bleeding mouth; CLTC at his bar mitzvah; Carson angrily berating the troops; Tosser and C. O. Cleo CO buggering each other. I had no control over these cerebral flashes. I was like a patron at an all-day movie, where a continuous stream of unrelated vignettes from a multitude of films had been strung together.

Now Jeremey Anvilhammer is typing orders—mine and Barlow's—the ones sending us to the field. I can see all of this and it is perfectly clear. And now I'm on a trail in the mountains, sweating profusely under the weight of my 80-pound rucksack. Now an explosion. I look up and see a soldier suspended in midair and then falling to the ground, where, upon impact, his body parts separate, head rolling one way, each arm detaching from the respective shoulder sockets, legs floating away, leaving only a bloody torso-stump in green fatigues, with empty sleeves and pant legs. I drop the rucksack from my back and bend toward the torso. I look, squinting to see the faded name on the blood-soaked fatigue shirt: Cumpton.

Then, a distant explosion rocked me from my reverie. I shook my head and realized I was shivering uncontrollably. My uniform was completely soaked through by the monsoon drizzle, as I stood staring at the sign reading "123rd Med-Evac Hospital." The hospital sat at the highest point of the basecamp, on a cliff overlooking the South China Sea.

This morning, despite the low ceiling and poor visibility, helicopters, one after another, were landing and depositing the dead and near-dead at the Med-Evac helipad. I watched the choppers come in, descend through the clouds, and put down gracefully. I observed medics and nurses rushing to the choppers pushing gurneys, onto which the wounded were placed. I noticed, too, that after the wounded were off-loaded, the helicopter crew gently shoved green zippered bags out onto the pad. I could only imagine, over the roar of the choppers, the sound of the dead bodies striking the concrete helipad. I wondered, did they squish, or thud, or plop? When the helicopters lifted off, the medics rolled the body bags onto litters and transported them into a small building adjacent to the hospital. The sign over the door of the building read "Morgue."

I now walked slowly into the hospital and up to a desk, above which hung a sign stating "Entry Protocol for Ambulatory Personnel." A long, typed list advised the walking wounded on the proper methods for availing themselves of military medical care. I looked past the deserted desk and down a long corridor filled with Vietnamese civilians who were standing, sitting or lying in the hallway. There was a tremendous din of sing-song talking and moaning, and an occasional outright, hysterical, pain-induced scream.

I was mesmerized by it all. It was a living nightmare. I had never seen so many people crammed into such a small space. The smell of urine, feces, and blood was overwhelming, and I choked back an urge to gag. I walked slowly down the corridor toward the Vietnamese. Several army medical personnel were tending to the civilians who were lying down and who appeared to be most seriously wounded. Among these, I noticed, were several small children and infants.

I felt nothing. I watched with a kind of morbid curiosity. How will they stop the bleeding on that chest wound? Why won't that trach tube go in? Can there really be that much blood in a small child's body?

I was shaken from my conscious reverie by a human voice. "Hey soldier, what the hell're you doing here?" an army medic had asked me. But I didn't hear the man. When I didn't respond, he tried again.

"You, troop, I'm talking to you!" the medic repeated and then asked, "Hey man, you alright? Look, you can't stay here. You're in the way. Is there something wrong with you?"

I looked at the medic for a few seconds before responding. "My wrist," I said pointing to my badly swollen left arm.

The medic looked closely at my wrist. "We gotta x-ray that arm. You come with me," he said and guided me along the corridor. We weaved our way through and around bleeding and moaning civilians, all the way down the long hallway to a doorway that read "Radiology."

"In here," the medic ordered and half pushed me through the doorway into a large, rectangular room with several curtained-off areas. In the center of the room was another line of Vietnamese wounded, lying on gurneys and waiting to be admitted to the x-ray area that was housed behind a curtain. I was immediately ushered to the head of the line. Several of the civilian Vietnamese were unconscious. Some looked dead and others moaned painfully, clutching bandaged wounds. I slipped on the blood-slicked concrete floor and would have fallen, if the medic had not caught me.

I asked the soldier, "Why are there only Vietnamese here?"

"We can handle them more efficiently if we segregate them from our guys, especially after a big attack like the one we had last night," the medic said, avoiding my eyes. I stared quizzically at the man.

"Well, you know, we don't want any trouble," he explained. "Some GIs don't like it too well when they see the gooks receiving our help, especially when they figure it's them that's causing all this shit."

The medic left after moving me to the head of the line in front of a groaning mamasan, who sat rocking a small child in her arms. The child appeared to be sleeping, although fitfully. The little girl's breathing was heavy and irregular, and on her face were dark specks, like black peppercorns. The specks seemed, incredibly, to form a question mark. The mark started across the top of the child's forehead, went diagonally down under one eye and across the bridge of her tiny nose, and then abruptly shot down her cheek, ending on the edge of her chin.

Amazingly, there was no blood, just parallel lines of red on each side of the black specks. The pattern on her face also reminded me of highway designation markings on a road map. I stared at her mother, who was weeping silently. She stared back at me with eyes that implored, indeed, begged me to help. To do something for her little girl. To help keep her alive.

Then, something inside me snapped. Turning quickly, I ran from the room. Out in the corridor, I sprinted in the opposite direction from which I had come. I had to get away. Away from the injured and dying. Away from their suffering and their imploring looks, their accusing eyes. Away, away, away.

I was now running aimlessly, searching for shelter, for sanctuary. I turned a corner and ran down another corridor, this one empty. My footfalls echoed loudly, as I ran on and on. Finally, I approached a dead end and stopped. My wrist throbbed painfully and I was shivering violently. I spotted a door to my left that read "Pediatric Ward." I opened it and entered a long room, slowly walking down an aisle with beds and cribs on each side.

The room was semi-dark and seemed deserted. As I moved farther into the room, I saw an indistinct figure at the far end of it. As I moved forward, the figure became clearer: a soldier performing some task. The man was whistling a happy tune and going about his work, as if he didn't have a care in the world.

I walked slowly toward the soldier and saw that the man was mopping an area of the floor near a small crib. Above the crib there was a jagged hole in the wall. Monsoon rain and wind blew through the hole, and water formed in small puddles on the floor. The worker, however, was concentrating on a puddle in the center of the aisle.

As I approached the whistling soldier, I could see a large pool of dark liquid in the half-light. The soldier, totally engrossed in his work and his tune, did not hear me approach. A knot began to form in the pit of my stomach, as I hoped against hope that the puddle was only rainwater. But I knew better even before asking.

"Hey buddy," I said softly. "What are you doing there?" The soldier hesitated only momentarily, not even looking at me, and resumed his task.

I tried again. "Say, man, what are you mopping up there?"

This time the man stopped his whistling and mopping and turned to face me. He was weeping silently and his face was filled with terrible pain and deep hurt.

"Excuse me," I uttered quickly. "I'll go."

I turned to leave, but before I could take more than a step, the man began to speak softly. I turned back to him.

"Lieutenant Dowling," he said. "Nurse Dowling. Super chick, great nurse." I watched as the soldier picked up the mop and squeezed out the blood into a half-filled bucket.

"Caught it in the neck. Jugular. Shrapnel just blew through there," he said, pointing to the hole in the wall of the ward. "She was feeding a gook baby when it happened. They found her on her knees slumped over the baby, like she was trying to protect it." His voice began to quaver.

"Was the baby wounded?" I forced myself to ask.

"No, man, that's the thing. The baby didn't even have a scratch on it."

"Then at least she saved the baby," I said hopefully.

"She tried to, man. She really did, but ... oh, my God." The soldier was now sobbing.

"She really wanted to protect the kid, but the baby rolled off her lap and into the … oh, shit, man … the fucking baby rolled face down into Nurse Dowling's blood and drowned."

I stumbled backward, turned, and ran aimlessly from the ward, out of the building and into the blowing monsoon. I went straight back through the rain to my hooch, where I dropped, wet and dripping, onto my cot and fell immediately into a deep and troubled sleep.

Decisions

I was awakened by a sharp pain in my left wrist. Standing over my cot was a soldier, who was gently probing my injured arm.

"Hey, what the hell," I said. Then I saw the combat medic patch on the collar of the soldier's green fatigue shirt.

"I don't think it's broken," the medic said over his shoulder to Specialist Five Hermey Dahler. Dahler had been concerned when I didn't show up for work after my trip to the Med-Evac Hospital, so he went to the hooch and found me asleep.

"Now take it easy, Augie," Dahler said. "When you didn't show up at the office, I called over to the hospital. But they didn't have any record of treating you, so I came over here and found you asleep. Man, you were sleeping like a baby. So I let you catch some z's for a couple of hours. Then I called the hospital and asked them to send a medic over to check you out."

"I still need this soldier to come with me over to the hospital and get this wrist x-rayed," the medic said to Dahler.

"Okay. Augie, you heard the guy. He's got a jeep right outside and he'll get you over there so they can get you fixed up," Dahler said.

The medic helped me off the cot and to my feet. I said, "I need to get cleaned up. I need to brush my teeth."

"Good luck with that," Dahler said. "The fucking latrine took a direct hit last night, remember? Anyway, they put up a tent with a makeshift toilet in it, if you need to take a shit. Otherwise, you can use the piss tube outside. There's no water to clean up or brush your teeth with, though, but there's supposed to be a water tanker truck coming soon."

I followed the medic outside, where I used the piss tube and then climbed into the jeep for the ride to the Med-Evac Hospital. This time, there were no long lines of civilians or soldiers waiting, so I was quickly x-rayed. The x-rays proved negative, but my wrist was wrapped in a soft cast and my arm was put into a sling. A medic then drove me back to the office.

When I got to my desk, an MP was waiting for me. I knew that I would eventually be questioned about Barlow's whereabouts, but I was hoping for a little more time to prepare myself.

"You Cumpton?" the MP asked me.

"Yeah. That's me."

"I need to ask you some questions about Spec Four Derek Barlow. Have you seen him in the last twenty-four hours?"

"No," I lied. "But everyone kind of scattered during last night's attack. He could be anywhere. Hell, he might have even been wounded—or worse."

"No, we checked the hospital and the morgue. And nobody around here has seen him. But everyone we talked to said you and him were buddies. We hoped you would know where we could find him."

"As I said, I haven't seen Derek. I'm kind of worried about him now, though, if you guys are trying to find him. What's up?" I said, trying to make it sound as casual as possible.

"We think he might have had something to do with Sergeant Carson's murder," the MP said, looking directly into my eyes.

"Derek? You shitting me? He would never do something like that. I hate to say this about the dead, but I don't know anyone who shed any tears when Carson was fragged. He was a real prick," I said and immediately wished I hadn't.

"Is that right, Cumpton? Well, we have statements from about ten troopers who heard Barlow publicly threaten to kill Carson over the past two weeks. By the way, where were you yesterday morning when the sergeant was murdered?" The MP once again stared directly at me.

"Hey, there's at least five guys that'll tell you they saw me around the time of Carson's death. I would never have risked spending the rest of my life in Long Binh Jail just to waste his sorry ass. And neither would Derek."

"Well," the MP said, "we'll see about that. I think your CO will be talking to you about this, too, Cumpton. If we find out you've been lying to us, you may find yourself down at LBJ anyway." The MP then left the office.

I sat at my desk and thought about the situation. I was sure I would have to face First Sergeant Buck Tosser and C.O. Cleo, CO before this was all over, and I hoped I would be able to keep my cool and not give them any clues about where they might find Barlow. I needed to go over to the CO's office anyway and see if Anvilhammer still expected me to get the Silver Star for Tosser. If so, I then needed to contact Barlow's friend at Division Personnel to see if the man really had the signed award and the orders for it.

I was exhausted and my wrist was killing me. With my arm in a sling, I sat at my desk and began to go through the stack of action reports and award recommendations. But I couldn't concentrate on anything except the situation I faced.

"Hey Augie," CLTC called to me from across the office. "I spoke with Hermey and we both think you should go back to the hooch and get some rest. You aren't any good to us now anyway with your arm in a sling. Go on. We'll see you after work. Maybe have a drink at the club. I think it's still there after last night. Anyway, go ahead and get some rest."

I nodded to CLTC and slowly ambled out of the office and toward the hooch. As I walked past the still-smoking remnants of the latrine, I saw that an olive-drab water tanker truck was now parked between the latrine and my hooch. A long, four-inch-diameter hose led from the tanker to a canvass-enclosed makeshift shower. A wooden pallet served as the shower floor.

Since the shower could only accommodate one person at a time, there was a line of about 30 soldiers, standing naked except for the rubber flip-flops they wore on their feet. They held towels and bars of soap, and they bitched at each soldier in the shower to "hurry up." There was still a light drizzle falling, so the troopers near the front of the line stood soaping themselves as they waited to rinse off in the shower.

There was also another line, where soldiers were filling canteens and jerry cans with drinking water from a spigot at the bottom of a large, plastic bladder. The dark green water bladder was fed by the tanker and hung suspended from a hook at the back of the truck. The bladder looked like the bloated carcass of some grotesque trophy fish. I went into my living area to get my canteen and then stood in line, waiting to fill it up so I could brush my teeth.

Then a short, rotund PFC walked up and addressed the two lines of men. "Is Spec Four Augustino Cumpton here?"

I was stunned by the sound of my own name being called. I looked up and raised my hand. "I'm Cumpton."

"Come with me, specialist. You're wanted at the Admin Head Shed," the small, portly clerk said and waddled off in the direction of the CO's office.

As I slowly made my way to the company headquarters, I struggled to get my thoughts together. I knew that I would be questioned by Tosser and Cleo about the whereabouts of Barlow. I would tell the same story to them that I had recounted to the MP, but I was convinced they would press me even more to tell them where Barlow was hiding. I would just have to play dumb.

I also wondered if Barlow had lied to me. Could he have really murdered Carson? Barlow was out of control after Vendetti's death, and he had made very loud and very public pronouncements about his desire to kill the sergeant. I still could not believe that he would go that far. But if not Barlow, then who could have done this? It was obvious that if Barlow was not the perpetrator, someone had gone to great lengths to frame him for the murder. And it was understandable that Barlow would assume that the deck was stacked against him because just about everyone had heard him threaten the sergeant in public.

On the other hand, Barlow's threats were just one person's publicly expressed sentiments that almost everyone else shared privately. It was no secret to the officers and other noncoms in the Administration Company that Carson was the worst kind of martinet. They had received numerous, serious accusations regarding the sergeant's bullying and harassing ways from the men under his command. So while things didn't look promising for Barlow, if he chose to face his accusers, the consequences of his decision to desert his post during wartime would compound his troubles. It might also put him in front of a firing squad if he was caught.

It was almost too much to process, as I entered the Administration Company office and followed the portly PFC up to Jeremey Anvilhammer's desk.

The small Indian wore a boonie hat with a large, silver peace button affixed to it and a white T-shirt inscribed with "Of all the things I've lost, I miss my mind the most."

"Here he is, Jeremey," the PFC said to Anvilhammer.

"Thanks, Marvin. You can go now," Anvilhammer said and the soldier left the office.

"Cumpton, have a seat," Anvilhammer said and looked up at me for the first time. "What happened to your arm? Oh, I know. You were pounding your pud with your left hand, missed a stroke, and threw your arm out of the socket? Right? You gotta be careful. I know it's tempting to use the left hand—I mean, I guess it's kinda like getting a little strange, if you're right handed." The little Indian was chuckling to himself.

"Cut out the bullshit, Anvilhammer. I suppose Tosser and Cleo want to grill me about Barlow. I'll tell them what I told everyone else. I don't know what happened to him," I said.

"Take it easy, Cumpton. Buck and the CO don't give a fuck about your buddy. That ain't why you're here. I wanted to see where you are with getting the Silver Star. Looks like Barlow skipped out and left you holding the bag. Well, we expect you to come through with the award, or your young ass is going to be out in the bush pounding the ground with the grunts. Christ, it's bad enough around here right now, but it's a cakewalk compared to the shit going down out there. And tomorrow's the beginning of Tet."

I stared at the Indian with undisguised contempt.

"You tell Tosser I'm still working on it, but it's going to take a little longer now that Barlow is out of the picture. It isn't as simple as just writing the award and putting it on a fancy army form. I have to get the fake orders signed and inserted into Tosser's 201 file, along with the official citation. And I have to be real careful or we all might be going to jail."

Anvilhammer quickly cut me off. "No one is going to jail but you, if you fuck this thing up. We will deny everything if you try to put this on us. Carson came to us the other day and accused Tosser of making you guys get him a Silver Star in exchange for keeping you and Barlow from being sent to the bush. That lifer son of a bitch had it figured out.

"But we told him the opposite was true—that you guys were going to do the award and then take it up the chain of command and blow the whistle on Tosser, say he forced you to do this, and hope the higher-ups believed you. That it would keep you here in Qui Dong instead of being transferred to the infantry. But all that shit got taken care of when Carson got himself fragged, right?" The little Indian winked at me.

"Just get the Silver Star for Buck and everything will be cool," Anvilhammer said.

I left the Head Shed in a state of shock. It was like someone had thrown a bucket of ice water in my face. Holy shit, these bastards had Carson fragged! The whole picture was now coming into frightening focus. I thought back to when Carson had confronted Barlow and me about the fake award citation. Carson had caught us red-handed. At first, we were worried about what would happen to us. But, after thinking things through, we became convinced that getting caught might actually be in our best interest. We would surely receive some type of punishment, but that would pale in comparison to what Tosser would face if Carson took the issue to division. But then, Tosser had Carson killed, and now things were back to square one: either get the award for Tosser or face spending my last weeks in-country out in the bush.

If I tried to take the information to the division, I would end up like Carson in a rubber body bag. And even if they didn't kill me, Tosser would deny any knowledge of the scheme, and I would not be able to prove what I was alleging. I might even face a court-martial for slandering the first sergeant.

It had truly been the most exhausting time of my life. I was both physically and emotionally drained. So much had happened in just the past couple of weeks. Barlow and I had been given Article 15's by Sergeant Carson for missing an inspection. That slight misstep had triggered an avalanche of negative actions that had resulted in Carson's death and Barlow's desertion. And now I was convinced the murder had been orchestrated by Tosser, who knew that Barlow would become the prime suspect. What a tangled mess.

As a result of all this, I felt I had no choice but to go through with trying to get Tosser the Silver Star. I would take this risk, but not just to avoid being ordered to the field as an infantryman. In fact, now I would welcome the transfer and gladly take my chances out in the boonies.

No, the real consequence of refusing to get the first sergeant the bogus award was much more frightening and compelling. If I refused to follow through with the deception, they would simply kill me like they had Carson. I was living a nightmare, except this was no dream. My life was truly on the line. I was in a country 10,000 miles away from home, where enemy soldiers were killing hundreds of American servicemen each week. Yet I was more likely to be murdered by one of my own countrymen than killed in action by the NVA or VC.

And so I had come to the depressing conclusion that I really didn't have any other option. If I had any hope of making it back to the World in one piece, I would need to somehow get the Silver Star for Tosser.

I went into the hooch and sat on my cot. How could this be happening to me? With just a short time to DEROS and the trip home, I was feeling the weight of the world on my shoulders. I tried to focus on something—anything—to relieve the overwhelming stress I was feeling. I had actually accepted the very real possibility that I might not make it back to the World and to my home in

Riverview.

How would my parents and the rest of my family deal with that awful news? It had been quite a while since I had written to my folks. I had always shielded them from the frightening reality of what I was experiencing in Vietnam. But now might be the last chance I would have to let them know how I really felt about them.

So I grabbed a legal pad from a small trunk that I used as a bedside table and began to write to Mom and Dad. When I finished, I sealed the letter and wrote instructions on the outside of the envelope for it to be given to them in the event I was killed. I would have the letter placed in my personnel file. So if I didn't make it home, I would at least leave my parents something that might help ease their pain.

At the same time, the letter would give me the opportunity to open up to them about some heartfelt matters I had repressed far too long. For me, it was always about family and, of course, Riverview, the sanctuary I could always retreat to when things got ugly here in Qui Dong.

After writing the letter, I walked over to division headquarters and met with Barlow's friend Cupernick. As Barlow had promised, things went smoothly, and Cupernick handed me a copy of the fake orders to show to Tosser, as well as a copy of the official award citation that would accompany it in Tosser's 201 file. I also handed Cupernick the letter to my parents and asked him to place it in my own file. Then I returned to my hooch.

Tomorrow I would go to the CO's office and give Anvilhammer proof that the orders for the Silver Star had been placed in Tosser's personnel file. Hopefully, that would placate the first sergeant. It was now 7:30 p.m., and it had begun to rain again. My wrist was throbbing, so I swallowed two of the Percocet tablets I had been given at the Med-Evac Hospital that afternoon. I quickly fell into a deep, coma-like sleep.

The Attack

While Augie slept the sleep of the near dead, General Phan was five miles away in an underground bunker, meeting with his senior commanders. The bunker was in the mountains that towered over the coastal plain and the basecamp at Qui Dong. It was a dark, moonless night, and the monsoon rains were steadily falling, creating perfect conditions, Phan thought. Finally, after years of planning, the general would launch his attack at 3:00 the next morning. At that time, he would give the order to begin the bombardment of the marine airbase and runway, and the perimeter defensive positions on the southern end of the American base.

High-explosive ordnance from three Russian-made 130 mm artillery guns and six 122 mm Katyusha rocket launchers would saturate the base with a devastating barrage. Simultaneously, lead elements of his infantry troops, which had moved to within 100 yards of the concertina wire along the defensive perimeter, would launch their 120mm mortars at the base.

After a half hour of sustained artillery and mortar fire, Phan would send wave after wave of his infantry at the Americans' defensive positions. He knew that these first infantrymen would be slaughtered, but he was confident that many who followed would be able to overrun the American perimeter guards. Then they would move inward, destroying planes and buildings, and killing as many Americans as possible, before air support from other US bases forced his troops to retreat.

While all this was taking place in the southern portion of the base, Phan's thirty-man sapper platoon would wait patiently in the northern sector of Qui Dong, as the Americans redirected most of their reinforcements to where the major attack was taking place. Then the sappers would attack and overrun the lightly defended Signal Battalion and Administration Company positions, and advance on the 123rd Division Headquarters and its Command and Control operations. There, they would destroy everything in their path. Finally, the sappers would move to the senior officer billets and kill everyone they encountered, especially, General Phan hoped, his nemesis these last few weeks, General Lawton "Bullseye" Carp.

*   *   *   *   *

It was 3:00 a.m. The enemy attack warning siren blared, once again too late for the troopers in our hooch, since it sounded five minutes after we had already been awakened by the distant bombardment of the marine airbase. We were all huddled in our sandbag bunker. So far, there did not seem to be any artillery or rocket fire directed at us, but, of course, that could change at any time. But after fifteen minutes in the bunker, we began to leave the protective enclosure and return to the hooch. The attack to the south seemed relentless and ongoing, and we knew things were serious. I also knew that soon, open-topped army trucks would be coming to transport us to the bunker line to reinforce the troops under attack.

"Okay, guys, time to saddle up!" Spec Five Hermey Dahler yelled to the men in our hooch. "You know the drill. Grab your flak jackets, M-16's, and helmets. Trucks'll be taking us down to the airbase. Dudes down there need our help to keep the gooks from overrunning their positions."

"You shitting me, Hermey? How'd that many dinks get close enough to attack?" PFC Richard Porter asked, as he pulled his flak jacket on over his fatigue shirt.

"I have no idea, Rich," Dahler replied. "But from the sound of it, this is definitely serious. Must be at least a company-sized or larger NVA unit. So make sure your weapon is cleaned and ready to rock 'n' roll."

I was struggling to put my flak jacket on using my one good arm.

"Hey Augie," Dahler said. "You can't go with us. No way, man. You'd be useless down there. You stay here. You, too, Toby. We need an NCO to keep the guys in the Admin Company like Cumpton here organized and ready. I also asked Rooster to hang with you guys here, since he was a grunt once—just in case."

I knew Hermey was right. I wouldn't even be able to carry, let alone fire, my M-16, and I would just be in the way down on the bunker line.

"Hey Toby!" Porter said loudly to CLTC. "Looks like you and Augie have to stay back here and defend the REMFS, while me and Hermey and the rest of us dudes get to go play GI Joe. We are gonna waste some gooks, man. Yeah, makes me proud to be a part of the mean, green, fightin' machine!"

"Richard, your eloquence and passion are inspiring, but I think you're underestimating the magnitude of our mission here," CLTC said to the former grunt. "We will be guarding important strategic facilities like the PX, the NCO Club and the remains of our latrine. And, of course, we will be protecting our fearless leaders Colonel Cleo and First Sergeant Tosser."

"Okay, knock off the bullshit," Dahler said to CLTC. "I hear the trucks coming. Okay, you guys kind of keep your eyes and ears open, and use that walkie-talkie to let us know if anything happens up here."

Just then Rooster ambled into the hooch. "Guess I gotta babysit these pukes. That right, Hermey?"

I couldn't resist. "You want it to be right?" I said, smiling at Rooster, who winked at me, offering his middle finger and a crooked grin.

After Dahler and the other troopers boarded the open-topped deuce and a half cargo trucks, CLTC asked Rooster to go through the Admin Company area and gather the other men who were left behind. Within fifteen minutes, Rooster had returned with twelve soldiers, including Duber who had purchased a guard duty walking post around the Administration Company, the Head Shed, and the hooches where Cleo, Tosser, and Anvilhammer lived.

"Okay guys, listen up," CLTC said, addressing our rag-tag group. "We're going to let you go back to your hooches for now, but be ready, just in case this thing down south spreads up here. And if that happens, we all probably need to head for the South China Sea and start swimming to Guam. Anyway, I'm sure this attack will be turned back, just like all the others have been, but just stay alert."

As the soldiers returned to their own respective living quarters, Rooster grabbed a couple of olive drab, metal folding chairs and moved them to the two opposite entrances of the hooch. I sat on one chair and Rooster the other. Each of us faced outward, staring at the monsoon drizzle, while CLTC stayed close to his walkie-talkie, adjusting the dials and monitoring the battle raging a few miles away.

* * * * *

It had been 35 minutes since the bombardment of the airbase to the south had begun, and now First Lieutenant Than Van Thieu, platoon leader of the NVA's 11th Sapper Battalion, had just received the go-ahead to begin his attack on the northern sector of the American basecamp. Lieutenant Thieu gave a silent command to one of his troops, who detonated a golf-ball-size piece of C-4 plastic explosive, blowing a hole in the barbed and concertina wire perimeter that was the first line of defense for the American base. The 30-man sapper platoon quickly entered through the breach in the wire. Two of the soldiers aimed and fired several RPG rounds at the elevated American bunkers, immediately destroying the three positions directly in front of where the sappers were attacking.

Several other sappers found and dismantled the American Claymore mines that were situated in the kill zone between the perimeter wire and the American defensive positions. The remainder of the platoon then charged the US bunkers, firing their A-K 47 rifles and tossing high-explosive satchel charges at and into the American elevated guard posts. Within three minutes, and with only two casualties, the sappers had penetrated the defensive perimeter of the 123rd Division, killing and wounding many of the Signal Battalion troopers, who were charged with providing security. Using maps drawn by local South Vietnamese civilians who worked at the base, Lieutenant Thieu led his troops silently and stealthily toward his first objective: the Division Administration Company.

* * * * *

"What the fuck is that?" Rooster said to himself, as he walked quickly down to CLTC's living area.

"You hear that shit, Chang?" the ex-grunt said to the diminutive man. "That's RPGs and AKs and satchel charges too. And that firefight is happenin' out there." Rooster pointed toward the American defensive positions some 400 yards from where they stood.

I had come into CLTC's area now too. Rooster and I looked intently at the little NCO.

CLTC looked up at Rooster and immediately picked up the walkie-talkie. He called the officer of the guard, who, after several seconds, came on the line. CLTC described what was taking place, listened intently for a moment, and then clicked off.

"Okay, listen up," he told us. "We have to expect the worst here. The OG just told me if the gooks break through, we're going to have to defend the hooches and the Administration Company Head Shed as best we can until they can get us some help. But he said their first priority up here would be to protect the Division Headquarters and the senior staff. So I guess we're on our own for a little while anyway."

I was shocked and speechless. CLTC stared at the floor for a moment and then continued.

"Rooster, I want you to gather up the dozen or so guys that are left here with us. Tell them to bring all their weapons, ammo, and grenades. Then go and set up a perimeter line here in the hooch area. Take two guys each and form a defensive line using the bunkers as firing positions. Put one guy on each end of the bunker. Set the perimeter line up from here to the Company Head Shed. Then find the CO and first sergeant and tell them what's going on. Duber should be around there. Tell him to stay there and help defend the Head Shed. Then come back here and we'll man the bunker outside our hooch. All we can do is try and hold them off until the cavalry arrives."

Rooster took off while I stood, momentarily stunned. "Hey Toby," I said, "I'll get Barlow's .45 caliber pistol. I can't hold an M-16, but I can shoot a pistol."

"Okay, Augie. I don't suppose either of us signed up for this John Wayne stuff, did we?" CLTC said, his voice dripping with irony.

*   *   *   *   *

Jeremey Anvilhammer had been sleeping in the hooch behind the Administration Company Head Shed when he was awakened by the battle raging down at the airbase. Once the attack shifted to the guard positions defending the Admin Company and Division HQ, the little Indian knew things were serious. Within five minutes both Buck Tosser and C.O. Cleo, CO arrived at the Head Shed. The NCO and officer compounds were 50 yards behind the Admin Company office. George Duber, who was pulling guard duty around the area, also arrived on the scene.

"What in the fucking world is going on, Top?" Cleo yelled to Tosser. He then punctuated the question with a volley of farts that hung in the heavy, humid air like gaseous shit clouds.

Tosser turned away from the colonel toward the bunker line and pinched his nose before he responded to his commanding officer.

"Sir, I can only guess there's sappers out there and they may be coming our way soon."

Just then, Rooster approached the group followed by two other GIs.

"Sir, Top, I think the dinks may be tryin' to get through here pretty soon," Rooster told them. "I'm guessin' they headin' for the Division HQ. You guys want, you can use these two troopers here to help defend this position, just in case that happens."

"Where's the rest of the enlisted men from the hooches around here?" the first sergeant asked Rooster. "We need to get them organized and ready to defend this position."

"Top, they all down at the airbase. Trucks took 'em when the NVA attacked there. Just left us with a dozen guys up here. I'm s'pose to gather 'em all up and form a line to defend the Admin Head Shed," Rooster said.

Tosser was incredulous. His face went completely pale. "Holy fucking shit," he whispered to himself. "Okay then," he said to Rooster. "We'll form up around here. You go ahead and get the rest of the troops in position. Dismissed soldier."

Rooster turned and headed back to his hooch to report to CLTC. Tosser positioned Duber, Anvilhammer, and the two troopers in defensive positions around the Head Shed and then joined Cleo, who had gone inside the building.

The attackers were definitely coming their way, Anvilhammer thought. "Hey guys," he said to Duber and the two other soldiers. "I gotta go back to my hooch and get my rifle and some ammo. I'll be right back."

When Anvilhammer got to his hooch, he crawled underneath the building. Moving to a point directly under the center of the hooch, he brushed aside the sand and dirt that covered a hatch to a trap door. He had paid one of the soldiers in the Admin Company $50 a few months back to dig him a four-foot-deep foxhole, just in case the base was ever overrun by the enemy. Without hesitation, he climbed down into the foxhole and pulled the trap door above him shut.

*   *   *   *   *

Lieutenant Thieu was pleased with the operation so far. His sappers had penetrated the American defensive positions and were slowly advancing toward the Administration Company area. He had only lost four men and had bloodied the Americans badly, destroying many of their defensive positions. He would now have to be vigilant because the American soldiers they had not neutralized would be forming up and attacking them from the rear.

No matter. They would carry out their mission until it was completed, or until they were all dead. This he had promised General Phan when the commander surprised him with a visit the day before. The general had impressed on him how important Thieu's mission would be in defeating the Americans at Qui Dong, and how proud his family would be of him. General Phan then gave the lieutenant a photograph of an American, a general, and ordered him to find and kill the man.

Thieu gathered his sappers around him and, on the crudely drawn map, pointed out where the Administration Company headquarters was situated. They would attack it and then move on to the Division Headquarters, destroying the command and control operations there. Then Thieu would lead his sappers to the senior officer billets and kill everyone in their path. He would personally look for the American general that his commander had shown him in the photograph and do everything in his power to execute the man.

*　　*　　*　　*　　*

The major battle on the bunker line guarding the Admin Head Shed and Division HQ had subsided. But there was still sporadic small-arms fire and the sound of explosions that might either be grenades or satchel charges, or both. The bad news, I thought, was that the sounds seemed to be getting louder and closer, indicating that the enemy was moving toward us.

Rooster was at the bunker opening that faced the direction from which the NVA attack was expected. CLTC and I were at the other end of the bunker, protecting the rear, but would join Rooster if the attack emanated from that direction. The floor of the bunker was dug four feet deep into the ground, providing us with a foxhole-like defensive position. But this foxhole was 20 feet long with a sandbag roof over it.

"Buckle up, dudes," Rooster spoke softly to CLTC and me. "The dinks are movin' our way. My guess is that they goin' for the Admin Head Shed first, but they gonna sweep this way too, so be ready.

"CLTC, if you see one comin' your way, open up with your '16, but not on automatic. Find a gook, aim, and fire single rounds. Remember, we gotta conserve ammo. But we can't let them git too close 'cause they probably got hand grenades and satchel charges, and they gonna try and throw 'em in here. That's the only thing we can't let them do, 'cause then we dead meat."

"Roger that, Rooster," CLTC replied.

"And Augie," Rooster continued, "I know that wrist is hurtin' you, but hold that .45 with both hands and squeeze, don't yank, on the trigger. I'm hopin' you won't have to shoot that thing because it ain't no good beyond about ten feet, and if the gooks are that close, we in deep shit."

"Got it, Rooster," I said, struggling to keep my composure as I strained to see out into the distance. The rain continued to fall, and an eerie, misty fog limited visibility even further. For the next ten minutes, there was no sound except the pitter-patter of the rain, which gave me hope that the attackers had retreated.

But just as I was about to speak, a blinding flash and then an ear-numbing explosion shook the bunker and rained sand and dirt down on us. Two more detonations and then several long bursts of automatic weapons fire followed. Rooster looked out to his right and could see a building completely engulfed in flames.

"That gotta be the Head Shed," he said, turning and addressing CLTC and me. We were still at the other end of the bunker.

"Has to be," CLTC replied, and then we both turned and duck-walked to where Rooster was kneeling in a firing position.

"Settle in next to me," Rooster said. "It sounds like them bad little dudes will be comin' from that direction." He pointed toward the burning Head Shed, some 75 yards from our bunker.

Just then, Rooster fired his weapon. One, two, three rounds outbound, as the brass casings popped out of his M-16.

"I can see two of them mothafuckers," he said and then fired again.

"You got one, Rooster," I said. "Oh, shit, now it looks like there's two more coming our way."

Then CLTC was firing his weapon. One of the sappers fell in a heap about 20 yards from our bunker. It seemed to me that everything was now in slow motion. I was between CLTC and Rooster. Then a round from Rooster's rifle took another NVA down, blowing half his face away. In the next instant, I felt the sting and spray of something warm on the side of my own face. When I turned toward CLTC, the little man was slumped over and there was a dime-sized hole in his neck, from which blood, with each beat of his heart, was spurting out.

I reached over to try and put my fingers on the wound to stanch the flow of blood, and in that instant, I saw a dark object coming toward the bunker, and then a flash ... then darkness.

The River Camp

"Wake up, Augie. Come on now, time to go."

I wiped the sleep from my eyes and looked up into the smiling face of my mother. The room was completely dark and I was a bit disoriented, but I could see that the sun had not yet risen.

"What time is it, Mom? And where are we going? It's still dark outside."

"Don't you remember, Augie? We're going up to Grandpa Salvatore's river camp today for a picnic. You'll be able to swim in the river and play all day long with your cousins. So get dressed. We're going up to the camp right now with Aunt Lia to get breakfast on before everyone gets there." Mom stroked my cheek softly for a moment and then left the room.

It was the summer of 1958 and I was 13 years old. I loved going up to the river camp. It was located about an hour from our home, along the Clear Fork River in an adjacent county, and in the foothills of the Allegheny Mountains. The headwaters of the river came rushing right out of a clear, cold spring underneath Bear Mountain, some forty miles from the camp. Grandpa had purchased the property right before World War II, so he could plant a larger vegetable garden to help feed his growing family. But he had more than enough room for the garden on this three-acre plot of land, most of which fronted the river.

Over the years, Grandpa and my uncles had built a simple, one-story cinder block camp house. The house had three bedrooms, two of them with bunk beds, and a large, open room that housed the kitchen, a dinner table, and a living area with three old couches. A poured-concrete porch surrounded three-quarters of the house. It was covered in the summer and fall with canvas, which was anchored to the ground by tent poles, stretched over the porch, and attached by hooks to the roof. There was no indoor plumbing, so my grandfather and uncles constructed an outhouse 30 feet downwind from the camp house. And there was a yard the size of a football field, where the horde of kids from the family could spend hours playing all manner of games.

Early that morning, Aunt Lia drove us to the camp in her 1951 Mercury

Monterey. Dad would come up later in the day after he completed his shift at the glass factory. But most everyone else in the family who planned to come to the camp that day would be there for breakfast. I shared the wide back seat of the old sedan with my cousins Frankie and Benito, while mom and Aunt Lia sat up front. The trunk was packed with paper bags full of fresh fruit, vegetables, warm bread from the bakery, soft drinks, and other picnic foods. There was also a large, metal cooler containing milk, cheese, butter, meat, and other food that required refrigeration.

Before we left town, we stopped at the South Pole Ice Company and picked up a one-foot square block of ice for the cooler. Except for the occasional coal truck, there were no other vehicles on the winding, two-lane blacktop that morning. The road began gently rising for several miles and eventually leveled off onto a ridgetop, where we could see the first signs of dawn beginning to light up the eastern horizon.

Soon we turned off the highway onto an old, unpaved forest service road that descended two miles to the Clear Fork River. There, we turned onto a rutted and narrow track that was more trail than road, and slowly made our way the final, long mile to the camp. This was the part of the trip that seemed to take the longest, since Aunt Lia had to drive very slowly to avoid ruts, tree roots, and large river stones along the way.

I could barely contain my excitement and anticipation as we slowly and ponderously made our way to the river camp. The first rays of dawn were like arrows of light that shot diagonally from the east, over steep ridges and onto the bank of the river opposite us. And then the sun crept over the ridgetops, bathing the river valley in warm light. The sun's heat drew a misty kind of fog from the cold water of the Clear Fork. Rounding one final bend, I could see the gate to the camp just to the left of us. When Aunt Lia stopped the car, Frankie, Benito, and I quickly opened the back door and ran over to the rusty old gate. We untied the rope knot securing it to a fence post and pulled the gate open for the Mercury to pass through. Then we headed for the river.

"Hey boys!" Aunt Lia yelled. "Don't go near that water yet! You have to wait until it warms up a bit. Come on back here and help us get the stuff out of the trunk and into the camp house."

As we unloaded the trunk and brought the contents into the kitchen, my mom and Aunt Lia began to open the windows and doors to air out the place.

Soon mom had the propane gas stove lit, and she and Aunt Lia began assembling and cooking a breakfast only an Italian-American could appreciate.

Along with the usual, traditional American breakfast foods, such as boxed cereal, bacon, and pancakes, we were treated to eggs scrambled with home-canned hot peppers in tomato sauce, wild mushrooms, provolone cheese, and pepperoni. In addition, there were loaves of fresh bread from the bakery, oven-roasted Italian sausage seasoned with fennel and hot red pepper flakes, and bowls of freshly cut oranges, bananas, wild blackberries, and apples.

And this was just breakfast. Every activity in our family revolved around food, so when my other aunts and uncles, along with their families, began to arrive at the camp, so did provisions for lunch and dinner. Aunt Lia coordinated the menu for the day and assigned different family members to provide the food for each meal.

After breakfast, we kids headed for the river. We pushed the floating dock from the riverbank into the chilly water and then swam out, pulling it by a rope to about 30 feet from the shore. Four 55-gallon metal drums provided flotation for the six-foot square wooden dock, upon which we played all sorts of games. One of our favorites was a version of "King of the Hill" we called, not surprisingly, "King of the River." The goal of the game was to throw one another off the dock into the river. The last person standing on the dock after the rest of us were too exhausted to continue the game was declared King of the River. I don't think I was ever "King" because there were always bigger and older cousins than me.

And we had serious pick-up basketball games, played on a dirt court located on one side of the outhouse. The goal was an old, bottomless wooden basket, attached to a backboard that was affixed to the outhouse roof. Uncle Giorgio had scribbled an inscription on the backboard in large, black letters that read "Shooting the Shit."

We also pitched horseshoes, played touch football, and watched as our uncles and adult cousins loudly played a mysterious Italian game they called "Mooda." I later discovered that, like so many of the Italian words I had heard spoken in my childhood, "Mooda" is actually pronounced "Mora." But in their Calabrian slang dialect, my family called the game "Mooda."

At the camp, Mooda was usually played with five persons per side. My uncles and older cousins would line up across from each other and, in loud voices, yell a number from one to ten in Italian. Simultaneously they would throw out from a clenched fist anywhere from no fingers (the still-clenched fist) to up to five digits. If the combination of what the two players displayed with their fingers matched the number one of them had yelled, then that player won the round.

"Dua," Uncle Sal said while throwing one finger.

At the same time, Uncle Dante, who was on the opposing team, yelled, "Quatro!" and held out three fingers, winning the first match.

"Bullshit, Dante! I saw you pull that other finger back. You had four of 'em out, and when you saw I threw one finger out, you pulled one back!" Uncle Sal said, accusing Dante of cheating.

"Sal, you always accuse the other guy of cheatin'," Dante replied. "That's what's bullshit. I won this round fair and square. Now git out of the way. I'm about to kick Giorgio's ass next."

The defeated team member—this time Uncle Sal—was out of the game and the winner would move on down the line to the next opponent. The game went on until one team completely eliminated the other.

And then the fun began. Since the game was usually played for beers, the losing team would be required to present the winners with their beer and would not be allowed to drink during the next game. And so it went on, for at least two hours, and then it was time for the midday meal.

Uncle Sal, his wife, Aunt Yolanda, and their family were in charge of lunch that day. And what a lunch it was! We were treated to an appetizer of boiled and then baked artichokes stuffed with a mixture of toasted breadcrumbs, garlic, red pepper flakes, and Pecorino Romano cheese. We also nibbled on roasted sweet red peppers in oil, garlic, basil, and lemon; paper-thin slices of Capicola; honeydew melon wrapped in Prosciutto; and large green olives stuffed with anchovies.

This was followed by baked cannelloni in marinara, rabbit braised in red wine with wild mushrooms, and a platter of chicken hearts and gizzards parboiled and then fried with onions and hot banana peppers. Of course, everything was accompanied by loaves of fresh Chestnut Bakery hard crust bread and jugs of Grandpa Salvatore's red wine. For dessert, Aunt Yolanda served a variety of cannolis and biscotti.

After lunch, we continued to play and swim for the rest of the afternoon, as Mom's younger sister, Aunt Maria, prepared the evening meal. The menu featured grilled baby goat; pasta in a sauce of white wine, garlic, oil, and parmesan cheese (or aglio e olio); and fried sweet red, yellow, and green peppers. Then we kids were treated to what Uncle Giorgio referred to as a "Snuffie Dessert" of marshmallows, which we toasted on sticks over the fire pit where the goat had been grilled.

While the menus and games might change from week to week, most of the river camp picnics followed the same type of schedule and I cherish the memories of those times.

Finally, at dusk, after a day of swimming, eating, and playing games, Frankie, Benito, and I piled into the back seat of Aunt Lia's old Mercury for the trip home. We were all asleep before we hit the hard road.

Aftermath

The NVA attack on the Army's 123rd Division and the marine airbase at Qui Dong was reported by the US Army's Public Information Office (PIO) in Saigon as a major defeat for the enemy. The lead paragraph in the PIO news release that was sent via teletype to the Associated Press and United Press International offices back in the states read as follows:

SAIGON (02 March 1970) – According to US sources at MACV, troopers from the US Army's 123rd Division and elements of the 24th Marine Air Wing yesterday repelled a large-scale enemy assault and soundly defeated a North Vietnamese Army regiment that attacked the basecamp at Qui Dong. American forces killed 372 North Vietnamese Army soldiers and captured 177. American casualties were light.

What the press release did not mention was that 112 US troops had been killed and another 207 had been wounded in the battle. The release also failed to report that seven F-4 Phantom jets and six helicopter gunships were destroyed on the ground, along with four aircraft hangars and several buildings, including the 123rd Division Administration Company Headquarters.

In actuality, the number of enemy soldiers killed that morning at Qui Dong exceeded 450, since many of the KIAs were carried out of the battle zone by their comrades. Yet, in contrast to the US Army's characterization of the battle as a defeat for the North Vietnamese, General Binh Duc Phan considered the engagement a victory. His infantrymen had breached the American defensive positions in both the southern sector, where the major battle had been fought, and in the north, where his sappers had executed a major surprise attack on the headquarters of the 123rd Division. The majority of the NVA soldiers killed in action during the battle met their fate from AH-1 Cobra attack helicopters and from fixed-wing aircraft, which dropped napalm and high explosives on the attackers, finally forcing them to retreat.

Even though his troops had suffered great losses during the engagement, General Phan was confident that he had clearly demonstrated to the US commanders in Saigon that no American base was immune from attack. More importantly, he knew his bold and aggressive assault would increase the political pressure in Washington to end the war and further fuel the growing antiwar sentiment in the US. His only regret was a personal one: His sappers were unable to locate and kill General Bullseye Carp, though Lieutenant Thieu and his entire sapper platoon had died trying.

*   *   *   *   *

"Hey buddy. You awake?" I could barely hear what the man standing over me was saying, as I slowly regained consciousness. My ears were ringing, my head was throbbing, and I was totally confused, but I knew it was Hermey Dahler.

Where was I? In the hospital? What had happened? My memory was slowly coming back to me, at first in bits and pieces, like finding one correct letter and then another to form a word in a crossword puzzle. Finally, and with brutally agonizing clarity, I remembered it all.

"Hermey, where's Rooster and CLTC? Tell me they're OK," I pleaded, as I tried to sit up. But I was too dizzy, and my head felt like it was about to explode.

Dahler was ashen faced as he quietly mumbled out a response.

"I'm sorry, Augie. There was nothing they could do for them. The guys that found you said Rooster was on top of you. Must have jumped on you when he saw the grenade coming toward the bunker. He and Toby are gone, man. I'm so sorry, Augie. Don't know what else to say.

"But you're going to be alright, man. Doc says you have a concussion and a burst ear drum, but otherwise you're fine, except for that wrist."

I looked at the hard cast on my left forearm and began to sob.

"I can't believe I made it and those guys are dead," I said to Dahler. "I remember trying to stop the bleeding in Toby's neck ... and then I saw this dark thing coming toward us and Rooster jumping toward me and ... Oh, dear Mother of God...."

Dahler tried to console me, but he knew there weren't any words to make things better. He and the rest of the guys in Awards and Decorations were grieving too. And everyone was pissed off.

"Fuck this place, man. And screw the politicians who sent us over here, and the clueless lifers that turned this war into a major clusterfuck," Dahler said, wiping tears from his own eyes.

He continued, "Augie, there was nothing anyone could do. It was a sapper attack on the Admin Company and then on the Division Headquarters. Killed a bunch of guys and blew the shit out of hooches and the Admin Head Shed. The dinks even got Tosser and Cleo. Threw a satchel charge in their office and killed them both. Duber got it too. Dinks fooled us. Had to be a diversionary attack on the airbase, when they really wanted to fuck-up the Division HQ. Anyway, man, so sorry you had to go through this."

Then Dahler grabbed my good arm and a smile began to form on his lips. "Hey dude," he said. "You are one serious short-timer. DEROS in twenty days and a wake-up! And with that early out, your young ass is going to be gone from this fucking army too."

I had applied for and had been granted an ETS, or Early Termination of Service. I had also enrolled in and been accepted into graduate school. The army could grant an "early out" to anyone who was completing a tour in Vietnam and who had less than 150 days remaining on their service commitment.

Dahler smiled down at me. "Shit, man, you'll be sipping cold ones and humping Rosy Rottencrotch back at the old U. You are one lucky SOB."

But I didn't feel lucky. I was grieving for my friends and I felt guilty that I was alive and they were not. I spent two days in the hospital and then I was released. Remarkably, my hooch had survived the attack, and the bunker that I had shared with Rooster and CLTC was still there too. But on closer inspection, I could see shredded sandbags and shrapnel pockmarks all along the corrugated steel roof and walls inside the bunker. Mercifully, though, there was no obvious sign that men had died there just a few days before.

As I sat on my cot inside the hooch, I felt relieved that I would not have to follow through with Tosser's bogus Silver Star. But I was also angry. Why did any of this need to happen? Getting caught wearing an unauthorized Spec-Five insignia had started a shit storm that had cascaded into a tragic chain of events leading to Carson's murder and my best friend deserting the army. And now the people responsible for this miserable situation were dead. Cleo and Tosser had paid the ultimate price, but I was still incensed at them and at that little rat Anvilhammer. I had heard that the crazy little Indian had survived. Maybe I could get him to admit that Tosser had ordered Carson's murder and get Derek off the hook.

* * * * *

It was late afternoon. I had visited the Awards and Decorations Office earlier and now I was back in the hooch. But I was determined to find Anvilhammer and confront him. I would extract the truth from the man and force him to come clean about Carson's death. Someone had retrieved the .45 Caliber pistol from the bunker and left it on my cot. I put the weapon under my fatigue shirt and headed toward the charred skeleton of the Administration Company Head Shed. Anvilhammer's hooch was about 25 yards behind the burned-out building. It had survived the sapper attack. I went inside the building and found Anvilhammer lying on his cot flipping through a Playboy magazine.

"Anvilhammer. Get up. We need to talk," I said staring down at the little buck-toothed Indian.

"Hey Cumpton. See you made it. Me too. Them fucking gooks are crazy bastards. Too bad about Top and the CO. I heard your spade buddy died saving your ass and ...."

Before Anvilhammer could complete the sentence, I pulled him up off the cot by his tee shirt and threw him to the floor.

"What the fuck you doing, man?" the Indian said as he stood now facing me.

I reached under my shirt and withdrew the .45 and pointed it at Anvilhammer's forehead.

"You little maggot. I ought to blow you away right here and now. You're going to tell me who killed Carson. I know Tosser had it done, and I know it wasn't Barlow who did it. Now tell me, or I swear I'll waste your sorry little ass."

"Now hold on, Cumpton. Shit, man, I'm just a clerk. I do what I'm told and I didn't kill Carson. I just thought it was Barlow like everyone else," Anvilhammer lied.

I was not impressed with the little man's response. "I don't believe you for one second. And that's about all you've got until I pull this trigger and send your sorry ass to the happy hunting grounds."

I cocked the hammer on the .45 with my thumb and moved to within a foot of Anvilhammer.

"Okay, okay, Cumpton. It was Duber. Tosser had Duber kill Carson. Told him he had to do it or Top was going to send him to the field. Told him what to do and even had him steal Barlow's M-16 and use it to waste Carson. And then he told Duber to put it back under Barlow's cot."

"Now listen up, Anvilhammer," I said. "You're going to go with me right now and you are going to repeat this story to the MP's."

"I can't do that, Cumpton. They might throw my butt in jail. Anyway, I'll just tell them you threatened me. Hell, everyone who had anything to do with Carson's death is dead too, except your buddy Barlow, and he deserted. It will be my word against yours. And the army don't like it when an enlisted man like you trashes an NCO—especially a dead one—without any proof to back it up. So you're either going to have to kill me, or just let it go," Anvilhammer said brashly, calling my bluff.

"So you do admit that it was Tosser who forced Duber to kill Carson? That right?"

"Sure, he done it. I'm the one brought Duber into Tosser's office. I saw the whole thing, but I ain't putting my ass on the line just so you can clear your buddy's name. Fuck him, and fuck you too," the little Indian said.

I smiled broadly at Anvilhammer. I looked over my shoulder and put the .45 back under my shirt. "Hermey, you there?" I said and watched as Spec Five Hermey Dahler appeared carrying a portable tape recorder.

"Yeah, man. I got it all."

*   *   *   *   *

On a sunny morning in late March of 1970, a Flying Tigers Airline Stretch DC 8, with 224 souls on board, used nearly all of the 10,000-foot runway at Cam Rahn Bay before lifting off the surface of South Vietnam. I had a window seat right over the wing of the giant plane, but I did not care to have one final look at the country that had taken so much from me. Vendetti, Rooster and CLTC were all dead, and Rooster died saving my life. My best friend, Derek Barlow, had deserted and was most likely dead or, at best, in a North Vietnamese prison camp. Derek would soon be exonerated for the murder of Carson, but he would never know that. And even if he was able to make his way back to Qui Dong, he would certainly face a court-martial for deserting his post during wartime.

I leaned back in my seat and tried to sleep. But that proved impossible. I had not been able to sleep for more than an hour at a time since I left the hospital after

CLTC and Rooster were killed. Rooster's last living act had been to save my life. Why had I survived? It was too much to process.

I could not comprehend the vagaries of fate. But I knew I would have to learn to accept that frustrating and unhappy conclusion, if I was ever to have any peace. In that moment, I remembered Uncle Sal's promise to take care of me when I got home. I could only hope so.

But in the meantime, I needed respite from these tortured thoughts, so I retreated to the one place that had always provided a sanctuary, where fear and trouble were kept at bay. To Riverview, the family, and those halcyon days of my youth.

About the Author

John H Brown served a year in Vietnam (1969-70) as an Army enlisted man in the Americal Division. After he retired from a career in public relations, he began writing Augie's War. John has also been a newspaper wine and food columnist for 37 years. He writes for the Charleston (WV) Gazette-Mail and for The State Journal - a statewide business weekly. He is a graduate of West Virginia University and lives in Charleston, West Virginia.

References

Album: *Abbey Road, The Beatles*

"Arriverderchi Roma" by Dean Martin
"Baby Love" by The Supremes
"Here Comes the Sun" by the Beatles
"I want to hold your hand" by The Beatles
"Purple Haze" by Jimi Hendrix
"Respect" by Aretha Franklin
"Stop in the Name of Love" by The Supremes
"The Green, Green, Grass of Home" by Tom Jones
"The Mickey Mouse Club March" by Jimmie Dodd
"The Orange Blossom Special" by Johnny Cash
"We Gotta Get Outta this Place" by Eric Burdon and the Animals
"Whistle While You Work" by Adriana Caselotti

Television shows

Fathers Knows Best
Davy Crockett
The Ed Sullivan Show
The Wild Kingdom
The Adventures of Rin Tin Tin

Films

The Bowery Boys

View other Black Rose Writing titles at www.blackrosewriting.com/books and use promo code **PRINT** to receive a **20% discount** when purchasing.

Made in the USA
Monee, IL
24 November 2020

49449359R00135